TREASURED CLAIM

A MYTHOS LEGACY NOVEL

Also By Jami Gold

Unintended Guardian (A Mythos Legacy Short Story)
Pure Sacrifice (A Mythos Legacy Novel, Book Two)
Ironclad Devotion (A Mythos Legacy Novel, Book Three)
Stone-Cold Heart (A Mythos Legacy Novel, Book Four)

TREASURED CLAIM

A MYTHOS LEGACY NOVEL

JAMI GOLD

BLUE PHOENIX PRESS

PHOENIX, ARIZONA

Blue Phoenix Press
18337 E San Tan Boulevard, #9435
Queen Creek, Arizona 85142
Visit our website at bluephoenixpress.com

This is a work of fiction. Names, characters, places, and incidents are a product of the author's imagination or are used fictitiously. Any resemblance to actual events, locales, or persons, living or dead, is coincidental.

The author acknowledges the trademark status and trademark owners of various products or copyright material mentioned throughout this work of fiction, including the following: GQ, Lex Luthor, Botox, Cosmopolitan, Mercedes-Benz, The Princess Bride, Tiffany and Co., Air France, and Queer Eye for the Straight Guy. The publication and use of these trademarks is not authorized, associated with, or sponsored by the trademark owners.

Ordering Information:
Quantity sales. Special discounts are available on quantity purchases by corporations, associations, and others. For details, contact the Publisher at the address or website above.

Treasured Claim / Jami Gold. -- 1st ed.

Publisher's Cataloging-in-Publication Data
provided by Five Rainbows Services

Gold, Jami.
    Treasured claim : a mythos legacy novel / Jami Gold.
       pages cm. – (Mythos legacy, bk. 1)
    ISBN: 978-1-942928-02-7 (pbk.)
    ISBN: 978-1-942928-01-0 (e-book)
    1. Shapeshifting—Fiction. 2. Billionaires—Fiction. 3. Dragons—Fiction. 4. Love stories.
I. Title.
PS3607.O436 T74 2015
813`.6—dc23

                                                                      2015903009

To join the author's mailing list and take advantage of
pre-order-only sale prices for new releases, visit
jamigold.com/mail

For my family —
Thank you for believing in me...

Chapter One

J EWELRY TRICKLED THROUGH ELAINA'S FINGERS, SCATTERING reflections across the peeling linoleum of her bathroom floor. Each piece hinted at how she'd acquired it for her collection— a broken clasp on a silver chain, earrings missing their backs, a loose sapphire she'd rescued from a sink drain. But the precious ornaments lacked the satisfying *clink* of gold coins when they landed in the safe-box at her knees.

Humans didn't make treasure like they used to. Such a shame.

She curled her fist around the last trophy—a brilliant ruby, almost the size of her palm. A weak dribble of energy from her talisman inched up her arm. She squeezed the gem harder.

It didn't help.

A sluggish rhythm still beat in her chest, and gnawing starvation still chilled her limbs. The pathetic recharge from her collection would barely keep her heart alive through the evening, much less until she *happened* to find another abandoned prize to claim.

Damn it. Her hand slumped to her lap, and she sat back on her heels. She didn't blame her ruby talisman. Neither it nor its sparkling companions had anything left to give.

Restraining her impulses was no longer an option. If she didn't take advantage of her natural talent to score an addition for her hoard at tonight's party, she *deserved* to die.

"Okay, I'll bring home a new friend for you." She kissed the gemstone. "I promise."

Jami Gold

Thievery wasn't as bad as committing murder, right? Besides, she'd already weakened herself by selling off a bracelet to buy an outfit for the ruse. For once, embracing her danger-junkie instinct despite the risk of exposure was logical.

One brilliant success coming up. Or a deadly failure. One of the two for sure.

She placed her ruby in the lockbox and stroked the facets in a final caress. Habit propelled her fingers through the steps required to protect the metal case: Activate triple security locks on the safe, insert the false bottom of the filing cabinet in her bathroom's closet, and engage the cabinet's deadbolt, which fell into place with a thud.

Full-strength dragons would laugh at the feeble defensive measures, but it wasn't as if she could afford anything better. Where was a hidden mountain cave when she needed one?

Elaina restacked her clothes in front of the cabinet, obscuring her hoard, and jiggled out the dress purchased for Phase Two of tonight's party. Red, sleeveless, and way too expensive. Strappy heels joined the gown in an insulated bag marked *Stefano's Fine Catering—Chicago, IL.*

She mentally reviewed her checklist. The kitchen assistant's uniform she'd swiped from work last week? She tugged the cuffs of the almost-too-small jacket. Check. Mandatory white gloves? Check. But she wouldn't put on the miserable things until the last possible minute. Hair pulled back in a health-code-friendly bun? Check. Hair color that matched her fake ID? Uh...

The cracked mirror over the sink revealed multicolored shades of blonde, auburn, and warm browns swirling through her hair. At the sight, a surge of cold invaded her limbs. Slip-ups like that would bring about her death, regardless of the strength of her heart.

She concentrated for a second, and the natural colors of her bun magically darkened under a solid wave of rich black. The worried expression spreading lines over her forehead was another matter. In her imagination, the furrows spelled out "I'm a reckless idiot."

As if this risky venture were her first choice. Or her twentieth.

After triple-checking her disguise, she left her apartment, descended the building's unlit stairwell, and walked the two blocks to the side street where her beater car was slightly less likely to be stolen. Creaks from its door hinges annoyed a dog behind a nearby gate. She ignored the deep barks and started her car. Or rather, *tried* to start her car.

"Oh no, you don't." She cranked the key again.

Nothing.

She slapped her palm against the dashboard, broadcasting her threat into the underlying mechanics. "If you don't start in the next thirty seconds, I swear I'm going to make an appointment for you at the junkyard."

Regardless of whether the rusted-out heap believed her, the engine sputtered to life, and she made it from inner Chicago to Stefano's headquarters on the outskirts without a single stall. She parked in a back corner of the lot, away from the lights and security cameras.

She relaxed, her spine sagging into the seat. Step one of Phase One complete.

Then she straightened and groaned. Arriving meant she'd have to cover her skin with the gloves Stefano required all his employees to wear. Her plan could have been so much simpler—not even requiring a Phase Two—without those fabric obstacles between her and survival. Stupid rules.

But she didn't have a choice. Stefano catered all the ritziest parties in the metro area because of his reputation for rule-following perfection.

Tonight was no exception. Right on schedule, the employees finished loading the carts, ovens, and trays into the delivery vehicles by the building. Time to go.

One last check in the rearview mirror verified her disguise, but that damned worried expression was still there too. She poked at her forehead. Yeah, as if stretching the skin flat would erase her concerns.

"I can do this. I was *born* to do this."

Technically, she was born to kill to get what she needed. At the thought, a memory flashed—her mother's lifeless face sparkling with blood—and she shoved it away. No, she'd die a cold death in the form of an extinguished heart before becoming like her father.

No one deserved to be murdered. Not even humans.

Despite the warm evening, a shiver skittered down her limbs, and her blood's temperature dropped another degree. Not much longer now.

Her mouth went dry, and she rubbed her arms, even though a summertime Death Valley heat wave wouldn't be enough to fix her low body temperature. Would it hurt to die? Would her heart stop beating before she froze to death? Or would her muscles freeze in place first, leaving her trapped in eternal hibernation?

She hissed at herself and threw open her car door. Neither of those was going to happen. She wouldn't let the situation come to that. Her plan *would* work.

With a tight grip on the insulated bag containing her gown, she crossed the parking lot and joined the workers climbing into the vans. No one gave her a second glance or questioned why the woman they knew as Linda, a front-office employee, was dressed for kitchen prep work tonight. Bravado was an art form—one she'd mastered. She squished into a seat and set the insulated container beside her.

Another employee eyed the bag. "Does that need to go in back with the rest?"

"No, this is extra serving ware, just in case. You know how Stefano is." She pasted an innocent smile on her face until the man shrugged and turned away.

Horns from the crushing weekend traffic accompanied them all the way to their North Shore destination. Through the van's windshield, the Wyatt estate finally came into view.

The building's grandeur had been impressive enough in daylight when she'd gone there to take notes for Stefano during his meeting with Mr. Wyatt's assistant. Now, landscape lights accented the dramatic columns and arched windows against the evening's twilight. The place did a fair impression of the impregnable fortresses in the stories of old she'd heard years ago from Nastav, her tutor.

As they neared, tingles spread over her skin, and her muscles tightened, even though she was in no shape for *fight* or *flight*. Last week's prep meeting at the mansion hadn't prompted that reaction from her senses. Something must have changed. Or had she run out of time already?

She pressed her fists into the bench seat and rolled her shoulders back. No, her heart was still beating. She'd make it.

Opportunities for a big score were the whole reason she'd applied for this job with Stefano. No more hoping for lost trinkets. No more freezing. No more starving.

And no killing required.

Maybe that weird feeling was anxiety. Given the stakes, she forgave herself. Especially as the mansion *was* an intimidating spectacle.

Next to her, a server around her age leaned forward and whistled. "I'd sure like to be the one to take Alexander Wyatt off the list of *Chicago's Most Eligible Bachelors.*"

The driver snapped around. "That's Mr. Wyatt to you. Stefano will have our heads if anyone is less than professional."

Masked by the darkness, the woman gave him the finger. Elaina stifled a snicker.

The van rolled up to the back entrance, joining Stefano's trucks already there for the afternoon's prep work. The vehicle's headlights spotlighted security guards at the door. Elaina clutched her bag and joined a group bustling into the mansion. Overhead cameras monitored everything in sight, and she kept her face down.

A guard shined his flashlight on her nametag. "Linda Jones."

Elaina suppressed the impulse to fidget with her jacket sleeves again. She'd sent the list of approved employees to Mr. Wyatt's staff, so she should be safe—unless Stefano had updated the file for some reason.

The guard checked off the name on the list and waved. "Go ahead."

She'd breached the castle's defenses. The thought tugged her lips into a curve. Maybe she shouldn't have been restraining her risk-taking instinct after all. The rush of danger lured her forward.

The elegant kitchen wasn't yet buzzing with activity, and she stashed her bag in one of the oversized ovens. Stefano used a portable kitchen for dishes that couldn't be prepared ahead of time— he'd never risk dirtying clients' appliances—so no one would look in the house ovens.

Her flagging energy weighed down her limbs, but the rest of the team would notice if a "kitchen assistant" didn't help with dinner preparations. The proper timing for the next phase couldn't come fast enough.

Faking patience and dealing with human food. Neither were her strong suits.

Hours passed with steady chores, and as she worked, she went over her mental dossier of the guest list. Although the riches around the Wyatt mansion would keep her heart beating for months, the building's security created an intangible barrier. She wasn't strong enough to force a bond with any of his possessions, so she couldn't remove them from his territory. But his guests...

Yes, the annual fundraising dinner put on by the famed Alexander Wyatt of Dakon Enterprises attracted everyone of importance in Illinois. And away from their homes—their territory—the adornments they wore should be vulnerable to her.

Servers hustled into the kitchen with dirty dessert plates. Finally, her cue for Phase Two.

She grabbed her bag and slipped into a storage room off an empty hallway. Those skin-covering, thwarters-of-jewelry-acquisition gloves came off first, followed quickly by the rest of the uniform. Within a minute, she'd stepped into her candy-red dress and heels. A second after that, her hair tumbled down her back, released from its bun. By the time she exited the room, she'd changed her hair's waves to blonde.

Laughter around a corner drew her to a cluster of women with freshly touched-up lipstick migrating to the ballroom. Prickles once again crept over her skin.

Okay, got it. Imminent death or something. She was working on that problem.

Time for her dinner. And if she was lucky, maybe she could nab some dessert too.

THE BIMBO BRIGADE AROUND ALEX POUTED AT HIS ATTEMPT TO retreat. Tonight was too important to risk upsetting any donors, even these women willing to throw themselves at him for the temptation of money. So much for their self-respect. He forced a smile to soften their disappointment, but his expression was as superficial as their charms.

"I'm very sorry, ladies, but my assistant needs me to assess the fundraising efforts." He disentangled himself from the group and strode toward George at the temporary stage.

Damned gold-diggers. Years of experience had taught him what that type was really like. His entire life, every woman on his arm had been lured to his father's side after the man flaunted his bigger wallet. He blamed his father for the betrayal more than the women he'd been shallow enough to choose.

Women of that type were simply locusts, greedy parasites marking their territory. As if he were a prize to be won.

Some prize.

They'd probably never realize the truth though. His charitable efforts could never make up for his failings. No one had ever recognized his dearly departed father as a fraud either, no matter how much Alex had wished for that exposé. Of all the skills to inherit from the old man.

As he neared the dais, a flash of red drew his eye to a woman entering the ballroom. Adrenaline surged through his body, throwing him off balance. Every nerve ending sprang to attention, focusing on her, and he stumbled into the side of the platform.

What the—? He caught himself on the edge of the raised floor and outright stared.

Sure, her red dress hugged every enticing curve, but he'd never reacted like this to any woman, much less recently. The longer he gawked at her, the more she struck him as unlike any woman he'd ever seen.

Her hair color defied description, shining pure blonde one minute and displaying streaks of reds and browns the next. Instead of jewelry for decoration, her skin shimmered with subtle rainbow colors, as though she'd bathed in body glitter that had sunk into her flesh. On anyone else, the effect would have looked ridiculous. On her, it was radiant.

Even the way she walked kick-started long-dormant lustful desires. She glided across the floor, each step a sinuous movement. An image of her body slinking across his burned itself onto the top of his all-time fantasy list.

His control washed away, his immunity to beauty lost in her

wake. A need consumed him. A need to hunt her. Dominate her. Conquer her.

Echoes of his father brought him up for a second, and he tugged at his collar. What the hell was he thinking? He'd spent years proving he *wasn't* like that bastard, and he wasn't about to let that change.

She scoped out the ballroom, but her arrival went unnoticed by the crowd, failing to trigger leers or jealous glances. They must have all been blind. Completely blind.

Her gaze skimmed over the other guests and then met his. They both froze. Her bright blue eyes glowed like the center of a flame. Her eyes narrowed almost imperceptibly, and then her attention veered elsewhere.

He shook himself, banishing a numb shock from his body. No one could look like her. She was an impossibility. But here she was, and—God help him—he needed to confront her no matter how much his reaction set off alarms in his mind.

Beside him, George finished prepping the ballroom security team, and Alex leaned toward his assistant. "Who's the woman in the red dress? I don't remember meeting her before dinner."

George set his to-do list on the platform, a peculiar quirk of needing empty hands to concentrate. He arched a brow at the hundreds of formally dressed guests. "Which woman in a red dress? There must be over thirty of them in here."

Alex tilted his head toward the cause of his fascination.

"The blonde?" George shrugged, dismissing the unique shades of her hair as easily as her beauty. "Doesn't look familiar. Probably someone's guest."

Alex paused, weighing George's theory. Maybe she was rendezvousing with a husband or boyfriend. But she didn't meet anyone else's gaze, and she didn't smile at anyone in recognition. Instead, she appeared serious, as though analyzing the crowd.

The compulsion firing his blood made the decision for him. For the first time in years, Alex would approach a woman for something other than business.

He couldn't decide if that was good, bad, or an impulsive risk he'd later regret.

Chapter Two

A TINGLE RAN DOWN THE BACK OF ELAINA'S NECK. DANGER. Danger here, among humans? Not likely.

She searched the ballroom for hidden threats. Tapestries on either side of an alcove caught her eye, where a red and bronze dragon confronted a knight brandishing a sword. Her fingernails sharpened into points. Well, that was...

Disturbing. But not dangerous.

No, she was probably just off-kilter because of the way that man, Alexander Wyatt, had stared at her. Could he know she didn't belong? Or had the assistant at his side identified her? Between her hair color change and her attempt to remain unobtrusive during the meeting with Stefano, she'd assumed Mr. Wyatt's assistant wouldn't recognize her.

It didn't matter. She needed more treasure to stay alive. Period. Giving up this opportunity wasn't an option.

If only her father wasn't obsessed with making her his next victim, she wouldn't be in this mess, having to live among humans and use up all her energy to evade him. It wasn't as though she'd snatched the most prized item from his collection for her *Zìwǒ* rite of passage.

Oh, wait. That's exactly what she'd done.

But he'd started it by threatening her in the first place. And now she didn't have a choice if she wanted to survive to tomorrow, much less to next week.

Besides, she could handle a little danger. If she let her instincts have any say, it might even be fun.

Just in case though, she concentrated on the biggest prize first. Her internal precious metal and gem detector sensed an opal and diamond pendant in the room. Probably the same necklace she'd seen the governor's wife wearing in pictures from other occasions. Perfect.

She aimed for the jewelry, but before she moved a foot, a warm hand caught her elbow and squeezed. Uh-oh.

The tingle she'd felt earlier intensified and, more surprisingly, carried a wave of valuable heat through her body, halting the shivers of her heart. She resisted the urge to move closer and instead calmly confronted the danger.

The host of the party stood beside her. "Excuse me, I don't believe we've met." He released her and extended his hand. "I'm Alexander Wyatt."

Her breath hitched at the sudden loss of warmth. Money-fueled power flowed around him like an aura, and his deep, resonant voice compelled her to meet his steel-gray eyes.

The magazine covers hadn't done justice to his appearance. On the surface, he looked younger than his thirty-one years, but the intensity of his gaze made him seem old enough to have witnessed her father's birth. His styled mahogany-brown hair and custom-tailored tux would turn heads even in a *GQ* spread. Come to think of it, he'd probably been on that cover too.

And in his pocket, diamonds—lots and lots of them. Her fingers twitched at the torture. So close and yet so impossible to acquire.

Power, looks, gems. Wow. Humans had never interested her before, but this one...

Dizziness swirled her thoughts, and she grasped his outstretched hand despite having perfect balance all her life. Lost in the whirlpool of his stare and the warmth of his touch, she forgot everything.

Except her name. Her real name.

"I'm Elaina Drake," she heard herself saying.

Her words echoed in her mind, and she recoiled, knees wobbling. Her chest caved with a sudden inability to breathe. What the hell had she done? Ten years of fake-ID anonymity broken by three little words spoken by an *idiot*.

An absolute idiot.

She yanked her hand away. Exit. Where was the damn exit?

He tilted his head, chasing her gaze. "Are you looking for someone?"

She stretched her fingers and forced her nails to reform into a shape less noticeable than their current points. He hadn't come to escort her off his property for crashing the party, so there was no need to panic—and certainly no need to freak out about her reaction to this human male.

Time to play nice rather than draw more attention to her presence. The faster she got away, the faster he'd forget her name, and the faster she could return to her hunt.

She went for blasé. "No, I'm just deciding where to start."

His grin that surfaced, broad and triumphant, could knock at least twenty IQ points off any woman's ability to think clearly. Liquid pooled in her mouth, and she nearly choked at the unfamiliar sensation. Her piecemeal self-education on human society—browsing the front covers at newsstands, reading the merchandise when she'd worked at a comic book shop, and various menial odd jobs—hadn't prepared her for this reaction from *her* body.

He offered his arm. "If you don't know everyone here, I'd be honored to make introductions, Elaina. May I call you that?"

"Yes, I mean, no." A quiet hiss escaped through her clenched teeth.

Damn it, her danger-junkie instincts were *not* helping. She had to get away from him before she completely lost her head. Not to mention what little remained of her security blanket of anonymity.

"That's not necessary, Mr. Wyatt."

"I insist."

He placed her hand over the crook of his elbow. His touch shocked her skin again, and a similar reaction glinted in his eyes.

He dipped his head to hers. "And please, call me Alex."

The quiet rumble of his voice sent shivers over her body, but the warmth of his touch strengthened the beat of her heart.

Once more, she succumbed to him. "Thank you, Alex."

The glow of victory in his expression was unmistakable.

He was dangerous all right.

Very, very dangerous.

ALEX COULDN'T HELP STARING AT THE WOMAN ON HIS ARM. SHE was even more gorgeous up close. And she smelled intoxicating, like an exotic blend of incense. The unusual fragrance complemented the slight foreign lilt of her accent, which he couldn't quite place. Eastern European maybe? Intriguing.

He stroked her fingers hooked over his elbow and savored the sensation of her skin. Sleek and lustrous as silk, the feel of her body spurred his fantasies into a gallop.

He would possess her.

A part of his brain sounded more alarms at the direction of his thoughts. Conquering? Possessing? That was too close to his father's modus operandi.

He blew off the warning. It had been too long since he'd been with a woman—and never one this attractive. The testosterone overload seemed darker simply because of his vow not to follow in the bastard's footsteps.

He *wasn't* his father. He still had his self-control, his constant companion.

It wasn't as if he was going to drag her out of the ballroom caveman-style. Probably.

He introduced her to the group clustered around Chicago's mayor. She stiffened when he said her name, as though inexperienced with being presented. By the time he was done with her, she'd be a pro.

The mayor's enthusiasm for Alex's new foundation gave him hope that he'd have the crowd's support. At a lull in the conversation, he excused them and steered Elaina toward several of his board members huddled near the string quartet. She tugged on his forearm after a few feet.

"Mr. Wyatt—" He raised a brow, and she huffed. "Alex. I'm quite capable of entertaining myself. You have a roomful of guests. You shouldn't concern yourself with me."

She glanced toward the doorway and shifted away from him.

He tightened his elbow against his ribs, holding her hand hostage.

Sure, he was out of practice, but a woman had never before itched to escape his presence. His internal guide to women made several suggestions. A few were even appropriate for public venues. Flattery had always worked in the past—that was worth a try.

"Perhaps I wanted the most beautiful woman in the room on my arm tonight."

Her gaze snapped back to him, and she recoiled. Not the reaction he'd hoped for.

"How ironic." She laughed, the hollow sound stomping on his intentions. "That I should be nothing but an ornament to you."

"No!"

The mayor silenced behind them, and others nearby stared. He led her away from the spotlight of the scene and stopped at a clearing between groups.

"I meant to compliment you." How could his praise be such a blunder as to be ironic? He'd apparently become far too cynical to predict multifaceted women. "Plenty of women here would be eager to hang on my arm. I assumed you'd welcome my attention."

The tips of her mouth twitched up. "I'm not like other women."

In other words, *not* a gold-digger. He couldn't help a grin. "Obviously. That confirms why you belong at my side."

Her eyes brightened, and she stood on tiptoe, placing her lips near his ear. Heat sped through his body in a race with his heartbeat.

"Maybe your name should be Lex instead of Alex." Her sultry whisper sounded more resonant than a feminine voice like hers should.

He pulled back and gave her a questioning look.

Her tone took on a shrewd edge. "As in, Lex Luthor. A filthy rich man who pretends to be nice with his charitable donations, and all the while he manipulates everything around him because he's used to getting his way."

His stomach sank, and just like that, he'd gotten his wish—someone had recognized him as an irredeemable fraud. Only now, he wished the truth had come from anyone but her.

His jaw must have dropped, because she pushed up his chin, closing his mouth. She slipped her hand from his elbow, but stroked her fingertips along his wrist.

"It's too bad the circumstances aren't different. I might have liked you."

A click on the marble floor from her heels accompanied each stride that took her away. The flutters of her dress drew his eye until he lost her in the crowd.

He stood there, off balance and disoriented. Had he really struck out with her? Or was she teasing him?

At the thought, he couldn't decide if he found her body or her mind more attractive. *This* was a woman who could match him for the relationship equivalent of a fair fight.

All he knew was that he would *not*—no matter what—allow himself to chase after her.

Yet.

Chapter Three

ELAINA WEAVED THROUGH THE GATHERING, SELF-BERATING thoughts piling high in her head. "Reckless idiot" summed them up.

Her logic warned her to abandon the ruined plan and slink toward the ballroom exit before Alex could corner her again. As though a hastily thought-out Plan B would be any better. Forget that.

Her danger-junkie instincts had the right idea this time. Suppressing them would accomplish nothing and kill her by morning. She searched for the grand prize of the diamond and opal necklace, and her senses aimed her toward Governor Boyce's wife, fifty feet away.

A shiver seized her heart at the memory of Alex's touch. She ignored it.

Between his money and his looks, the guy was clearly used to getting everything he wanted. Good thing dragons couldn't love, so she was immune to his charms.

His warmth didn't tempt her. His powerful aura didn't affect her. Nope, not at all. She was here to do a job, and she wouldn't let him get to her.

Reckless? Abso-friggin-lutely.

She joined the group clustered around Governor Boyce just as he was introducing his wife to the gathering. Showtime. Salvaging the plan, Elaina dismissed the distraction of her inconvenient reaction to "Lex" and gathered her wayward thoughts.

"Mrs. Boyce, it's such a pleasure to meet you."

She hid her left arm behind her back and shook the woman's hand. At the touch of bare skin, she mentally called to the pendant around the woman's neck.

Elaina's left palm remained empty. Damn it, that man had flustered her.

Or maybe she wasn't strong enough to do a summoning.

No, she refused to believe that. She *could* do this. As long as her determination to acquire an object was stronger than the wearer's attachment to it, she could take ownership—a nifty trick thanks to her DNA—and starvation made her damned determined.

Desperate even.

She changed her approach and lightly pumped their handshake, faking excitement. "I admire your unflagging support for your husband's career. He's a great asset to the state, and I'm sure you must be the foundation of his success."

A flush rose to Mrs. Boyce's cheeks. "Why, thank you."

If the woman's emotions toward Elaina softened enough, the necklace's resistance to her call might diminish. Elaina concentrated harder.

A second later, the jewelry vanished from Mrs. Boyce's collarbone and materialized in Elaina's hidden hand. A giddy laugh bubbled up her throat. She'd normally suppress the not-quite-human sound, but she needed to draw the others' attention from Mrs. Boyce so they wouldn't notice the disappearance.

"No, thank *you*." She released Mrs. Boyce and gave the woman a genuine smile.

Elaina's smooth, practiced motion to lift the hair off her neck brought the pendant unseen to her bare skin. Against her flesh, the necklace bonded to its new owner—and became invisible to humans.

A sudden rush fried her thoughts. *Oh, um, wow.* That was new.

The energy kick from the bonding satiated her starvation and then some, the necklace's strength explaining its earlier reluctance. The overflow buzzed inside her head, and she excused herself from the group before she started giggling like one of her drug-using neighbors.

She'd won. She should definitely indulge her recklessness more often.

ALEX RESTRAINED HIMSELF FROM SCANNING THE BALLROOM FOR HIS obsession. He might have finally found a woman with enough self-respect to stand up to him.

Maybe before, he'd subconsciously chosen the wrong women to prevent a heartbreaking betrayal, as his father had never believed in a fair fight. As a result of too many lost battles, Alex yearned for fairness and equality. But now that he didn't have to contend with his father's sick need to best him in every way possible, he was in no hurry to make his move.

He would *not* seek out Elaina yet, no matter what his instincts wanted to do to her. Right now.

Instead, he worked the crowd, promoting his new foundation. Encouraging donations tonight was just the first step. He needed ongoing partners for the foundation to succeed.

After his spiel, a mob gathered, picking his brain with endless finance questions. In the midst of a debate on the Fed's interest rate policy, a tap on his shoulder startled him. One of his security personnel stood behind him.

"Sir." The man leaned forward and spoke in an undertone. "I'm sorry to bother you, but we have an issue."

Perfect. Just the excuse he needed to escape the political jousting. He took leave of the group and followed the guard to the security control room down a back hallway of the manor.

His security manager greeted him. "Mr. Wyatt, I'm sorry to pull you away from your guests."

"It's all right, Baxter. What's the problem?"

"Governor Boyce's wife was wearing an irreplaceable heirloom necklace this evening. She noticed a few minutes ago that it was missing, and she asked us"—he indicated the guard beside him—"to begin a quiet search for it."

All but one of the monitors on the wall behind Baxter displayed real-time feeds from cameras throughout the mansion and grounds. According to the time stamp in the corner, the remaining screen had been cued to show the ballroom from several minutes earlier.

"We're not sure what happened to it. In one frame we can see her wearing the necklace, and in the next frame, it's gone."

"Did it fall?"

The guard shook his head. "I've already checked the floor in the vicinity, and the lady said it hadn't slipped down her dress."

Baxter motioned toward the monitors. "We have an unobstructed view from this camera angle. If it fell, we'd have seen it happen." His gaze flicked to the screen and back. "I'd like permission to question one of your guests about the situation."

Christ. Alex clasped his hands behind his back, the potential fiasco playing in his mind. No matter what, one of his guests—investors in his cause—would hold him responsible. Either he'd let down the governor and his wife, the people he most needed on board with his foundation, or he'd offend this other guest.

Tension constricted his grip around his right wrist. "You'd better have a good reason for that request."

"Let me show you the incident, and you can decide for yourself." Baxter adjusted the monitor's settings and zoomed in on Mrs. Boyce among the milling crowd.

Cold seized Alex's chest at the image. There, in front of the governor's wife, stood Elaina.

At least he thought it was Elaina. It looked like her, but then again, it didn't. This woman was a full-on blonde, and her skin didn't shimmer. Her facial features were slightly different as well, plainer and less angular. What the hell?

His gut churned as Baxter played the clip. The women shook hands and exchanged pleasantries. And then the necklace disappeared.

Even though he already knew the answer, he forced his dry mouth to open. "This woman is the guest you wish to question?"

"Yes. She—"

"She never touched it." He didn't recognize his voice through the defensive tone.

Baxter cringed. "Let me play it again, and this time, watch her other hand."

With the second viewing, the agitation in his gut twisted harder.

As Baxter had pointed out, Elaina's left hand—assuming it was Elaina—remained behind her back until after the disappearance. Then she stroked her neck. True, the pose was odd, as though she was hiding something in that hand, but she hadn't touched the necklace.

"That doesn't prove anything."

"Of course, Mr. Wyatt." Baxter straightened. "We certainly don't have enough to justify involving the police. I'd thought it wise to question the person closest to Mrs. Boyce, but we'll investigate the best we can without disturbing your guests."

No, that dread in his stomach meant something, and he had to figure out the significance. Maybe this incident explained his mental alarms or those urges to hunt her down. And there was the mystery of her appearance as well.

He gave a sharp nod. "We'll question her together."

Then he'd get his answers.

THE ENERGY RUSH FROM HER NEW ACQUISITIONS MADE ELAINA light-headed, and she had to concentrate on steadying her steps across the ballroom floor. She'd gotten the necklace she'd come for, as well as a bonus dessert of a diamond tennis bracelet and drop earrings from other guests. Her ruby talisman would be glad for the fresh additions to her hoard when she recharged tomorrow too. When had she ever felt this satisfied? Oh, never.

She should leave. Really.

So why hadn't she grabbed the opportunity to escape?

Maybe she was *too* happy. What was the human term? Intoxicated? Drunk?

That must be it. She certainly wasn't seeking an excuse to give in to temptation and search for the man infecting her thoughts.

Nope. Not going to happen.

Proving her denial, she spun on her heel and started her escape. Stefano's crew should have finished the cleanup by now for her to leave the same way she'd arrived.

She rounded the doorway from the ballroom, aiming toward the storage closet. Twenty feet ahead, Alex entered the hallway with two burly-looking guys and stopped short.

Uh-oh. The anti-party-crashing police. Her knees locked in place, and her mind blanked.

Like an inebriated human, she couldn't make her brain focus on anything, much less an exit plan. Instead, the mass of cells in her skull noted in a detached way that maybe she should be careful about over-indulging in the future. Not helpful.

Alex's heated gaze swept over her, scrutinizing her neckline for some reason. His expression hardened, and he stalked closer. He seized her upper arm and yanked her toward him.

"My office," he ground out. "Now."

Yep. Busted.

Chapter Four

ALEX THRUST ELAINA AWAY ONCE THEY REACHED THE privacy of his office. Any other woman might have stumbled in those heels, but not her. No, as he somehow knew she would, she easily kept her balance, despite the uneven edge of the area rug over the hardwood floor. Then she swiveled toward him, slow and deliberate, as though flaunting the evidence of her crime.

His security guards stopped mid-stride and gave him a double take, no doubt surprised by his brutish behavior. He didn't give a damn about his father's influence or his public image right now. This thief was worse than all the gold-diggers in the ballroom added together.

"What the hell were you thinking?" He jabbed toward the necklace brazenly hanging around her neck, where her skin once again shimmered with iridescence. "Did you think you'd be able to walk out of here with it?"

Her eyes narrowed, taking in the two guards, and then she considered him. "I'm sorry, Mr. Wyatt. There must be a misunderstanding. Walk out with what?"

"That necklace. The one belonging to Mrs. Boyce. The one you're wearing now that you didn't have on before."

She flinched, and her fingers splayed over her collarbone, as though attempting to hide the jewelry. "I'm wearing a necklace?"

Her irrational question sharpened his need to do...

Something to her.

His security manager entered the room before anything regrettable happened. The two other guards spread out between his desk and the door, covering the various angles. Alex forced his shoulders to relax.

"Baxter, call the police for Ms. Elaina Drake, if that's even her real name, and reclaim that necklace."

Baxter turned to her, then Alex, and then back to her. His brows pulled low, even though the situation didn't warrant that level of confusion.

She openly sized up the man and gave him an innocent smile. "I'm sorry, Baxter, is it? Mr. Wyatt seems to be under the impression that I'm in possession of a necklace." She raised her hands and slowly twirled in her form-hugging dress. "However, I clearly don't have any place to hide something like that." She opened her palms. "I don't even have a purse."

Alex's jaw slackened at her gall.

One corner of her lips twitched up into a teasing curve. "Unless this is all an elaborate setup for a strip search."

"What the hell do you mean by tha—?"

Shouts cut off his exclamation, and Alex found his biceps grasped from behind. He'd apparently stormed closer to the maddening woman without realizing it.

He whirled on his captor. "Get your hands off me."

Baxter paled and released him. "Sorry, sir, I was trying to protect you from trouble."

"Your *job* is to get that necklace." He scanned her from head to toe. "And that bracelet and those earrings she didn't have on before while you're at it."

Elaina ignored him and kept her attention on Baxter. "How much abuse am I to tolerate from this man simply because he's rich? Earlier, I made it clear to him that I wasn't interested in his company, yet he continues to find reasons to harass me."

Harass her? The word normally would have stopped him cold, but confronting a thief was *not* harassment.

"I'm sorry, ma'am." Baxter held up his hands. "This is a terrible mistake. I take full responsibility. I'd spoken to Mr. Wyatt about you a few moments ago, and he must have misinterpreted my concerns. You're free to go, of course."

"The hell she is." Alex seized her arm. "You're all blind."

He yanked at the necklace, but couldn't get a grip on the pendant, as though it was an illusion. What the—? Were his eyes playing tricks on him?

She wrenched his hand away from her neck. Hard.

"Do you *enjoy* having restraining orders filed against you? This won't help your reputation, *Lex*." At her emphasis of the name, she gave him an alluring look through her lashes.

A shiver coursed through him, and his body clenched, wanting to take her on his desk this second. Damn his raging hormones to hell. How was the woman messing with his control like this?

If he couldn't trust his control, he couldn't trust himself, much less his eyes. She'd already made him think she was more beautiful than she really was, with the hair and the skin and everything. And now she'd deceived him into seeing non-existent jewelry to make him look like a fool. If he didn't know better, he'd say she'd bewitched him.

Not that he believed in witches. But if she'd created the problem, she could undo it.

Before he could state his demand, she had the audacity to address his security manager. "Baxter, maybe you should see if someone tampered with Mr. Wyatt's food or medication. Surely he's not always like this." She placed a wrist on his forehead, as though checking his temperature—which *was* quickly rising—and gave him a wink. "Unless, of course, we need to add an addiction to hallucinogenic drugs to your list of faults."

The teasing statement rang in his ears. It didn't matter that it was as false this time as it had been years before. No one accused him of that. Not anymore.

God, this was fun. Maybe it was the energy buzz talking, but Elaina hadn't enjoyed herself this much in over ten years. This kind of danger she could handle.

Sure, unlike any other human, Alex could somehow see the jewelry. But her brain was in no shape to puzzle over that mystery yet. Her mind would clear eventually, and she could wait.

After all, no one else could see the necklace, so Alex couldn't prove anything. And the more he protested, the more innocent she seemed in comparison.

Then his gray eyes flashed like a sword in sunlight. "Leave us."

Alex tightened his grasp on her arm and directed his glare toward Baxter, adding weight to the command. The guards focused on their security boss as well.

Her throat constricted, as though the necklace had become a noose. They wouldn't leave her. Would they?

Just in case, she slid the pendant along the chain to the back of her neck while no one was watching her. Futile? Yes, but she had to do what she could to protect her treasure. Maybe if Alex didn't see the jewel, he'd forget about it.

Alex lifted his chin. "That. Was. An. Order."

Baxter signaled to the brute squad, and all three members of the security team slinked to the office door. She struggled against Alex's vice-like grip, sobriety returning in an instant.

"You can't be serious. You're leaving me alone with *him*?"

At least Baxter had the decency to act ashamed, his sturdy frame rounding.

Over his shoulder, Alex added, "Shut the door behind you."

Click. No noise had ever sounded more ominous, and chills spread over her skin despite Alex's touch. She was abandoned to the man she'd just had way too much fun provoking.

Technically, she could defend herself against any mere human, but the death—or even just an assault—of a multi-millionaire would land her real name in the news and reveal her whereabouts to her father in two seconds flat. More to the point, using up her energy to do something forceful would put her back where she started.

Her reluctance had nothing to do with the fact that she didn't want to harm *this* human in particular. Nothing at all.

"I should warn you that I can scream—loudly. Your guests will hear me."

He scowled down at her. "I'm not going to *hurt* you."

As if to emphasize his words, he released her arm. However when she stepped back, he kept pace, continuing to loom over her even as the backs of her heels thumped into the wood-paneled wall behind his massive desk.

The thrill of danger radiating from him did odd things to her thoughts. Her logic shouted at her to find a way to escape, but the rush pulsing through her body enticed her to stay, to explore these new sensations. Being a danger junkie had taken on a whole different meaning.

His broad shoulders caged her in, blocking the easy way out. "Fix it." His hand circled in the air. "Take away this spell or whatever it is you did."

His request interrupted her appreciation of his jaw line. "*What?*"

Had she pushed him too far? Had he snapped?

"Spell? Like a witch?" She scoffed. "Is *that* what you think I am?"

She wasn't leaning closer so she could smell him. She wasn't. Even though he smelled enticingly sharp and clean, not like soap, but like cold steel, it didn't affect her at all.

Despite her denial, her head tilted, placing her nose within inches of his neck. She drew in a lungful of his scent. Between the afterglow of her acquisitions and his nearness, her drunken mood returned, stronger and more reckless than before.

"I can one hundred percent guarantee you that I'm not a witch."

"Then why am I seeing things?" He caressed her bare arms, seemingly without realizing it. "Feeling things?"

Energy from his touch warmed her body, and she longed for more. Much more.

"Maybe you have a jewelry fetish? And an active imagination?"

His lips beckoned her gaze. How would they feel against hers? Not a kiss of course. She simply wanted to touch one body part to another to experience that tingling sensation there.

He stroked her arms more forcefully, pinning her to the wall. A wave of heat flowed through her body, building into a craving. She stifled a gasp and angled her head up to his.

"What about your hair?" He bent closer, his breath wafting over her. "And your skin?"

A static field hovered between their lips, only millimeters apart. She closed her eyes, her voice a soft murmur. "What about them?"

"Your hair shifts between multiple colors, and your skin shimmers."

No! Her knees gave out, and only his embrace kept her from crumpling to the floor.

"Y–You don't exist." Her insistence was weaker than intended, no thanks to an attack of hyperventilation, and the solid strength of his arms proving her wrong didn't help either.

Apparently, his kind was more than just a bedtime story told to scare younglings away from the human world. The danger she'd felt earlier now made sense. She'd recklessly stumbled upon the one human who saw the real her. The one man who could pinpoint her heart.

The one man who could kill her.

Would kill her.

Right now.

Chapter Five

NO WORD COULD ADEQUATELY DESCRIBE ALEX'S STATE OF mind. In the last few minutes, his emotions had twisted from bitter fury to rampant lust. As soon as her teasing had become more acquiescent, his control had returned—at least of everything except his libido.

And now Elaina had collapsed, trembling against his chest. *This* he could handle.

"You know I exist. You feel me." He tightened his arms around her and kissed her temple. A spicy cinnamon flavor danced on the tip of his tongue.

She straightened and pushed against him. "Please don't do that."

"Don't deny what you want."

Her gaze dropped to his tuxedo shirt. "But mortal enemies don't kiss."

A laugh burst from his throat, reverberating off the paneling of his office. Mortal enemies? That was the most ridiculous rejection he'd ever heard.

She peered up at him, a crease forming between her eyebrows.

His laughter faded. "You can't be serious."

In answer, she wriggled under his arms and scrambled for the door.

"Elaina." Hell, was that even her real name? He lunged and snagged her wrist. "Elaina, no." She fought his grip, but he had too many questions for which he wanted answers to lose this battle. "You don't get to leave." Not yet.

After a moment, her body went limp. Her eyes downcast, she appeared broken and defeated. This woman was more than multifaceted. She was unfathomable. He steered her toward his desk and set her in his chair.

He crouched in front of her. "Explain."

"Please..."

He strained to hear her.

"Make it quick. That's all I ask."

"Make what—?" The meaning of her words sank in, and his hands shot up and cradled her face. "Damn it, I said I wasn't going to hurt you, and I'm certainly no rapist."

His control might be on shaky ground, but he'd never stoop to abuse. Never.

The furrow between her brows deepened. "I didn't think you were going to rape me."

"Then what did you mean, make it quick?"

Her fingers curled tight and rested on her chest. "When you kill me."

Dizziness swept over him, the accusation spiking his blood pressure. His hands slipped, and he clenched the arms of the chair, needing something solid to balance out her whiplash-worthy switch from temptress to victim.

With every ounce of patience he had, plus some, he forced calm into his voice. "Why do you think I would kill you?"

Her chin dipped to her collarbone. "Your kind is driven to kill my kind."

"My *kind*? What—male, rich, used to getting what he wants— that makes me a *murderer*?" As far as he knew, not even his father had been that bad.

"You don't know what you are?" Her eyes flashed bright blue, confirming her irises did indeed glow, and her fingertip skated over the back of his wrist. "Although... We wouldn't be having this conversation if you had those instincts. Maybe you're just a mutant."

He rocked back on his heels. From murderer to mutant?

Yet he couldn't write her off as a special brand of crazy and send her away. Especially not when her touch sent shivers up his arm that triggered every possible desire. Or when a compulsion to know and understand her burned inside him.

"Elaina—" He paused. "Is that your real name?"

She gave a slight smile. "Yes. You're the first human I've told. You should feel honored."

Bizarre as it was, and despite her odd choice of words, he did feel more extraordinary, simply by being around her.

"Elaina, I don't understand." Anything. "Who did you think I was?"

She stroked his right forearm, making his hairs stand up in response. "A knight. Haven't you ever read fairy tales? Knights always kill my kind."

A *knight*? A sharp grunt tore from his chest. "Sorry to disappoint you, but I'm no knight. Believe me."

"I want to believe you." Her tone softened at that admission, and she tilted her head. "Can you prove it?"

"Prove it? Knights don't exist, unless you count honorary titles like Sir Paul McCartney."

She focused on him, as though searching for something. "Where is my heart?"

His gaze skipped to the tops of her rounded breasts, eager for the excuse to stare. He let his fingertip leisurely explore a path from her collarbone to the neckline her dress. Who was he to argue with her request?

She clasped his wrist, and her voice rose in pitch. "You don't see it?" Her fingers intertwined with his. "You really *aren't* a knight."

Part of him wanted to be offended at the implication he was somehow less important because of that fact, but her happiness at the observation overruled the impulse.

He moved their joined hands and traced her lush lips with his thumb. "Why did you think I was?"

A soft brush of air tickled his knuckles, and blue smoldered in her gaze. Her voice now seemed to be weak for an entirely different reason. "Supposedly, the only human who can see our genuine form is the one true knight. All younglings are warned to stay away from humans because of the risk of encountering him."

She flinched and yanked out of his grasp. Her hand swept through the air, as though to erase her previous statement. "Anyway, when you said you could see my real hair and skin, I assumed you were this knight."

Her real hair. Her real skin. Her glowing eyes. She'd been warned to stay away from *humans*. All the details of her explanation—of her appearance—finally clicked into place.

She didn't think she was human. Even crazier, his instincts told him to believe her.

"Does that mean I'm not imagining things when I see your eyes glow? Or your skin shimmer like a rainbow?"

A smile lit up her features, shining brighter than the reflections off her cheeks. "You think my skin looks like a rainbow?"

Her radiant expression struck him numb, and his arms fell to his sides. Jesus. Words failed him, and he answered with a silent nod.

"Thank you. That's a more attractive picture than my description for it." She beat him to his next question, grimacing. "Fish scales."

"You don't have scales."

"In this form, they're microscopic."

In this form? His brain struggled to keep up. "You're not human. That's what you're telling me?"

"You tell me, since you can see the real me. Do I look human to you?"

At her question, something shifted in her appearance. Nothing specifically changed, but all her differences suddenly seemed...

More.

Her eyes blazed more vibrantly. Her skin shone with its iridescence. And the blonde shade in her hair no longer overpowered the other colors, instead becoming one of many that moved and danced from one wave to another.

His heart stuttered in his chest, and he lifted a lock of her hair. The curl changed from blonde to red to brown and then lightened again. Magic.

He barely believed what he was witnessing. He'd thought she was gorgeous before. In truth, she was stunning beyond imagination.

Treasured Claim

"What did you do?"

"I stopped projecting a human image."

Yes, that made sense—assuming any of this made sense. A double exposure wasn't subduing the truth anymore. He saw only the reality. The reality no one else saw.

Her unsuppressed beauty spurred on the instinct to conquer her. His reaction probably should have concerned him, but he couldn't say why.

Unable to resist, he captured her wrist and once again marveled at the lustrous texture of her skin. "What are you?"

A playful tone curved her lips. "Why should I tell you?"

His mouth opened, but he couldn't come up with a reason that didn't involve the threat of hunting her down until she revealed the truth.

She focused on his hand's strokes along her arm. "We're known in various languages as *dráko, dragua—*"

"Dracula!" He jerked back. "A vampire?"

She rolled her eyes. "Not Dracula. Drag-*guh*-ua." Her volume dipped along with her shoulders. "That one's Albanian." She shook herself and gave him a mischievous look. "How about *drakon*? Or—"

"Dragon," he whispered, as though speaking louder would wake him from this dream.

"Dragon." She matter-of-factly confirmed with a tip of her chin.

He didn't know which of them was more insane: her for saying she was a dragon or him for believing her. No human could look the way she did. And as strange as her claim sounded, the possibility *felt* natural. Felt normal. Felt like a truth he'd always suspected.

He found himself edging closer to her. "I should have known. I've always been fascinated by dragons."

Obsessed, in fact. His childhood go-to coping mechanism was dreaming of their homeland, which he imagined as a magical place where the stars danced like diamonds in the night sky.

His gaze lingered over her curves. "But I have to admit, you're not what I expected."

"We're born humanoid and have to shapeshift to the big winged serpent you're imagining. And before you ask—no, I can't show you my dragon form."

"It *would* be a shame to ruin this dress."

She laughed. "Shifting doesn't work like that. Clothes stay with our humanoid form." Her lashes lowered. "But it doesn't matter. I'm not powerful enough yet."

He cradled her cheeks, itching with the need to touch her, hold her. Dragon or not, her distress proved she was vulnerable, and that made her even more appealing.

Nothing she'd told him changed his attraction to her. If anything, knowing her secret increased the urge to capture her. Maybe even keep her.

Temptation lurked. Perhaps he could use the information to make her stay.

Chapter Six

"**W**HY DID YOU TELL ME ALL THIS?"

Alex's question caught Elaina off guard, and she jerked up. "I don't know."

That statement wasn't true, but she didn't want to admit how his queries compelled her to reveal her secrets. How she longed to have him know her. How he affected her.

Her gaze drifted to his lips, which probably explained the truth more than she intended. She forced her attention to the lapel of his tuxedo.

A knock rapped on the door, and Baxter poked his head inside Alex's office. "Er, sorry to interrupt, Mr. Wyatt, but George is on his way. He needs to finalize the arrangements for the presentation. I thought I should warn you."

Alex released her. "Wait here."

He strode toward the door, his focus on Baxter. "I commend you for checking on my guest's wellbeing, but next time, wait for my permission to enter. As you can see..."

The rest of his reprimand was drowned out by the click of the door closing—and being locked.

She should have jumped immediately at the opportunity to flee, but the sudden removal of Alex's touch, or more precisely, his heat, shocked her heart. How he managed to warm her, she didn't know and wasn't complaining, but right now, its loss was damned inconvenient. Precious seconds ticked by while she waited for her heartbeat to stabilize.

God, why was she such an idiot around him? Sure, at first she hadn't fought to get away because escaping a knight was impossible, and if death was a given, she'd rather embrace a quick demise than suffer the way her mother had. But even after discovering he was nothing more than a mutant, she'd babbled like a stupid, doe-eyed girl as soon as he'd looked in her direction. *Here, let's tell the powerful man all our secrets.* Idiot.

This was why she restrained her risk-taking instincts. Dragons were simply too unstable to rely on their instincts and still act logical and mature. And idiotic recklessness was a sure way to slip up and gain her father's attention. She couldn't afford mistakes.

As soon as she felt steady enough, she rushed to the large picture window. Several-inch-thick glass stood between her and the outside. Since when was glass that thick? She tapped on the window. The resonance was all wrong, deep and deadened.

Her forehead sagged against the window. It was probably some bulletproof, unbreakable, polycarbonate-something-or-other. Apparently, multi-kajillionaires worried about their safety.

She swept through his office, tapping at various spots on the side and outer walls. The results were the same. Solid mass lay behind the wood paneling. Escape wouldn't come from simply busting through thin plaster or drywall. Heat vents? Too small. Ceiling? Floor? Still solid.

Her hiss broke the quiet of her tiptoeing around the room. The sole exit point was through the door. She laid her ear against the wood. Muffled voices sounded on the other side.

She glared at the doorknob. Forget about this place being an "impregnable" fortress, it was more like "inescapable."

Her only choice was to use up all her new energy by breaking the lock, dealing with however many security guards stood outside, fleeing from the mansion, and oh yeah, somehow finding a way back to her car. And as a bonus, the violent exit would land her name and picture on the news as a wanted criminal.

Perfect. Her father would find her for sure.

Her gaze landed on the chair at Alex's desk. If she was honest with herself, she'd broken the secrets of her kind because of more than just her tipsy mood. Ever since she'd escaped her father, she'd been *in* the human world, but not one of them. Then this man—this *human* man—affected her more profoundly than she'd ever thought possible.

So, should she make herself the top story of the late night news? Or should she stay and see how things played out with the man who was *not* a knight, *not* driven to kill her, and whose touch strengthened her heart and weakened her knees? His calm acceptance of her nature proved he wasn't a typical human.

With all its rules, human society had never welcomed her, but what if *he* did? What would it feel like to fit in somewhere?

A small voice reminded her that she *couldn't* get what she really wanted. Dragons were incapable of real relationships. But would it be so bad to see where things *could* go with him?

The lock on the door clicked, and she hurriedly retook her position in the chair.

Alex entered, closed the door, and stood in front of her. "Now, what am I to do with you?"

She reached for him, eager to feel his warmth wash over her body. He obligingly returned to his crouch, bringing his eyes level with hers. His palm settled on her cheek, banishing her shivers, and his thumb brushed her lips once more.

"Tell me everything. How do weak dragons like you become more powerful?"

The heady sensation of his touch scrambled her thoughts again, and she sank against his palm. "Dragons get energy from their hoard. The more treasure they have, the stronger their potential, like having access to a grocery store. And the more fresh or unused their treasure is, the more they can draw on that strength, like having fresh food in the fridge." Her eyelids fluttered closed. "The oldest and most powerful dragons have constant access to an all-you-can-eat buffet, with the clichéd huge caves filled with endless piles of gold and gems you read about in fairy tales. I have less than a quarter of a square foot."

His fingers tensed against her skin, and his thumb pressed on the chain at her neck. "The jewelry isn't an illusion, is it?"

The warm feelings inside her shriveled, and she opened her eyes. Damn. Of course he wouldn't be okay with her taking things. Those problematic human rules again. It'd never work between them.

He stood and went into full "menacing" mode, complete with cold glare and stiff jaw. Time to go.

She dove to one side. He trapped her before she'd lunged more than two feet and tossed her back into the chair. Its wheeled legs thumped off the area rug and rumbled over the hardwood floor and into the wall.

"You're not leaving until you return the necklace." His chin lifted. "And the earrings and bracelet for that matter."

She rose, clutching the pendant in her fist. "I need them. I *earned* them."

"You *earned* them. Really?" His stance widened, and he crossed his arms. "It looks to me as though you stole them."

"Dragons don't use words like 'stealing.' We—"

"Rather convenient."

"Treasure must choose to bind to us. We can't summon or claim an item if its connection to its current owner is too strong." Taunting him, she marched forward and matched his pose. "So, yes, I *earned* them."

"What about the original owner? What about the money they had to *earn* to afford it in the first place?" The corners of his eyes tightened. "Do you at least leave them a nice little thank you note?"

Hair lifted at the nape of her neck at the signs registering from her body. Energized. Hyperaware of his every muscle twitch. A desire to get closer to him.

The more dangerous he was, the more excited she became. Definitely an unsafe combination.

And talking through this wouldn't help either. He'd never understand. Humans couldn't.

"I'm sorry. I didn't mean for it to happen like this. I didn't mean for you and I—" Her throat constricted. "It doesn't matter if you understand or not. I need these, and well, quite frankly, you can't take them from me so there's no point arguing about it."

"Bullshit." He pulled a cell phone from his tuxedo's inner pocket. "You can't rationalize your way out of this. You're stealing. I'll turn you over to the cops and let them deal with you."

"What are you going to tell them? That I stole a necklace they can't see? Or forcibly remove from my body?" She took the decorative quill pen from his desk and playfully swirled the feather around the pendant. "They can't touch me, and you know it."

His eyes assumed a flinty cast, and the sense of power around him flared. She shuffled back. His influence could get her locked up regardless of the lack of proof.

Helpless and imprisoned under her real name. So not good.

She replaced the pen in its holder and tried another approach. "Have you ever been poor? I mean, a real you-don't-know-where-your-next-meal-is-coming-from poor?"

He exhaled. "No."

"That's what my life's been like for ten years, Alex. Ten years. I've been on my own since I was fourteen. The only one of my kind living among humans, the only one in the Americas at all. Ten years of scrounging a lost earring here, a discarded engagement ring there. Until I finally collected enough to do a real summoning."

She grasped the necklace. "This is my energy—this is my food. If I don't have enough treasure, I starve, and my heart stops beating." Admitting her weakness went against her nature, and the points of her nails instinctively sharpened, ready to defend herself from anyone who assumed her helpless. "I'm sorry this messes up Mrs. Boyce's day, I really am. But if I give it up, I die."

"Why did you take that if you came here to steal—or whatever you want to call it—from me?"

"I came here for your guests."

"And you were going to pick them clean?"

She couldn't help grumbling, "I was on my way out when you dragged me in here." She resisted poking him with a sharpened nail to emphasize her point. Barely. "I told you, this isn't about greed or stealing. I'm just trying to survive."

He leaned back against his desk and stared at her, arms crossed over his chest again. Although the distance between them gave her some needed breathing room, a shiver traveled through her heart at the loss of his heat.

Rather than squirm under his attention, she returned to his desk chair and tipped her chin. "So are we at an impasse? Am I to stay here forever because you refuse to let me go and yet can't do anything to change the situation?"

Unexpectedly, he laughed. "No, the gossip pages would have a field day with that. I can already imagine the rumors flying around the ballroom as it is."

"Rumors?"

"In case you've forgotten, I'm supposed to be hosting a party out there." He slipped his cell phone into his pocket and jerked his head, indicating beyond the door. "Several hundred of the most powerful and influential people in the state—and instead of pandering to them, I disappeared with a beautiful woman."

"Oh. *Oh*..." The implications of his words mingled awkwardly in her thoughts. "I'm sorry." And she meant it.

"I'm not." One corner of his mouth quirked up. "Truthfully, if it wasn't necessary for building fundraising partnerships, I'd never host these parties. I hate them."

Despite the uncertainty hanging over the situation, she offered him an impish smile. "In that case, you're welcome."

Instead of scowling at her, he laughed again, and then he stood and strode toward her. "I propose a trade. I'll give you something in exchange for everything you took."

She leaned forward, unable to hide her shock. "You'd do that?"

A flicker of surprise crossed his features, as though he couldn't believe his proposal either. Then he gave a single, sharp nod. "Yes."

Respect for this man, this human, burned within her, more than she'd ever felt for any other being. He'd proven her wrong. On some level, he *did* understand.

"Why?" Her voice was so quiet she wasn't sure she'd spoken aloud, but she couldn't help the question.

He seemed too good to be true. And she desperately wanted him to be true.

ALEX PIVOTED AWAY, HIDING WHATEVER HIS EXPRESSION MIGHT reveal. He roamed to the picture window across his office, the darkness outside masking his thoughts. Why *was* he willing to help her?

The discovery that she was the ultimate gold-digger, literally, had revolted him at first. Yet it hadn't stunted his desire for her—maybe because her claims of starvation rang true. After everything he'd endured with his father, fair fights were more interesting than easy victories over a weaker opponent. But he doubted that was the limit of his reasoning.

Outside, a haunting full moon rose from the horizon, glistening off the ripples of Lake Michigan. Through the thick air, the glowing orb shone huge and reddish. Unnatural. Despite appearances, this was the same moon he knew well.

Like the moon, was this woman someone he could relate to no matter her form? The long list of differences between them didn't change his craving for her. Instead, the secrets she'd revealed filled in a piece of him he hadn't realized was missing. A piece he didn't want to lose again.

He studied her in the reflection on the glass. She'd picked up the feather quill again and was distractedly stroking its length. Without trying, she was the sexiest woman he'd ever known. Everything about her stirred his desire to keep her beside him. On some level, his urges were worrisome—possibly even reminiscent of his father's attitudes—but he needed her close in a way that felt like destiny, not contempt.

He returned and sat on the edge of his desk. "To answer your question, I won't allow anyone to harm my guests. But I also won't make you starve. I'm helping you fix this situation."

Her hands stopped their sensual movement. "Fix it?"

"Can you return the bracelet and the earrings the same way you took them?"

"I suppose. I'm not sure it's ever been tried."

"The necklace will have to be 'found' in the ballroom somewhere, as Mrs. Boyce has already noticed it missing."

She pointed the feather at him. "Why do you care about protecting my reputation in front of these people?"

His stomach hollowed at the uncertainty her question implied. If she didn't cooperate, he'd be forced to have her escorted out. Away from him. The thought propelled him to his feet. He wanted to hold her, grab her—restrain her if necessary. His plan was the only outcome he could accept.

"Because you're going to be my date for the evening."

Her eyes opened wide, and then one brow rose. "I should have known." She stood and tapped the quill against her lips. "Let me get this straight. The deal is, I return the jewelry and pretend to be Mr. Bossypants's doting arm ornament, and in exchange you'll give me something I deem of equal or greater value?"

Christ, she didn't have to make it sound like that. He didn't need to *pay* for anyone's company. "Your words, not mine."

"But that's the deal, right?" She replaced the quill in its holder.

His jaw clenched so hard his blood pressure rose and pounded in his ears. Jesus, what he wouldn't do to force her to submit.

His entire foundation was at risk because of her. The governor would never cooperate with the statewide expansion plan if a thief walked out with his wife's jewelry. And God only knew how long he had until the owners of the other items discovered their losses. If multiple thefts were reported at his party, everyone would hold him responsible. All potential donors down the drain. For the sake of everything he'd worked for, he had to control himself.

"Yes. That's the deal."

She stuck out her hand and gave him a triumphant grin. "Agreed."

His chest sank at her display of glee. He shook on their arrangement without enthusiasm, the joy sucked out of his victory. Her claim of starvation notwithstanding, she had a mercenary streak as deep as any other gold-digger.

And he'd approved letting her determine what was of equal or greater value. Wonderful.

She sat on top of his desk and crossed her legs, shifting the open slit of her dress up her shapely thighs an inch or so. He stifled a groan. She knew how to push his buttons—the bad ones *and* the good ones.

"So..." Her playful tone matched her mischievous expression. "Let's see what you have to buy me off."

He yanked his money clip from his pocket and separated the wad of cash. "Just tell me how much this is going to cost."

But her attention didn't follow the dollar bills. A quiet squeal escaped her, and she hopped off his desk and hovered closer to the money clip itself.

"Ooo, 3.64 total carat weight, G and H color, VS2 clarity

diamonds set in 47.5 grams of fourteen-karat white gold."

"Uh, yeah." He almost smiled at her unusual talent. "No, 3.64 carats? I paid for 3.75."

"Trust me." She flashed a smug grin. "I'm never wrong."

"I'll take your word for it." He flipped the clip right-side up, and his thumb brushed the embedded diamonds forming a winged serpent shape on the clip's surface.

She sucked in a breath. "You weren't lying."

"I told you, dragons have always fascinated me."

"Okay, I'll take it."

His fingers tightened around the clip. "What do you mean, you'll take it?"

"I *mean...*" She drew out the word and gave him a *duh* look. "I'll take that for the trade."

"In exchange for what, the bracelet or the earrings?"

"All of it."

His ingrained desire for fairness almost prompted him to protest that although the money clip hadn't been cheap, it was far from the value of all three items, but he caught himself in time.

She deciphered his expression anyway. "Human monetary values don't match the energy I receive from an object. The stronger the connection between an object and its current owner, the more valuable it is to me. And you clearly don't want to give that up. *If* I can take it from you—and that's a big 'if'—the energy I'd get from it would surpass what I receive from all of these." She gestured to the stolen jewelry.

He shook his head at her candor. She certainly didn't fit under a tidy *good* or *bad* label. More importantly, she'd proven him flat-out wrong. She might need gold to survive, but she was *nothing* like the gold-diggers he'd known.

Under his breath, he muttered, "You're absolutely maddening."

She gave him a saucy smile. "From you, I'll take that as a compliment." She patted his wooden desktop. "I need you to put it here."

"You haven't turned over the jewelry yet."

"I need their energy to claim that from you." She shrugged. "If you don't trust me, we can stand here all night."

"Why can't I just give it to you?"

"I have to overcome your connection to the clip to claim it and establish my bond. Without that bond, I can't get energy from treasure no matter how much it's worth in human terms." She tapped a fingertip against her lips, which teased him with a curve. "The other option for overcoming your connection to the clip is killing you, but I've taken a vow of non-violence. And I don't think dying would be your preference either."

His brow climbed high on his forehead. Beautiful, witty, truthful, intriguing...

The money clip clattered to the desk with his decision to trust her.

She stretched her hand toward the desk but didn't touch the clip. Her eyes closed, and her features tensed in concentration. Nothing happened.

She eyed him and grimaced. "I told you I wasn't very strong."

Her face screwed up once more. Any lingering suspicions he had about her vanished. She hadn't tried to take advantage of him, and she hadn't been lying about her weakness.

Again, nothing happened to the money clip. But this time, she wobbled on her feet.

He grasped her other arm. The desire to protect her was as strong as his urge to overpower her, and that contradiction was going to be the end of him.

Chapter Seven

ELAINA'S LINK TO THE MONEY CLIP INCREASED WHEN ALEX'S fingers closed around her and spread warmth through her body. Of course. She should have thought of that.

She'd had the idea of getting the clip out of his possession to weaken his connection to it, but hadn't considered how to strengthen hers. Just as holding Mrs. Boyce's hand had allowed her to acquire the necklace, Alex's touch increased her ability to claim his treasure in his territory.

With the added boost, she concentrated again on her summons. The clip disappeared from Alex's desktop and materialized in her palm. She exhaled with relief at the same time Alex released her and staggered back.

"Holy shit."

She stifled a roll of her eyes. "What did you think was going to happen?"

He stared at his trembling fingers. As though they'd gone numb, he shook out his wrist.

"I don't know. It'd fly through the air or something. I hadn't thought about it."

She slid the clip down the bodice of her dress, where it bonded to her skin with a heady rush of energy. Her hand slipped from her neckline, and she braced herself on the desk. Maybe becoming inebriated in front of Alex wasn't the smartest idea.

As though he'd read her mind, he leaned forward, checking out the current location of the clip. Her body wanted him even closer.

Bad idea. Really bad idea.

She distracted them both by giving him the necklace. Discarding the pendant removed her claim—and some of her energy—settling the buzzing in her brain.

"If you want me to try to replace these"—she jangled the bracelet on her wrist—"I'll need to leave them on for the time being."

"Uh, sure." He still sounded stunned.

She closed her eyes and concentrated on recreating her human appearance.

Warm air floated across her cheek, and his deep voice rumbled at her ear. "What are you doing?"

Her eyes shot open, and she tottered back from his invasion of her personal space. "If you expect me to go out there again, shouldn't I look human?"

"You're beautiful the way you are. Leave your hair."

Her fingers instinctively stretched and curled. Of course he'd have instructions on how to fulfill her duties as his arm decoration. As though treasure had value only as property.

"First of all, you know this 'arm trophy' thing doesn't work because no one else sees me as you do. My human projection is plain and unremarkable by design. And secondly, you can't control me the way you do everyone else. I'll leave the colors, but not the swirling."

He waved, as though equally unconcerned about others' impressions of her looks and others' right to see the shifting colors. As if that was even an option.

If people recognized she wasn't a pure blonde anymore, she'd make him deal with their confusion. Would serve him right. She subdued her skin and eye differences and froze the changeling shades of her hair into a fixed pattern.

He opened the office door, revealing one of the brutes standing in the hallway.

Alex hitched his thumb down the hall. "Tell Baxter to have the ballroom team complete another low-key search for the necklace."

After the guard acknowledged, Alex led her to the ballroom. Before the guests noticed their arrival, he discreetly dropped the necklace behind a potted tree beside the entrance.

The jewelry's sense of abandonment called to her. Back when she'd had the chance, she should have reassured the pendant that it was on its way home. Too late now.

Alex linked her hand over his left elbow and had her point out the women missing the other pieces. As they crossed the ballroom, the bleached and spackled one she'd taken the earrings from motioned in their direction.

"Alex! I was wondering where you'd gone off to." She sidled closer in a cloud of heavy perfume and air-kissed his cheek. "I was about to feel neglected."

The woman turned alongside him and backed up a step. Elaina had to slip out of Alex's arm to avoid being run over. The woman then had the nerve to reach for Alex's now-empty forearm.

He smoothly shuffled Elaina to his other side and pivoted away from the woman's advance. "*Mrs.* Reid, have you met Ms. Drake yet?"

The temptation to give the bitch a few nasty dragon claw scars faded at his emphasis of the woman's married status, especially when he focused his dazzling grin on Elaina. He brushed his knuckles along her neck down to where the pendant had lain on her collarbone.

"We were unavoidably detained."

She blinked. Yeah, *that* would quell the rumor mill.

Mrs. Reid pulled her mouth into something between a smile and a sneer—although that could have been the Botox. "Ms. Drake, is it? I hadn't realized you were here with Alex."

Elaina shook the woman's hand and concentrated on sending the earrings back into the woman's earlobes, maybe with a tad more force than required. But she had to make sure this untested technique worked, right?

Mrs. Reid squeaked and yanked her arm away. She rubbed her earlobes and was unsurprised at finding her earrings there. One disappearance fixed and unnoticed.

The elegant older woman she'd taken the bracelet from joined their conversation. "How do you know Mr. Wyatt?"

Before Elaina could shoot Alex a questioning look, he easily answered, "She's a jewelry appraiser. We met when I needed several items examined."

Impressive. That was a good line.

"Elaina Drake." She held the woman's hand and sent the bracelet to her wrist. "It's nice to meet you again."

The long sleeves of the woman's gown had probably prevented her from realizing the loss of her jewelry either. Alex squeezed Elaina's hand against him. She took that as a thank you.

Mrs. Reid dropped her fingers from her earlobes. "A jewelry appraiser, huh?"

"Yes," Alex answered for her. He met Elaina's gaze with raised brows, a reminder for her to play along. "I'd say she's the best in the world."

Between the intensity of his stare and the compliment, she didn't mind her obligation.

Mrs. Reid huffed. "That's quite a recommendation. I should have you do an appraisal of my wedding ring. I keep asking Henry for the paperwork so I can update our insurance, but he's so busy, you know."

Elaina didn't even glance at the lifeless rock on the woman's finger. "You don't need an appraisal."

"You sound like Henry. It's three carats. I need it insured."

Elaina widened her eyes in faked innocence. "Your insurance covers cubic zirconia?"

"Cubic—?" Mouth agape, the woman stormed off across the ballroom. "Henry!"

The crowd that had gathered around them during the exchange snickered at the outburst. Before Elaina could check Alex's reaction to the insult of his guest, a feedback squeal broke over loudspeakers. Everyone jostled for a view of the other end of the ballroom, where a thin, dark-haired man—Alex's assistant—stood on a low platform. He adjusted the microphone.

"Good evening, ladies and gentlemen. If I could have your attention for a moment, we're about to start the presentation."

Alex leaned close and whispered, "Ready for the spotlight?"

The taste of dirty coal rose up her throat, and she choked. He began walking toward the dais, and she yanked him back. "Spotlight?"

"A short speech and a few pictures. Not a big deal."

"No." Her voice hissed despite the lack of sibilant consonants.

"No pictures."

His shoulders jerked. "No—?"

"No cameras, nothing like that." She didn't try to hide that the idea terrified her. For good measure, she even added a "please."

He took in her expression and then looked away and nodded with an odd tilt of his head. "Stay here."

After that firm instruction, he maneuvered through the crowd, accepting their enthusiastic greetings on his way. Once he was out of sight and her heartbeat stopped fluttering at his absence, she scoped out her escape options around the room. Sure, she'd promised to stay through the evening, but she'd returned the other jewelry pieces already. Letting photographers document her location wasn't part of the job description.

Up ahead, Alex climbed the platform and took the microphone. She retreated a few steps for a clear view of the ballroom entrance. A hand pressed against her back, halting her movement.

Baxter, Alex's security guy, prowled closer. "I'm glad you'll be remaining with us for the evening."

The message came through clearly. He'd prevent her from leaving unless she wanted to use up all the energy she'd gained tonight. And making any kind of scene would bring out every camera phone in the place. So much for that idea.

Alex's voice from the stage intensified, recapturing her awareness. "No children should have to experience violence in their home. To that end, I'm establishing the Safe Home, Safe Child Foundation, which will work to prevent child abuse and assist children in dangerous situations. Because of your generosity, we'll be able to establish and maintain shelters throughout Chicagoland. And if I can count on your ongoing support and cooperation, we'll be able to expand our efforts across the state, providing safety to those most vulnerable."

She found herself nodding along with the crowd. Protecting the young was a good cause in any society.

"As promised, rather than match your donation, I've added a zero to the amount donated tonight." He chuckled. "I suspect some of you opened your wallets extra wide because you knew how much it would cost me." He glanced at his assistant and jokingly grumbled, "Remind me to pack a bag lunch for the rest of my life."

A wave of laughter rippled over the audience.

"Thanks to all of you, I'm pleased to present this check for fifty-seven million dollars to the Safe Home, Safe Child Foundation."

She echoed the crowd's gasp. Fifty-seven million dollars?

Applause burst through the ballroom. Beside her, guests compared their shock at the number. Apparently, matching the total was his usual approach for encouraging donations at his annual fundraising party. But for whatever reason, this year he'd drastically changed the rules.

After the presentation and official pictures, Alex descended the platform and was quickly mobbed. Elaina edged away, hoping to escape in the chaos. Baxter seized her arm and jostled through the throng toward Alex. The man was too good at his job.

As soon as they neared, Alex hooked her hand over his elbow. "Thank you for seeing to her, Baxter."

The men shared a look that held too much understanding of her intentions. She wanted to be upset at the thwarting of her plans, but the warmth settling around her heart wouldn't let her.

She leaned close, pressing more of her body against Alex. "That check was rather generous of you."

His chin dipped. "It's for a good cause."

She did a double take. Since when was he humble?

As the night wore on, his behavior continued to conflict with her expectations of how a guy like him would act with an "arm ornament." He treated her with respect, was attentive, and had Baxter take her aside every time someone brought out a camera for a picture with him. Was he just putting on a show? And if so, for what purpose?

His line for introducing her added to her confusion. "She's going to be my special advisor for tangible assets and unique investments."

An ongoing arrangement? That wasn't part of their deal. She didn't fit in with humans.

Yet Baxter's constant presence proved Alex wanted to keep her around. How far would he go? Would he expose her secrets if she didn't go along with his demands? Skimming the cover headlines of *Cosmo* hadn't prepared her for this situation.

She fell quiet and swallowed, conflict playing out in her mind.

No matter what a part of her might wish for, it was pointless to hope for more than simple blackmail between them. Dragons weren't capable of more. Period. End of discussion.

Once the crowd around them thinned, he steered her close. "I do believe it's time for a dance."

His husky voice vibrated through her body. She refused to look up at him and place her nose closer to his neck. As it was, his scent invaded her senses, inviting her to breathe deeper.

Distracting herself from the idea, she listened for the music's deep, repetitive thumps, but heard only soft vibratos. *That* was dance music? The sounds produced by the stringed instruments in the alcove were nothing like those resonating through her apartment walls every night. Others seemed to agree with her. Only a few couples swayed together on the wood floor near the musicians.

"Won't that make us the center of attention?"

He motioned to Baxter, and she recognized the signal as his directive to keep cameras away. Then he led her to the dance floor. "It's too late to worry about that now."

True. He'd already given the gossipmongers plenty of material.

"Why'd you do it?" She suppressed a shudder as his arm slid over her bare back and set her skin on fire.

He gave her a blank look. "Do what?"

His graceful movements impressed her. Even though she didn't know the first thing about this dance, he effortlessly guided her through the rhythm of the music.

"You know." She squeezed him, attempting to shake an answer out of him, but it only resulted in them dancing closer. "If you were worried about your reputation, why'd you encourage the rumors?"

"Rumors were going to happen whether I said anything or not. Just showing up with a woman on my arm for the first time in three ye—" He cut himself off and tilted his head away.

"Three years?"

He didn't deny it, and he didn't face her. His hold on her body tensed, yet their smooth sweeps of the dance floor continued, hiding the nature of their conversation from observers.

"Alex"—she lowered her volume—"what happened three years

ago?"

His gaze snapped back to hers. "How do you do that?"

At his accusing tone, she almost stumbled. "Do what?"

"Any other person would ask *why*. Why haven't I been with a woman lately? And I could make up something, like how I hadn't met the right person. But you get to the root of the issue, asking *what* happened to cause the change."

His fingers caressed her back, as though she were a stringed instrument for him to play. Mild shocks zipped through her body.

He gave her a rueful smile. "And that's a harder question to duck."

Her mouth twitched into a curve. "Sorry."

"No, you're not."

She stiffened. Had she upset him?

His expression unwound until it revealed nothing. "My father died three years ago."

"I'm sorry." Her voice held only sincerity this time.

"Don't be." His eyes sharpened, glinting with ferocity. "My father was a miserable, arrogant, controlling bastard." He grunted. "He was everything you think I am."

She flinched, although she couldn't say why. "I don't think all that of you."

His severe look softened, his irises melting to liquid silver.

The glimpse of his vulnerability turned her thoughts to goo. Before she did something she'd regret, she attempted to change the mood. "I certainly don't think you're *miserable*."

He laughed, just as she'd hoped. "What am I going to do with you?"

Her yearning for his touch broke through every defensive wall of safety around her. Surrender was a valid option if he would give her what she wanted. What she suddenly needed.

"Kiss me."

His incredulous expression matched her reaction to the impulsive words. He leaned closer, and her heartbeat quickened in response.

Her plans forgotten, she wasn't going to take back her request.

Chapter Eight

ALEX EMBRACED HIS GOOD FORTUNE. ELAINA'S EYES HAD widened after she'd spoken, as though she hadn't meant to say the words, but he wasn't going to give her a chance to change her mind.

He slanted his mouth over hers and tightened his arm across her back, cradling her closer. Her lips, warm and soft, gave in to him.

She moaned, echoing his pleasure. The vibration traveled through his body, blazing a trail of arousal. Unable to hold himself back, he stopped any pretext of ballroom dancing.

His tongue flicked over her lips, demanding. She gasped and opened her mouth. Her fingers twisted into his hair, tugging him to her.

He obliged and swept his tongue inside. A sweet-spicy flavor hit his senses, and he was starving for more of a taste. A whole feast in fact. Intoxicated by their connection, he crushed her against him. The pressure was all that contained his rapidly beating heart.

Another second, and they'd be putting on an indecent show for the crowd.

A cheer shrieked from the other end of the ballroom. Elaina pulled away and focused on his tuxedo lapel.

He scanned the room. At least they weren't the center of attention. Mrs. Boyce's joy at having her necklace returned to her by his security team had captured his guests' interest.

"It's okay," he murmured into Elaina's hair. "No one noticed."

She peered up at him and swallowed. "How could kissing be like that? Was that normal?"

"Nothing about you is normal."

He'd almost forgotten they had an audience, and he *had* forgotten to care about the potential repercussions from that.

He admitted, "That wasn't normal for me either."

"Oh god, Alex." She laid her head and palm on his chest. "I didn't know."

He stroked her back, wishing he could feel all of her against him. "That better be a good reaction. I *will* be kissing you again."

"Yes, it was good. So good it scares me."

He knew what she meant. Losing control wasn't an option, but something about her made it seem like a good idea. At the thought of experiencing that sensation with her in bed, his fingers moved to her shoulder blades, following the curves along her spine.

She shuddered against his touch and straightened. Her gaze darted away. "I need to go. Now."

The compulsion he'd felt all evening to hunt her down and keep her close concentrated into this moment. He couldn't let her leave.

"Look at me."

She did as he asked, but her expression didn't explain her sudden request. Her eyes shone with an emotion he couldn't figure out. Embarrassment? Confusion? Fear?

"I know I promised, but I can't stay any longer." Her lips rolled into a tight line. "Please, let me go."

He ached to fist his hand in her hair and restrain her, force her to stay, force her to do what he wanted. Against his will, his imagination played out the scene.

The images soured, his dominant nature becoming dangerous. Brutal. Unforgiving.

Chills spread from his heart to his disloyal fingers. He'd made his vow to maintain control for a reason. He couldn't—wouldn't—force her to stay.

Movement along the wall near the musicians caught his eye. Several guests huddled around a cell phone, which disappeared as soon as they noticed his spying.

Goddammit. A camera phone. Apparently, his behavior with Elaina hadn't escaped detection after all. With the display he'd put on, he couldn't blame Baxter for missing one. The man had probably had his hands full.

At least she hadn't observed the group behind her. Given her current mood, if she saw the camera, she'd take off without leaving him a way to track her down again.

Behind her view, he signaled Baxter to go after the photographer and mouthed the word *delete*. Then he led her away from the intrusive guests. "I'll have my driver take you home."

Another guard took Baxter's place at his side, and he texted his driver, James, to meet him at the garage. But as soon as they left the dance floor, crowds surrounded him again.

It took him a half hour to break away from the mob. She remained subdued at his side, not saying a word even after they reached the calm outside the ballroom.

During their trip through the winding hallways of the mansion, he kept his distance, his arms stiff at his sides. No matter what he wanted or how badly he wanted it, this was not the time to test his self-control.

Once they reached the garage, he pulled James aside. "Don't leave her alone until she's safely inside her house."

James's dark eyes flicked to Elaina and back, the muscles around them tight and alert, and he gave a strong nod. As Alex's de facto bodyguard off the grounds, he probably assumed he'd been given the task of protecting her. Alex let him believe that. It was better than admitting he simply wanted to learn where she lived.

He returned to Elaina and clasped his hands behind his back, where they wouldn't be tempted to do any damage. "Don't worry. James will get you home."

She stretched and kissed his cheek. "Thank you."

"I'll be in touch."

James escorted her away, and Alex tried to ignore the instincts ripping him in two. The only thing keeping his adrenaline from spiking into the danger level was the knowledge he *would* see her again.

As though his life depended on it, he swore this was *not* goodbye.

Elaina didn't bother turning on the lights inside her apartment. Her night vision allowed her to make it to the kitchen chair, where she collapsed.

Her skin still tingled and quivered at the nexus Alex had unintentionally stroked, right where her wings would eventually emerge. She rubbed her spine against the back of the chair, as though she could scrape away the disconcerting feeling.

God, what the hell had happened tonight? The whole evening had set off unfamiliar sensations in her body, and his touch had awakened parts she'd never heard from before. The sensory overload was way more than she could handle.

If she hadn't left... No, she wouldn't let her thoughts go there.

But she couldn't stop all her thoughts, too many of which were nothing more than a jumbled pile of conflicting desires and needs. Like the fine chain of a pendant so hopelessly tangled she might as well get used to the new length.

Because the truth was—she was an addict.

In the years since fleeing across the ocean, she'd become so complacent that she'd forgotten the strength of her instincts. Forgotten the dangerous excitement of the constant near misses with her father. Forgotten how adrenaline had been a comforting presence after her mother's death.

The rush from her acquisitions tonight was beyond anything she'd ever experienced, and not just because of the energy surge. The danger junkie she'd unleashed inside her wanted more.

Forget abandoned pieces. Forget the guilt issue. At the party, part of her had become convinced that stealing treasure was the only way to go.

And then she'd discovered an even bigger rush: embracing danger.

Literally.

The threatening vibe radiating from Alex kicked her addiction to a stratospheric level. And embracing him—kissing him—

intensified that buzz by a thousand. A million.

That was bad. Very bad. She could easily lose herself in him and forget her goals. He *was* incredibly dangerous to her, even though he wasn't a knight.

On top of that, if she let Alex draw her into his world, with photographers and gossipmongers reporting on his every move, the chances of her father tracking her down became a question of *when* and not *if.* The last time her father had gotten close, thousands of acres in Europe had burned to the ground in a supposed forest fire. If he found her here, all of Chicago would become a smoking monument of destruction.

At her kitchen table, she flipped Alex's money clip over in her palm. Her thumb caressed the dragon shape on its surface, and her forehead thumped onto the tabletop.

She *really* was an idiot. A huge, almost overpowering part of her wanted to return to him.

And then what? Even in the best-case scenario, without the threat from her father, they'd have a hard time making things work between them. They'd argue about her taking jewelry. Or worse, she'd capitulate to his human laws and stay weak forever, unable to ignite her heart and change form, constantly on the verge of death.

No, it was better this way. Love wasn't possible for dragons, and it didn't conquer all anyway. Her mother had paid the price for that fallacy.

Elaina needed to stick to her plan, or she'd die by her father's hand as well. She sat up and once more ground her spine against the back of the chair, attempting to erase her body's reactions along with any thoughts of Alex.

Besides, for all she knew, kissing anyone would give her the same rush.

Chapter Nine

ALEX TOSSED IN HIS BED. AGAIN. THE TOO-BRIGHT NUMBERS on the clock announced a time of just past four a.m. Instead of crashing after an insanely long day, he punched his pillow and adjusted its height for the hundredth time.

Every time he closed his eyes, the nightmare vision of becoming violent with Elaina haunted him. The fear was crazy though—the disturbing thought *wasn't* going to become reality.

Given everything with his father, Alex prided himself on being Mr. Self-Control. He'd never even been close to abusive before. One little mental image was no reason to think he'd suddenly lose all self-discipline around Elaina.

His attempt to sleep also wasn't helped by an obsessive need to see her. Right now. Despite the early hour, a suspicion gnawed at his gut that he wouldn't get another chance. Of all the things he should be thinking about—like how she wasn't human and how he should be freaking out at that fact—his mind instead fixated on rationalizing his need to get to her.

When the clock displayed 5:17, the relentless internal debate drove him to surrender. After disentangling from his bedcovers, he took a quick shower, threw on a T-shirt and jeans, and slipped a ball cap onto his still-damp hair. His pocket bulged with several extra hundreds for an I-know-I'm-dragging-you-out-of-bed-way-too-early-on-a-Sunday-morning bonus in preparation for his next stop—the gatehouse apartment where his driver lived with his girlfriend.

James's last text the previous night had mentioned he was returning to Elaina's place today. Something about helping her pick up her car. Alex was simply kicking off the plan earlier than anticipated and tagging along. Not a problem.

By the time James parked in front of Elaina's apartment building in one of the many sketchy areas of Uptown, Alex wished he'd instead surrendered to sleep, and the world outside was merely the product of a bad dream. Graffiti-covered plywood boarded over most of the ground-level windows on the block, vagrants slumped in sidewalk alcoves, and the least rundown structure in the area was a methadone clinic across the street.

From within the car, he examined the mid-rise building James indicated. "Are you sure this is the right place?"

"I walked her up to her apartment, just like you said. She asked me to drop her off at her car at work, but I insisted on taking her home. I told her I'd pick her up and drive her to her car sometime today."

"Thank you for offering your personal time to her." Hiring James despite his spotty record was one of the best impulsive decisions Alex had ever made. "She's expecting you, right?"

"Sort of. We didn't set a time."

A man stumbled past them on the sidewalk, yelling into an imaginary phone held to his ear. The ragged trench coat on the man's thin frame and the grizzled beard on his gaunt face made it unlikely a Bluetooth headset was to blame for the invisible nature of his one-sided conversation.

Alex's heart sank under the grim reality of the neighborhood. Even *he* didn't have enough money to fix all of Chicago's problems.

Uptown rightly had a reputation as the city's dumping grounds for the mentally ill, the homeless, and the drug addicted. Too many times, all three labels would apply to the same person.

And Elaina lived in this place. The thought made him sick.

"Which apartment is hers?"

James leaned forward and peered up through the windshield, the early morning sun adding an orange cast to his otherwise dark, clean-shaven scalp. "That fifth floor unit with a light on."

Her light was on? This early? The ominous feeling in his gut ratcheted up a notch.

"You can earn your wingman stripes by taking me to her apartment."

They entered the building, dodging the broken glass littering the sidewalk along the way. The building's entrance wasn't locked. In fact, the door didn't have a lock anymore, appearing to have been busted out long ago.

At her apartment upstairs, Alex directed James to knock while he held back. A security chain rasped, and the door cracked open. A sliver of light spilled into the dim, unlit corridor.

"James, hi." Surprise pitched Elaina's voice higher than usual. "I wasn't expecting you this early. Um, come in for a second." She unhooked the chain and swung the door wide. "Let me find my keys."

Alex strode forward. "Actually, he was delivering me."

She stood silent and frozen, one hand gripping the doorknob, as though using it for balance. Neither the early hour or her simple low-cut T-shirt and jeans diminished her beauty.

The sight electrified his mood, and a grin burst onto his face. "Good morning, Elaina."

Her hand moved from the door handle to her hip. "You have a lot of nerve coming here."

Uh... Not quite the welcome he'd hoped for. Yes, it was early, but they'd parted on good terms the previous night. Hadn't they?

He signaled James. "Go watch the car."

The man puffed out his cheeks and released a breath. "In this neighborhood, I'm more worried about *your* safety."

"The car, James."

His driver grunted and relinquished his bodyguard duties. Alex entered her studio apartment and closed the door. "You're angry. Why?"

"Unless you're here to apologize for destroying my life, I don't have anything to say to you."

"*Destroying* your life?" He swept a hand over his face, hiding an eye roll. "How do you figure that?"

She didn't answer. Instead, she spun to an old laptop on a scuffed-up table, fingered the touchpad for a second, and waved him toward the keyboard. "Take a look, and see if you're still confused."

He sat in the room's only chair, the uneven legs thumping the linoleum with his shifting weight, and scanned the computer screen. Shit. The local gossip column.

MISCHIEVOUS MUSINGS BY MOI

How the mighty have fallen...

Alexander Wyatt appeared back on Moi's radar in spectacular fashion last night—with another lavish display of moolah the man has become famous for. At an invitation-only celebratory dinner (celebrating his fabulousness, that is) at his sumptuous North Shore manor, he announced his return to the playboy ranks by showing off his latest acquisition, a Ms. Elena Drake. While we welcome Alex back to these fine pages, we shudder to think this woman was the best he could come up with for his coming-out party. Come now, Alex, we know you've already used up all the local bimbos with bra sizes bigger than their IQs, but really...

Although Alex introduced Ms. Drake to his guests as a jewelry appraiser, Moi could find no records of any certifications for said occupation—or of this woman's supposed name at all. Either she's managed to pull the wool over our favorite lady-killer's eyes, or Alex picked her up off a street corner minutes before his soirée. Neither alternative bodes well for our boy.

An unflattering photograph of their kiss graced the top of the article, and a close-up of Elaina—or at least the mundane version of her that cameras and others were able to see—was posted next to Moi's snarky comment of "but really..." Double shit.

Alex's throat worked, but too many bad memories created a nausea-induced lump he couldn't get past. He drew circles on the touchpad and tried to think of a response.

Christ, this was bad. No, horrific. With the references to his past behavior, he had to do major damage control on her impression of him. Worse, the article had decimated her reputation. Whether Baxter had missed deleting all the pictures on that camera phone the previous night or there had been a second photographer, the damage was done. Her urgent pleas to avoid cameras echoed in his mind with an I-told-you-so indictment.

If he were a weaker man, he would flee rather than attempt to fix this. His obsession wouldn't let him consider it. His best option now was telling her the God's-honest truth.

"I have so many apologies to make I don't know where to begin." He pivoted in the chair toward her. "I'm sorry you were dragged into this. I—"

"*You* dragged me into this, with that stupid deal of yours." Her hands were back on her hips, accusing. "You're obviously not a stranger to this column, and you mentioned how rumors fly around you. So you knew this would happen, and yet you dragged me into it anyway."

When she put it like that, he sounded like a first-class jerk. His instincts gave him several unhelpful suggestions for a response, most of which involved tossing her onto the twin-size bed in the corner of her studio apartment for another make-out session. He ignored them all and remained sitting.

"I knew people would make comments, but I never thought they'd attack *you*. I'll admit I'm a selfish bastard who wanted to be with you more than I wanted to avoid innuendos, but believe me, if I had the power, I'd be protecting you from crap like that, not purposely subjecting you to it."

Her arms fell to her sides. He grabbed the opportunity to continue, now that she seemed to be listening. "I'll do everything I can to fix this. I don't want you hurt."

For a second, she softened, but then she scoffed. "And you expect me to believe you? Chicago's favorite playboy?"

Heat slid up his cheeks, and he glanced away. "That was a long time ago."

Despite the accusation, he couldn't give up and let her go. The more he saw her, touched her, witnessed her strength, the more he wanted to keep her. *Needed* to keep her.

He finally swallowed past the lump in his throat and met her gaze. Somehow, he had to salvage her opinion.

"You're right. About everything you believe about me."

Her eyebrow arched.

His stomach roiled, and he steadied himself for his confession. "I used to be the playboy you'd expect of an irresponsible 'trust fund kid.' In those days, I appeared in the gossip columns for the rotating arm-candy more often than I appeared in the business section."

His shoulders rounded, and he shrugged away the memories. "Then my father died."

She crossed her arms over her chest. "Is that supposed to make me feel better?"

Her reaction hit him like a physical blow. "Well, no. I just wanted you to know why that columnist would jump to those conclusions. But I've changed. Completely."

"Really? No offense, but the fact that your father died doesn't automatically lead to a total personality transplant."

Damn, she wasn't making this easy. He rubbed his cheeks. How could he explain without going into all the issues surrounding his father?

"After college, I used my trust fund money to start Dakon Enterprises. Truthfully, I was too self-destructive to run it properly, but like a target of Midas's golden touch, the company grew in value despite my neglect. It did so well, in fact, that—"

"You're going to have to let me know when I should feel sympathy for you, because I'm not feeling it yet."

Maybe it was his imagination, but he thought he detected a hint of amusement behind her words. A lopsided grin warmed his face at the possibility. "Will do."

He straightened. "Dakon Enterprises did so well that after my father died, I was able to gain controlling interest of his company. At first, I thought it was perfect." His hand slashed through the air. "The ultimate vanquishing of my father."

Memories weighed down his arm. "Then I dug into the financials past the official annual reports and learned how close he'd been to bankruptcy. He'd used every fraudulent accounting practice known to man—and had probably invented several new ones—to cover up the problems." He rubbed the back of his neck. "The issues were so bad I considered walking away from my investment and letting his company take that last step into hell."

An imagined laugh from his father cackled in his mind. The man would have loved the idea of besting Alex from the grave.

"I couldn't let my father win." He forced himself to sit upright. "For the first time in my life, I had a real goal—bringing my new subsidiary back from the brink of failure. I no longer had the time for, or interest in, being a playboy. Along with the absence of my father, the experience taught me responsibility and maturity better than anyone who knew me before would have believed possible."

The tale had skipped several therapy-worthy complications, but it seemed to have done the trick regardless. Her arms now hung loosely clasped in front of her.

He opened a palm. "That would be the part where I hope you understand how and why I changed. But no sympathy required."

"Good. You're not going to get any from me. Fine, you've had three years where you had to work. Congratulations on joining the real world. Barely. In your view, I *stole* last night, but that was the first time, and I did it to survive. I *work* for everything else. Treasures do me no good if I have to sell them off to live day-to-day."

She swept her arm across the small room. "And you see what I can afford despite that constant work. But not you... *You've* been successful enough in your quest to defeat your father that you have all this money for throwing around at fancy parties and donating—"

"I don't throw money around. I host parties for building fund-raising partnerships. Once a year. I told you I hate them. And my donations aren't frivolous."

"That's right." She pointed at him, accusing. "You're trying to buy your redemption."

His jaw unhinged, and his skin crawled, hot and too tight. Like the previous night, she'd effortlessly uncovered his hidden agenda. He had no comeback because she was right.

At his silence, she continued her point. "So with your success, what's to stop you from returning to your past attitudes and behavior?"

"Because I *am* trying to buy redemption." His growled response made her recoil a half step. "You can't have it both ways, Elaina. If

Treasured Claim

I haven't changed, I don't have a reason for my donations. If I have changed, then yes, I'm trying to make up for my past."

"Fine, maybe you've changed." She rolled her shoulders. "Then I expect you to have my name and picture removed from that article."

"I'll do everything possible to fix your reputation."

"I don't care about my reputation. *I* wasn't the one claiming I'm a jewelry appraiser." She slapped the table. "But get my name and picture off that article. That's all that matters."

With that, she marched into her bathroom, as though dismissing him. But he didn't intend to leave. If only that damned article hadn't interrupted his plan—as vague as it had been.

He tapped her laptop's touchpad, bringing the computer back from its screensaver of falling gold coins, and reviewed the offending column. His contacts at the paper could revise the article for him, but the issue was potentially bigger than that, as the pictures could have been sold to others too. He needed to cut this off at the source.

Given the number of guests at last night's party, the list of who could have provided information to Moi stretched rather long. He clicked the *refresh* icon to see if any comments had been posted yet. Thirty seconds later, the page was still loading.

Good lord, this computer was a piece of shit. Or maybe she was on dial-up. Or maybe it was the dozens of other tabs she'd opened in the web browser.

Well, no wonder the thing was slow. This ancient laptop couldn't handle that kind of memory usage.

He scanned the tabs.

Washington, DC Area Public Transportation Guide.

Washington, DC apts/housing for rent classifieds.

Washington, DC food/beverage/hospitality jobs classifieds.

His gut twisted. Shit. He shot up from the chair and started toward her bathroom. At the same time, his cell phone trilled in his pocket. The clamor overwhelmed the small room, and he scrambled to answer it before it rang again.

"This is Alex."

"Alexander Wyatt? Of Dakon Enterprises fame?"

The male voice didn't sound familiar. Alex pulled the phone

away from his ear and checked caller ID. It claimed the call was from James's phone.

He moved toward the window. What the hell had happened to James? "Yes. Who is this?"

"Right. And I'm Obama's second cousin twice-removed."

"Excuse me?" On the street below, a police officer with a hand by his ear stood next to Alex's car. "Officer, what's going on? Is James okay?"

The cop angled his head up. "You're in this building here?"

"Yes. What's—"

The line clicked off, and the police officer motioned James out of the car. The cop yanked on James's oversized bicep and shoved him toward the building entrance below.

Just what he needed, more chaos to manage.

Elaina emerged from the bathroom with an armload of clothes and laid them on the bed beside the window. He wanted to see her in—and out of—all of them.

"We're about to get a visitor." He lifted his phone. "Apparently, James ran into an issue with a cop downstairs."

"Police drive by all the time. Living on a main street in a crime-ridden neighborhood isn't all bad." Unconcerned, she returned to the bathroom.

A knock rapped from the hall a moment later, and Alex opened the door. The uniformed man he'd seen below was manhandling James in the hallway.

The policeman took in Alex's features but didn't seem to recognize him in his casual clothes. "Let's see your ID." He checked Alex's license, and then he cleared his throat and dropped James's arm. "Mr. Wyatt, I'm sorry. I didn't mean to disturb you."

"Officer...?"

He dipped his chin for a belated show of respect. "Officer Reynolds, sir."

A quick scan of James confirmed his driver was unharmed. Alex returned his attention to the cop. "Why were you treating one of my employees like a criminal?"

"Er, when a car like your Benz shows up in this neighborhood, it usually means one of two things—a drug dealer or stolen. I approached your vehicle and requested license and registration. I noted your name on the registration and figured he'd"—the cop indicated James beside him—"stolen it."

Alex put on his best you'd-better-not-be-making-racist-assumptions scowl.

The cop swallowed. "Er, he doesn't have a chauffeur's license, and his record showed a prior conviction for grand theft auto."

"Yes, I'm aware of James's background. He's my private driver, and we live outside city limits. He doesn't need a chauffeur's license."

Officer Reynolds shifted, his balance bouncing from one foot to the other. "Of course, sir. Once again, I'm sorry I disturbed you."

"James deserves your apology more than I do."

The cop mumbled something vaguely remorseful and returned the cell phone to James. Alex tilted his head, and James slinked away at the hint to return to the car while he had the chance.

Elaina appeared in the doorway next to Alex. "Before you go, Officer"—sweetness dripped from her tone—"could you escort this man from the building? I'm in danger because of him."

Alex swallowed a groan. "Elaina."

"Danger?" By the cop's tone, he seemed to be seriously considering her words.

Alex held her shoulder. "If you're truly in danger, let me help."

"No offense, Mr. Wyatt, but she'd be better off working with the police if there's a threat." Officer Reynolds motioned to the hallway. "I can take you to the station if you'd like to make a report."

The man's leer traveled up and down her body, and Alex was tempted to punch him. First the gossip column, then the stuff about D.C., and now this?

If he was going to keep her from escaping, he had to gain control of the situation. An idea occurred to him and was reinforced by a survey of Elaina's tiny apartment—clean despite its overall shabbiness.

His lie came easily. "I came here this morning to ask you to move in with me."

Yes, impulsive beyond belief. But it was far from the first impulsive decision he'd made in his life. Most of them had even turned out well.

"Alex..." Her voice was barely above a breath.

He stroked her cheek, keeping his touch light despite his determination. "Let me help. Give me a chance to fix things."

She leaned into his palm, placing her future in his hands. But a second later, her expression hardened, and she straightened. She spun toward the police officer.

And kissed him.

Alex yanked her back from the doorway. "What the hell are you doing?"

While the cop drew a hand across his mouth and cycled through several bewildered expressions, she frowned and met Alex's gaze. "An experiment."

"An *experiment*?"

"Yes. And it didn't work."

She tugged out of his grasp and moved to her bed. As she bent over the piles of clothes, organizing the heap without a care for the man she'd just kissed, the cop leaned and checked out her ass.

Alex ground his teeth. "Goodbye, Officer Reynolds."

He slammed the door in the man's face. That was nothing compared to his first instinct, which would have gotten him arrested. His obsession with her threatened everything. He needed to accept that they were too different from each other before he went insane.

But that was asking the impossible. Maybe that was proof he'd already lost his mind.

The wall in front of him beckoned. Punch it? Or bang his head on it?

He resisted both destructive options and approached Elaina. "I don't know what your issue is—whether this is a dragon thing, or you think this is all a game—but you can't ask me to bury a story about you and then pull a stunt like that. How much do you want to bet that cop is blabbing about everything on police radio, right now?"

Her gaze shot to his. "Oh."

"Yeah, *oh*."

She sank onto the bed and draped an arm over the stack she'd created. "I made things harder for you to erase, didn't I?" She straightened a button on the top shirt and cleared her throat. "I'm sorry. That was rather idiotic and impulsive of me."

Her honest apology added to his bafflement. Just when he'd wished he could convince himself to abandon the hunt, she showed him another side that struck a chord deep within him.

He crouched in front of her and stroked her hair. For a long moment, they stared into each other's eyes.

His fingertips skimmed down her neck, and her gaze flitted to his lips. He took that as a request. He braced himself on the edge of the mattress and leaned forward to kiss her—this beautiful, maddening, intoxicating woman who enticed him in every way possible.

And made him not care about the consequences.

Chapter Ten

THE WAR GOING ON INSIDE ELAINA'S MIND ROARED LOUDER
with every inch Alex moved closer. It would have been
easier if her experiment had turned out differently. But no.
She'd felt nothing. No warmth, no tingle, no rush at all from
her kiss with the cop. It wasn't the kissing.

It was Alex.

She'd run out of strength to push him away. She hadn't been
able to escape before he'd arrived and tempted her again, and his
honesty had defused her anger from that gossip column. Now she
quivered, anticipating the hit from her new drug of choice.

His lips touched hers, and she melted against him. She needed
this. She needed him. Fire lit her nerve endings, and all thoughts of
being scared, of worrying about her father, of her goals for the future fled.

She opened her mouth, allowing his tongue access. He tasted
clean, almost tangy. His flavor sharpened her senses. More alive
than ever before and yet somehow closer to death.

He pulled away, and she couldn't help a whimper. But then his
lips trailed down her neck. Heated shivers followed, rolling
through her limbs. Oh...

She slid her fingers under his hat and tangled them in his hair.
His cap flopped to the floor, and she tugged him harder against
her.

Without her realizing it, her legs had parted, and he came

forward on his knees between them. She scooted toward the edge of the bed and pressed into him. Close wasn't close enough.

He slipped an arm around her and drew her to his chest. The heat of his body added to the warmth his touch brought to her heart. Desperate need burned within her in response.

His muscles rippled under his T-shirt, and she had the urge to trace their lines with her fingers—or maybe her tongue. Damn, she was losing it.

That truth didn't stop her thighs from falling farther apart. Or stop her feet from wrapping behind his legs and tugging him even closer.

His mouth on her neck was driving her crazy. And the spot between the tops of her thighs wanted—needed—something.

His hardness touched the spot, and her body shuddered. "Alex..."

One strong hand tucked under her bottom, and he lifted them onto the middle of her twin-size bed together. His other hand shoved her hard-earned outfits to the floor.

She glanced at the untidy heap. "My clothes!"

He laid her on her back and followed her down, rumbling into her neck, "I'll buy you new ones."

His deep, nearly growling, voice sent shock waves through her body. Did he have to be so sexy? She forgot about her clothes, along with everything else, and arched into him.

A moment later, he planted his elbow on the mattress and propped himself up. Strength and intensity glinted in his silvery-gray eyes. In response, her heartbeat swelled in power.

"Now that I have you right where I want you." He emphasized his position by pressing his body into hers and using his free hand to pin her wrists on the bedspread. "You need to answer one question."

His head dipped, placing his lips out of reach of hers. "Will..."

She stretched up to him, and he leaned back.

"You..."

His body closed in again, taunting.

"Move..."

The tip of his tongue flicked her lips.

"In..."

He avoided her attempt once more.

"With..."

She broke free of his grasp and yanked his head to hers. Their mouths met, and she couldn't stifle her moan.

Dragon strength good. Using extra energy to steal that kiss was totally worth it.

Prickles skated across her skin. Electric sensations danced wherever their bodies touched.

She anchored her calf across his jeans and nudged him onto her. A cry escaped with her body's response, like a lit fuse sparking along her limbs. Any more aroused, and she'd explode.

His mouth moved frantically across her earlobes, neck, and collarbone, echoing her desperation. "You need to say yes. I want you. I want you so much."

His hips thrust against hers, and she gasped at the pressure—the delicious pressure. All thoughts of resistance or fear were crowded out by her hopeless need to experience *this*. She was lost. Utterly lost.

"Yes, I—"

He thrust again, and she curled her hips up to his.

"Damn it, *yes*, I want you too."

He angled away and studied her. "You mean that?"

She lifted her head to chase his lips, but they were out of reach. A handful of his shirt scrunched in her fist, answering his question. A devious grin flashed across his face, and he pushed himself farther above her.

"Alex, *please*." She yanked on his shirt, untucking it from his jeans.

"*Please?* Please, what? Please take this off?" He knelt for a second and wrestled off his T-shirt. "Well, since you asked so nicely."

She gaped at his chiseled abs and swallowed, her mouth watering. Her fingertips skimmed from his chest to his back.

He flung his shirt across her apartment and bent down to her again, dipping below her collarbone. His hair ruffled her neck, and his muscles bunched and flexed under her palms.

He inched up her shirt from her waist, and her skin tingled with the sensation of flesh touching flesh. Just when she thought this experience couldn't get any better, his fingers slipped under her bra and glided over her nipple.

A shudder blasted through her body, almost levitating her off the bed, and she gasped in a hiss.

"You like that, huh?" He sounded amused at how easily he could play her.

One hand slid her shirt up near her shoulders, and his other hand released her bra clasp. His eyelids drooped at the view. "Oh God, I have to taste you."

Uh... She drew back. "*Taste* me?"

"Yes." A groan rumbled through his ribs. "I'm going to lick you..." His tongue flicked her nipple. "And suck you..."

His lips closed over her nub, erect and eager for more. A squeak escaped through her pinched lips.

"All over."

She nodded, not sure what noises she'd make if she opened her mouth. How much more could her body take? And here she'd thought kissing had sent her over the edge.

Apparently, the urge to use tongues like this wasn't unique to dragons after all. Silly her for not investigating the sexual behavior of humans. How was she to know that she'd ever get this opportunity? Especially since she'd never looked for it—or wanted it—before.

He leaned over her and winked. "And something tells me you're going to like it." His mouth sought her other breast and gave it the same treatment.

"Uh... Ah, yes." Her breath stuttered with each circle of his tongue around her nipple. "Umm, I just didn't know humans did this."

His lips slipped from her, and he raised his head. "How could you not—?" His brows pulled together in a slight grimace. "You've never done this before."

His tone, almost like a croak, set her on edge. What was he getting at?

Oh. Heat gathered in her neck and threatened to creep into her cheeks. Damn it, she never blushed.

"Get off." She shoved him away. "Get off me."

He sat up, unresisting. She held back from launching him off the bed.

No, she did *not* "do" insecure. Fine, she didn't know what she was doing—unlike all her neighbors and the readers of the "50 Ways to Please Your Lover" articles she saw on magazine covers. But she wasn't a human and never would be. Human expectations shouldn't apply to her. She'd never tried to fit in with their ideas of relationships, and she wasn't going to start now.

Her chin lifted. She straightened her shirt and met his wide-eyed gaze.

His mouth worked through several shapes before he formed the words. "You're a *virgin*?"

Humans. They turned the simplest thing into a big deal.

"Yes. In fact, until last night, I was a virgin in *every* sense of the word, as I'd never even kissed anyone."

She shot him a look, daring him to insult her. It wasn't her goal in life to fit in with human rules, and nothing he could say would change that.

Chapter Eleven

OLY SHIT. AND HERE HE'D THOUGHT HIS THREE-YEAR stretch was mind-boggling. No wonder she hadn't questioned his admission during last night's dance.

He'd been her first kiss. The concept repeated itself in Alex's brain several times, and still, he struggled to wrap his head around the idea.

Perhaps he could have deduced some of her situation if he'd paid attention to her words the previous night—"How could kissing be like that?" But he'd been rather overwhelmed at the time. Hell, she'd made him feel as if that had been his first kiss too. This probably explained...

"That *experiment* with the cop?"

She huffed and stood from the bed. "Go ahead and feed your ego." Her wild gesturing almost smacked him. "I wanted to see if my reaction was to the kissing or to—" She stopped and fisted her hands.

"Me." His statement earned him a glare.

"All right, fine. Yes, you. Happy now?" Before he could answer that, yes, he was happy—thrilled in fact—she continued her rant. "I might be naïve about human logistics, but I've seen enough *Cosmo* covers to recognize I don't meet your expectations. And you know what I say to that? Too bad. I'm normal for me."

He rose and swept her into his arms. "And I like you just the way you are."

"You—? You do?"

"Why is that such a surprise? I'm an arrogant bastard, remember? I love the idea that I was your first kiss, and if I get my way, I'll be your first everything." He squeezed her tight. "You're mine alone to treasure. Mine, mine, mine."

Her musical laugh rewarded his possessiveness. Once it faded, however, her expression tightened. "Are you sure? I mean, compared to the *Cosmo* headlines and my neighbors here—"

"Your neighbors? In this place, they're probably all hookers and drug addicts. They're less normal than you are." He kissed her forehead. "Stop comparing yourself to anything in *Cosmo* or to anyone else. You're unique and that's why..."

He refused to finish that statement. The line restraining his impulsiveness had to be drawn somewhere. "And that's why I like you."

The blue glow of her eyes flared. A blink later, the ceiling filled his view.

She'd shoved him back onto the bed faster than he could see, much less react. Luckily, he'd landed lengthways on the twin-size mattress, or else he'd have banged into the wall. She straddled his hips and pinned his wrists.

Her breath left a heated trail up his chest. "So I shouldn't restrain myself if I want to do something dragon-like?"

With the air knocked out of his lungs, his voice came out as a strangled whisper. "No..."

A hiss—an honest-to-God hiss—tickled his earlobe and sharpened points dug into the backs of his hands where she held them.

Brief questions, wondering if he should be freaked out or concerned for his safety, floated through his head and then abandoned him just as quickly. The lone coherent thought in his mind was that she was slinking across his body, exactly as he'd fantasized. If only she was wearing fewer clothes.

Her breasts pressed against him, but her damned shirt was in the way. "Tell me, Alex. Show me what to do. I want this." She rocked her hips on his.

Fuck. God, did he want her.

But not like this.

Okay, one part of him would take her any way it could, but her virginity changed everything. Triggered his protective nature even more. He couldn't treat this like a hot-and-heavy hookup.

Every male instinct he had protested, but he strained out of her hold. "If I get to be your first, you're going to have that experience someplace nicer than here."

"What's wrong with my apartment?" Her mouth drew down. "I worked hard to afford it."

That depressing thought dampened his insistent horniness. He caught his frown before it darkened his features.

"Trust me. I'll make it worth it." He bounced against the mattress. "Think of what we can do with the room on a king-size bed."

Her giggle chased his words, and he lifted both of them upright on the floor. Once she settled her feet under her, he stroked the nape of her neck and met her gaze.

The thought of keeping her reinforced his earlier impulsive decision. He *did* want her to stay with him.

"Come on, beautiful, let me show you to your new home. The one you deserve."

Right as she melted in his arms, his cell phone rang again. Damn it.

He glanced at the screen. "Hang on, it's James."

She gave him a mischievous grin and swirled her tongue on his neck, right when he switched on the phone. Oh, *hell.*

"Yeah?" The word was almost a groan into the microphone, and he cleared his throat. "What's up?"

"The paps are here."

"Shit!" Paparazzi? That was *not* what he needed. He pressed a finger to Elaina's questioning lips. "How bad is it?"

Shuffling sounds emerged from the phone's speaker, as though James was checking the area. "I see two right now. Colin from the *Investigator* and some sleazeball from that *TotalAccess* website. But if they're here, others might be on their way."

Double shit. "Are they watching the car or the building?"

"Hard to say. They're both hanging back by half a block. But I know their cars as well as they know yours."

Think, damn it. If he emerged from the building with Elaina now, they'd be all over the front pages of those tabloid rags, and he'd never get a chance to clean up his mess.

"Hang on." He pressed mute on the cell. "Is there anyone in the building who's my height and build?" He cut off Elaina's questions. "Answer me."

"Um, I guess. The guy across the hall is pretty tall."

Alex went into the hallway and pounded on the opposite door. The muffled "go away" didn't deter him. "I'll give you a hundred bucks if you open this door and let me talk to—"

The door swung wide. The man standing in the doorway wasn't as broad of shoulder as Alex was, but he would do. Alex passed the promised bill to the guy.

"I'll give you another hundred if you put on a baseball cap and go to the car waiting out front. The driver will give you a third one if you get in and let him drive you someplace." Alex took in the man's narrow frame. "A breakfast place. And he'll pay for that too."

The guy inspected the hundred in his grasp and apparently decided Alex was for real. He slid on a cap and extended his hand. The desperation he must have to go willingly into a stranger's car wasn't lost on Alex.

After sending the guy on his way, Alex returned to Elaina's apartment and un-muted his phone to fill in James. "I'm sending down a decoy. Get him in the car and drive off. See if you can lure them away."

"What about you? Should I swing back around to pick you up?"

"We'll see. Others might show up in the meantime. The decoy's expecting a hundred dollars and a hot breakfast somewhere. Give me a call once you're finished with him and in the clear. Then we'll figure out the rest."

"You got it, boss."

Alex switched off the phone and met Elaina's narrowed gaze. Shit. This would not go well.

"James said a couple of reporters are down the street. They must have heard that cop mention where I was on the police scanners. James is going to try to lead them away with the decoy."

"Reporters? You mean paparazzi are right outside my *apartment?*" Her pitch rose so high on the last word she nearly squeaked.

There was nothing he could deny, so he nodded.

She became a flurry of activity, lunging and closing her laptop. "They have my real name." She grabbed a laptop bag from a kitchen cabinet and stuffed the computer and cables inside. "They have my picture." Her fingers refastened her bra clasp so quickly he hardly scored a peek. "They have my address." She stormed past him to her bathroom. "I am so dead."

He followed her and stood in the doorway. "Relax, we'll figure out something."

She crouched beside a steel cabinet in a closet at the far end and glared up at him. "There is no 'we,' Alex."

At her scathing tone, he staggered against the doorframe. She ignored his reaction and ran through the most complicated set of switches, hidden cubbyholes, and combination locks he'd ever seen.

The whole time, she muttered to herself, "Sure, the article spelled my name wrong, but he's smart enough to work that out. And the untouched hair? That'll be the sword in the heart. I couldn't have given him better directions if I tried."

"Who's *he*?"

"I knew it was only a matter of time." A small lockbox sat inside the cabinet's secret compartment, and she cradled the case to her chest. "No. No, it'll be okay."

Alex trailed her whirlwind back into the kitchen. "What are you scared of?"

She ignored him and unsuccessfully tried to shove the box into the bag with her laptop.

"Damn it, talk to me." He elbowed her out of the way and stuffed the safe into the bag for her. "If I knew the problem, I could work on a solution."

While he zipped the case closed, she crossed her arms. "I think I've had enough of your *help*. You're the reason I'm in this mess."

The truth hurt. Badly.

She held out her hand for her bag. He didn't pass it over right away, and she jiggled her arm, demanding the tote.

His cell phone chose that minute to ring again. He noted the caller. "Yes, James?"

"Figured you'd want an update. At least one of them followed, but I think one stayed behind."

"Thanks for trying. Give me a call after—"

Elaina yanked the strap from his grasp. "Bye, I'm..." She shook her head and marched toward her apartment door.

He hung up with James and snagged her elbow. "Don't. One reporter is still out there."

She gave him a withering roll of her eyes. "This building is infested with drug pushers. Don't you think they have a back way out for when the cops come by?"

"I'm coming with you." He reclaimed his shirt and cap from the floor.

"If you want to follow me to learn the way out, suit yourself. But you aren't doing anything *with* me." Matching her words, she strode down the hall while he was still pulling on his shirt.

He closed the door behind him. "Don't you want to lock this?"

Her hand spun in a careless wave. "Whatever."

What about all those clothes she'd been so worried about? "Toss me your keys."

A jangling pile of metal just missed his head. She'd thrown her key ring *at* him. Yeah, definitely pissed.

It took a moment to figure out which key went to her door. He caught up to her heading down the stairs and held out the key ring. "Here."

"Don't need 'em."

What the hell? He slipped the keys into his pocket. She shoved open the stairwell's door to the fourth floor hallway and stormed toward the rear of the building.

Up ahead, a graffiti-decorated board covered the busted-out window at the end of the dark hall. Like a pendulum, the board swung to the side, and she let herself through the opening. The fire escape for the back of the building was outside.

Somebody had boarded over the route to the fire escape? Good lord, how many code violations did this dump have?

He avoided the broken glass edging the window frame and followed her onto the grating. She lifted the strap of her laptop bag over her head so it lay diagonal across her body, freeing her arms. But instead of descending the ladder, she climbed onto the railing four stories above the pavement below.

"No!" He dove to grab her.

His hand closed on empty air.

She vaulted to the mostly flat roof of the two-story building across the alley and landed safely, with nary a hair on her now-brunette head out of place.

"Jesus Christ. Are you trying to kill yourself?"

A touch of a grin appeared on her features. "Oh come on, the druggies do it all the time."

Yeah, while they hallucinated that they could *fly*.

She took off across the roof. "Feel free to stop following me anytime."

It finally dawned on him. She was *trying* to lose him. She was running away from more than the paparazzi. Someone had her scared, and she was simply running away. She wasn't ever returning to her apartment. If he didn't keep up with her, he'd lose her forever.

His mouth went dry at the thought, and his racing heartbeat yelled at him to catch her before she got away.

Shit. His options were rather limited. If he took the fire escape ladder to the narrow alley below, a ten-foot-tall barbed-wire fence would stand between him and Elaina. It was jump or say goodbye to the back of her head.

Every cell of his being joined his pounding heart in shouting that he couldn't let her escape. Losing her might, in fact, kill him. Hopefully, trying to keep her wouldn't do the same.

He climbed onto the railing and tried not to look down. Sure, he was in good shape, but Harvard lacked a men's gymnastics team. Like a good little elitist rich boy, he'd taken up sailing and fencing. And the elegance of those sports was quite different from the reality of balancing thirty-some feet over a blacktop littered with broken bottles and used syringes. Gossip headlines would bleed onto the front page if he died here, at the foot of Drugs and Hookers "R" Us.

So don't die. Simple enough.

He took a deep breath and crouched for more thrust.

And leaped.

Chapter Twelve

AT HIS INHALATION, ELAINA SPUN AND WATCHED HIS sculpted body spring through the air. Her muscles tensed at the sight. He was only human after all. Although she was leaving him, she didn't want him to get hurt. Hell, half the reason she was leaving was so that he—and everyone else in Chicago—*wouldn't* get hurt.

His powerful thighs filled out his jeans at his landing, and he took two steps forward before getting his balance. Must. Not. Drool.

He looked up and caught her ogling him. His broad grin could have equally applied to his successful jump or her gawking. Damn him.

The air in her lungs burst out in a huff, and she refocused on her goal. The sloping far corner of the roof led her to a convenient covered dumpster below. Alex continued following her, dropping the short distance to the dumpster and then to the pavement.

She wasn't impressed with either his determination or the muscles rippling under his T-shirt. At all.

She was also a liar.

His grin had grown to light up his face. "Now where?"

"*You* can go to the side street that way." She jabbed in a direction away from her route. "And have James pick you up."

Without another glance at him, she left her apartment building behind, walking down a narrow driveway between twin sets of security fences and crumbling structures. Thick shrubbery along the fences and buildings kept the location hidden from the surrounding roads.

Footfalls echoed behind her. "I'm going wherever you're going." Of course he was. "Stalker."

"I can't be a stalker if you want me here. Tell me to leave you alone, and I will. But we both know you won't."

Arrogant bastard.

He kept going with his delusions. "There *is* something between us. There *is* a 'we.'"

She whirled around to tell him off. Unlike her neighbor, she couldn't be bought. Not when it was a matter of life and death for her to escape.

But Alex was much closer than she'd expected. As in, toe-to-toe close. The hand she'd extended to point in anger landed on his chest, and she gasped.

He raised a brow at her hand and then lifted his gaze to hers. The determination that must have driven him to make the leap over the alley still shone like steel in his eyes, sharp and unbendable. His fingers slid through her hair, and her traitorous muscles leaned into his touch.

"Go on," he whispered in a husky voice, thick with the challenge of baiting her. "Tell me."

Her jaw tightened, flat-out refusing to open so she could contradict him. Despite the risks, she couldn't deny that she wanted to keep him, claim him as she'd claimed the treasure in her satchel. Damn it.

She spun around and stomped off. His dark chuckle followed her.

Another security fence stood between them and the side street at the end of the driveway. She elbowed her laptop bag toward her back, jumped, and hooked the top of the tall fence. At least it wasn't covered in barbed wire. The last thing she needed was getting rips in her only set of clothes.

Alex palmed her butt while helping her over the edge, sending flickers of warmth to inappropriate places. Maybe his middle name was Temptation.

On the other side of the fence, she stuck close to the overgrown

Jami Gold

bushes along the sidewalk to the right. Alex's footsteps caught up to her again once he made it over the fence, and she motioned for him to stay behind her. They were approaching the intersection where this side street met the major cross street near her building.

This would be the trickiest part of her escape. The main thoroughfare in front of her apartment building was one intersection to the east of this one. So how could she cross the road without being seen by the paparazzi down the block? Sure, as a brunette, she might not draw their attention anymore. Then again, they might be used to their targets wearing wigs. And any photographs here would make the neighborhood a target for her father's destruction.

Beside her, Alex had moved away, closer to the curb of the side street.

"Alex," she hissed, "if you get me caught, so help me, I *will* kill you."

He pivoted from surveying the opposite direction and met her glare. "We need to cross that street up ahead, right?"

She didn't bother to argue with the "we" aspect of his sentence and nodded.

He seized her wrist and dragged her across the empty side street beside them. She opened her mouth to yell at him, but he shushed her and led them between the cars parked along the far curb. Once there, he edged them closer to the intersection they needed to traverse.

When he glanced away from the cross street again, she figured out his plan. This side street was a one-way road running the same direction they wanted to go. If a car approached the intersection without its turn signals on, maybe they could follow alongside as it crossed to the other side and let the vehicle shield their passage from any paparazzi at the corner of the next block.

Huh. That was a decent plan.

She stopped fighting his grip, and his lips formed a smug curve. "See? I can help you."

"Don't congratulate yourself until we see if it works."

Lucky for him, the first vehicle to arrive at the intersection without turn signals was a white delivery van. They shot to its flank and jogged alongside. Once on the other side of the cross street, she circled through the connecting alleys back toward the road at a point halfway between the two intersections.

While they stood in the shadow of a building at the alley's entrance, Alex leaned into her and whispered, "Now what?"

She hitched her thumb toward the sidewalk. Ten feet away was a bus stop.

"A bus?" He grimaced. "The climax to this great escape is a bus?"

"I didn't ask for your approval." She checked her watch. "You have two minutes to decide if your desire to stalk me is greater than your distaste for public transportation." Assuming the bus was on time.

His grin flashed again. Great. He'd taken it as a challenge.

A few minutes later, the CTA bus rumbled down the street toward their hiding place. As soon as the bus crossed the intersection of the main thoroughfare down the block, she darted out and stood at the sign. Hopefully, no one would spot her, as the bus blocked most of the view of the sidewalk. Once the bus stopped, Alex loped beside her, keeping his head down for his hat to shield his face.

She inserted her Transit Card into the farebox twice and indicated Alex to the driver. "For him." The driver didn't spare them a glance, and they took a row near the back of the bus.

Alex slouched in his seat by the window. "You didn't have to pay for me."

"Really? Did you have the correct change out and ready, or would you be standing there like an idiot, letting the driver get a good look at you while you fumbled around?"

He rubbed the back of his neck. "Okay, thanks." He pulled out his cell phone. "Where does this bus go?" When she pointed toward the front of the bus, he tapped the phone on the chair, as though silently counting to ten, and then cleared his throat. "Where should I have James pick us up?"

"You can have James pick *you* up anywhere you'd like." In answer to his arched brows, she leaned back into the unforgiving bus seat. "I'm serious. There is no *we*. I'm doing what I have to do, and I'm sorry, but that doesn't include you."

"And what do you have to do? Run? There has to be another

option."

"Believe me, I wish there was." She'd never meant the sentiment more truthfully.

He twisted toward her and stroked her cheek. "You're stuck with me following you no matter what. You may as well tell me the problem and see if I can help."

Did he have to be so damned determined? And understanding? And perfect?

Her failure to push him away after the stalker accusation had proven how much she *wanted* him in her life, where she could claim him as her own. Despite the impossibility. Despite the danger. Despite the risks. *This* man tapped into needs she hadn't realized existed, but now they throbbed, raw and exposed.

Her eyes closed with his caresses. She was so tired. The research for yet another move had kept her from sleeping at all the previous night, much less enjoying a regenerative sleep, and their sudden departure had prevented her from recharging with her talisman this morning.

Her successful acquisition notwithstanding, the energy maintaining her heart was still dangerously low. It would be nice to let someone—especially *this* someone—help her with things.

Her logic rejected the idea. Yes, it would be nice. But even if she *could* find a way to fit into his human life, there was nothing he could do.

She straightened and offered him the truth. "Unless you know how to prevent a 371-year-old dragon from turning Chicago into a burning wasteland in his obsession to kill me, you can't help."

Chapter Thirteen

A DRAGON? ANOTHER ONE? *HERE?*

Alex internally cursed his reaction when Elaina's expression, which had almost appeared hopeful a moment before, closed down and became wary.

He forced his facial muscles to relax. "I don't offhand, but I can try to figure it out."

"Forget it." She shrugged his arm away and fell into a quiet mood.

Several minutes later, he followed her lead and stepped off the bus behind her. Without a word of explanation, she trudged up the sidewalk. He trailed her, his brain buzzing with her revelation.

Of course there were other dragons. She'd come from somewhere after all, and she'd talked about growing up among them. But accepting a beautiful, non-threatening dragon—who couldn't shapeshift into the big serpent thing anyway—was vastly different from accepting a powerful and dangerous dragon. Especially as he'd always imagined them as having their own homeland far—*far*—from humans.

She'd talked about a "him" and how the gossip column had been like giving "him" directions to her. Given how long this "him" had been around to collect treasure, he likely *could* shapeshift into a winged serpent.

A serpent dragon in Chicago. His body ached at the idea, as though the creature's tail had already leveled him with a sideswipe. No wonder she was running.

After two blocks, the side street ended at a main road. In front of him, Elaina's shoulders rounded, like from fatigue or despair, perhaps both. She crossed the intersection without checking if he was still following her.

On the other side, an unmarked set of wooden stairs led up an embankment, and she gripped the handrail while she climbed. If he didn't know better, he'd think she was using it for balance, her innate grace nowhere to be seen.

She paused and swayed, and he rushed to offer her an arm. He didn't expect her to accept his support, but she had a death grip on him by the time they reached the top of the steps.

What was wrong with her? Sure, she looked tired, but he couldn't detect any other symptoms. Then again, dragon sickness was a mystery. Did they become feverish, go pale, or something else?

He rubbed at his temple where a headache gathered. Dealing with helplessness out of his own ignorance wasn't one of his strengths.

A Metra rail station sat off to the left at the top of the embankment. He guessed that to be their destination and steered them toward the building to buy tickets.

"No, it's okay." She straightened and fumbled through the side pocket of her bag. "I have at least two rides left on this." Her fingers clutched a ten-ride ticket as evidence.

Had she finally accepted his assistance? She'd offered him passage—in advance.

He clasped her wrist and scanned the ticket. "Are you sure there's enough for both of us? You're not trying to ditch me again, are you?"

"I don't have a choice right now."

That wasn't reassuring.

"Are you okay? Is there anything I can do?"

Her eyelids drooped. "Let's get over there for the northbound train."

They rode the Metra for two stops, and then she directed them to exit. Any other time, he'd be celebrating his victory over her. Instead, her apparent illness left a sour taste in his mouth.

Treasured Claim

The white columned station here in Morton Grove was nicer than the glorified shed for the one in town. She once again steadied herself on his forearm and led them south. Broad lawns fronted the office parks they passed, and the smell of freshly cut grass finally erased the lingering scents from the bus that he'd rather not identify.

He'd given up trying to figure out her destination. The phrase "along for the ride" applied perfectly to this situation.

A couple of blocks later, she released him and dug through her bag. He followed her across the lawn toward a parking lot. Half-hidden by a low-hanging tree, a rust bucket of a car marked their destination.

He stopped, his limbs heavy and numb. Damn it. He should have known. This whole time, her goal had been to escape. She'd needed to get to her car when James hadn't been able to deliver her here this morning.

She took the driver's seat, and he stood in the open door in a last ditch effort to prevent her from leaving. But no convincing words came to him.

Even his aggressive instincts remained silent. Now that he knew the reason for her fear, his protective nature overwhelmed any impulses to force her to stay.

He rested his forearms on the roof, his head sagging between them. What the hell was he going to do now? Nothing he'd done or said had changed her mind. She still wanted to leave, probably to move halfway across the country if the tabs on her web browser were any indication, and he'd lose her forever.

Crazy urges to follow her cross-country, relocating his headquarters if need be, whispered persuasively in his head. After everything he'd learned in the past twelve or so hours, he wasn't sure he had enough logic remaining to resist his impulsiveness.

Several quiet clicks interrupted his internal debate. She hadn't started the engine. Had she changed her mind? Inside the car, she hunched over the steering wheel, in much the same position his body had just held.

"It's okay." He rubbed her shoulders. "We'll figure out something."

She sat back and slapped the steering wheel. "You stupid,

no-good piece of junk. I need you to work. You do *not* get to slack off today, you understand?"

Wonderful. She wasn't upset about leaving him. She was upset she *couldn't* leave him.

"Slide over, let me try."

She obeyed without protest, and he settled inside and turned the key. Another quiet click, like a dead battery or loose connection. He tugged the switch to pop the hood.

"Stay here. I'll take a look."

She hugged her bag and gave a silent nod.

One engine problem was immediately obvious. The battery terminals had corroded so much the cables weren't making a good connection. He needed something to scrape off the crud.

His hands went to his pockets, and he felt her discarded apartment keys. If she wasn't going back there, she wouldn't care about gunk all over them. He disconnected the cables and got to work.

Several minutes later, the terminals were clean enough to reconnect the cables. Inside the car, she'd slumped against the passenger door during the wait. He turned the key in the ignition again. Bingo. Still enough charge in the battery.

She didn't move at the rumble of the engine, dead asleep. He watched her long enough to be sure and then allowed himself a fist pump. Now *he* was in charge of their destination.

After gently closing the hood, he returned to the car and edged her bag out of the way to click her seatbelt into place. The satchel slid to the floor from her lap. In her sleep, she whimpered and shimmied closer to him, snuggling under his arm. A contented sigh curved her lips.

This was more like it.

His sense of triumph leaked away at the sight of her vulnerability. His chest constricted until it was hard to breathe. He'd never been more lacking in the knowledge of how to protect someone. He didn't have the slightest idea of how to take care of a human, much less a weak and defenseless dragon.

Well... Right now, she seemed to need sleep. And he just so happened to have a luxury bed at home. Rationalization or not, it was a good plan.

Chapter Fourteen

ELAINA STRETCHED, WAKING FROM THE MOST WONDERFUL dream. In her dream, she'd been holding a priceless, life-size golden statue of a man, encrusted with countless diamonds, polished silver orbs for eyes, and rubies so deeply colored they were almost opaque for hair.

She hadn't slept that well for as long as she could remember. And no doubt, she'd needed it. All that stupid stuff with Alex had distracted her from—

Damn!

She opened her eyes and saw the gaze of her distraction inches in front of her, their bodies entangled on a bed. Oh, no, no, no. She moved to pull away, but her leg was hooked over his hip, one hand was up the front of his shirt, and her other hand was inside the back of his shirt.

He smoothed her hair back from her temple. "Shh. It's okay. You're safe. How are you feeling?"

"*Feeling?*" She gulped. Yeah, as if she would admit that to Mr. Arrogant.

"Did the sleep help? Or are you still feeling sick?"

Now his question made sense. "I don't get sick. I was just tired. I hadn't slept last night to—" Everything came back to her, and she sat up and scanned the bedroom. "Where's my bag?"

"Relax." He rested a palm on her knee and reached past her to the floor. "It's right here." He set the case with her most important possessions on the mattress.

She twisted and surveyed the carpet by the nightstand on her side of the bed. "I wasn't holding it?"

His voice dropped low and teasing. "There wasn't enough room between us for you to hold that *and* me."

Damn it. Don't blush, don't blush.

She instead questioned the facts that didn't make any sense. How could she have recharged if she hadn't been holding at least her talisman? Had she drained energy from Alex somehow?

She searched his appearance for signs of weakness. "How are *you* feeling?"

A broad grin stretched his cheeks, and he slid a hand up her leg. "Fantastic." A shadow crossed his face. "And starved." He grabbed the phone off his nightstand behind him. "What do you want? It's almost dinner time, but I can have the kitchen make anything you wish."

"I don't eat food." For that matter, she felt as though she'd feasted on an all-you-can-eat buffet.

He sat back. "You don't eat?"

For a second, she thought this difference between them would be the one to push him beyond his ability to tolerate. Then he leaned closer.

"Have you ever tried food to experience the taste of it?" When she shook her head, he raised a finger. "More opportunities for me to be your first."

With that, he once again easily accepted her nature. She'd never thought a human would understand her.

Of course in the next moment, he ignored her protests and made a call to his staff to ask for a bunch of foods she recognized from Stefano's menu choices. He returned the handset to its cradle and arched his brows in an overconfident expression.

"It'll take the kitchen about forty-five minutes to get that together. So we have time to—"

"Talk." She clutched her bag to her chest, scrambled off the bed, and took several steps backward. "How did I get here? *Why* am I here?"

He swept a hand through his hair. "You fell asleep while I fixed your car. I drove us here, put you on the bed, and you moaned until I held you."

Her elbows tucked in closer, and she cringed. She'd moaned because, to have a regenerative sleep, dragons needed the security of their treasure. Or apparently, the security of being in the arms of a gorgeous hunk.

"That doesn't answer my other question. This is your house, right? Why am I *here*?"

"Did you expect me to drive you all the way to Washington, D.C.?"

He knew about that? Damn, he'd seen her laptop.

"No. But why here?"

"*Here* is safe. The paparazzi don't know you're here, and the people on my staff have signed the tightest NDAs imaginable." Before she could ask, he explained, "Non-disclosure agreements tied to their very well-funded retirement accounts. Trust me, they won't leak anything to the media."

"It's too late to hide everything. Remember the cop?"

"I took care of that already. Nothing about *you* had been mentioned on the police scanners or reported yet, and a donation to the Chicago Police Memorial Fund convinced the Police Superintendent to issue a direct order to Officer Reynolds for absolute silence."

For someone who claimed he didn't throw money around, he sure used it frequently to buy the outcome he wanted. Not everyone was for sale.

"And how long do you expect me to stay here?"

He rose from the bed and approached her, his T-shirt straightening and covering her view of his abs. "Expect you—? You're not my prisoner." He didn't seem to notice that she backed away from him until she hit the wall. "I still *want* to help you. This is a safe place for you to stay while we come up with a plan."

She scoffed and surveyed the room to distract herself from his temptations. The dark wood furniture, deep red accents, and oh yeah, the *dragon*-carved headboard on the huge four-poster bed left no doubt in her mind whose room this was.

"Safe? Is that why you put me up in *your* room? So you could keep me *safe*?"

His lips quirked up in a curve, and he closed the distance

between them. His fingers slid through her hair. Against her wishes, her head pressed into his palm.

He laid a gentle kiss on the exposed side of her neck. "You agreed to move in with me."

Between his touch and whispered words, fire spread through her body, and her arms hung limp at her sides, her bag forgotten. Still, she fought. "That was before everything happened that made it easy for him to find me."

"No..." Another nibble on her neck. "The only thing that changed between your answer and now was the paparazzi hearing that I visited Uptown today." He moved lower and placed a kiss on her collarbone. "Neither of us will ever go back there, and I can issue a press release about a charity project in the area."

He rested his forehead on hers, forcing her to focus on him. "Problem solved."

At that pronouncement, he swept in for a kiss that singed her insides. He squeezed her against his body, and she couldn't remember her reasons for disagreeing with him.

"Um, I guess I can stay," she mumbled to his lips.

Her fingers betrayed her feigned hesitancy. They let her jewels slip to the floor so she could tug him harder to her mouth.

Several minutes later, he leaned back, his eyes twinkling. "Good, because I already had all your stuff moved here."

"All my stuff?"

Instead of answering, he led her to a walk-in closet twice as big as her old apartment. There, neatly hung and folded, were his clothes on the left and her clothes on the right. At the front of the closet, her multi-locking cabinet with hidden compartment sat tucked into the corner.

She wanted to be mad at his presumption, but she couldn't manage it. The fact that he'd retrieved her belongings so she wouldn't lose everything struck her speechless. No one had done anything so thoughtful for her before, much less something this complex and important. The effort he'd put into making this situation work for her outweighed any thoughts of how she hadn't gotten a vote.

She rubbed the fabric of her clothes for confirmation that she wasn't still dreaming. The silky material of the dress she'd worn the previous night slid through her fingertips.

This was real. He'd rescued *everything*. For her.

The lump in her throat got in the way of her attempt to speak. She swallowed and tried again. "How did you get all this?"

"I had James go to your place in his pickup truck. The paparazzi wouldn't pay attention to it." One corner of his lips curved up. "Especially since that's his hunting vehicle with all the add-ons."

"Thank you. And tell James thank you too, please." The reality of her new situation sank in to her consciousness. "You really want me here, don't you?"

His eyes shone. "More than I've ever wanted anything."

Her head seemed to spin as wildly as her thoughts, and she focused on her feet, quieting the internal debate. His attitude proved he thought he could take anything he desired, but it was hard to complain when he used that power for her benefit. He was likely one of the few humans on the planet who *could* assist her, and she couldn't help wanting to stay despite the danger.

He probably should have heard all the facts before entangling himself with her. Of course, between trying to get away from him and the desperately needed sleep, she'd never had the chance to tell him everything. Even so, he knew the basics of what they were up against and had done all this anyway.

Too bad dragons couldn't love, because for once, she wished it could be possible.

She let her fingertips skate along his jawbone, marveling at the strength revealed in him. Her hand stilled when she noticed his skin was paler than before.

"Are you okay?" Maybe she *had* drained something from him.

"I was busy arranging all this." He indicated her clothes and kissed her palm. "I didn't get to catch up on my sleep as much as you did."

"You didn't sleep well last night either?"

"Not a wink. Perhaps I shouldn't have let you leave."

"What, and miss seeing you make that leap across the alley? Not a chance." She nudged him toward the bedroom. "Why don't you rest until your dinner is ready? I'll organize my stuff in here."

"I was going to suggest something more entertaining, but I like the idea of you making yourself at home."

At his exit toward the bedroom, her heartbeat did its usual stutter with his absence. A moment later, her mind cleared. What was she doing? She couldn't make this her new home. Could she?

Worst case, her father couldn't get here for a couple of weeks, so she could give Alex a few days, maybe a week, to try to erase the leak of her name and picture on that gossip article. If that didn't work, at least she'd have her stuff for the next move. In the meantime, she was merely rearranging her things, *not* moving into her new home.

Of course, the paltry number of outfits on her side didn't fill even a tenth of the space, but it was enough to hide her locking cabinet. After her safe-box of treasure was secured under the false bottom, the phone rang. The second ring earned her attention. Apparently, Alex had fallen asleep. At the third ring, she stood by his bedside table and hesitated, watching for a sign that he would awaken.

She snatched the handset mid-fourth ring, deciding to let him sleep, and leaned away from the bed to keep her volume low. "Hello?"

"Good evening, Miss Drake. Dinner is ready. Where would you like to be served?"

"Um..." As if she would know?

She glanced at the bed, where Alex grinned, wide-awake. The insufferable man had been testing to see how much she'd make herself at home.

"They want to know where you want dinner."

She held out the phone, but he refused to take it. "Tell them to deliver the food here."

The instruction passed on, she hung up and then yanked the pillow from under his head and swung. The pillow smacked him with a satisfying *whump*. A second later, he wrestled her onto the mattress. She kept rolling—away from him—thanks to her quick reflexes.

She stood on the far side of the bed and held out her hands. "Stop trying to turn this into more than it is. I don't *fit* into your life here, Alex."

He walked on his knees across the mattress toward her. "If you don't feel as though you belong here, why did you answer *my* phone?"

"I'm serious. This isn't a game." She wished for another pillow to toss at him but settled for a shove against his chest, which barely knocked him off balance from his kneel on the bed. "I can't be bought, unlike everything else in your life, because my needs don't have a price."

He ignored her statement, trapping her wrists as if to drag her back onto the mattress. She decided to lay the truth out for him.

"Running and hiding are what's kept me alive for the past ten years. If my father learns I'm here, he'll destroy everything in his quest to track me down, laying waste to all of Chicago to ensure my death. Staying hidden is my only choice, not to mention the best choice for the humans here, and low-key doesn't fit in with your life."

ALEX FROZE, HIS BRAIN BELATEDLY TRYING TO PROCESS HER WORDS. "Your father? Your father is the 300-whatever-year-old dragon you were talking about?"

Jesus. And he thought *he* had daddy issues.

A knock interrupted them before he could ask for the details. He stood. "Enter."

After the table for two in the corner of his room was set for its inaugural dinner, he and Elaina were alone once more. He held out a chair for her. "Please join me for dinner."

Her reactions to the various foods he offered were fascinating. Every new bite would start with her doubtful, then she'd roll the food around on her tongue, and finally she'd compare it to something she could comprehend. The creamy wild mushroom soup felt "as smooth as gold," and the sip of Merlot was like "liquid rubies."

She took a piece of the New York strip steak and coughed. "How do you swallow this?"

He held back a laugh. "You have to chew it first."

Her jaw worked for a second, and then she grimaced and brought her napkin to her mouth. "Ugh."

"You don't like it?"

"It's like a lump of coal. I don't know how you stand it."

He restrained a snort. How dangerous could dragons be if they weren't even carnivores?

Now that she'd declared herself done with the sampling, he started his questions.

"Talk to me about this father of yours. Why does he want to kill you? And can't you kill him first? Chop off his head or something?" If he remembered correctly, that technique worked on mythical creatures in stories.

She didn't answer him. Instead, she picked up the steak knife and studied it for a second. Her arm extended in front of her, and she flipped the point of the knife toward her body.

His stomach clenched at the image, and his mind denied what he was seeing. Time moved slowly, too slowly, and he couldn't grab her wrist in time.

She plunged the knife into her chest.

Chapter Fifteen

ALEX'S STRANGLED SHOUT HADN'T YET ERUPTED FROM HIS throat when he realized the knife hadn't gone into Elaina's skin. Thank the holy what-the-fuck-was-that. He looked up from his new position of kneeling at her feet after he'd lunged toward her.

"Sorry." She lifted his chin and closed his mouth. "I should have warned you, huh?"

While he debated how to answer, she offered, "Dragon scales are harder than metal, even in this form. My skin can't be cut by anything other than dragon claws or teeth. Dragons have but one weak spot in their armor where they can be stabbed."

He vaguely recalled more of the mythology. "Over their heart."

"Correct. But dragon hearts aren't here." She tapped alongside her left breast, where she'd aimed the blade. "Only the one true knight—or other dragons—can see the real location of our heart and hurt us."

He was hardly listening. The knife seized his attention, where she absently ran her fingertip along the edge, proving her invulnerability.

"Then maybe we should search for this knight. Pay him to take care of your father."

A noise suspiciously like a whimper sounded from her, and then she cleared her throat. "No, thanks. The knight's ability comes from magic, not genetics, so his instinct *compels* him to kill dragons." A shudder overtook her body, and she hugged her stomach. "He couldn't resist killing me too. Even if you tried to find him on your own, he'd assume you'd learned about knights by talking to a dragon. And since my father's not the talking type, the knight would stalk you to find your source of information, obsessed with hunting me down."

That explained her sudden fear the previous night when she'd thought him this knight. She'd honestly believed he'd slay her on the spot. He squeezed her leg, reminding her that he was still there, offering his protection.

She uncurled her body. "It'll take years—*decades*—for me to collect enough treasure to shapeshift into my dragon form. Until then, I don't even have claws, teeth, or fire for protection."

"Can't *you* attack him?"

"What part of 'I can't protect myself' don't you understand? If I can't defend myself, how could I possibly be strong enough to attack—even if I hadn't taken a vow of non-violence? No, running is my only choice."

He hated the whiff of resignation in her attitude, but he didn't have a better answer for her. During his questions, she'd continued stroking the edge of the blade, and his focus skipped between her fingertip and the spot the knife-tip had hit, checking for any sign of damage.

"Are you sure you're okay?"

She rolled her eyes and tugged her low-cut T-shirt even lower, showing her unblemished skin. "See?"

Oh yes, he saw. He saw perfection. The rounded top of her breast was unmarked in any way, appearing ripe and ready to eat. The sight erased all questions about her father.

He nibbled at the unharmed spot. "There's a shortage of perfect breasts in this world. It would be a pity to damage yours."

At her scoff, he pulled back. "What? You've never seen *The Princess Bride*? I've been waiting my whole life to use that line."

She laughed and pushed him away. "Go finish your dinner."

"As you wish." He winked.

But when he sat in his chair and picked up his steak knife, the image of the blade rushing toward her stuck in his mind. He dropped the knife and shoved his plate away.

She looked at his mostly untouched food. "I thought you were starving. You need to keep up your strength."

He couldn't admit that he didn't want to touch the pointed utensil again. That probably wasn't high on the list of attributes that impressed females of any species.

She slid the plate back toward him. "I'm serious. I'm worried I might be draining energy from you. Sleep helps dragons recharge, *when* we're in contact with our treasure. But I wasn't touching my bag with my lockbox—I was touching you."

"And yet you recharged anyway?"

"Yes, I, uh, I dreamed I was holding treasure."

Spots of color appeared on her cheeks. He hadn't known she *could* blush.

That must have been some dream. He was arrogant enough to guess it had something to do with him.

As though she knew exactly where his assumptions had gone, she hissed, and the blue of her irises flared, giving him a split-second warning to sit back before she launched herself at him. She landed, straddling his lap, and her sharp nails dug into his jaw and neck. Her glare briefly made him wonder if full-dragons could burn things simply by looking at them.

"Eat or I'll *make* you eat."

God, her dominant shit turned him on. This, more than anything, hinted at how well-matched they could be. He squeezed her ass against him to let her feel how much he liked it.

"I'm counting on it." He kissed a trail from her earlobe to the low neckline of her T-shirt. "We both know you want me to have the strength later to show you a few *things*."

She leaned away, as though about to deny his words. He continued nibbling across her chest until her head dropped back. He ground her hips down on him again, and her breath caught.

"Okay, yeah, that sounds like a plan."

Good girl. To continue this game where they could somehow both be dominant, he indicated the table. "Now feed me."

With no objection, she twisted on his lap toward his plate. Could there be anything sexier? A gorgeous woman, her ass and inner thighs rubbing against him when she moved, her shirt tight in all the right places as she leaned toward the table, and to top it all off, she was serving him. He was tempted to skip to dessert.

Her hand hovered over his knife, but after a hesitation, she avoided it. The nail on her index finger extended into a three-inch-long claw, erasing any doubts of her lethal potential. She sliced through his steak like butter.

She noticed his attention and dropped her arm to her lap. "Sorry, that's probably pretty freaky."

"No," he lied.

In truth, the image was disconcerting, but nothing he'd reject more than any other of her differences. He caught her wrist and placed a kiss on the smooth top side of the talon.

"Though things could get interesting with these later when I make you lose your mind." He swirled his tongue in her palm.

"What? Oh..." Her fingers reflexively curled. "So far, just this one changes, and it grows only when I want it to." She held up her hand, showing the transformation to her normal curved nail.

Good to know. Of course, her fingernails were rather pointy on their own.

He stroked his thumb over her knuckles. "As long as I survive the experience well enough to repeat it, I have no problem with you losing control."

Those ground rules likely would have made a normal man pause, but he was in too deep to care.

The glow of her eyes wavered. "How did you get to be so..."

"Perfect?"

He expected her to reject his statement. When she nodded speechlessly instead, his throat thickened, turning breathing into a struggle.

He had to keep this woman. And the best way to make that happen was to understand her situation.

"I'll eat if you tell me everything there is to know about this father of yours. Where is he? Why is he after you? Everything. Agreed?"

Rather than appearing defensive at this line of discussion, she brought his fork laden with a piece of steak. Once he took the offered bite, she began. "When I was a youngling, I always thought I was lucky. I mean, I had a happy family—my parents were *together*, and that's unheard of in dragon society."

"Unheard of?"

Her brows pulled together, and she fetched him another forkful. "I guess I need to start with Dragonology 101."

He couldn't confirm her observation because of his mouthful of food, but she seemed to understand the meaning of his "go ahead" gesture.

"Dragons don't have the concept of community that humans do because they're too jealous of each other's hoards and too protective of their own. The only times dragons interact are with younglings, like how my teacher Nastav did, or for procreation."

He wasn't sure he wanted to know how procreation worked with two full-dragons, and fortunately, she didn't go into the details.

"Other than when we're young and receive lessons, dragons are solitary creatures." Although she spoke matter-of-factly, a note of sadness sounded in her words. "The whole idea of *any* type of education is recent, as before Nastav, no dragon had ever volunteered for the job. I think the adults thought him rather senile." Fondness shone in her eyes. "He *is* extremely old."

The society, if it could be called that, she described didn't sound appealing. And based on her tone, he guessed she didn't miss any of it other than her teacher.

After another bite of food, she shrugged. "Anyway, against that environment, my parents were rebels. Or I should say, my mother was. I think she was the dragon version of a hippie. She believed in love." Elaina scoffed. "She believed dragons *could* love. And she thought she loved my father. So she convinced him to stay with her so they could raise me together."

What did that scoff mean? It sounded as though Elaina didn't believe in love. Or worse, that she didn't think dragons could love. Rather than pursue a conversation he wasn't ready for anyway, he concentrated on the promising aspect of her explanation.

"Does that mean it would be safe for me to meet your mother?"

"You can't. She's dead."

Damn it. What an ass. He'd missed the past-tense clue.

"My father killed her when I was fourteen." Her voice quieted. "I don't know what provoked him, but I saw the end of his attack. He carved her with countless slashes but never pierced her heart, so her death dragged on until she lost too much blood. Right up to the end, my mother was proclaiming her love for him, begging him not to do this to her, asking him to trust in their love."

No wonder she'd taken a vow of non-violence. Alex squeezed her tight. "I'm sorry."

She twisted away, hiding her face, and stabbed another piece of food. Hunger was the last thing on his mind after all that, but he accepted the mouthful to keep her talking.

"Normally, dragons stay with one of their parents for their first twenty-five years. Then they need to leave before their parent worries the child will kill them for their treasure. If younglings stay too long, their parent might kill them instead."

Wonderful. What a beautiful portrait of dragon family life she painted.

"But you left ten years ago." He put the pieces together. "After your mother's death."

"One of the few rituals of dragon society is called *Zìwǒ*, our rite of passage. Younglings must be strong enough to steal an item from their parent's cache but not so strong that their parent feels their entire hoard is in danger. After a youngling successfully steals something from their parent and escapes, they're considered an adult."

"You used the word *stealing*." His eyebrow lifted on a tease. "I thought you said what dragons did wasn't stealing."

She dipped her chin, and a tiny smile spread across her features. "True. In this context, *stealing* is the best way to describe it. Younglings aren't strong enough to *claim* anything from their parent's collection, so it's simply a physical grabbing and running. If they escape from their parent's territory, the item bonds to them and becomes their talisman, the conduit for accessing the energy of the rest of their hoard and the core of all their strength. Parents are supposed to let the matter drop and consider themselves lucky they didn't lose more treasure."

"Your father didn't let the matter drop," he guessed.

"It's more complicated than that." She winced and gave him another bite. "He went crazy after killing my mother."

Alex would argue her father was crazy before that—for the killing itself—but didn't interrupt.

"I sneaked away while he stayed with her body. He sat and watched her for a long time. Days, nearly a week. I almost thought he regretted what he'd done. If he had, I could have forgiven him, and we still could have tried being a family."

Her voice dropped into an abyss on the word *family*, and her spine curled inward, pained, protecting. Cold crept up Alex's limbs, and his heartbeat became sluggish. He didn't want to hear the next part of her story.

"But as soon as he saw me, he became enraged again, spouting craziness about how he had to get rid of me and my whole existence. His reaction didn't make any sense—it was personal, about *me*, which was all the more terrifying. So I hid." Her voice broke. "And then he ripped my mother's body into pieces and screamed that it was all her fault."

"I'm so sorry." His words were meaningless against her memories.

"At that moment, I knew he'd lost his mind. He'd come after me next unless I got away from him. Even though no youngling had ever survived it at that age, I decided to go through my *Zìwǒ* early. I took the ruby my mother had given him, the only thing of *his* I'd want."

Her hands twisted after she fed him a bite of vegetables. "He sensed when I stole the gem and chased me through the tunnels. I escaped through a narrow passage that was too tight for him to follow me at full speed."

"Tunnels?" He sipped his wine and tried to picture her story. "Like underground?"

"Yes, I grew up in a cave. Other than me, all dragons live in caves inside the mountains of Europe and Asia." Her brows arched, as though daring him to comment. "Your point?"

He gave her a casual shrug, showing that he wasn't judging her.

"Once I crossed the boundary of his territory, the ruby bonded to me, giving me enough strength to survive on my own, but just barely. Dragons are supposed to stay with their parent until the age of twenty-five so their parent's treasure can keep their heart beating while they're growing. I didn't get that benefit. Instead, every ounce of energy I acquired went to keeping my heart going.

I'm a runt compared to other dragons."

No question she was petite. He'd assumed that was simply the way she was and not a sign of how unhealthy she'd been for ten years. Once again, his protective instinct reared, and he moved to pull her closer, keep her safe in his arms.

She interrupted his consoling attempt by resuming her story. "My father chased me across Europe and Asia for the next four years. If I hadn't learned how to fake my way through human society, he'd have caught me long ago. I never lost him for more than a few weeks until I moved to America."

"Have you seen him since then?"

"No, I don't think he can imagine that I'd come here."

"Why not?"

If her father was *that* intent on hunting her down, after losing track of her for the six years she'd been here, wouldn't he have followed every possibility?

"Because *he* can't imagine coming here, with all the logistics of integrating into human society enough to acquire an ID and pass the scrutiny of airport security. I mean, he'd find a way if he had proof I was here, like that picture, but otherwise, he'll assume I'm somewhere over there."

Her words from the previous night came back to him, how she was the only dragon living among humans. Until this moment, he hadn't understood how different dragon society was, how separate they were from humans despite being born humanoid.

Logically, those differences should have prompted him to question whether they could be truly compatible, but he couldn't make himself think of her as strange. The more he learned, the more she amazed him. She'd accomplished so much and come so far on her own.

"Other dragons don't live in apartments and have regular jobs, I take it?"

She snickered. "Other dragons don't know how to work a doorknob, much less drive a car or anything else *normal*."

"No cars? How did he chase you?" An image of her and her father jogging across Europe and Asia came to mind. She couldn't have meant he'd *literally* chased her like that.

"I traveled by train, bus, hitchhiking, you name it. He flew."

"I thought you said he couldn't get through airport—"

She placed her finger against his lips. "No, he *flew*."

Oh... Dragon. Wings. Flying. Jesus. Now it made sense that her father wouldn't have thought about her flying—in an *airplane*—over the ocean. Of course, this confirmed her father could change into his dragon form. Wonderful.

"And the Atlantic is too big for him to fly across on his own?"

After she verified his guess, he asked the obvious. "How do you know he's still searching for you? It's been six years since he's seen you and ten years since whatever it was provoked him to start all this. Perhaps he's cooled down since then."

"If you saw how relentless he was, you wouldn't question it." She grimaced and ducked her head. "One time I was sloppy, and he caught up to me in Greece. By the time I escaped, his attempts to kill me triggered huge fires that devastated homes and killed people."

Her shoulders hunched, and she shivered on his lap.

"People *died* because of me. I'm not willing to risk that happening again on the off-chance that he's no longer insane."

He couldn't fathom the psychosis behind her father's behavior. The situation was different from what he'd experienced, and these dragon attitudes didn't add up in his mind. But he let the matter drop—for now. Later, after he knew more about dragons in general, he might be able to make better sense of it.

"Okay, you've been living in relative peace since coming here, and you need to keep your presence under wraps to maintain that peace. The immediate problem is you have to build up your treasure collection beyond mere survival so you're not always on the verge of starvation. But I get the feeling that what you really want is simply to stop worrying."

She stiffened, and her fingers fanned against her collarbone.

He sat back. "What did I get wrong?"

"Nothing." Before he could ask, she added, "And that's what's so surprising. You understand this, Alex. You understand *me*."

That was quite a compliment coming from her, especially since he wouldn't go as far as claiming he understood everything.

She stroked along his jaw. "I don't know how you can be so accepting of everything. Why *aren't* you freaking out? We're so different, and yet you act as though it's no big deal."

"Because with you it *doesn't* feel like a big deal." He tugged on her hips. "This feels natural enough to me. You're just you, and I like you however you are."

The glow in her eyes wavered again, as though it might be a dragon-type of tearing up. Her attention settled on his lips. Dinner was over.

Time for dessert.

He held her tight and stood from the chair. Her legs wrapped around his hips, and he carried her to the bed. Their bed.

She stretched up to him from the mattress. He kissed her palm and yanked off his shirt. She began removing her shirt as well, and he stopped her.

"I'll do it."

She nodded and cast her gaze across his chest. Those bench presses he did to keep in shape were worth every drop of sweat. Her appreciation justified barbells of solid gold.

He lay next to her, his hand entwined with hers at the bottom of her shirt. He propped himself on his other elbow and skimmed his fingers over her hair.

"I'm going to make this good for you. I promise."

"I know. I trust you."

And if that wasn't a damnable amount of responsibility, he didn't know what was. He rocked forward, ready to start with a gentle kiss. But she had other ideas, and her free arm yanked him hard to her mouth.

Jesus. Their lips and tongues played, sucked, and nibbled. How the hell was he supposed to stay in control of himself if she kept up this shit? He clenched the hem of her shirt with his struggle to restrain himself from ravaging her.

Her leg hooked over his hip and pulled him onto her. While he was distracted by that, his fingers sneaked under her shirt, seemingly on their own. She arched, encouraging his fingertips to slide higher.

His restraint shredded, held in check by the thinnest strand. He couldn't stop himself from admitting, "I want you so much."

"Then take me." Her hips pressed into his, emphasizing her words.

Fuck. A mental twang accompanied the breaking of the last wisp of his composure. Screw it. He'd have to hope she'd speak up if something bothered her.

His hands moved frantically now, nudging up her top. She didn't resist, her arms rising for him to tug off her T-shirt. And she didn't protest when he tossed it to the floor behind him.

Her lacy red bra beckoned like a present waiting to be unwrapped. He placed a few kisses onto the rounded tops of her breasts while he unfastened the bra's clasp.

With that article of clothing out of the way, he paused, drinking in the vision of heaven before him. Her breasts were perfect—that hadn't just been a line. The ideal size and shape for her, and a deep red tinted her nipples. The sharp contrast of color against her iridescent skin added to their allure.

He traced around the curves, and she shuddered. Her nipples hardened, tightening into delectable peaks.

God, she was so responsive to the smallest touch. He circled closer and closer to his target. When he reached her nipple, she hissed and arched into his palm. He pinched the bud, and she writhed beneath him.

Her hand stroked his cheek, and he looked up. Crap, he probably should have been paying attention to her face more, but he'd been so damn fascinated by her body he couldn't help it. She didn't seem upset in the least though, and a luscious smile spread across her mouth.

"Do it, Alex. Taste me." She pressed on the back of his head.

He didn't need a second invitation. His lips latched onto her nipple. Unlike last time, he didn't stick with shallow nibbles and licks. He filled his whole mouth with her softness and sucked.

She gasped, and her fingers tightened in his hair. He let her fullness slip from his hold and gently bit at the hardened nub. At the same time, he pinched and twisted her other nipple.

"Oh god, yes." Her voice was breathless and shaky, and her body squirmed in encouragement. With her responsiveness, it would be easy to make this great for her.

He shifted slightly to reach her other breast with his mouth, and her hand moved from his hair to his side. While he sucked and bit and pinched, she circled her fingers in the hair trailing down from his navel. The touch sent sparks to his cock, constricted in his jeans.

Her fingertips hooked into his waistband. "Now I'm wondering where else you're hiding this extra hair."

He chuckled against her breast. "Why don't you go exploring?"

She shoved him onto his back, rolling them together, and straddled his hips. "Well, I can see some here..." She brushed along his waistband. "But it seems as though it might go lower, so I'll have to take a peek to make sure."

A broad grin stretched his lips, and he rested his head in his palms, restraining himself so she could take the lead for a minute. "By all means, satisfy your curiosity, beautiful."

Her eyes flashed in response to his words. This was going to be good.

Chapter Sixteen

ELAINA DIDN'T KNOW WHERE TO START. HER BODY WANTED everything at once. The kissing, his attention to her breasts, the feel of their skin together, the heat between her thighs. Each made her feel as if she'd explode, and yet her body longed for more.

The whole situation was unreal. The answer to her dreams, to the desires she'd kept hidden from even herself, was right before her.

When Alex had said that what she really wanted was the simple freedom from worry, the truth had hit her: Even if she no longer worried about her father, she wouldn't go back to the caves. The human world, as ill-fitting as it was, was more her home now. She wanted to stay.

With Alex.

And he made it seem as though that was possible. As though he could help her fit in. As though he could keep her safe. As though he *would* be able to protect her from her father's eyes.

She'd always hidden through the power of anonymity, but what if the power of money could hide her as well? The possibility was tempting. This *man* was tempting.

The thought of exploring his body freed her fingers from paralysis. The idea of body hair was so strange and intriguing.

She unbuttoned his jeans and slid the zipper open. His soft, curly hair disappeared under the waistband of his... What were those shorts things called? Panties didn't sound right, but magazine cover headlines rarely discussed men's underclothing details.

His abs jumped when she touched the area. And something *moved* under the material.

She had her suspicions, but wasn't sure how much her scattered self-education had put together the snippets of information properly. Beyond curious, she crawled backward so she could tug his jeans down and out of the way.

He watched her with a smug expression, the muscles of his chest and arms standing out in sharp definition as his hands rested behind his head. "Let me know if you want help."

"Nope." She dragged the thick fabric over his knees. Once his jeans and socks were off, she started her investigation with his feet.

A stroke on the arch of his foot made him flinch. "Ticklish."

"Ticklish? Is that a good or bad feeling?"

His shoulders bunched against his bent arms with his shrug. "It's not necessarily good or bad. It just is." His brow jumped. "You're not ticklish? Anywhere?"

"I don't think so."

She slid up his sculpted calves to his powerful thighs. Light hair dusted his skin, and she kneaded the ridges of muscles. The closer she got to the top and inner sides of his thighs, the more the *something* inside his shorts jumped.

Curiosity finally got the best of her. Her fingers caught the waistband, and she pulled. She had to stretch the elastic over the bulge hidden by the fabric.

Once the mystery was revealed, she stopped and stared, awestruck. This thing matched her guess in a vague sense, but in the flesh, it was still so foreign compared to anything on her body she didn't know what to make of it.

Before she could stop herself from voicing the inane question on the tip of her tongue, she blurted, "What is this?"

He barked a laugh. "Guys have a hundred different words for it. You can call it whatever you want. As long as you're not too rough with it, it'll be a slave to your whims."

Ooo, she liked the sound of "slave to her whims" much better than all the coarse words for it she'd heard during her time among humans.

His gaze piercing, he curled his fingers around hers before she could investigate further. "But how could you *not* know?"

"What do you mean? What part of *virgin* makes that a surprise?"

"It's just..." His brows tightened. "After everything you said about being on your own, I figured you must have spent some time on the streets, and that you would have seen *everything*. You do know how this works, right?"

"I know the basics." She shrugged and drew circles on his abs. "I lived on the street most of my years, but I never felt part of the human world, so I didn't pay attention to the specifics. I mean, how much do you pay attention to the mating practices of squirrels?"

He snorted. "I'm a squirrel now?"

"No." She focused on her slave and grinned. "Definitely not a squirrel. But until recently, humans and their society didn't concern me, so I paid attention only on a need-to-know basis." She caressed lower and looked through her lashes. "Now, can I get back to learning about everything I missed? This is something I *need* to know. Right now."

He laughed and used his feet to finish removing his clothes, and she continued where she'd left off at the tops of his thighs. Every move of her fingers caused her slave to rise above his abs.

His hair was thicker here, but the protuberance was smooth and reddish. Her strokes set her slave bouncing enthusiastically. She couldn't help a giggle, which earned a groan from Alex.

One of his forearms now covered his eyes, and he grimaced, as though in pain. She stopped her caresses. "Are you okay?"

"First, guys tend to feel insecure when women laugh at..." He waved, indicating the area. "Second, this is driving me crazy. I feel as though I'm going to explode."

Him too? Then she must have been doing something right.

She wrapped her fingers around her slave. How rough would be too rough? She gently squeezed. Alex stiffened and gave another groan. A good groan. Maybe she'd figured out how to do this after all.

Her thumb rubbed the tip, the velvety texture surprising her. It was unlike the skin anywhere else on his body. A drop of moisture clung to the end.

Alex's heavy-lidded eyes gazed at her hungrily. She squeezed again, and his hips thrust into her hand.

"My turn." On his growl, he grasped her torso and tossed her back onto the bed.

His lips skated over her abdomen while he unbuttoned her jeans. The spot at the top of her thighs felt heavier with anticipation.

In much the same way she had, he removed her jeans and caressed her skin. But his lips also joined in, kissing and nibbling up her legs.

As always, his touch sent warm shocks through her body. The tingles set off a cascade of wet heat between her thighs.

The heel of his palm pressed onto her panties when he reached the top of her legs, and she bit back a moan. Her hips lifted off the bed, encouraging him to remove the last of her clothes. He took the hint and slid her panties down. Like her reaction to him, he stopped when they were only partly to her knees, his brows furrowed.

Her gut tightened. "Is something wrong?"

How bizarre *was* she compared to human women?

He shook himself and met her gaze. "Nothing wrong, beautiful. I hadn't realized my body hair fascinated you because you don't have any." Before she could wonder what to think about that difference, he squeezed her thigh reassuringly. "And that's not a problem."

Once they were both completely naked, he eased her legs apart, skimmed a finger along her inner thigh, and lay down beside her. His fingertip circled the opening at the top of her legs, making her squirm. The spot was demanding he do something different, but she didn't know what.

He whispered in her ear, "How are you doing? Good?"

At his question, his finger slipped between the folds of her skin. She gasped and her knees fell apart, offering him better access. Oh, yes. *This* was what she needed.

He slid a second finger inside, and her hips moved forward, wanting more. His thumb rubbed against a hard spot at the top of her opening.

She gripped the bed covers with the electric sensations. "Alex!"

"Shh. Relax. It's okay. Just breathe."

Easy for him to say. She'd never felt anything so shocking. It was as if he'd found a secret button connecting to every nerve ending in her body. While his thumb circled and pressed on the spot, invisible threads gave him control over her body like a marionette.

His fingers took up their rhythm again, adding to the overwhelming feelings, and her hips surprised her by arching up to him, begging for more.

"That's it, beautiful. Let yourself feel." He slid down the bed and tugged her nipple into his mouth, sending her past the point of being able to think.

"Oh god." She had so much she wanted to say, but words were beyond her. "Make me feel. Make me feel. Make me feel." Although she knew she was babbling, she couldn't halt the flow.

He increased the speed of his fingers and thumb, and his teeth lightly bit down on her nipple. Her hips answered in kind, desperately rocking into his hand. She was being propelled toward a pinnacle, somehow both terrifying and enticing.

"Alex, please!"

His fingers pressed harder, and he switched to her other breast, biting less gently now. Her nails dug into the bed covers, and her legs shook with tension.

"Come for me, Elaina. Come for me."

Her body obeyed, shuddering its release. The tingles of energy from his touch turned into a rush beyond the biggest treasure claiming. Time stood still while waves of pleasure engulfed her body. Devoured her body. Ravaged her body.

She'd never known anything could feel like this. This exquisite explosion of sensation. This perfection of ecstasy. This glimpse of her soul.

Eventually, her knees fell to the mattress, her legs seemingly made of goo.

Oh god. She *felt*. She felt everything. Every feeling, every emotion, was within her grasp.

Most of all, she knew—she wanted him. She needed him. She claimed him.

Water leaked from her eyes.

Dragons didn't cry.

The proof that her body wasn't obeying the rules dampened her temples. That fact both scared her and made her hopeful in ways she couldn't understand or explain. In truth, the whole experience couldn't be put into words. At least not yet.

His fingers stilled. He slid up next to her and searched her face, pausing on the wet tracks at her temples. "Are you okay?"

She answered his worry by capturing his lips with a kiss. A kiss of desperation, of need, of the desire to tell him everything she couldn't express in words. She pressed into him so hard they rolled together, ending up with him on his back and her straddling his hips.

Her slick folds rested on top of him, spreading moisture along his length. She curved to kiss his neck, and their bodies slipped against each other, rubbing in all the right places. His hands clamped onto her hips with his groan.

She straightened, nibbling her way down his chest, pausing to test his reaction to her tongue swirling around his nipple. The skin hardened, and he gave a grunt. Interesting.

When she moved to the other one, he growled, "Are you trying to kill me?"

She sat up, her muscles tense. Was she doing something wrong?

But he didn't seem mad. In fact, his hands went to her breasts, kneading them, and his eyes looked wild.

He forced them to roll again, shoving her onto her back with him above her. His strength surprised her, and she didn't think she could have stopped him. Good thing she didn't want this to stop.

He propped himself up and locked gazes with her. "I'm going to take this as slow as I can. It might hurt a bit because it's your first time, but it will get better, I promise. It'll help for you to stay relaxed."

"I trust you."

"Speaking of that..." He started to move away, reaching for his nightstand.

She grabbed his shoulder. "Where are you—?"

"Condom."

"Why? I'm a virgin and immune to human diseases." She'd seen enough PSA signs about condoms to know they were yet another human thing that didn't apply to her.

"There's still pregnancy."

"Human and dragon? Not going to happen."

"Oh." For a second, his enthusiasm dimmed.

Before she could worry about his reaction, he lifted himself above her again. Ropes of muscles stood out in stark relief on his arm as he balanced and used his other hand to adjust his length below. The tip pressed against her opening, and he slowly rocked his hips forward.

Oh god. Everything she thought she knew about how this worked disintegrated compared to the real thing.

He slid inside her, spreading her, filling her. Filling an emptiness she hadn't known existed.

She grasped his hips, and he stilled. "You okay?"

"Yes, yes, big yes. More, please."

"That's my girl, using words like *big* and *more*. I like that." He came down to his elbows, their chests together. "I like that a lot." His kiss showed her how much, his tongue filling her mouth at the same time he slipped further into her.

She wanted more. She wanted everything.

He drew away from her lips, and she whispered encouragement before he could back off and check on her again. "Give me more, Alex. Give me everything. I want you."

He must have heard her because his movements became less gentle. With a final hard push, he was completely inside her.

His torso stiffened, and she cut him off before he could say anything. "I'm fine." She let her nails dig into his butt, and she pulled him into her. "And if you keep holding yourself back, I'll have to punish you."

His dark chuckle was wickedly seductive. "We'll play that game another time, beautiful."

As she was trying to think of a retort, he angled his hips back and thrust them forward. All thoughts fell out of her head at the sensation.

Oh, yes. He did it again. Yes, yes, yes.

She wanted her hands everywhere, and they moved crazily

with her desire. Tangling in his hair. Sliding across his back muscles. Squeezing his butt.

He matched her frantic movements by increasing the tempo of his thrusts. Their hips found a natural rhythm, a point and counter-point to maximize the friction between them.

Her legs bent farther, spreading wider, and the different angle let him hit new places within her. Deep wasn't deep enough.

As though he recognized her needs, he rose up on his arms again and pounded into her. Ruthless, relentless. And she loved every bit of it, couldn't get enough. She grasped his butt and tugged at the pace of his thrusts, adding to his force as he slammed into her.

Yes, that was hitting the spot. Tension built within her again.

"Yes, Alex, yes."

Almost. She knew what to expect now and rode the crest. She hissed. Yes, yes, yes...

Her body clenched, squeezing him, taking everything it could from him. Again, the rush of energy bound her to him tighter than the strongest claim of treasure. Every muscle vibrated in ecstasy, and she never wanted the pleasure to end. This was where she belonged—the two of them together.

His body answered, his features contorting into a grimace, and he grunted with a final thrust. A shudder swept through him, and he collapsed, catching himself on his elbows rather than squishing her.

For a quiet moment, the only sound was their heavy breathing. Then he rolled to her side and ran his fingers through her hair. "Are you okay?"

Her emotions bubbled out on a giggle. "I'm so much better than *okay* it's not even the same language." She gave him a kiss and met his gaze. "I don't know the words to describe how perfect, fantastic, amazing—"

He squished her against him. "God, Elaina, I love you."

She stiffened. Love? That thing dragons were incapable of?

The weight of inadequacy crushed her. She'd never be who Alex wanted her to be.

Who she wished she could be.

Chapter Seventeen

ALEX BIT BACK A CURSE AS ELAINA FROZE IN HIS ARMS. HE hadn't meant for his declaration of love to slip out. He'd swallowed the words earlier at her apartment, but after the best sex of his life, he couldn't help his impulsiveness. When her body moved once more, she withdrew from his hold.

Christ. She balked more than his Mercedes SLS AMG on regular gasoline.

If he was going to get her to stay—without needing handcuffs— he had to get her to trust him. What was the dragon-spoiling equivalent of premium grade fuel?

"I want to help you. What if I added treasure to your collection?"

She halted her retreat. "You'd do that?"

"If that's what it takes to help you avoid starvation, then of course."

Her expression became so blank he couldn't tell what she was thinking.

He caressed her thigh and tried again. "I've never liked unfair fights. I want you strong, as strong as you can be. That's what I mean by wanting to help you. I want us to be a team. A *we*."

She leaned farther away from him. "You're going to help me steal treasure?"

"Not stealing. You can build up your collection and get energy in other ways. I've seen it. The harder it is for you to take something, the more energy you get from it, right?"

"It's more complicated than that." He circled his wrist in an impatient wave until she conceded, "In general, that's a fair assumption."

He rose up on the bed. If he could *prove* to her that staying with him didn't mean remaining weak, maybe she'd be less likely to run.

"Do you have to see something to take it? How close do you have to be?" He indicated the nightstand on her side of the bed. "Could you take the ring in the top drawer over there?"

She rolled toward the end table. "The 8.16 grams of fourteen-karat yellow gold, inset with a twelve-millimeter square of onyx?"

"That's the one."

"And you want me to *take* it from you?" Her vocal pitch climbed with her confusion.

"If you *can*."

Her puzzlement flickered to being offended before finally settling on determination, just as he knew it would. She huffed, sat up, and stretched an open hand toward the nightstand.

He scooted behind her and rested his chin on her bare shoulder. "That's right, beautiful. Show me what you can do."

The muscles of her back tensed against his chest with her concentration. A moment later, prickles spread on his skin where they touched, and the ring appeared in her palm.

"I did it." She sounded surprised.

He spun her around and kissed her forehead. "I knew you could."

"No, you don't understand. Summoning something without having laid eyes on it? And from several feet away? I've done that with abandoned pieces before, like a ring that had fallen down a storm drain, but nothing that had an owner."

"This will make you stronger?"

Her fingers closed around the ring. She inhaled sharply, and her eyes flashed. A charge like static electricity raised the hairs on his forearms.

The fact that he sensed when she bonded to an item emphasized how connected they were. How connected they could be—if only she'd allow it to happen.

"Yes, this makes me stronger."

She unfurled her hand, and the ring still lay there, but he guessed it would now be invisible to others. And that meant his plan would work.

"Now do you understand how I can help you?"

Her gaze shot up to his. Despite her open mouth, no words came out.

He scooted closer on the bed and cradled her cheeks. "I don't want you to be weak, and I want you to be able to stay here with me—without stealing. If that means I have to supply you with a steady diet of jewelry..." A grin broke across his face. "Well, I wouldn't be the first guy to do that to keep his woman happy."

Instead of happiness, a bittersweet tightness creased her expression. "If only I could stay with you *and* remain hidden."

The wish in her declaration gripped his chest. *If only...* Then everything would be perfect.

"What if I also help you hide from your father? We don't have to go out in public. I'll get rid of that article with your name and picture. No one other than my staff has to know you're here. Just..." He stroked her lips. "Stay with me."

"You're saying that you not only promise to provide me with treasure, but you'd also keep me hidden—even if that means we're never *together* in front of anyone other than your staff? No more arm ornament appearances? No more paparazzi?"

She was right to question him. These were huge promises, life-altering promises, promises he didn't know how to keep, but he needed to try. She was worth it. The alternative of letting her go was too horrible to contemplate.

"Yes, that's what I'm saying." He met her gaze. "I can give you what you want, what you need. I promise."

She tucked her legs closer on the mattress, and her empty hand rubbed her abdomen. "Why? Why do you want me to stay here so much that you'd do all that for me?"

Her question proved that she'd dismissed his earlier admission of love. Maybe that was for the best. For now anyway. Time might help her adjust to the idea.

But that meant he couldn't answer her question honestly. She'd freak out again if he revealed his suspicions of how perfect she was for him. That she challenged him like no other woman. That she fascinated him like no other woman. That she was strong like no other woman. And even though she wasn't human, that he understood her like no other woman.

Instead of scaring her off with all of that, he gave her an ambivalent shrug. "I'm used to getting what *I* want. And I want you."

His answer seemed to mollify her, and she lifted her hand. "You're okay with me having this?"

He hadn't wanted to think about the thing.

"It belonged to my father." He tilted his head and pointed to a spot on his jaw. "This is what that ring means to me."

Her fingertip skimmed his jawline, and she examined the mark he indicated. "This is a scar?"

Right. Her super-strong dragon scales meant she wasn't familiar with scars.

At his nod, she searched his face for an answer to a question he didn't know. "He did this to you? On purpose?"

He nodded again, and her expression twisted into open-mouthed horror. Given the story of her father's attack against her mother, he hadn't thought this blemish was anything in comparison.

"How old were you?" Her voice was clipped.

"Eight. I made the 'mistake' of getting between his fist and my mother." His wry smile tensed into a grimace. "I never let him touch her like that again."

The blue fire in her eyes dimmed. "But you were a youngling—a child."

"That fact doesn't stop monsters. He stopped only when I was big enough to fight back."

She touched his jaw again. "An adult has threatened a pre-Zìwǒ-age youngling only once in all history. But I'm less vulnerable than you, especially back when you were a child."

The glow of her eyes wavered, and she leaned closer. Her tender kiss on his scar caught him by surprise. He'd never have guessed gentleness was in her repertoire.

She examined the rest of his body. Each mark she found earned another soft kiss, from the indentation at his hairline where his father had smashed a bourbon bottle on his forehead to the faint crisscrossing white lines on his knees caused by his father shoving him onto the broken glass of his mother's favorite crystal vase. Elaina honored each mark that had protected his mother.

Something inside him cracked at the gesture.

By the time she finished, he was lying on the bed, quiet and acquiescent while she moved his limbs with her search. His eyes were open, but they weren't focused on the ceiling above him. Memories clouded his vision.

After hundreds of beatings, he'd thought they'd all blurred together. Her recognition of the scars had unleashed the origin of each one in vivid detail.

She stretched out alongside him and touched his temple. "I'm sorry."

Her voice broke the spell. She slid her hand back from his skin, and a drop of clear liquid clung to her fingertip.

The sight made him feel weak. Hot tension quickly followed, and bitterness filled his mouth. "She should have left him."

"Why do you think she didn't?"

A humorless laugh punched the air between them. "I asked her that same question every day until she died." He forced the words out through clenched teeth. "She claimed he'd have made sure we were penniless and homeless, if we got out alive at all."

"You don't believe her?"

The way Elaina worded it—using *don't* instead of *didn't*—shoved his lingering resentment into the open.

"In public, she still stood beside him as his dutiful wife at every function and accepted all the fancy dresses and jewelry he gave her. You tell me. Maybe she simply loved the money more than she loved—"

He cut off the thought, but Elaina finished it anyway. "More than she loved you."

She propped herself up on her elbow. "Alex, you're incredibly strong inside. Stronger than most, dragon or human. I pushed you away, and you didn't yield. Call it arrogance or call it determination, the fact is, most people would have given up. You didn't. Instead of stopping you, obstacles have made you stronger."

Her insight floated past him without making an impact.

She dragged his chin toward her. "I bet that each of his attacks

Jami Gold

made you more resolved, and that you refused to show him weakness. You took his abuse in stoic silence, didn't you?"

He couldn't ignore her direct question and angled away from her. "I cried out the first time."

"Probably from surprise more than anything else. But after that?"

He didn't need to answer her. She already knew.

She lay down and snuggled next to him. "You're understandably disappointed your mother didn't have the strength to stand up to him the way you did. But you don't know what kind of emotional abuse she endured once their bedroom door closed every night. Her choices don't mean she didn't love you."

His eyelids pinched closed. Nothing had ever been easy when it came to how he felt toward his mother.

Protecting her had made him feel strong and powerful, yet accusations had always simmered below the surface. Intentional or not, she'd put him into the position where he'd needed to let his body be pummeled to shield her, and he couldn't help the resentment he still harbored inside.

Elaina's light touch smoothed his eyebrows, which had furrowed without him realizing it. "Did she ever blame you for his attacks?"

His eyes popped open. "No." He breathed deep, releasing the tightness around his chest, relieved he could give her credit for something. "She blamed herself, saying parents were supposed to protect their children, not the other way around. She begged me not to do it. She hated what he did to me."

The memory of that last night washed over him. "I thought she'd finally leave him when I landed in the hospital at fifteen years old with a concussion, a fractured arm, two broken legs, and three broken ribs. My father gave the doctors a story about how I was a drug addict and the dealer had set his goons on me. A simple blood test would have showed me to be clean, but no one questioned my father. It was much easier to believe the spoiled rich kid had gotten in over his head."

The flow of memories sharpened like acid. "She was so upset I thought for sure she'd tell them the truth. Instead, she..."

The silence stretched out.

After several moments, Elaina drew a shaky breath, understanding what he couldn't yet say. "She loved you."

"Then why did she kill herself?" His voice was barely a whisper. "Why did she leave me?"

Elaina kissed the left side of his chest. "Your heart knows the answer to that question."

The straightforward response reignited his anger. "Because she was weak."

"No, Alex. Because she loved you more than her own life." His gaze shot to hers, but she didn't let him deny her statement. "You said it yourself. She blamed herself. You put up with the abuse to protect her."

The truth slammed into him, unleashing his thoughts fast enough to make him dizzy.

His mother had killed herself so he wouldn't need to protect her anymore. She'd sacrificed herself to set him free.

He wanted to be furious with her for coming to such a ridiculous conclusion, but he had to admit things had improved afterward. The months of physical therapy had triggered his commitment to a workout regimen.

By the time he'd fully recovered and was no longer under the doctors' observation, he was bigger and stronger than his father— or at least big enough to even the odds. And without the worry of needing to be on the defensive to protect her, he'd gone on the offensive after the first punch, eager to finally confront the man in a fair fight.

That was the end of the abuse. Of the physical kind at least.

"She..." He choked out the words. "She loved me."

She'd loved him so much that she died for him. She'd done it to protect *him*.

That truth broke through his mental walls, shattering everything he'd believed for the past sixteen years. He'd filled his head with blame, disrespect, and resentment for his mother, for not loving him as much as he loved her.

Despite the abuse she'd lived through before his intervention, he'd never seen her as a victim of his father. He'd seen her only as being weak.

But as with most things, the truth was more complicated than that. *Love* was more complicated than that. Love wasn't always expressed in the ways he expected.

ELAINA HELD ALEX'S SLEEPING FORM AND TRAILED HER FINGERS down his back. There was no longer any question. She cared about this man.

Not only did he understand her better than anyone ever had, but she also understood him. His extravagant donation the previous night to establish shelters for victims of abuse now made perfect sense. Likewise, his determination to salvage his father's business was, at heart, about proving himself a better man.

She suspected he'd never told anyone his history previously. And he'd certainly never confronted his buried emotions before.

Their families weren't messed up in the same way, but the similarities gave her insight into his situation. Her hand stilled, and she suppressed a shudder.

No wonder he had that steely resolve. She couldn't imagine what it would take to willingly allow someone to hurt her. And how much love someone had to be capable of to *want* to accept pain on behalf of another.

She sucked in a breath until his scent filled her lungs. Her flesh tingled from more than simply the touch of his skin against hers.

This man deserved to be loved. And she wished she could give it to him.

Before she'd wanted to leave him out of fear—now she wanted to stay out of selfishness. Even though she could never be who he wanted her to be, who he was worthy of, she couldn't muster the willpower to give this up. Her embrace tightened around him at that realization.

Beyond the fact that he *did* have the power to give her the protection she needed, he was perfect in every other way as well. Any man she was going to be with had to be strong. Alex met that requirement and then some. His inner strength complemented her physical strength, matching it so well she *wanted* him to be dominating. Most of all, she didn't want to be alone anymore.

Even if Alex couldn't remove the gossip article, his promise to shield her from exposure going forward was more important. The chances of her father—who wasn't even integrated into human society—seeing a single instance of her name and picture within a human newspaper from Chicago were, in truth, laughably remote. And shutting this wonderful man out of her life over such an impossibility would be the height of stupidity.

No, she would stay. She would keep him. And she would be happy for the first time in her life.

Maybe the fact that she cared about him would be enough. For both of them.

Chapter Eighteen

ELAINA WOKE TO THE SOUND OF HER OWN MOANS. HER treasure wasn't in her grasp.

Alex's sharp scent wafted close, and gentle lips kissed her forehead. "Good morning, beautiful."

She opened her eyes and found him standing beside the bed in a business suit, sans the jacket. "You're *dressed* already."

"It's Monday morning." He chuckled. "I have to go to work."

Her arms felt empty without him. "How are you feeling? Did I drain energy from you?"

"I feel great. Wonderful, in fact." He sat beside her on the mattress, and his gaze turned serious. "Thank you."

"For what?"

"You know what." He massaged his temples for a moment and then smoothed his hair. "I'm not there yet, but I think I've started to forgive her."

An invisible weight perched on her chest, and her throat thickened. She took his hand and kissed his fingers. Words about how much he deserved to feel loved threatened to spill from her mouth. If that happened, she'd succumb to guilt. And she didn't do guilt.

Instead, she offered, "I'm glad."

"My schedule is full of meetings today, but I'll be back for dinner. The house staff knows you're here and will help you with anything you need."

He bent down and gave her a soft kiss. Before he could pull

away, she grasped his tie and deepened their embrace.

Their moans echoed each other, and his hands took advantage of her still-naked state, skating across her skin. She wrapped her other hand around his shoulder, ready to tip him beside her on the bed, but he broke away.

His eyes glinted, amusement lighting them from within. "Whether you're denying me or giving me what I want, you always manage to have the upper hand." He pressed a finger against her mouth, preventing her retort. "I stayed in bed with you as long as I could. I'm already running late."

Her lower lip stuck out in a pout.

He stood, putting distance between them, and grinned. "Does that mean you'll miss me while I'm gone?"

Her limbs stiffened. The intensity of how much she'd miss him constricted her throat.

His grin faded. "You *will* be here when I come home." Despite his firm instruction, the statement ended on a questioning tone.

"Yes." She gave a long exhale. "And I'll miss you."

He picked up his suit jacket from the corner of the mattress and walked backward toward the door. "It's taking every ounce of willpower I have to leave right now."

His gaze traveled over her body, and his hungry expression let her know exactly what he was thinking. She stretched, sensuously moving her limbs to torture him.

His look turned even more heated. "I wish I could stay, just to teach you a lesson."

A wince creased his features, and he left the room on the sound of her chuckle. Emptiness followed with his absence. She'd have to find a way to fill her day or else start moping. The second option didn't sound appealing at all.

Stefano's was closed on Mondays, as most of the staff worked events on the weekends, so she couldn't occupy her time with that. Come to think of it, did she still need that job?

She'd taken the position to get the inside scoop on Chicago's most lavish parties, but if Alex was serious about helping her acquire more treasure without stealing, the place had lost its allure. And he probably wouldn't want her to keep the job anyway, as he was smart enough to figure out her motive for working there.

So where did that leave her? She'd had to hustle for the past ten years to survive. But now he'd taken responsibility for both of her goals—acquiring treasure and hiding from her father—so what was left for her to do? Lying around as a "kept woman" was contrary to her personality.

All the doubts about how she'd fit into his life returned to haunt her. Her bravado faltered with her scan of his sumptuous bedroom.

She didn't belong with humans at all, much less here. Every soft fold of the high-thread-count sheets tangled about her legs confirmed that fact.

And yet she wanted to stay—she'd promised to stay. Rationalizations, defensiveness, and anger at the circumstances fought for her thoughts.

His willingness to help her increase her hoard in exchange for following his rules was rather close to "buying" her, like how he handled everything else he wanted. On the other hand, except for the lure of danger, she'd never wanted to resort to thievery anyway.

Could her goals *really* work within human society? Could she live by his rules and still get everything she needed? Could she fit in with humans—at least this one?

An uneasy decision formed in her mind, the one thing on which all her conflicting emotions agreed. She would stay—at least until he came home.

The morning ended up passing quickly while she distracted herself from a case of heartburn with an exploration of his bedroom. Every drawer, every niche, and every shelf came under her examination.

The rationalizing part of her brain claimed she was simply trying to familiarize herself with where she was now living. But that was a lie.

The defensive and angry part of her sought a sign of *something*. She didn't know what. Maybe proof that he'd lied to her, wasn't who he claimed, or hadn't really changed. Something that would make it easier to leave later that evening. Yet even as she searched for this evidence, she desperately hoped not to find it.

Her hunt uncovered nothing. No pictures of former girlfriends.

No old love letters. Not even a speeding ticket.

She closed the last drawer and regarded the room. That hadn't made her feel better at all. The truth was just...

She sighed and swept her palm over the bare top of the nightstand. *Sad.*

His room—his life—was sterile. He'd buried the memories of his father by getting rid of everything that reminded him of his life before. Now that she understood that history, his reinvention made sense. She wasn't going to find anything because there was nothing to find.

A knock at the door interrupted her exploration. She stepped away from the nightstand. "Yes?"

The door opened partway, and the skinny form of Alex's assistant froze. Then he backed up and closed the door.

The wood muffled his voice. "Let me know when you're decent."

She checked her attire. The shirt she'd snagged from Alex's side of the closet—for no reason whatsoever—was buttoned up respectably high, and the hem fell low enough to cover her panties. It's not as though she was still naked.

Fine. Whatever. This only emphasized how difficult it was to fit in with humans and their rules—expecting her to cover her skin all the time. Bah.

She put on jeans but left her feet bare. That'd show them.

She opened the door. "Better?"

He scowled and swept into the room. "I'm George Barbour, Alex's assistant. I heard about the uniform and nametag in the closet downstairs, 'Linda Jones.'" His nose wrinkled, as though he found being in her presence disgusting, and he waved, indicating her clothes. "You might have him fooled, but that kind of display won't work on me."

Nice. She hoped this George wasn't like the legendary Saint George who killed dragons, or she'd really be in trouble. "Was there a reason you stopped by?"

He gripped his laptop case and tensed. On instinct, she stepped back a second before he elbowed past her and laid his bag on the table she and Alex had used for dinner the previous night. His hands empty, he motioned for her to take the chair opposite him and didn't start his explanation until she sat.

"Alex thought you might be feeling..." He cleared his throat. "Bored." He looked past her, as though she didn't deserve his attention. "He thinks you might like my help with a project."

"A project?"

His mouth pinched tight, reinforcing his attitude about this assignment. "He's under the impression that you're *not* just a gold-digger. And he thinks you'd enjoy starting a business—he mentioned jewelry appraisal—and that you'd need help getting it started."

"*That's* what he sent you for?"

"Disappointed?" He met her eyes and leaned forward. "Believe me, I'd like nothing more than to return to the office with the news that you weren't interested in work that didn't involve"—he glanced at the bed at the other end of the room—"lying down."

The man was so off base about her she laughed. "You speak your mind. I can see why he keeps you around." He blinked hard, and she grabbed the opportunity to keep him off balance. "Do you *really* think Alex wants to help me start a business simply out of the goodness of his heart? Or do you think his goal might be to keep me busy so I'll stay out of trouble?"

George opened and then closed his mouth. Obviously, he'd assumed his boss was lovesick stupid when it came to her. In contrast, she assumed Alex was smart enough to have ulterior motives. Which of them was giving more respect to Alex now?

George answered her questions with a begrudging smile. "Touché."

"You're an intelligent man." She patted his hand and winked. "Assumptions don't suit you. Yes, I sneaked into the party—for reasons unrelated to your boss—but I was in the process of moving across the country yesterday when he kidnapped me and brought me here."

"Nice try. I'm not that gullible."

"What would *you* call it when I'm in my car, ready to leave, and the next thing I know, I wake up here? In his bed?" She gestured toward the door. "Ask any of the staff who were around when he carried me inside the house—unconscious. For that matter, ask James if I had any say over whether my stuff was moved here or if

I was *still* unconscious when it all happened."

He flinched. "Seriously?"

"Seriously. In case you haven't noticed, your boss doesn't take *no* for an answer." She giggled to let him know she wasn't complaining.

"Yeah, I'd call that kidnapped." He groaned the sigh of a man who wouldn't put anything past his boss. "But if you're not a gold-digger, why aren't you protesting the cage, no matter how gilded?"

"It would be a cage only if I *was* in it for the money. I'm not trapped. After I woke up, he convinced me to stay for the time being. I *do* like him—as a person, not a wallet—and I'm not giving up anything by living here that I can't get back easily." She'd started from scratch more times than she could count, and she could do it again if the situation worsened.

"I'll admit." His jaw shifted, revealing a chink in his attitude. "You're not at all the type I expected Alex to choose."

Was that almost a compliment? "That's my point—I'm not a *type* at all, much less a gold-digger using sex to ensnare him. For that matter, until last night, I was a virgin."

George snorted and did a double take, and she halted mid-rant. She'd forgotten how much importance humans attached to that status. But maybe his surprise would break through his beliefs more than her planned tirade.

She nodded, slow and deliberate, emphasizing her words. After letting that information sink in enough to elicit a few random stammers, she grinned and extended her hand.

"Hi, I'm Elaina Drake, and I'm not in control of this situation."

He laughed and shook her hand. "It's nice to meet you, Miss Drake." He scratched below his ear. "Does this mean you *are* interested in starting a business?"

Honestly, it wasn't the worst idea. After all, she'd been wondering how to fill her time and fit in here. And once again, Alex had shown how well he understood her.

There was just one little problem.

"Wouldn't I have to complete a bunch of paperwork to set it up?" Government forms required a name, and now that she'd used her real name, her fake IDs weren't any help.

George removed a laptop from his case and opened it on the

table. "Not if we set it up properly." He gave her a sidelong glance. "Alex warned me of your paperwork phobia."

Of course he did. The man thought of everything.

Warmth that had nothing to do with his touch spread through her. He might have been a trust fund kid, but there was a reason his companies were going stronger than ever. While other rich playboys wasted their money until they had nothing left, he'd learned what it took to run a business. Or several. He was, quite frankly, amazing.

George indicated the document on his screen. "We can establish the business in Alex's name. Then you and Alex would sign this agreement giving you control of all assets. As long as the company stays privately held, this contract would never need to be made public."

She sat back, stunned at the thought already put into the plan. No wonder George had seen her as a risk.

"And he's okay with all this?"

"Alex has authorized any start-up funds you need, from certifications to office space."

A lump formed in her throat. The man was too good for her.

George took in her expression. "You really *aren't* in control of this situation, are you?"

That was putting it mildly. "Why is he doing all this?" The 'for me' went unspoken.

"Alex's relationships with women have always been complicated."

"You mean his mother?"

George's face scrunched, his confusion confirming that others weren't aware of the abuse in Alex's family. "No, I mean the women he dated."

Oh yes, she couldn't forget about his playboy past. Her lips twisted in a grimace.

George shrugged. "None of them stuck around long. They always gravitated to his father within a few weeks."

"His father? Why would any self-respecting woman ever go out with *him*?"

George laughed. "Maybe that was the problem—they had no respect, for themselves or otherwise."

"No." She tapped a nail on the table, measuring what she knew of the abusive man. "His father did it on purpose. To beat his son at something, he stole anything and everything Alex cared about."

She sat back as the full picture of Alex's messed-up history came into view.

"Until Alex simply stopped caring."

George propped up his head, openly scrutinizing her. A moment later, he dropped his hand and pointed in her direction. "I thought Alex was dating again simply because he'd finally gotten over his father's death, but this is deeper than that. You made him care because you understand him." He leaned back and dipped his chin. "Congratulations."

Yes, she understood now. Just as much as Alex *literally* saw the real her no one else saw, she saw the real him.

He'd never intended to become a playboy. His father had driven Alex to self-destructive behaviors, where each "failure" reinforced his mother's rejection, and he relived the pain of feeling "not good enough" over and over. The realization sat heavily on her shoulders.

At whatever expression had formed on her face, George's tone gentled. "So should we get everything ready for you to sign or no?"

A shiver skated across her skin. Between this new insight into Alex's abandonment issues and the risk of her actions harming his business reputation, she sat paralyzed, unable to answer George.

The power to hurt Alex resided in her hands, and he knew it, willingly giving her the capability. He trusted her enough to offer this opportunity. For the first time in her life, she had the chance to live how *she* wanted, not just focused on avoiding the threat of her father.

Possibilities—real possibilities—floated through her head. Alex's understanding made it seem as though she *could* learn to live among humans, following their rules. Maybe a jewelry appraisal business could also include a design aspect, so she'd at least be able to play with the precious metals and gems passing through her hands. And as long as she laid low and didn't risk another paparazzi incident, she might even be able to relax and enjoy life.

Enjoy life with Alex.

So the question was, echoing back to her uncertainty that morning, if she didn't have to worry about treasure or her father, what did she *want*?

The answer quivered on the tip of her tongue, and she forced out the word. "Yes."

That one word instruction for George to establish a business for her carried more weight than her agreement to move in with Alex. She'd bounced around crappy apartments so frequently the place she lived was inconsequential. As she'd told George, she hadn't given up anything by living here. The decision to move out could happen as easily as the decision to move in. But this...

Starting a business together was the epitome of teamwork. That "we" he wanted them to have. She wouldn't be able to walk away without leaving a financial and emotional mess for him to clean up in her wake.

This meant she wouldn't be leaving once he arrived home later that evening.

This meant she was going to stay with him.

This was a commitment.

Chapter Nineteen

ALEX THREW A "GOODNIGHT" TO JAMES OVER HIS SHOULDER and crossed the garage. His churning thoughts drowned out any response from his driver. After a full day of meetings, fifty-one voicemails waited for him, and as of number fifty, not one was from home.

Was that a good sign or not?

His phone intoned, *"Next message."*

"This is Dirk from TotalAccess, and I have pictures of your escape yesterday from Hookerville on a CTA bus and Metra train."

Alex froze and nearly dropped the phone.

The guttural voice continued, *"Something tells me there's more than a simple pussy pounding behind this, so I'll give you 'til six p.m. tonight to give me your side of the story. Otherwise, I'm running the pictures of you and the skank as is."*

"End of messages."

Shit. Now what?

He checked the clock on his cell phone. 5:47 p.m. That was barely enough time to go inside and make sure his gut was right about Elaina not fleeing during the day, much less break the news to her and figure out a plan. No, he had to deal with this himself.

The missed call icon on the display glowed unblinkingly, unconcerned at the havoc it was causing. He loosened his tie and tapped the icon to return the call. There was no other choice.

Halfway through the first ring, the guy answered. "Ah, the

great Alexander Wyatt. I was just reviewing the article we're going to run tomorrow. It's—"

"Save it. Unless those pictures are of me assassinating the governor, no one cares. The only reason I called you back is to find out how you obtained my private number."

First rule of dealing with bullies: Make them think they don't have any power.

"Are you telling me there's nothing special about this hooker? You two sure look cozy in these security camera pictures. If you ask me, that's a weird way to treat someone who had enough articles about you around her apartment to qualify as a stalker."

"I'll be sure to let the police know you broke in to her apartment."

"The door was unlocked."

"Right. After you picked the lock. Or had one of her neighbors do it."

The guy ignored his accusations. "In fact, the whole situation screams exposé to me. What is it about this whore that got your attention?"

Blood rushed to Alex's head. Everyone from the Moi columnist to this scumbag had jumped to the *whore* assumption. He wouldn't use that word to describe the gold-diggers he knew, much less someone like Elaina.

The misogynist's questions continued. "Why did you have your lackey move her stuff to your place? What does she have on you that would lead to that development? Who is she, and why is she so important?"

Alex rubbed his temple until it hurt. This guy wasn't pursuing a typical gossip article.

He wanted to make this about Elaina, her background, her secrets, and her current location. He wanted all the details that would unravel yesterday's efforts and invalidate the promise Alex had given her. More importantly, any exposure was guaranteed to send her running.

And without knowing how well she'd covered her tracks, who knew if this guy could discover the truth about a dragon living among them. Goddammit.

His instincts wanted to send a hired thug after the slimeball, but that was something his father would have done. He forced his shoulders back and resisted the urge. For now.

A keyboard clicked in the background. "You ready to tell me what's really going on?"

"No, I need you to forget the story."

The man's loud guffaw crackled the phone's speaker. "Sorry, dude, not gonna happen. I suppose if you offered me twenty mill'..." His blackmail attempt trailed off in invitation.

"Then you'd run a story about a suspected cover-up or 'leak' the story to someone else for a cut."

The laugh on the other end of the line turned quiet and shrewd. "Smart man. So how do you plan on tempting me?"

Alex answered without thinking. "An exclusive."

The silence on the other end of the line gave him hope. At least the jerk wasn't laughing anymore.

His offer went against everything he'd promised Elaina last night, but he needed a delay long enough to come up with a way to keep her safe despite any publicity. Assuming they were still together in several months. Assuming she was still inside the house right now. Assuming she didn't find out about this deal and kill him.

"I'll grant you an exclusive for the full details if you forget the story for six months."

"You had me going until the *six months* thing. That's a lifetime in this business. What would prevent one of my competitors from scooping the story? No can do, amigo. I'll give you a week."

There was no way in hell he could get things under control in a week. He applied his killer business-negotiation skills, but the only power he had in this situation was hoping the guy wanted the inside story more than whatever he could uncover on his own. After several minutes of debate and posturing, they reached an agreement, but the final compromise left him barely enough time to get a plan into place.

The guy growled into the phone. "All right, I'll grant you two months, but this exclusive better be something good. She was blackmailing you for a dark family secret or a hush-hush wedding or something. If not, I'll publish every piece of dirt I can find on you, and I'll make up several others."

Of course he would. Alex had no doubt the man had recorded their conversation despite the illegalities.

"It will be."

"Then we have a deal. Nice doing business with you, Mr. Wyatt."

The line clicked off, and Alex squeezed his phone. What the hell had he done?

He'd sold his soul for a two-month reprieve—that's what.

His to-do list had grown more intimidating. To paraphrase Prince Humperdinck from *The Princess Bride*, he had a skittish girlfriend to deceive, a murderous dragon to thwart, a tabloid reporter to outsmart, and a story better than the truth to concoct. He was swamped.

For a man who'd thrived on control, he sure didn't have much of it anymore.

A *crack* echoed off the garage's surrounding concrete. He gawked at the source of the noise—his cell phone. A spiderweb of lines fractured the near-indestructible screen.

He loosened his death grip around the case. Defective piece of crap. He jammed the phone into his pocket and entered the house.

The portly figure of his house manager waited for him inside. He passed his briefcase to her. "Everything okay on the home front today, Madge?"

"All's quiet." She followed him toward his office. "We never did see Miss Drake, however. Not even at lunchtime."

He whirled on her mid-stride in the hallway. "She never came out of the room?"

Madge paled and shuffled back. "No. George went up to meet with her, and I assumed I would have heard if there was a problem." She cleared her throat. "I'm sorry, sir. I should have checked on her."

"Don't worry about it." He chastised himself for his temper. More evidence of his control issues becoming a bad habit. His steps resumed and quickened. "I'm sure everything's fine."

Everything *was* fine. Logically, he knew that to be the case.

For one thing, if George was still up there, that meant she hadn't fled. For another thing, George was definitely not like Alex's father, in more ways than one. But Elaina's experiment with the cop the day before proved she didn't restrain her impulses, and the fact they'd stayed in the *bedroom* the whole time didn't help his paranoia.

His evening ritual to put everything away in his home office and catch up with Madge continued as normal until he patted his pockets and felt both his broken cell phone and the surprise he'd picked up on the way home. The reminder of the abrupt change in his mood in the past half hour prompted a grimace.

After excusing Madge with a request to replace his phone, he stood in front of the beach landscape painting on the far wall of his office. The scene resembled the pictures of the Caribbean property he'd won in a high-stakes poker game before his lifestyle overhaul. If things ever calmed down, he'd take Elaina and finally visit the place.

He swung the frame forward and revealed the safe in the wall. Once the small box from his pocket was secured, he bounded up the stairs toward his bedroom.

A trill of her musical laugh spilled into the hallway through the open door. His hair stiffened along the back of his neck, and he forced his muscles to relax before he entered the room.

Elaina and George leaned close, discussing whatever was on his laptop screen on the table in front of them. Their backs were to the door, and neither had noticed his entrance.

As he watched, Elaina laughed again at something George muttered, and she playfully shoved her shoulder against his. Alex cleared his throat with a growl.

She whirled around, and at the sight of him, her expression transformed like in a slow-motion movie scene. A smile grew to dominate her features, and her eyes flashed a brilliant blue. Then, as though the movie accelerated to super-speed, she launched herself at him and wrapped her legs around his hips. He barely managed to stay upright under the attack, and when her lips plundered his, his weakened knees didn't help.

His awareness narrowed to her alone. Her mouth tangling with his, her hair swirled around his fingers, her hands clutching him with desperate need, her breasts pressed against his chest, her legs asking him to never let her go. Under her touch, he was alive.

A minute later, she released him and slid to the hardwood floor.

A mischievous sparkle lit her eye.

"Sorry, that's probably not the kind of show you want to give someone who works for you."

Still lost in her kiss, he grunted a "Huh?"

She explained her meaning with a tilt of her head back to George. The man's eyebrows had lifted high on his forehead.

Ah. Apparently he couldn't resist making scenes with Elaina. He couldn't resist a lot of things when it came to her.

Elaina stretched on her tiptoes and whispered, "I missed you so much I couldn't help it."

He squeezed her against him. *This* was what he needed to get him through the next two months of deception. She might be the source of chaos in his life, but she was also the cure.

Only when he knew he wouldn't spout words that would make her uncomfortable did he trust himself to speak. "I missed you too, beautiful."

The sparkle in her eyes brightened. Before the situation spiraled out of control, he tossed a *you'll finish with her later* look in George's direction. The door latch clicked closed, and she immediately drove him to the bed and straddled him.

Her tongue teased his lips, but she pressed his shoulders to the mattress, preventing him from capturing her mouth. She leaned back and regarded him. "You missed me?"

Despite her hold, his hands were free to slide up her thighs. "Your expression when you noticed me was the best thing I've seen all day."

"You were worried about something." Her shoulders dropped, and her voice lowered. "I told you I would be here. Did you not believe me?"

"No, it wasn't that."

He relaxed his grip on her legs, hiding his tension. If he told her about the threatened exposé on her or about his deal with the devil, she'd run. Instead, he stuck to the less incriminating reason.

"I wasn't expecting you and George to hang out here," he paused, stifling a wince, "in the bedroom."

The creases tightening her eyes softened. "You don't need to be jealous of anyone, especially not a *gay* man."

"If anyone could convince him to give women a try, it would be you." The statement earned a scoff from her, and he avoided her penetrating stare. He couldn't help trying to justify the lamest excuse ever. "You kissed that cop—"

Her lips cut off his words, and her tongue stopped the rest of the thought. He let her have her way with him, forcing the negativity away.

She released his shoulders and scraped her nails through his hair. He slipped his fingers under her shirt.

Or rather, *his* shirt. A chuckle burst from him at the realization. She pulled back questioningly.

"You're wearing one of my shirts." He brushed along her waist. "Don't you know that's one of the sexiest things you can wear?"

A scolding look crossed her face. "You're changing the subject." Her fingertip traced his mouth. "Don't you know that experiment proved you're the only one for me?"

Her words, echoing his own but answering his doubt, heated through his chest. The declaration she wasn't ready to hear threatened to escape his lips, and he sucked in a breath, holding the words inside. A slow exhale helped cool off the intense urge.

"You're perfect." He clamped his mouth shut, determined to make that statement the end of the conversation.

"As are you." The light in her eyes wavered. She blinked quickly and fumbled with his tie. "How do I get these clothes off you?"

The phone's ring interrupted them. He eased himself from her arms and grabbed the handset. "Yes?"

"Sorry to disturb you, sir, but dinner is ready. Did you want me to have it sent up, or should I hold it for you?"

He wanted to be frustrated with the chef, but a check of the clock showed that he usually made his appearance in the dining room by now. "Is Madge still around?"

"I believe so. Let me verify that for you, sir." A moment later, the man returned. "Yes, sir, she's here."

"We'll be down in a minute. Have Madge wait for me." He hung up and tapped Elaina's chin. "Hold your thought for later. I need dinner, and I want to introduce you around."

Twenty minutes later, Madge hovered at his elbow, frowning pointedly at Elaina's untouched plate, while he and Elaina sat at the dining room table.

Before the woman could comment, he promised, "She'll raid the refrigerator. Don't worry about her."

"But she hasn't eaten all—"

He cut off her protest with a sharp glance. "There's nothing to worry about, Madge. Put it out of your mind."

The woman dipped her chin. "It was a pleasure meeting you, Miss Drake." She adjusted her thin, wireframe glasses and attended Alex. "Was there anything else you needed from me, sir?"

"No, and thank you for taking care of this." He indicated the new cell phone beside his plate. Good thing Madge had picked up an upgrade for him already—he wouldn't have been able to go without his phone for long. Hopefully this one wouldn't be another dud.

After the woman left, he reassured Elaina. "Sometimes Madge tries to be a surrogate mother, and every once in a while, I have to set her straight. I appreciate that you tasted everything yesterday, but I don't expect that to be a regular thing."

"Definitely not." A weak smile shone through her slight green pallor. "I discovered my stomach wasn't designed for digesting food."

He lowered his fork. "Then what does it do?"

"It's the furnace for fire-breathing." She rubbed the back of her neck and shrugged. "I think that means I had the ultimate case of heartburn today."

He bit back a laugh and reached for her hand. "I won't ask you to do it again."

"Good." She squeezed an acknowledgement and then stroked his wrist. "George told me what you paid to get that web article deleted. Thank you."

He swallowed, slowly and calmly. "He did, did he?"

"Don't blame him. I wrangled it out of him because I wanted to know how far you'd go to keep your promise." An uncomfortable edge colored her chuckle. "Pretty far, I learned. But now I know I can trust you to deliver on your promise, so there's that. Thank you."

"You're welcome." His voice sounded flat to his ears. Better than the alternative of sounding guilty.

He slid away from her hand and stabbed a piece of prime rib.

"While I'm eating, tell me what you and George decided to do."

Anything to keep him from thinking about the deal with Dirk—and the deadline looming over everything he planned. Anything to distract himself from the fact that his promise had already been shattered and that he'd have to lie to the woman he loved every day for the next two months. Anything to silence the doubt about whether she'd be safer if he let her run.

He *would* find a way to protect her.

Chapter Twenty

W HILE HE ATE DINNER, ALEX ENCOURAGED ELAINA TO dominate the conversation. With luck, the distraction would help his food digest and not swell with sickness over his lies.

Her voice reflected her excitement as she told him about her day. His suggestions for the jewelry appraisal company had met with her approval, and before long, the conversation turned into her gushing about his thoughtfulness. He let her believe his attention to detail was special for her, rather than his standard operating procedure when it came to business.

At least, it *had* been his normal approach. The consequences of his sloppiness when it came to Elaina pointed out the cost of failure. He vowed to do better by her.

She finished her tale and regarded his now-empty plate. Her tone became tentative. "Are you sure about all this? I mean, you're putting your business name on the line for me."

"For us," he corrected. "I told you, I'll do whatever it takes to make this work."

That *whatever* encompassed things he couldn't admit without losing her. So much for ever having a simple evening together like a normal couple.

"That reminds me. I have a surprise for you." He placed his napkin on his plate. "I picked up something on my way home, and we're going to play hide-and-seek and see if you can find it." He guided her to the hallway. "I've hidden a diamond tennis bracelet somewhere in the house. Can you feel it?"

She matched his playful attitude, and for the next fifteen minutes, she walked several feet, stopped and concentrated, and then set off again. The manor's maze of hallways forced her to make a few unnecessary turns, but she never went in the wrong direction. Finally, she stood in front of the beach landscape painting in his office.

He reached for the latch on the frame, but before he could reveal the safe, she touched his elbow. "Let me try it first."

Her grip on his arm tightened with her effort, but nothing happened.

He wrapped her into a hug. "You'll get there. I'm proud you were able to find it in this huge house." Then the meaning behind her attempt sank in. "Safes don't stop dragons?"

"It depends on the dragon's strength. Unless an item has been abandoned, every piece has a base attachment to its owner. Things like sentimental value, security measures on the house itself, and safes all increase the level of attachment. Now that I live here, the house security doesn't hold me back, but the intention behind a safe does." She circled her fingers on his chest. "It would be near-impossible for me to overcome that barrier yet, but you'd just acquired the bracelet, so I was hoping for a miracle."

"You'll be able to soon. I have no doubt of that." He opened the safe. "What about now?"

"Now you've taken away the safe's intent to protect its contents."

The way she spoke made it sound as if his safe was conscious of its purpose. He was still puzzling over that when the bracelet appeared in her hand. The sconce lights around his office reflected in the hundreds of tiny facets on the string of diamonds.

Glittering sparkles shifted with each tilt of her palm. "It's beautiful."

"Just like you."

"I–I don't know what to say. I haven't earned this."

He took the bracelet and latched it around her wrist. "This is the first payment on my promise to provide you with treasure for keeping your side of the bargain and not taking things anymore.

You deserve it if I say you do." He caressed her face. "And I say you do."

"Oh, Alex."

The glow of her eyes intensified, and she leaned into his hand. Static electricity whispered over his skin as the bracelet bonded to her. Providing her with energy made every penny he'd spent worth it. He could do this. *They* could do this—if she'd let him.

"I need you to tell me only one thing—is this what you want?"

"Yes." Her voice sounded choked. "I do. I want you more than you can imagine."

"Then this will work because that's what we both want." He stroked her lips. "And I can imagine quite a bit because I want you just as much."

"Don't make me prove how much I want you." A sharp tap against his abdomen brought his focus down to where she waved her pointy nails. "Are you going to take these clothes off, or am I going to slice them off you?"

He undid his tie. "Let's save that demonstration for less expensive clothes."

He spotted his open office door. She caught his meaning and stretched out her arm. The door slammed shut on its own.

He rocked back on his heels, and his gaze shot to her.

An impish light shone in her eye. "You taught me I could do that the other day when you had me push the jewelry away to return the pieces." One tip of her mouth curved up. "Did you know those doorknobs are solid brass?"

Just when he thought he'd accepted that she wasn't human, something new reminded him how special she was. And every crazy dragon thing stoked his urge to take her.

He made quick work of the rest of his clothes. Chair, sofa, or desk? Oh hell, might as well go for the full CEO-sex-in-the-office fantasy and take her on his desk.

A sweep cleared his desktop of the quill pen, lamp, phone, and stack of papers from his briefcase. Her lips quirked at the pile on the floor. He half-sat-half-leaned on the wood and hooked his finger, beckoning.

She ignored his demand and reached behind her, under the shirt she'd borrowed from him. A series of dance-like motions of her arms released a lacy white bra, which fell to the rug. His cock hardened at the slow torture.

Her gaze never left his as she undid the button of her jeans and eased the waistband down her thighs. One bare foot and then the other gracefully stepped from the material.

The smooth curves of her calves captured his attention. The sight of her legs under his shirt distracted him from being annoyed. She hadn't come to his summons yet, but God, he could get used to this. Her underwear joined the heap on the floor, and only then did she sidle closer, her hips swinging in temptation.

He reached for those hips as soon as she was near and drew her toward him. She'd left on his shirt—and nothing else. And that fact was a bigger turn-on than he'd thought possible.

"Unbutton the top four buttons," he ordered, his voice rough with need.

Her tongue darted out and wet her lips, and her delicate fingers closed around each button. As soon as her hands dropped out of the way, he nosed the material aside and sucked a good portion of her breast into his mouth. Desperation drove him past gentleness. How he could need her so much he didn't know, but he wanted to take her and claim her hard.

She didn't seem to mind. Her spine arched, and her head tipped back, giving him easier access.

"Yes, Alex, yes."

His mouth moved to her other breast, and his teeth bit at her skin. Raw desire consumed his thoughts, and he wanted to fuck her until she couldn't take anymore.

He nudged his knee between her legs. She moaned and angled herself to press against his thigh. Her wetness spread across his skin. And if she was wet already, that meant he didn't need to wait any longer.

His fingers slipped under her shirt, and he lifted her onto his lap. She understood and knelt on the desk on either side of him. Once she was in place, he yanked her down onto his aching cock.

They cried out as one, and he kneaded her ass with his craving. Her half-lidded eyes showed her pleasure.

He pressed into her hips, and she followed along, riding up and down his flesh. She was so slick and tight. And he was...

Home. Home to the only place that mattered—being with her.

All too soon though, she wasn't going along with his lead. Instead, her slow, torturous movements were driving him mad. His fingers dug into her skin to force her down onto him, but she was too strong.

She rose up on her knees to tease his tip and refused to indulge his wishes. Her hips circled, adding to the cruelty. The heated glow in her eyes proved that despite her lack of experience, she knew exactly what she was doing, daring him to overpower her.

That was a dangerous proposition. Tonight was not for holding himself back.

He gave her one last bite on her nipple in warning and stood, gripping her legs around his hips. A sexy *mmm* vibrated her body in answer. He swung around, facing the end of his desk, and laid her out before him, her legs dangling off the edge.

Now this was more like it. The view of her presented for his pleasure filled him with unrestrained lust. Even better, this position gave him all the advantage while leaving her none.

Finally. A need to control *something* raged through him, building until he couldn't deny it any longer. She was his to conquer. His to dominate. His to own. He seized her wrists and pinned them next to her shoulders.

A growl escaped him. "You've been a bad girl."

She batted her lashes and bit her lip, feigning contrition. "I know."

"I must punish you now." He plunged into her as hard as he could.

She gasped. "I know."

"You"—thrust—"will do"—thrust—"what"—thrust—"I tell you."

The force of his movements slid her across the desk several inches. He yanked her close again and ground into her. She moaned and wrapped her calves around his hips.

He shoved into her, harder and deeper, unconcerned with the brutality of his action.

"You"—thrust—"will"—thrust—"obey"—thrust—"me."

"Yes." Her voice was breathy. "I will obey you."

He punctuated each word with another sadistic thrust. "You. Are. Mine."

Her legs tightened around him, and her hips lifted off the desktop. The better angle encouraged him to double his vicious motions.

"I. Own. You."

Her walls clenched on his cock with a squeeze that matched his ferocity. "Yes." She gasped again. "I'm yours."

One last violent thrust seated him deep into her tightness. His release came with his husky declaration. "Forever."

Her legs shuddered and fell limp. She regarded him with languid eyes. "Forever."

After a moment, his mind cleared, and he noticed the odd angle of his desk. What the hell had just happened?

He'd broken his desk—his *solid* cherry wood desk—with the force of his driving movements. He'd attacked her with enough aggression to leave any other woman bruised and unable to walk for days. He'd completely, one hundred percent, lost control.

His stomach twisted, and he unhanded her. "Christ, I'm sorry. Are you okay?"

She blinked and gave him a slow smile. Her arm stretched in a sensuous movement. "Don't you *dare* apologize for that." Her grin deepened. "Or else I'll have to punish you."

Her reaction eased the clenching in his gut, but his legs shook with the aftereffects of his assault. Hell, *he* might not be able to walk for days.

"I don't think I'd survive."

"Then you should do what you're told." She sat up and pressed their chests together. Her sharp nails trailed across his back. "Shouldn't you?"

He managed a smile at her reminder of their dual-domination game. "I suppose."

She approved of his answer and teased his lips. But even as he enjoyed their kiss, his fears about his behavior refused to leave him alone.

He'd never acted that viciously with anyone before, much less a woman. She didn't deserve to receive the force of his frustration at everything else in his life.

And yes, he *needed* to keep her, but all the talk of obeying and owning? Where had that come from? On every level, he'd failed her, and he'd failed himself.

What the hell had happened to his famed self-control? The discipline he'd always prided within himself—from his lack of tears during his father's beatings to his business acumen—had abandoned him.

Beyond the façade he'd hidden behind, he'd discovered something very dark and dangerous inside himself. Something that endangered his ability to have a relationship with anyone, much less the woman who brought his monster to the surface more than ever before. Something that revealed how deep his similarities to his father went. Something that scared him.

He vowed not to let it take hold again, even if that meant keeping an emotional distance from her. He *wouldn't* surrender his control. And he hoped he could keep that promise.

Chapter Twenty-One

ELAINA STOOD ON THE SIDEWALK AT A POSH OFFICE PARK AND shivered uncontrollably. Rain that was threatening to turn to snow dripped from her umbrella. Late autumn cold soaked into her bones, adding another level of impatience for Alex's arrival. What was taking him so long?

Maybe the fire inside fully-grown dragons kept them warm, but in her case, cold weather was her nemesis, endangering her body temperature and sapping her energy. And having to wear all these layers of clothes drove her crazy.

Her assistant, Susan, didn't seem to mind the wet or the chill. "I can't wait to see what Mr. Wyatt thinks of everything. You haven't let him peek, have you? Do you think he'll like it?"

The woman prattled endlessly, but she'd proved her efficiency during the past two months while they prepared every aspect of the business. Elaina wouldn't have been able to accomplish a tenth as much without the chatterbox.

"I haven't let him peek, and I hope he likes it, but if he doesn't get here in the next thirty seconds, he's going to miss the 'grand opening' on account of me freezing to death."

The approach of Alex's weekend sports car accelerated her heartbeat. His regular contributions to her treasure hoard had strengthened her abilities enough to sense all metals, precious and non-precious alike. The sleek aluminum shape called to her awareness before the silver coupe even coasted into the parking lot, especially as the area was otherwise empty this Saturday morning.

Alex splashed through the puddles and wrapped her in a hug. "Sorry I'm late. I had to stop at the bank on my way."

His body's warmth eased her chill, and she relaxed into him. "I forgive you."

They'd spent precious little time together the past couple of months due to his work schedule. If she didn't know how much his businesses meant to him, she'd suspect he was avoiding her.

At least when they were together, all was right with the world. Even today, when she wanted to be mad he hadn't let his "people" take care of his banking for him, all that mattered was that she was in his arms now.

She snuggled deeper into his embrace. Most couples probably wished they had more time together, and that similarity only emphasized how well she'd been able to fit in with humans over the past couple of months. Heck, she was even the *boss* of one.

Thank goodness she hadn't let fears of her father prevent her from experiencing this happiness. Sticking around to make things work with Alex had been one of the best decisions of her life.

No, *the* best one of all.

Behind her, the click of Susan's heels on the concrete brought Elaina back from bliss.

She peered behind Alex. A quiver that had nothing to do with the weather tickled her forearms. "No guard with you today?"

"Today's special. Just for us."

At the reminder of why they were here, she dismissed the oddity and waved toward the building. "Are you ready to see it?"

He released her and checked out the sign beside the door. "*Dakon's Designs. Custom Jewelry and Appraisal.* Very nice. I like it."

The loss of his body heat prompted another shiver, and raindrops fell from the shimmying umbrella onto his shoulder. He regarded her for a second and frowned.

"Let's get you inside." He held the umbrella while she unlocked and opened the door.

"Ta-da," she managed between her chattering teeth. "A lame grand opening, I know. But I wanted a special ceremony, just for you."

She didn't need to explain that this occasion, with no witnesses other than her NDA-bound assistant, would be the only time they could appear together at her office. He knew perfectly well the promises he'd made to her, and not just because the subject of potential dinner parties or charity meet-and-greets came up in weekly invitations.

"Special for me? That works." He winked. "Now you hold this." He passed the umbrella to Susan. "And I'll hold this."

He scooped Elaina into his arms and—ignoring her surprised *whoop*—carried her over the threshold into her new office. What had gotten into him? And her giggles weren't professional in the slightest.

While Susan wrestled the umbrella closed, Alex set Elaina on her feet. "Congratulations, beautiful. You did it."

"All thanks to you."

She pressed her body to his, from her legs to her lips. He cradled her cheeks in his palms, giving her the skin-to-skin contact she needed to feel the deep warmth of his energy. His kiss singed her from the inside out and chased the remaining chill from her bones.

Susan's voice interrupted them. "I thought carrying over the threshold was a wedding thing."

Alex shifted his jaw. "My building, my rules."

Elaina hooked his arm and steered him close. Logically, she knew Susan would never dare flirt with Alex, but dragons couldn't help being possessive of their treasure. "This is the reception area, and over there is—"

"My desk," Susan cut in. "And see, we have couches for visitors and everything. And there's..."

While Susan rambled on, Alex raised his brow at Elaina, perhaps in a show of sympathy.

Honestly, however, Susan's enthusiasm covered for Elaina's nerves. His approval of how she'd spent his money meant everything to her.

Ever since she'd realized months ago that he'd given her the power to hurt him, she'd concentrated on the business aspect. *That* part she could make sure she honored.

The emotional aspect was more difficult. Which option led to the bigger crime? Lying to him by encouraging his assumptions about their relationship's potential, or telling the truth—that dragons were incapable of love?

So far, her desire to protect him from feeling rejected or abandoned had made her decide deceiving him was the better way to go. Especially because she *was* making this living-among-humans thing work, and she wasn't going to give it up without a reason.

A *really* big reason.

Susan snapped her fingers. "Oh, show Mr. Wyatt that fancy hand-security thing." But as soon as Elaina directed him toward her office, Susan piped in again. "Her door doesn't have a keyhole. Did you notice that? That's because it opens only when her palm goes on that metal plate."

Elaina subtly shook her head before he could question the expensive security measure. Her office was actually more secure than that—and had cost a fraction of palm-recognition technology.

She placed her hand against the plate, which was more for show to explain away how the door *was* secured, and concentrated on the bolts in the doorframe. They retracted at her mental instruction, and the door opened.

Her office beyond was as simple and elegant as the reception area. The left wall held her new certification documents, the paperwork humans tended to trust. Her desk and three chairs filled most of the space. Humans couldn't detect the stash of gems and metals hidden in the wall behind her desk.

Susan continued her tour. "Did you notice that we don't have any jewelry cases? We sell only custom pieces that have been special ordered. We're going to take pictures as Ms. Drake finishes orders and create a portfolio of her work. She's fantastic."

Unable to take any more of the chattering, Elaina gave Susan a significant glance. "Will you wait out in the reception area for a minute? I'll need you to take a picture before you go."

"Of course, Ms. Drake." Susan closed the door behind her.

Elaina restrained herself from jumping at the latch's *click*. The privacy was necessary for giving Alex his surprise, if only she could stop freaking out at the thought. When had she gotten all these weaknesses like worry and insecurity?

Stupid, worthless emotions.

If *those* emotions were possible, why couldn't dragons experience the *love* one too?

Alex folded Elaina into his embrace. "I'm proud of you."

"You don't think I wasted your money? I don't have your talent for business."

"You've done a great job." He kissed her forehead. "And it was your idea to add the custom jewelry."

"I'm probably the only dragon in all of history to *not* claim every bit of precious metal and gems I can get my hands on."

It was time. She leaned back and straightened his collar.

"Did you want a demonstration?"

"You know I love seeing what you can do."

She led him to a chair in front of her desk. "Get ready for my magic trick."

He rubbed his palms together and perched forward in the seat. His eagerness restored her composure, and she took her chair behind the desk and swiveled toward the wall. Brushed bronze covered the lower half of the wall in her office like modern paneling. The molecules of the metal shifted and exposed a drawer front, which opened at her thought.

She removed the envelope she'd prepared earlier and dumped the contents onto her palm. A 12.5 gram lump of fourteen-karat white gold, dozens of G and H color, VS2 clarity small diamonds with a 1.75 total carat weight, and .45 carats worth of tiny rubies tumbled into her hand. She extended her arm over her desk for him to inspect the pile.

His focus sharpened, lighting up his face, especially when she closed her fingers around the raw materials. Her thoughts directed the objects' dance inside her fist.

The gold shifted into shape, and the diamonds and rubies lined up to match the pattern in her mind before embedding themselves in the metal. A final mental caress ensured the piece was smooth and all of the gems secure.

She unfolded her hand and revealed the ring. A square of diamonds edged the top flat surface. Inside the square, more diamonds formed a script letter *A* in the upper-left corner and an *E* in the lower-right corner. The rubies created an ampersand symbol in the middle, overlapping and connecting the letters.

"Abracadabra."

Alex sucked in a breath. He reached for the ring and then hesitated.

"Take it." She stretched toward him. "I made it for you."

His gaze snapped to hers. "You didn't have to do that."

"I wanted to. You've done so much for me. Consider this my thank you."

He picked up the ring. "*A* and *E*."

He swallowed and didn't say a word.

"What's wrong? Do you not like it?"

She knew it was a stupid idea. It was impossible to think of a gift for a man who had everything.

"I can change it. Make something else." She made a grab for the ring.

His fingers tightened around it, and he scooted back in his chair. "No, it's perfect."

"I sold some of my old stuff to pay for the materials, so this didn't come from your money or anything."

She knew she was rambling, but she couldn't help it. Thinking of others, anticipating their wants and needs, knowing what they would like—all of that came naturally to humans, not dragons. This was *way* outside her comfort zone.

His expression darkened. "What did you sell?"

She flinched, his tone slicing through her like a claw. "What difference does it make?"

"Because I'm trying to help you get stronger." He held up the ring. "And if you sold any of your treasure to pay for this, then it's not worth it."

"My treasure is *mine*, to do with as I please. If I wanted to sell a piece of abandoned jewelry that I'd already drained and didn't add much to my hoard's strength to stupid humans who wanted to give me a lot of money for it, that's my choice."

His volume lowered. "Is that what happened?"

"Yes." She gave him a scathing glare. "I'm not stupid, Alex. You know abandoned pieces are little more than a snack to me. So yes, I took something that had been meaningless and turned it into something *with* meaning." She huffed. "At least, that's what I was *trying* to do."

He stood and stalked to her side. "Stand up." His voice was rough.

She peeked up at him and suppressed a shudder. Muscles popped out along his jaw.

"I said. Stand. Up."

She lifted her chin and rose to confront the man whose opinion now meant too much to her. "I did nothing wrong, and nothing you say will change that."

She'd barely straightened her legs when he trapped her in an embrace.

"I'll tell you what you did wrong." His voice cracked. "You thought you needed to use your own money to give me a gift. You worried I wouldn't like it. And worse, you made me fall in love with you all over again."

She stiffened like a cornered animal. Whatever had gotten into him today was *not* good.

He squeezed her tight. "No, you don't get to escape this. I. Love. You." His headshake ruffled the top of her hair. "I don't know what crazy ideas your *Cosmo* education gave you, but it's been two months. I won't lie anymore and pretend that's not how I feel. I would do anything for you." He kissed her forehead and pulled back. "And *that*—my dear, beautiful Elaina—is love."

She pinched her eyelids closed. This conversation could *not* happen. This conversation was ten times worse than the all-too-common impression of him being distant the past couple of months. Hell, she'd take seeing him only on weekends if it meant avoiding this conversation.

She cared about this man, yes, more than she'd thought possible. But even if she admitted her willingness to do anything for him as well, the confession would mean nothing. Her parents had shared that devotion, and it hadn't been enough to keep her mother alive. There must be more to love than simply that.

Whatever piece of the emotion that dragons were missing would always elude her. And if she acknowledged that, she'd have to concede that Alex deserved to be with a human who could give him the real thing.

The dirty taste of charcoal wafted up her throat at the thought of losing him. They'd dodged the bullet with that gossip article months ago, and her father hadn't shown up to act the part of the boogeyman. So she certainly wasn't going to let something else undo that success story.

A distraction. She needed a distraction.

She tried to smile, but her expression was probably more bitter-sweet than anything. "Now isn't a good time for this conversation. Susan's waiting in the next room to take a picture of your ring."

The muscles in his jaw twitched, and he released her. "You're right, but we'll continue this soon."

Soon? That's what she was afraid of.

Chapter Twenty-Two

DESPITE ELAINA'S HOPES FOR A REPRIEVE, "SOON" TURNED out to be later that day when Alex took her shopping for a business wardrobe *and* a new car, bending his promise to keep her out of the public eye to the breaking point. He rationalized the promise-bending by limiting her interactions to only a pre-screened private shopper.

Back in his sports car, she slunk below the window frame. "It's not just about the promise, Alex. You're spending too much on me."

"You don't get to decide that. Whether you want to hear it or not, I love you, and I'll show it however I want."

It wasn't that she didn't appreciate his gifts—she did, greatly—but the more he put into the relationship, the more her deception twisted her insides. Between her lies and these new feelings of shame, she hardly recognized, much less respected, herself anymore.

She noted the scene outside the car window and changed the subject. "Where are we going?"

He'd taken her into downtown Chicago for the shopping trip, and now he drove up Michigan Avenue. She was going to kill him if he bent his promise any more.

He regarded her. "Do you trust me?" The question raised her suspicions beyond where they were already, but before she could ask anything, he raised a finger. "Answer me."

Her nails tapped out an impatient rhythm on the door handle. "Yes."

She'd probably regret that answer, but it was the truth. Damn him.

"Then close your eyes." After she obeyed, the car stopped. "Keep them closed until I tell you." At that order, his door opened and shut.

Muffled voices sounded by the trunk, and she thought she heard a "Thanks, James."

Alex's driver was *here*? Why now and not earlier? The trust he was asking of her piled higher and higher.

Cold wind blew across her cheeks when her door opened. Rain beat onto an umbrella overhead, and the rumble of James's truck pulled away on a busy street alongside them.

Alex captured her hand, spreading the tingles of his touch. "Come with me."

She let him lead her, her heels clicking on cement. The various sensations from humanity and the density of the city buildings around them overwhelmed her newly strengthened talent with countless sources of tickling awareness.

Cars whizzed by on one side, their metal frames and the jewelry and watches of the occupants a constant distraction. At her elbow, the priceless décor of the high-end buildings they passed—even the copper wiring and pipes from the hulking skyscrapers—added to the chaos and kept her from being able to pinpoint any specific origin.

A knock on glass drew her attention to the structure on her right. She nearly swayed with the powerful impressions behind the surface. Hinges *swished*, and warmth poured over her exposed skin from the open door.

A woman's voice spoke. "Good evening, Mr. Wyatt. We're ready for you."

Alex led her inside, and a click and ruffle of nylon signaled the closing of the umbrella. "Eyes still closed. That's my beautiful."

Honestly, the impact of her surroundings weighed on her so heavily she wasn't sure she *could* open her eyelids. A tug-of-war between the pressure of a high security location and the lure of treasure spun her thoughts. Where had he taken her?

His sharp scent cut through her muddled senses, and his lips brushed her ear. "I have a surprise for you, but it requires you to follow the rules—no matter what."

The past two months had been *all* about following the rules and resisting temptation. What *was* this place that he felt the need to remind her again? She nodded her understanding anyway.

He moved to her side and held her hand. "Open your eyes."

His instruction gave her the strength to overcome the chaotic pressure around her, and she pried her eyelids apart.

A prim woman stood a few feet away. "Welcome to Tiffany's."

A feast for her senses encircled her. Every type of precious metal and gem vied for her attention, sparkling and gleaming in the jewelry store's strategic lighting.

Alex's fingers gripped tight, supporting her. "Are you okay?"

She hadn't realized she'd been hyperventilating.

"Easy, beautiful. We're going to walk around so you can see everything, and then you'll pick one to take home. Anything you want. Understand?"

She forced her breathing to slow and nodded again. Nice surprise. No wonder he'd been acting oddly.

He led her around the store, and if not for his arm at her waist, she might have stumbled. Her body acted as though she waded through a sea of orphaned children, all tugging at her limbs, begging her to pick them.

The employee followed at a discreet distance, ready to answer any questions. Not likely. Elaina knew more about each piece than anyone here would.

After they completed a full circuit, Alex brought her to the farthest point from any jewelry and signaled the employee. "Give us a minute."

The woman retreated, and Alex stood in front of Elaina. "What do you think? Anything in particular appeal to you?"

She intertwined her fingers with his, trying to ignore the surrounding cacophony. "The security here is incredible."

His brows popped high, and he grinned. "*That's* what you noticed?"

She laughed and tension eased from her shoulders. "Not only that. But it means for the most part, any item here would have the same effect on me."

"For the most part?"

She risked a glance to one counter. "The pieces with rubies seem stronger."

"Because your talisman is a ruby?"

Her gaze shot back to his. One day she'd stop being so surprised at how well he understood her. "Probably."

"Any thoughts on whether you could take something from here?"

She bounced on her toes. "I'd like to try."

"Just the one thing though."

She stretched up and gave him a quick peck. "Promise."

He deepened the kiss, pulling her close. No matter how many times they'd done this, his touch never failed to electrify her skin and fill her heart with warmth.

A minute later, he rested his forehead on hers. "Time to pick out your ruby prize, beautiful."

Now that she concentrated only on the items at the single counter, she could listen to one piece at a time more easily. A teardrop-shaped ruby pendant bordered by tiny diamonds called to her the loudest. It was the highest-quality ruby in the collection—and it came with the biggest price tag. She forced her attention to slide to a bracelet instead.

Alex wasn't fooled. "That necklace?"

"No, it's too much."

He motioned the employee over. "We'll take the pendant necklace here."

Before the woman could unlock the case, he pressed his credit card into her hand. While he kept the employee occupied with ringing up the purchase down the counter, Elaina noted the locations of security cameras and shifted to block their view of disappearing jewelry.

She hadn't been kidding about the security here acting as an effective barrier. The sense of territory was even stronger than Alex's home had been before she'd moved in. She concentrated and called to the necklace.

It didn't budge.

She placed her palm against the glass, refusing to give up. *Come home. Come home to me.* She tempted the ruby with thoughts of his big brother in her lockbox.

The necklace materialized under her hand.

Alex and the employee finished their transaction, and he nestled into Elaina's hair, as though giving her a kiss, and lowered his voice to a breath. "Leave it on the counter, and I'll handle it."

She stepped back from the glass. The employee did a double take at the pendant lying on top of the case, but Alex gave her a charming smile.

"On second thought, don't bother boxing that up for us. She's decided to wear it home after all."

"Oh... Yes, of course, sir."

He picked up the necklace and fastened it around Elaina's neck. Before she could adjust the pendant for bonding to her skin, he spun her toward him and slipped the chain under her collar.

"*Now* it's yours."

Energy from the claiming surged through her, and he caught her in a kiss. Only his embrace kept her from collapsing into a heap from the intense burst.

Once the dizziness faded, she returned the kiss and moaned, wanting to take him right here in the middle of Tiffany and Co. Nothing could be more arousing than being surrounded by treasure while enjoying passionate sex with Alex.

He chuckled and leaned back. "A good one?"

She probably had the stupidest grin on her face, but she didn't care. "Oh yeah."

"Hopefully that means now is a good time to give you something else without you wanting to claim it."

She readied her protest that he'd already given her too much. Then Alex lowered himself to one knee and looked up at her.

Oh no. Not this.

Chapter Twenty-Three

ELAINA'S HEART PLUMMETED AND CRATERED THE FLOOR OF Tiffany and Co., where Alex knelt before her. The only person she'd ever cared about, and she'd have to hurt him.

He ignored her head shaking and pulled out a small case she hadn't sensed on him because of the overwhelming stimuli everywhere. A case that explained both his rendezvous with James, as Alex must not have wanted her to sense it in the car during their shopping trips, and his earlier trip to the bank, where it had probably been in a safe deposit box.

"Elaina, I love you enough that I'd buy this whole store for you if you'd let me, but I'll settle for spending forever with you."

He opened the box and revealed a fourteen-karat white gold ring. She gasped. Two pear shaped diamonds flanked a round brilliant diamond, and their quality was near perfection: E color, IF clarity with a 3.98 total carat weight. It was beyond beautiful.

"This was my mother's, and you're the only one worthy to wear it. I've made no secret of the fact that I want you, and now I want you as my wife. Will you marry me?"

Time stood still as she debated her answer. If she turned him down, who knew how he'd react. Public humiliation was never good, especially for someone like him, with his history. If she accepted, she'd merely be delaying the inevitable.

Either way, the Tiffany's employee hovered in the background, a silent witness. Hopefully Alex had paid off the woman generously enough to prevent her from squealing to the tabloids. Of course, that she wished for a bribe proved how screwed up the situation was.

Damn it, why had he put her in this position?

Because I've strung him along for months with my lies.

The odd combination of her selfishness and her refusal to hurt him meant he'd believed her increasing affection equaled love. And now she'd lost the opportunity to explain that her inability to feel that emotion wasn't his fault. No matter what she said, he'd take it as yet another rejection by a woman he loved.

He must have seen her internal debate reflected on her features because he rose and moved closer. His voice was for her ears only. "I'll give you time to figure out your answer, but I ask you to wear this in the meantime."

She silently extended her left hand. It was the coward's way out, continuing to encourage him, but she rationalized that it was better than hurting him in public.

Victory glinted in his eyes, his fearlessness at confronting uncertainty on display for all to see. Maybe he'd had this compromise in mind the whole time. A compromise in which she could give him almost everything he asked for simply by not saying *no.*

He slid the band onto her ring finger. Good manners prompted her to say "thank you" for his gifts even though humans would likely label the sickening sensation inside her ribs as nausea.

"Thank you for trusting me. And for not claiming this one." He gave her a smile she couldn't match. "I'm claiming *you* this time."

His heartfelt words sharpened the ill feeling in her ribs. She knew what he was getting at. This ring wasn't to be made invisible. This ring was for everyone to see.

The significance of this ring to him—its tie to his mother—and its stunning beauty placed it far outside of what she'd earned. She probably couldn't claim the ring if she tried.

Her nod was meaningless, but he kissed her for it just the same.

Dragons didn't cry. Whether it was a physiological or emotional thing, she didn't know. Yet tears had leaked from her eyes twice in her life. Once after her mother died, and once after Alex first brought her to ecstasy. The moisture threatening to overflow today was closer to the first circumstance.

Ten years of stealing from humans and nothing compared to the self-loathing shredding her now, leaving her in wretched pieces strung together by lies.

Before, she'd taken things humans valued mostly for vanity and monetary reasons. This time, she'd stolen something far more valuable—Alex's heart.

At the thought of what she'd become, pain built in her chest until she nearly wished for death. He deserved so much better, so much more.

She could no longer justify or defend her claim on him. She had to let him go.

The tension in her chest yanked at the tangle of emotions between them until energy drained from her limbs. She had to let him go.

She broke off their kiss and stepped back. She had to let him go.

His thumbs smoothed her furrowed brows. "It will be all right, I promise."

If only that could be true.

He thanked the employee, opened the umbrella, and led Elaina into the rain, which splattered in slushy drops like sleet. The cold wind worsened her mood, and she silently vowed to empty the store if the security video found its way online.

Their drive home passed in silence, Alex's awareness directed to navigating the slick roads. The pendant made its presence known by strengthening her abilities more than any piece other than her talisman. She no longer wondered how her father had sensed when she'd taken the ruby from him.

A lonely diamond called out to her as they glided past the landscape. Instinctively, she summoned the gem. A diamond solitaire ring materialized in her palm.

While she stared at her accomplishment, open-mouthed, Alex noticed the hitchhiker in her hand. "Where did that come from?"

"I don't know. It had been abandoned, but I'm not sure where." She concentrated on the impression from the ring's memory. "I think it had been lost inside a car at a junkyard."

He peered through the wet gloom beyond the window. "There's no salvage yard around here."

"I..."

The size of her achievement stunned her into speechlessness. She'd never been able to summon anything farther away than a few feet. Yes, it had been abandoned, but still...

She stroked the pendant under her blouse. "The necklace gave me the strength to do it. Thank you again."

She put the ring on her right ring finger to complete the bonding. Her deep inhale at the rush of energy garnered a smile from Alex—until he glanced over.

His fingers squeaked against the leather steering wheel, his grip tightening. He swore under his breath.

Her own emotions were in too much turmoil to figure out his. She'd thought he would be happy she was getting stronger.

At home, he burst out of the vehicle and smashed his door closed, rocking the lightweight sports car on its tires. As soon as she climbed out from her seat, Alex was waiting.

A *boom* echoed through the garage when he slammed her door. He loomed over her, sending her stumbling back against the car. "Why is it that you can wear *that* engagement ring without a problem, but I practically have to beg you to wear mine?"

Splashes from drips off the car's underside almost drowned out her whisper. "You know the answer to that."

"Tell me."

She raised her right hand. "Because this one is meaningless other than being a trophy." She lifted her left hand. "And this one is more than I deserve."

A grimace etched his face, and he pounded on the car's roof. "Why do you say you don't deserve it?"

They were no longer in public. She had no right to string him along any more. Her heart ached with the pain she was going to cause him. But she had to let him go.

She touched his cheek and tried to memorize the angles of his jaw, the curve of his eyebrows, the smell of his body. Everything she would never have again.

She swallowed back the tears threatening to fall once more. Unable to resist, she gave him one last tender kiss. But even the usual tingles between them had abandoned her.

A moment later, she pulled away and forced herself to meet his gaze. Her throat closed up, unwilling to say the words.

He deserves better. He deserves to know.

"I don't deserve this ring—or you—because I don't love you."

Her voice cracked, but not as much as her heart.

Chapter Twenty-Four

O F ALL THE THINGS ALEX HAD EXPECTED TO HEAR, THAT wasn't one of them. He staggered back, breaking eye contact with Elaina as his legs wobbled under his weight, which suddenly felt ten times heavier. His thoughts skittered from one raw reaction to another, every possibility clamoring at once.

She didn't lo—? He couldn't even finish the thought. Lingering fears of whether his mother had loved him echoed with Elaina's answer.

No, it wasn't possible. Unless the past two months of near-perfection between them had all been a lie. The idea twisted his pain into anger. She *had* to love him. He'd make her see that.

His phone rang before he could respond. Several more trills reverberated through the garage. This conversation couldn't wait, but he needed to take this call for the final step of his two-month-long plan to protect her. Shit.

"Go to my office. I'll be there in a minute."

After she trudged off to the house, he picked up his phone, impatient to get past this confrontation. "I gave you the headline you wanted."

Dirk from *TotalAccess* guffawed in his ear. "Yeah, I'll say. A credible witness, a PR fantasy, even video. But you still haven't told me the story behind the whore."

"If you ever use words like that to describe my fiancée again, I'll drag you through mud so deep you'll be shitting it for years.

This isn't *Pretty Woman.* Being poor and living in a bad area of town isn't a crime."

"Take it easy, dude. Her old neighbor across the hall already told me your woman was a loner. Thought she was a junkie, actually."

He swallowed a curse. Of course the guy had checked into Elaina's life during the past two months.

"She's never done drugs either. And if you—"

"Yeah, yeah, no insinuating. Got it. Then you've gotta give me something real. How did you two meet?"

This question he'd prepared for. "I was searching for a jewelry appraisal business for investment purposes, and—"

"*Investment* purposes?" The man's voice sounded incredulous.

Alex stuck to his story. "I diversify. If you need financial advice, I can give you the names of my advisors. Perhaps if you acted on their suggestions as I do, you wouldn't be living in your mother's basement while she's locked up for DUI."

Surveillance was a two-way street.

"Just an innocent question, dude."

"I met Elaina Drake—and that's *E-L-A-I-N-A*—because she was looking for a job as a jewelry appraiser. She'd recently moved into the area and had the skills, but not the certification. I had her check an item of mine to see if she knew her stuff. She told me more about it than the guy who'd sold it to me. She's brilliant."

"Aww, sweet story. 'Cept you left out the part where she rented her apartment under a different name. Things like that make a guy like me suspicious."

"She didn't want her father, Volus Drake—and that's *V-O-L-U-S*—finding her. So yes, she muddied her tracks a bit. Witness Protection doesn't step in when the U.S. doesn't have jurisdiction, and he's a criminal in Europe."

"No kidding." The guy's tone was more dismissive than surprised.

"It's the truth. Check with the FBI. Now if you don't mind, I have unfinished business with my fiancée. I trust I've provided enough story for you?"

"Yeah, I'll make it work."

"Then this arrangement is over."

Alex hung up the phone and pressed his fingertips to his throbbing temples. There was no going back now.

Click. Forty feet away, the door leading to the house shut.

Shit! Alex chased after Elaina, nearly tripping over her discarded coat in the doorway. "I can explain!"

Inside the house, she scrambled up the stairs, and then she twisted and fell into a crouch at the top. Her fingernails sharpened into points.

He bounded up the steps without slowing down. Her eyes widened, and she took off along the hallway again toward their bedroom. Her expression set off alarms in his mind, but he couldn't stop to listen.

Artwork rattled against the walls, his barreling strides thumping through the hall, and he let his long coat slide off his shoulders to the floor. He slammed their bedroom door behind him, leapt over the bed, and propelled himself off the mattress toward her. His momentum carried him to the entrance of their bedroom closet, where he tackled her to the floor. He pinned her on her stomach to keep her claws from ripping into him.

"Christ, woman, let me explain."

Her chest heaved for breath, and her ass pressed into him with her struggles. The curves of her body under his were distracting, but despite his growing hard-on, he didn't move away. At least here, she *had* to listen to him.

"It's not what you think."

"I heard you, Alex." Her words pitched high like a sob. "I heard it all."

"It's not what it sounded like. Trust me."

On a whisper, she admitted, "I do. Damn you, I still do trust you."

She stopped fighting his grasp.

At her surrender, his emotions tangled into something he didn't recognize. She wasn't supposed to react like this. She wasn't supposed to accept defeat.

He needed her to be strong. Strong enough to play their dual-domination game. Strong enough to demand answers from him. Strong enough to keep him in line.

Dark thoughts clouded his mind, wanting to push her, corner

her. He ground his hips against her ass.

"I'm going to take you. Conquer you. Make you mine forever." His voice was hard and taunting.

Her body arched into his, rubbing him temptingly, and she turned her head to the side and bit her lip. "Please... I want to be with you more than I ever wanted anything in my life."

"Liar."

She couldn't want to be with him that much and yet not love him. One of those claims had to be a lie.

And the fact that she'd run for their bedroom raised suspicions that burned through his stomach and had him wishing for industrial-strength handcuffs.

His heartbeat nearly exploded at the thought that she might leave him. The pain dug deep inside him and thrummed a deadly warning: *Don't let her leave. Don't let her leave. Don't let her leave.*

She nibbled on her lip again. "Are you going to punish me?"

Her high-pitched tone of submission shot through him like lightning. The instincts he'd restrained for the past two months exploded in a fiery burst, shattering his earlier vow along with his self-control.

He gathered her wrists in one hand and used his other hand to undo his pants and release his aching cock. The new skirt that showed off her great ass was already halfway up to her waist from their tumble to the floor. He shoved the fabric the rest of the way. A quick yank ripped away the fragile tights and delicate red panties, and he angled his cock at her entrance.

For a second, his fears seized him, and he choked out a whisper. "Please stop me."

Her only resistance was to squirm, wiggling her bottom. Rather than helping him regain control, the pathetic response teased the tip of his cock and triggered the return of his darker urges. He plunged himself into her. She gave a squealing gasp and pushed against his invasion by lifting her ass.

Her feeble protest encouraged him. He thrust deeper, surprised to discover she wasn't dry as expected. Instead, her wetness enfolded him, and his length slid into her. His victory made his roiling emotions even more chaotic.

"You were coming up here to leave me, weren't you?"

He slammed into her, their skin squeaking on the polished floor. He dug his fingers into her wrists, and he pulled her hair out of the way with his free hand.

His voice was a harsh rasp. "Did you forget that I *own* you?"

His claim sounded nonsensical, even to his own ears, but he couldn't stop the raw flow of panic and desperation. He thrust again as hard as he could, as though he could nail her down and prevent her from fleeing.

"Promise you'll never leave me." He wound his hand around her hair, tugging it back, and his words broke into a vulnerable plea. "Don't ever leave me."

Her lashes fluttered, and she licked her lips. "I promise."

His thrusts sped up. "You promise?"

She sucked in a breath between his attacks. "Yes."

She's lying. "You'll never leave me?" Lying, lying, lying—he punctuated each thought with a hard thrust, punishing her.

Her gasps came faster now. "Never."

"Say it." He yanked her hair. "Say, *Alex, I will never leave you.*"

Her nails dug into the hardwood, leaving gouges on the floor, and every muscle of her body became taut, clenching around his cock.

She panted out the words past gritted teeth. "I promise you, Alex. I'll never leave you."

At her pledge, he found his release. An irrational wish that he could get her pregnant despite the impossibility crossed his mind. All the better to mark his territory in a primal conquest.

A few minutes later, the fire in his body cooled, and he noticed her labored breathing under him. The truth bulldozed its way into his thoughts and left him nauseated and trembling.

He was a brute and an asshole. The wide eyes she'd had at the top of the stairs could only mean one thing: He'd bullied her into fearing him. And for good reason.

Even now, his hand yanked on her hair tight enough to cut into his skin. Hell, he'd gone caveman.

No, worse than that.

He'd thought this strong woman would keep him in line, keep him from turning into his father. But she hadn't been able to. She hadn't even fought back.

Why would she let him do that to her? His mind drew a blank.

Only one explanation made sense. Sometime in the past two months, he must have broken her. And now...

He'd raped her.

Chapter Twenty-Five

LEX GAGGED ON THE ACIDIC TANG OF THE BILE SURGING up his throat. "Oh God, I'm sorry."

He knelt to give her breathing room and unwound her hair from his hand, locks tangling in his haste. A snarl of hair tightened on his ring—the stunning ring she'd made for him, the ungrateful bastard—and he slowed down to keep from yanking on her scalp more than he already had. His hands shook uncontrollably, and he couldn't grasp the strands.

"Sorry, sorry, sorry." No wonder she didn't love him—he was a goddamned monster.

The bit of her forehead he could see on her angled face furrowed at his words. "Why are you apologizing to me?"

"For starters, I just fucking"—he choked out the word—"*raped* you."

"Rape?" She scoffed. "That *wasn't* rape."

He punched the closet floor with his free hand, unable to release the knot in her hair and escape the situation.

"You're stronger than this." He caressed her cheek. "Don't let me break you. I don't want you to be weak."

At his plea, she seized his forearm, her pointy, claw-like nails pricking his skin.

His breath burst from his lungs, and their bedroom closet's ceiling now filled his view. Pain radiated from the top of his skull. The agony increased as his back complained about something. What the—?

His body and brain struggled to catch up with the fact that she'd flipped him faster than he could perceive. Before he could inhale, she landed on his abdomen, straddling him. Her nails lightly dug into his shoulders, not enough to break the skin, but enough to let him know she could.

Red streaked through her hair in an angry dance of flames. "Don't *ever* underestimate a dragon. We are *never* weak compared to humans."

"But you didn't stop me."

"Because I didn't want you to stop." Her tone effectively added 'duh' to the end of her statement. "Choosing to be submissive isn't weak. It's a choice *I* made because that's what I wanted."

He stretched his fingers, where her hair had freed itself from his ring, and searched the ceiling as if it held the answers. "But you ran from me. I scared you."

She hissed. "I ran because I didn't want to accidentally injure *you.*"

His gaze fell back onto her. "Oh."

"You would *never* be able to force me to do something against my will." The talon on her index finger lightly slid across his neck, making her meaning clear.

He wanted to believe her. He wanted to absolve himself of this guilt. He replayed his attack in his mind, noting how she'd wiggled and lifted her ass to accommodate him, how she'd flirted with her lashes and lips, how she'd practically begged him to "punish" her, and how she'd come for him.

But did the reality change the fact that he'd completely lost control?

She poked his collarbone. "Whatever you're thinking, stop it. This does not make you like your father."

An invisible weight compressed his chest more than the mass of her body on him. "Yes, it does. I'm as much of a monster as he was."

"No, Alex." She leaned close, filling his vision. "You aren't like him. You *aren't* him."

"In the only way I care about, I *am* like him. I lost control and turned to violence."

"Dominating and aggressive behavior during sex is *not* abuse." She tapped her ribs. "My *choice* to be submissive with you doesn't make you a rapist. I consented. I consented before you did a damn thing. And if you weren't so blinded by your fears, my consent would have been blinking-lights obvious to you."

"But I shouldn't have lost control."

"Why not? You *can't* hurt me." Her brow cocked high at an angle. "And I rather like that you want me that badly."

His face tightened, his conflicted thoughts warring inside and out. He'd wanted a strong woman to stand up to him, and he'd gotten more than he bargained for with Elaina. Her long-ago demonstration with the steak knife proved he *couldn't* hurt her, and she was as strong mentally as she was physically. And that meant she had a point.

He kept thinking of her as human, and she wasn't. The normal rules didn't apply to her—or to them together.

The only reason he'd had power in that situation was because she'd given it to him. A gift. She trusted him *that* much. The idea humbled him.

Even though he still didn't forgive himself for losing control with her—the one person he didn't want to lose control with—the imagined weight on his chest floated away.

Her eyes narrowed, hard and flinty. "Now if you're done beating yourself up about that, let's talk about how you thought so little of me that you assumed you'd *broken* me." Blue fire intensified in her gaze. "Get over yourself. Yes, I care about what you think of me, and yes, I've changed my behavior to be with you, but that does *not* mean I'm *broken*. Give me more credit than that." Her claw prodded his collarbone. "Do I make myself clear?"

He couldn't help a grin. "Yes, ma'am."

"Don't smirk at me as though everything between us is magically all better." She pressed her fist into her abdomen, and her spine bowed. "You still owe me an explanation for that phone call."

He nodded and then winced, his head aching at the movement.

"The day after you moved here, one of the tabloid reporters called me. I don't know how he found my direct number, but the guy is good. Too good. He had pictures of us escaping your apartment from the public transportation security cameras. He was going to do an exposé on *you*—everything from the fact that you were living here to your background, uncovering who knows what in the process."

Her body stiffened, but she didn't interrupt.

"The only way he wouldn't pursue it was if I offered him something better. In exchange for two months of silence, I had to promise him a bigger, exclusive story. I pre-arranged everything with Tiffany's PR department so he'd get access."

"*That's* why you were so public today?" Her entire body sagged. "You asking me to marry you was just a *stunt*?"

"No. God, no." He brushed her cheek. "I *do* love you, and I *do* want to marry you. I never lied about any of that. The only thing I did was neglect to tell you that we had an expiration date on our privacy. You have to believe me about that."

She exhaled, and he couldn't tell if it was from frustration or resignation. "What was supposed to happen at the end of these two months? And why did you make sure he knew how to spell my name and give him my father's name?"

"Bait." His explanation made her eyes widen. "You've lived in fear for ten years, and I don't want you to spend the next ten years afraid too. We need to know if he's still searching for you."

She smacked his hand away from her cheek. "Of course he's still searching for me."

"Good." When she jerked back, he rushed to explain. "I pulled some strings to get his name on the terrorist watch list, the No-Fly list, everything I could think of. He'll never make it past customs to get to you. And the Feds have the firepower to deal with him if he goes full-dragon on them."

"And then what? Even if their weapons *can* damage him—which I *doubt*—how many people would get hurt in the process? I can't let that happen again. You *promised* to hide me."

"I know it's a risk. But we couldn't keep you a secret forever. You said you wanted to be free from worry, so rather than wondering and worrying, I wanted to confront the question so we can find a resolution."

She tensed, her thighs squeezing his sides. "Listen to yourself. *You* wanted to confront this. What about what *I* wanted?" Her body shook against him. "What about all the sacrifices I've made to *prevent* humans from being hurt? I asked you to make that promise for a reason beyond just *my* life and security. You disrespected everything important to me because of what *you* wanted. This was about *you*."

His face heated as if he had a fever. And here she'd said she couldn't breathe fire.

Maybe confessing would change her mood, at least enough so he could breathe. "You're right. I didn't tell you about the exposé and the plan I'd come up with because..."

He needed her. He needed her more than he allowed himself to consciously recognize, as though losing her would destroy him, kill him. As though keeping her close was his reason for living.

Admitting how much he needed her would never be easy, especially not when things were so precarious between them, but if he wanted them to have a chance at moving forward, he had to.

"Because I was afraid of losing you."

Her muscles relaxed, seemingly from disappointment.

"You talk of all this teamwork and 'we,' but you don't trust me. Not really. That's what hurts more than anything. I committed to you the day I agreed to start a business with you, yet you lied to me out of a lack of faith in that commitment."

She'd committed to him? Her simple declaration slapped him upside the head. His fixation on deceiving her meant he'd missed noticing that two months had gone by without her alluding to running away a single time.

Her fingers stretched and curled. "You don't give me credit for everything I've given up for you. I haven't stolen a single piece of jewelry since we met, even though it would make me stronger in a hurry. Why? Because *you* wouldn't like it. Tell me, who's acting more like a *we*?"

His stomach hardened like armor, but it couldn't protect him from the truth. He hadn't *accepted* her differences. He'd ignored them to the point of disrespecting her. She'd met him much further than halfway, choosing to change everything and live by human rules to be with him.

In return, he'd given her expensive trinkets, as though he *was* trying to "buy" her. Amazingly, resentment hadn't sounded in her tone, only a statement of fact.

"I can fix this."

She flinched, and her chin trembled. "Don't you remember? We *shouldn't* be together. I don't love you."

The back of his throat burned with a rawness he couldn't swallow away. He still didn't believe her, but at least his anger had cooled.

An urgent tapping sound caught his attention before he could argue with her claim. "You promised not to leave me, so we don't need to figure this out right now." He motioned for them to stand. "I suspect that's a member of my staff checking on us. Let's get presentable so we can send them away, and we'll come back to this later."

Much later. After he figured out how to convince a stubborn dragon that she was wrong about her own damn feelings.

Chapter Twenty-Six

ELAINA LET ALEX PERSUADE HER TO REASSEMBLE THEIR clothes, and she filled in the blanks with non-ripped replacements. The shattered pieces of their relationship weren't so easy to put back together.

She'd trusted that he'd use his money and influence to keep her safe, and he'd obviously been busy doing just that—at least in his mind. Yes, she'd said she wanted to be free from worry, but they'd never talked about how to make that happen. Or more importantly, how far *she* was willing to go.

Maybe it was a good thing to delay the rest of the conversation. At least until she had a better handle on what her options were.

The great sex they'd just shared—when he *wasn't* holding himself back and being distant—showed once again how perfect they could be for each other. If it weren't for the "dragons can't love" issue and the fact that they'd both been lying to each other for the past two months, their relationship would be ideal. Luckily, they had days before that reporter's article could bring her father here.

Decent again, she followed Alex to the knocking on the bedroom door. Baxter, his security manager, stood in the doorway.

"Sorry to disturb you, ah..." Baxter's eyes bugged out and focused behind them.

She and Alex twisted around. Behind them, the mattress listed off the foundation, both nightstands lay toppled, and one of the drapes hung limply, half-ripped from the curtain rod with her claw marks scoring the wall. The disheveled result of Alex's flying scramble to tackle her turned her on all over again.

Alex cleared his throat. "You couldn't reach me by phone, I take it."

That was probably a good guess. The house phone had been torn from the wall, and Alex's cell phone lay in pieces, as though it had crashed into the far wall and popped the battery from the case.

She gave Alex a grin, hoping he got the message that if they figured out a way to stay together, she wanted to repeat the experience. Maybe someday he'd believe her about how much she liked his aggressiveness. The stronger he was, the less she worried about hurting him.

Alex's brows furrowed, and then he regarded Baxter. "Why did you need me?"

Baxter glowered at her before answering. "We caught an intruder."

All business, Alex ushered them into the hallway. "Tell me everything."

Baxter scrutinized her again. A shiver fluttered in her chest. What did his attention imply? Was this simply about his dislike of her, or did the intruder have something to do with her?

Alex led them through the mansion's hallways and clarified, "Tell *us* everything."

"We caught him skulking around the grounds. Normally, we'd have turned him over to the police, but I don't think this guy is a paparazzo." Baxter stopped them outside the door of the security office. "We found a gun on him."

Alex jerked back. "A gun?"

At Alex's reaction, she had to stop her arm from instinctively reaching for his hand. Bullets couldn't hurt her any more than knives, but Alex was vulnerable to human weapons.

She turned to Baxter for a distraction from her forgot-she-was-supposed-to-be-mad-at-Alex impulse. "Why does that mean he's not part of the paparazzi?"

Baxter looked inclined to ignore her question, but Alex gave him a pointed stare. Her ribs squeezed, and she dropped her gaze. Yep, Baxter's reaction was all about not liking her presence here.

Even after two months, she still hadn't won over most of the house staff. Their loss, right?

Baxter cleared his throat. "It's difficult to carry a concealed weapon *legally* in Illinois."

Alex grumbled under his breath, "Because criminals would never break *those* laws."

"Yes, but paparazzi would have no reason to risk a weapons violation." Baxter stepped back from the door. "We can call the police if you'd rather not get involved, but you asked me to inform you of any unusual security issues."

She answered Alex's unspoken question. "My father would have no reason to carry a gun. It's not him."

"All right. Let's find out who he is."

Baxter opened the door. The two guards inside scoped out their group and then returned their attention to a dumpy-looking, middle-aged man in a chair. The guy's eyes landed on her and widened.

Uh-oh. Did that reaction mean this intruder *did* have something to do with her? It had probably been a bad idea to let him see her. Too late now.

She scanned the room, the various sources of metal making an impression on her heightened awareness. Handcuffs locked the guy's wrists behind his back. His gun sat securely in the small safe under Baxter's desk. And a metal blade was in his shoe.

"Have you checked his shoes for weapons?"

Baxter twitched and stared at her. "What?"

Alex crossed his arms. "Take his shoes."

While the other guards loomed over the man, Baxter removed the guy's shoes and found the catch that released the blade. He clicked his tongue and met her eyes for a millisecond. "Good call."

She subtly signaled Alex that the guy was now clean. He grabbed another chair and straddled it backward, challenging the man. "Who are you, and why are you here?"

The man didn't answer, so Baxter tapped his foot. "Mr. Wyatt can make things easier or much, *much* harder for you with the police, so I'd suggest you cooperate."

The guy remained silent. Obviously, he wasn't going to play nice.

Time to make him uncomfortable. Maybe Baxter's pressure

would then be more effective.

Non-precious metals used to be difficult for her to manipulate. Before, she had to be close to the material, like the bolts in her office door. Now, the ruby pendant around her neck acted as a direct conduit to the energy of her entire hoard.

At her mental instruction, the steel handcuffs around the guy's wrists warped, biting into his skin.

He gasped, and his eyes locked onto her. "Okay, okay, I'll talk."

His reaction told her almost everything she needed to know. He knew who—and to some extent, *what*—she was. "Who sent you?"

"I don't know their names." An East Coast accent flavored his voice. "Some mafia goons maybe. I know I shouldn't have gotten involved with them, but they were offering a lot of money, and with the economy, my P.I. business ain't what it used to be."

"You're a private investigator?" Baxter's tone scolded the man, as though he should have known better.

"Yeah, Douglas Watkins." He shifted in his seat. "Believe you me, I'm not happy about being here either."

Alex leaned over the back of his chair. "What did they want you to do for them?"

"They wanted me to track down this lady." His chin tipped in her direction. "They've paid me for a couple of years actually, even though I never found shit until the other month." He shrugged. "It was easy money. I ran a few searches and took their cash."

Alex nearly growled. "Then what happened?"

"Her name popped up in a search. I told my contacts. I figured that would be the end of it because the search results showed her in the Chicago area—not my stomping grounds. But my contacts wanted me to come out here anyway and check it out. They said their client wouldn't be happy if it turned out to be a dead end."

Ringing sounded in her ears, and she fought back her panic. "Did they say who this client was?"

"Some guy in Russia, I think. Or maybe Eastern Europe. They acted like the guy was very, *very* powerful. Not someone to mess with. At that point, I was ready to bow out. The last thing I wanted to do was get myself in deeper. 'Specially once they told me to be careful around her if she was the real deal."

She wanted to ask him more questions, but she couldn't risk

exposing the truth to Baxter and the guards. What she knew was bad enough that a part of her wanted to deny it. Wanted to deny that Douglas's contacts knew the truth because the "client" had told them. Wanted to deny that her father had discovered a way to lengthen his reach.

But the temptation to dig up dirt on her was likely too much for Baxter to resist. "What did they tell you?"

Douglas paled, and beads of sweat erupted on his forehead. "That she wouldn't even need to touch me to kill me."

The world no longer contained the sense of up or down, and her limbs crumpled under her.

Chapter Twenty-Seven

A FLURRY OF MOVEMENT BURST AROUND ELAINA, AND Baxter's office darkened. Everyone was probably scrambling to get away from her at the news of her deadly capability.

No, wait. Alex was carrying her. Well, *he* wasn't worried about the fact that she could turn any piece of metal into a weapon.

She couldn't say the same about herself. She didn't *want* to be lethal, but Douglas's simple statement had forced her to confront that horrible truth.

Alex had taken her into the hallway, and he peered down at her. "Are you okay?"

"What happened?"

"I think you fainted."

"I *don't* faint."

His lips twisted, as though he was trying to suppress a grin. "Your eyes glazed over, you lost your balance, and you were about to fall when I caught you and brought you out here to get some air."

"Precisely. That doesn't mean I fainted." She shoved out of his hold and stood. All her fears returned, and her heart pounded so hard she half-expected to hear the beat echoing in the vacant corridor. "You know what this means."

"He *has* been searching for you all this time."

"More than that. He's integrated enough into human society to use them to do his footwork over here. Your plan for baiting him won't work. He doesn't have to come out of hiding to get me, and those terrorist watch lists keeping him out of the country won't protect me."

He tucked her against him, absorbing her trembles. "Yes, but these guys can't actually hurt you, right? No matter how dangerous this mafia group is, they're less dangerous than your father. And if he's using criminals, we can take away his eyes and ears by working with the police to have them arrested." Before she could launch into another protest, he spun to the door. "Let's see how bad the situation is."

She followed. He might be right about the risk being low, but just the fact that her father *knew* where she was felt perilous.

Back in the room, Alex strode over to Douglas. "What have you reported to your contacts?"

Douglas's gaze darted from Alex to her. "Nothing."

Baxter held up a cell phone. "According to the call logs, he made a call to a New Jersey number a half hour before we captured him."

The liar licked a drop of sweat rolling toward his mouth. "It wasn't my fault. I told you, I wanted out. But my contacts refused to let me go. They said if I didn't come here, they'd take my baby sister. She's supposed to graduate from college next spring. The first in the family."

Alex's expression remained hard and intimidating, but his shoulders slumped a fraction. "Tell us everything."

"After finding this lady's name linked with yours, I called my contacts." He nodded toward his cell on Baxter's desk. "I told them I didn't have anything yet, but that I was going in tonight to search for the proof they wanted."

Alex's left hand grasped his right wrist behind his back, as though he was afraid his arm would act on its own and do something he'd regret. Douglas might not have provided evidence yet, but with the gossip column coming out any hour, that fact hardly mattered.

Of course, Alex *was* right about humans' limited ability to damage her.

She forced strength into her voice. "Do you know what they

planned to do to me?"

"I heard them joke about a cement overcoat once, but I don't know what they really intended."

"Cement overcoat?"

For once, Baxter didn't ignore her. "Encasing someone in cement. It's a joke about how the mob kills people."

She caught herself on the edge of Baxter's desk. Alex glanced her way and stiffened.

Given his reaction to her expression, she must look rather stricken. And no wonder. An organized group could theoretically subdue her long enough to bury her in a solid concrete slab. Metal, she could manipulate. Concrete? Not a bit. She'd be powerless—and they could transport her back to Europe.

The threat of such helplessness squeezed her body until she couldn't breathe. She needed to get out. Run. Get air. Escape.

Alex clasped Baxter's shoulder. "Hold him here until we figure out our plan."

He tucked her close and steered her to his office. On the couch, he settled her beside him and rocked them together with a rhythmic plea for her to breathe normally. The security of his presence loosened her lungs enough to hold the black spots at bay.

He waited for her hyperventilating to calm. "What's going through that head of yours?"

Did she have thoughts? "I think I'm numb. The idea that he's working with humans now..."

"If I'd known that, I would have handled that *TotalAccess* jerk differently."

She held in a whimper. The night had been one crisis after another, but Alex's lies hardly mattered anymore.

Reality pushed its way into her awareness. She'd run out of time to make this playing-by-human-rules experiment work. If she stayed, she wouldn't get the chance to grow stronger.

Everything she'd worked for and hoped for was pointless. And no solutions made themselves known in her mind.

In fact, her head felt empty. That deadened reaction subdued the panic, and any blame and "should have" ideas were pointless to dwell on. Logic crept into the void.

She'd run out of options, and only one thing remained a

possibility. She should flee. She should abandon the human world and their rules. She should leave Alex and her guilt for not loving him the way he deserved.

That made the most sense, right? All evening, she'd known she had to let him go, and this was simply more proof that her rationalizations had to end.

Yet if she fled, she'd also be up against the human underworld on her own. They probably knew better than she did how to hide in the shadows, and their knowledge of how to capture her gave them the advantage.

Unless she renounced her vow of non-violence, all she could do was continue to run—from a larger, well-organized group this time. As if running from a full-strength dragon hadn't been hard enough.

Alex seemed to read her mind. "I won't let you run."

"You have to." Her words rushed out before he could argue the point. "It's safer for me. It's safer for you. It's safer for everyone. Anyway, we shouldn't be together, remember?"

"That's just a lie you tell yourself." He cradled her tight. "Don't turn that into an excuse to leave. You *do* love me. I know it."

A flood of emotions engulfed her. "I wish I did." A choked sob escaped her throat. "I truly wish I did. But dragons can't love."

"You're wrong. Your mother *loved*. You know she did, or else she would have defended herself from your father's attack."

She pulled away and wrapped her arms around her waist.

He gripped her shoulders and twisted her toward him. "No, I'm tired of this. Even if you don't believe me, stop judging what you think you should feel for me by human rules that you picked up from a stupid magazine. I love you as you are."

"But you deserve to be with someone who can love you back."

"Give *me* credit to know the right woman for me." He held her gaze. "Fine, your messed-up parents keep you from believing you can use the word 'love.' Then don't say it. I don't care. I want you. Nothing has changed that. And I know you want me. That's all that matters. That's all that ever mattered."

She broke eye contact. "But that's *not* all that matters. I can't stay. It's too risky."

"Not really. If we're dealing with humans, there's more I can do. Politicians and celebrities deal with assassination attempts all the time." He tipped up her chin. "We can buy time by forcing your father to start over with a different group. We'll disappear for a while and let the authorities catch these guys."

"Disappear?"

He glanced at the beach painting over his safe on the far wall. "I own some property that doesn't show up in official records." He shrugged and offered a sheepish grin. "Won it in a poker game in my previous life."

She blinked, his idea lighting a flame of hope in her chest. Could she really stay with him? Were these crises *not* the end of the line?

As fast as hope tossed celebratory confetti in her mind, practicalities played the role of party-pooper. "You can't leave all your business obligations." She injected as much logic as she could into her tone. "He's not searching for you. I'll go, and you can send for me when it's safe."

His body became so rigid that tendons stood out on the side of his neck. "No. I'd never forgive myself if something happened when I wasn't with you."

She slumped into the couch cushions. She'd never win this argument.

This man had endured years of abuse for a woman he felt conflicted about. Now with Elaina, his aggressiveness in bed—or out of bed actually—proved their relationship tapped into similar primal emotions. His drive to protect her would likely be unstoppable, and he'd follow her no matter where she went. No matter how much she begged him to stay out of danger.

Maybe she could go along with his plan long enough to escape the immediate danger in Chicago. That way she wouldn't be fighting him and the mafia at the same time.

She could always leave Alex later if the situation demanded it. And given that secluding themselves somewhere off-the-books might not provide her the opportunity to gain more treasure, the situation *would* demand it. Time would be working against her.

"We'll do what you think is best." She had no doubt he'd do everything possible to keep her safe. If only he had the same instincts for himself.

He stood and lifted her to her feet. "Go and pack whatever you're going to need. We'll leave in an hour."

"An hour? You'll have everything ready to go that soon?"

"I've been anticipating this possibility for a while, especially if we'd gotten word that your father had taken the bait. My staff is already briefed on the details."

Wow. He *had* been busy the past two months. She couldn't help appreciating his efforts. "You're amazing."

He strode toward his desk and picked up the phone, as though he hadn't heard her. She moved to the door to start her packing.

Behind her, his soft voice reached her ears. "Let's see if I can keep you alive before we decide if that's true."

Her hand froze on the doorknob, dueling insights stiffening her muscles. Was he worried he *wouldn't* be able to protect her? Or did he fear she'd sacrifice herself the way his mother had? She considered reassuring him, but he'd already punched in a phone number.

"Good evening, Madge. I'm sorry to be calling you so late, but I'm enacting the Paladin Plan." He paused. "Yes, that's right. You still have those notes I gave you?"

He noticed Elaina standing by the door. "Madge, hold on a minute." He pressed a button on his phone. "It'll be fine. Now go. Oh, and the place we're going is warm."

He flashed her a grin, knowing how she'd react to that news. At least this trip might not be all bad.

An hour later, she tapped her nails on the kitchen counter. One large suitcase stood beside her, packed with a good portion of her casual clothes, while one carry-on bag with her laptop and safebox leaned against the cabinet. Thank goodness Alex had bought her a slim new laptop a while ago.

She was as ready for this trip to nowhere-ville as she could be. She'd even managed to contact her assistant, Susan, and put a hold on all of their business plans until she knew more about the situation. With luck, that hold wouldn't have to last forever.

A few feet away, Madge wrung her hands as they waited for Alex. His confident strides sounded on the stonework from the hallway, echoed by the clacking wheels of the suitcases George dragged behind him.

Alex nodded approvingly at her packing and gave her a light

kiss. The restraint in his lips revealed his stress level more than his expression did.

In light of the emotional chaos of the evening, her reaction to the news about her father had remained subdued. The promise of this trip had almost seemed like an adventure in comparison. But his worry reminded her of all the obstacles they had yet to overcome. And most importantly, everything he was doing for her. Everything she wasn't even sure she wanted him to do.

Baxter jogged into the room. "Douglas agreed to help the FBI track down his contacts in exchange for dropping the charges and getting protection for his sister. My men are escorting him to the Chicago FBI office right now."

"Good. Then we should be back in a couple of weeks."

George distributed new phones to Alex and Elaina. "All outgoing calls from these are routed through a service to shield you. You can safely call anyone without them seeing your real number or location."

George indicated himself, Madge, and Baxter. "Only our three cells will be able to get through to you directly. All other callers will be routed to voicemail, so you'll have to check your messages frequently."

Elaina hefted the bulky handset and surrendered her old cell to George. "I miss my smart phone already."

"You'll be glad for the satellite phone when you get there."

Madge huffed and looked over the rims of her glasses at George. "Why are you going along with this crazy plan? This is like something off a stupid TV show."

"What would you have me do? Handcuff my boss to his desk?"

"I'd help," Elaina blurted.

Alex narrowed his eyes at her. Oops, had she said that aloud?

Elaina straightened her shoulders. "What? You know I wish you wouldn't take this risk. You can't drop all your company obligations for me."

"Are you saying I don't deserve a vacation now and then?"

"Of course not. But that's not what this is."

"Says who? I haven't taken a vacation in three years. Is it out of line to go on a celebratory trip with my fiancée?"

Oh no, not this. Again. Her heart twisted in so many directions from the stresses of the "engagement," their arguments and lies, and the threat from the mafia and her father that a sick feeling crept up her throat.

Madge did a double take. "Fiancée? You're engaged?"

Alex glanced at Elaina. She didn't know how to deny his claim without causing a scene in front of his staff.

The woman took the silence as confirmation, and her expression brightened. "Congratulations!"

Madge pulled Elaina and Alex into a hug. Since when did any member of his house staff ever care for Elaina?

Elaina cleared her throat, but the woman was oblivious to the sense of awkwardness. A snicker sounded behind her. George must have said something to the staff. Sometimes the man was too observant.

"I'm so happy for you both." Madge finally released them and gestured toward the door. "Okay, go, go. What are you waiting for? Enjoy your vacation."

Elaina tugged up her luggage handles and muttered under her breath to Alex. "Manipulator."

He smirked. "And damn good at it."

She couldn't argue with that.

George snapped his fingers. "I can use this to deflect questions about this trip too. I'll issue a press release with the announcement of your engagement holiday."

Alex gave her a grin as big as his ego. "See? No problem."

Uh-huh. No problem? That would be quite a switch from the last couple of hours.

Baxter put a fingertip to his ear, concentrating on his earpiece, and swore. "We have a problem. Douglas gave my men the slip on the way to the FBI meeting."

"*Shit.*"

Saying "I told you so" didn't even cross her mind. She was too busy trying to stay upright despite the shakiness in her limbs.

"I'm sorry, Mr. Wyatt. We—"

"It's not your fault. I'm the one who decided to trust him."

"Orders, sir?"

Alex's features became a mask of concentration. "Were you able to confirm his name and P.I. information?"

"Not yet."

"Then we have no way of knowing how much of his story was true. For all we know, he's a *member* of this New Jersey group. It'd be safest to assume the worst. Madge, give James a call. We'll need him to drive his truck."

While Madge, Baxter, and Alex adjusted plans for bringing in Alex's driver for help, George caught Elaina's eye. His sagging posture reflected the same realization she'd had. Their best lead for catching her father's minions had disappeared. If they didn't get a break soon, this going-into-hiding plan would be a one-way trip.

Chapter Twenty-Eight

A HALF HOUR LATER, ELAINA, ALEX, AND BAXTER HID IN the darkened living room of James's gatehouse apartment. While Alex and Baxter filled James in on the plan, Elaina scanned the yard beyond with her senses, trying to detect if anyone was watching them through the accumulating snow.

James's girlfriend, Peggy, settled on the adjacent couch. "Can I get you anything?"

"Hmm?" Elaina relaxed her grip on the chair. "No, thank you."

"When I was little, I used to dream my life would be perfect if I were white. Then I could be a princess and marry some rich white prince who would rescue me from a fiery dragon." She indicated Alex and chuckled with a wry edge. "It's not quite like the fairy tales, is it?"

Tension shot through Elaina. Did Peggy know too much? But the woman's dry tone was more ironic than awed.

Elaina shook her surprise away before her expression revealed anything. "Fairy tales are full of lies. Don't believe them."

Peggy half-laughed, half-snorted. "Yeah, you're right about that. I finally figured out that I could be the princess of my own life, no matter my color, and that I shouldn't wait for any man to rescue me. We don't need a fairy tale to find happiness." Her focus shifted to James, and her dark features lit with an inner glow. "Forget the damn prince. You can't help who you fall in love with, but he's the right man for me."

Elaina followed her gaze to the men, who hunched on the floor over a large map with a red-tinted flashlight. Just like with his businesses, Alex was in his element here, preparing, detailing, and coming up with plan A, B, C, and D. Plans that were more complicated than necessary because of her inability to defy Alex and simply take off and never look back. She couldn't do it. She couldn't hurt him like that.

Despite everything—despite the lies and the hurt and the impossibility—she still wanted to be with him. She still wanted to give them every possible chance.

"No," she agreed, "you can't help how you feel."

Peggy plucked a twig from Elaina's jacket. "Did you crawl through the bushes to get here from the house?"

She rolled her eyes. "Almost."

The woman's easy-going manner made her feel as though they'd been friends for years. The kind of friend she could ask for advice about men.

Or more specifically, *a* man. The only man who mattered.

"Do you mind if I ask why you and James aren't married?"

"You mean, if I love him, why aren't we married yet?" Peggy gave her a sideways smile. "There's more to marriage than just love. My grandparents celebrated their fiftieth wedding anniversary last year. They said the secret to their happiness was commitment, respect, and being each other's best friends. James and I have most of that, but we're working on the respect thing."

"He doesn't respect you?"

"No, it's not that." Peggy pulled her cloud of textured dark hair back and secured the bun with a band from her wrist. "I'm finishing my associate degree. Then I'll be able to get a real job and won't just be 'the girlfriend' mooching off him. I'm more independent than that."

"I understand." After all, that same reason was a big part of why she wanted the jewelry appraisal business to succeed.

Peggy bent closer like a conspirator. "Are you hoping Mr. Wyatt will ask you to marry him?"

Elaina rubbed her gloved palms together, and the fabric hiding the ring on her finger squeaked. Too bad that friction warmth couldn't make a dent to the cold stiffening her hands.

"He's already asked."

The woman's eyes widened and then narrowed. "You haven't said *yes* yet?"

After Elaina didn't disagree, Peggy wagged a finger. "Smart woman. Money doesn't buy happiness." She patted Elaina's knee. "He definitely seems to love you though. See if you can get that 'commitment, respect, and best friends' thing going. Then you'll know."

Elaina's insides flipped over at the woman's innocent comment. Alex had complained about how her unusual self-education and old neighbors had corrupted her concept of relationships. Was love *not* the end-all, be-all determining factor?

Alex caught her staring at him and grinned. "Ready, beautiful?" Confidence filled his tone again, evaporating another layer of her anger.

"Say the word."

Baxter checked his watch. "It's been almost twenty minutes since George and Madge left in your car. Hopefully, anyone watching would have followed the car to the airport."

Alex subtly tipped his chin, indicating the yard, and she gave a slight shake of her head. Her sensory range didn't extend far, but no one with a watch, cell phone, keys, or weapon was hiding around the entrance to the manor's grounds.

The group crept down to the garage and lined the suitcases along the sides of James's truck bed. Alex climbed up and piled blankets in the back of the pickup between the rows of luggage.

Peggy scrutinized the space, her lips pressed tight, and gave Elaina a friendly hug. "Good luck, girlfriend."

"Thank you." Maybe someday she'd come back and find a way to fit in—really fit in—with the rest of these humans.

Alex helped Elaina onto the truck bed. They nestled into the blankets, lying down in the back of the pickup.

Alex wrapped her in an embrace. "I'll do what I can to keep you warm."

Cold seeped into her bones from the metal beneath them. She didn't tell him it was a lost cause. Whatever damage this exposure to the weather triggered wasn't his fault. She was the one who'd made the decision to go along with his plan.

Jami Gold

Peggy crawled over the suitcases and tucked the blankets around them. She squeezed Elaina's shoulder. "Be safe."

The woman probably didn't hear Elaina's reply of "Thanks," muffled by Alex's chest and layers of jacket and blanket, but Alex echoed the sentiment for her.

Then the dim light in the garage disappeared, blocked by the material James attached to cover the back of his truck. Only Alex's arms and the whisper of his breathing remained in the world.

A moment later, the truck engine roared, and even Alex's steady breath was lost to the rumbling darkness. A drone accompanied the garage door opening, and the truck backed out onto the driveway. The movement previewed the motion sickness she feared would crop up with this escape. Her finely tuned sense of balance needed more input than unchanging blackness.

Peggy called over the noise of the truck. "Fine. Have fun on your stupid hunting trip. But if you're not back in time for dinner with grandma tomorrow, you're going to wish you hadn't given me a matching shotgun for Christmas last year."

Elaina's amusement at the woman's performance vanished when the truck pulled onto the road. Motion sickness became the least of her issues. The blankets provided little cushion against the cold, much less the bumps of the pavement.

Normally, jostling wouldn't be a problem. Her scales protected her from a hell of a lot, and her natural healing abilities made blunt force trauma a non-issue. Too bad tonight was different.

She snuggled closer to Alex and buried her face against his neck. Maybe this was sending mixed messages about the state of their relationship, but she was too desperate to care.

It didn't matter. Even the skin-to-skin contact didn't help. Her cheek registered his warmth, but it didn't sink into her bones like usual. How could she fix what was broken when she'd never understood how the bonus of his heat worked?

The truck hit a pothole, and the punishing impact damaged the muscles underneath. Her body acted as though she'd lost her claim on a good chunk of her treasure, far more than she could afford. How could she be so fragile right after gaining the ruby pendant?

Was the cold to blame? No doubt, the icy thief was stealing much of the extra oomph from the necklace. Something—maybe the bitter temperature or maybe something more—was destroying her inside, leaving only a vulnerable shell.

Whatever the cause, bruises formed on top of bruises, and her body's efforts to keep her warm *and* heal itself drained the energy she still possessed. From being at her strongest ever to becoming dangerously weak, it had been a hell of a rollercoaster day.

She only hoped she'd survive to tomorrow.

Miles zoomed by under the truck's tires. Occasionally, a hard swerve would send Alex and her rolling, the suitcases sliding and squishing them together. Sure, they were laying together in the dark, but there was nothing romantic about this.

Hour after hour passed in the noisy, freezing, jolting truck bed. Her uncontrollable shivers were interrupted only when potholes bounced her around, and with each landing, she slammed her skull, shoulder, and hip against the unforgiving metal.

Repeat. Endlessly.

How much longer would this torture last? She hadn't seen the route Alex and James had decided on.

Exhaustion finally caught up to her, and she passed out—unconscious, and closer to death than she dared to admit. Not to Alex, and especially not to herself.

Chapter Twenty-Nine

ELAINA WOKE LATER, STILL IN ALEX'S ARMS, BUT THEY WERE now in the cab of the pickup beside James. Clear morning sunlight streamed through the truck's windows.

"Where are we?"

Alex gazed down, his eyes bulging and wild, and he clutched her with a tense grip. "Christ, it's about time. Are you okay? When we stopped hours ago, your skin was cold to the touch, and I couldn't wake you."

"I'm okay," she lied.

Whether the lie fell from her lips because she couldn't talk about the issue in front of James or because she didn't want to admit how weak she was, she wasn't sure. Alex's touch still wasn't warming her inside, even though the hot air blasting from the vents kept the cab toasty. Was that bonus between them permanently broken?

She sat up in his lap. The truck sped through a snow-covered landscape. Ahead, a big city broke the horizon, but she didn't recognize the skyline.

"Where we are?" she repeated.

"We're almost to Minneapolis-St. Paul. James is going to drop us off at the airport and then return to Chicago to cover our tracks."

"No one followed us?"

James looked over and grinned. "I think someone was following at first. I had to lose them—without driving as though I had a reason to try to lose them."

She restrained herself from knocking that expression off his face but didn't hold back her grumble. "I'm delighted *someone* had fun last night."

James scrubbed his smooth scalp and returned his attention to the road. "Yeah, I heard the back wasn't very nice. Sorry about that."

She leaned around Alex and checked out the rear window. "You're sure we lost them?"

"Positive." James verified with Alex, who agreed. "To go along with the hunting story, I drove up to northern Wisconsin last night. Miles of country roads with no one on them. Over the crest of a hill, I killed the lights and pulled off the road at the bottom. After ten minutes passed without another car catching up to us, I knew we were safe."

"That's when he fetched us from the back." Alex squeezed her against him. "But that was hours ago. Are you sure you're okay?"

"The less said about it, the better."

When she was strong, she was stronger than a human, but when she was weak, she was disturbingly vulnerable. Between the stress, cold, and healing of the physical abuse, the previous night's escape had depleted the energy from the last several weeks' worth of acquisitions.

And for whatever reason, not only was Alex's touch not warming her, but her sleep in his arms also hadn't been recharging. She was damned lucky she'd woken at all.

Had something changed the energy dynamics between them? His marriage proposal maybe? Or her rejection of his proposal? Had one of those changed her "claim" on him? She drove the questions from her mind before she started hyperventilating again.

The hard part of their travel didn't end at the airport, as they alternated airline flights, car rentals, and taxi drives to hopscotch from Minnesota, Colorado, Missouri, and Tampa, Florida on their way to Miami. According to Alex, the broken itinerary would make it harder for anyone to track them, even if the bogus names they used for the airlines were exposed.

They'd done all they could by paying cash for everything and using fake IDs. Luckily, she still had her old IDs, and Alex had picked one up as part of his preparation.

Despite the 48-hour travel marathon and her energy deficit, she wasn't going to complain. The man who had protested a couple of months ago about traveling on a bus had now accompanied her in the cheap seats on bargain airlines.

Maybe she could have used the journey to break away from Alex and leave in the chaos, but once again, she couldn't help wanting to give them every opportunity to figure out a plan together.

After hitching a rollicking boat ride to Abaco Island in the Bahamas the next morning with a well-compensated fisherman—thus avoiding an airline ticket trail—Elaina was beyond ready for the journey to end. Their last obstacle was to locate the caretaker of Alex's private island, whom he'd never met.

The *Buttercup*, his island's main boat, was docked in the Marsh Harbour marina on Abaco Island as planned, but their guide was nowhere to be seen. As the sun dipped lower, every unanswered phone call to his island's custodian caused Alex's face to tighten.

Mid-afternoon had deepened into late afternoon by the time an older man stumbled up the pier, struggling under the weight of several boxes. Alex grimaced and sprang to his feet.

"Let me help you with those." He took the top two cartons off the tower.

The islander eyed Alex and Elaina over the top of the now-lower pile. "Thanks. You must be Mr. Roberts."

Was this the custodian? His Bahamian accent turned *thanks* to *tanks* and *must be* into *mus-see*. But even forgiving the accent's effect on his pronunciation, he hadn't called Alex anything close to *Mr. Wyatt*—or the phony name from his fake ID.

"Uh, yes. These go in the boat?"

The man confirmed and led them onto the *Buttercup*. The boat was bigger than it had appeared from the dock. The swimming platform off the back opened to a patio-like area behind the enclosed section of the boat.

Her steps halted inside the glass door. No small fishing boat, this thing was a yacht.

Treasured Claim

Boxes currently buried the cushioned benches lining the sides, but that clutter didn't detract from the gorgeous mahogany wood or gleaming fixtures at the helm. Toward the front, stairs led below the expansive windows down to a lower level with a granite-counter-topped kitchenette.

The stress of the journey slipped from her shoulders. As far as she was concerned, they'd arrived at their destination.

Alex checked out the lower hall, drawing her attention to the master bedroom below. "Not bad. I'm glad that broker I bought it through didn't steer me wrong."

"True, true." Their guide shook Alex's hand in a friendly greeting. "I happy to meet you, Chief. Welcome to the Bahamas. You family to the Billy Roberts?"

"Uh, not that I know of. His people settled in the area though, right?"

The caretaker's head of graying hair bobbed. "I's *Lenny* Roberts. I's a Roberts like you. You can call me Uncle Lenny."

Alex's lips twitched into a grin. She wasn't sure which irony he found more amusing—the idea of him and the dark-skinned man sharing genetics or that he wasn't a "Roberts" at all.

After they finished loading all the boxes and luggage, they followed "Uncle" Lenny up spiral stairs on the back deck to a second level over the enclosed section of the boat. Other than a roof, this level was open to the air. The men took the two control chairs at the front, and she settled on a cushioned L-shaped bench beside a table in the back corner.

A few minutes later, they were underway. Tropical breezes teased her hair, and she stretched out on the bench, surveying the view.

Turquoise water churned in their wake. Palm trees covered the main island to their right. Narrow barrier islands broke the surface of the ocean to their left. She breathed deeply, her worries about how long they'd have to stay here lessened by the hot sunshine.

Up front, Alex was getting Uncle Lenny's rundown on the boat's controls and his disagreements with the island's previous "grabalishus" owner. Despite Uncle Lenny's complaints about the greediness of his former employer, his singsong accent lulled her to unwind and close her eyes.

A few minutes later, Alex's voice sounded above her. "You know, the bright sunlight makes your skin shimmer more than usual. If the locals could see it, they'd think you were a mermaid, or maybe a survivor of the lost city of Atlantis."

"Yes, because a dragon isn't exotic enough."

He laughed, loud and genuine. The sound lightened the worry weighing down her heart. After the last couple of days, it was good to see him happy and relaxed again. For a moment, she let herself forget the difficulties facing them.

She sat up and grinned at him. "So, 'Mr. Roberts,' where is your pirate ship *Revenge?*"

He joined her on the bench and wrapped an arm around her shoulders. "You figured that out?"

"You've only made me watch *The Princess Bride* about seven times."

Not that she was complaining. She was glad to be included in his favorite memories of his mother by watching "their" movie together.

Her finger ran teasingly down his open collar. "I should hope I could figure out the 'Dread Pirate Roberts' reference. Especially with this boat being named *Buttercup.*"

"It's true that I love you for your brains." He kissed her forehead and tipped his chin, indicating ahead of them. "*Revenge* is the name of the sailboat. More appropriate, don't you think?"

"It sounds perfect. Now if only you had let me summon that first class passenger's jewelry yesterday, you'd have been all set as a pirate."

A shadow fell over his expression. "Don't bring that up again. There are laws against that behavior. End of story."

Easy for him to say. Those earrings might mean the difference between life and death, and she'd practically told him as much during the flight.

Once again, she debated at what point she should give up this experiment to follow the human rules he insisted upon and leave him. How could both options feel *too* selfish?

By staying, she was salvaging their relationship and respecting his rules, but she was also risking the financial state of his businesses and endangering his life. On the other hand, if she left, she'd protect him and his companies, but she'd hurt him emotionally.

Neither option was a clear-cut winner from her perspective either. She *wanted* to stay with him, but sticking around kept her weak. Leaving would be the hardest thing she'd ever done and being on her own might be *more* dangerous, but then she could ignore his rules and collect as much treasure as she needed.

She wanted to scream at the impossibility of the decision. None of the choices made sense for either of them—emotionally or logically or any other way.

Alex had returned his attention to the view. "Uncle Lenny's been getting the beachfront guesthouse ready for us. He said a hurricane several years back took out the main house at the top of the island. The guy I won the place from neglected to mention that. I'd always wondered why he called it a money pit and seemed happy to let it go."

The engine changed pitch a few moments later, and they moved to the front of the bridge. Up ahead, an island of green greeted them.

Uncle Lenny pointed out the beacon light at the northwest end of the island, which had been used to signal Marsh Harbour behind them in decades past. Two L-shaped walls of stone jutted from the western shore, creating a breakwater to protect the marina area. A sturdy pier extended from the beach, and a large golf cart awaited their arrival.

After Uncle Lenny expertly docked the *Buttercup* and they loaded the golf cart with the boxes and luggage, he drove them over the sandy paths cut through jungle-like foliage. The trail took them around a marina canal carved into the rock bed of the island, and she glimpsed the *Revenge* through the trees as they went by.

Past the canal, the path veered back toward shore, and a quarter mile of pristine pink sand beach lay in front of them. She now understood the draw of a tropical paradise.

An immaculate bright yellow cottage perched at the tree line. Caribbean blue shutters and doors decorated the outside, and white gingerbread trim supported the covered front porch. Vivid red flowers bloomed nearby, a parrot chattered at them before flying away, and a gentle breeze rustled the palm and ficus trees shading the house. And as a bonus, the warm weather wouldn't eat up as much of her energy in the struggle to maintain body heat.

After they'd outfitted the one room cottage with their supplies, she went out to the front porch. Waves at the beach sang a peaceful lullaby.

Alex stood behind her and folded her into his arms. "Not bad at all."

"I agree." Salty air filled her lungs. "I shouldn't like it, but I do."

"It's beautiful. Why shouldn't you like it?"

She didn't want to detail the depths of her fatigue. Knowing him, if she mentioned the problem, he'd insist on doing something even more risky. She couldn't be responsible for endangering him any more than she already had. Besides, their journey's end meant things might not be as dire as she feared.

With luck, her remaining energy would last long enough for her to come up with an Alex-compliant plan for how to obtain more jewelry while out here in the middle of nowhere. Or even better, now that they'd arrived, maybe being in Alex's arms tonight would give her a bonus recharge.

She spun in his embrace. His touch didn't elicit the tingles she'd become used to—not a good sign for the potential of rebuilding her strength. Instead of dwelling on whether the energy drain was permanent, she twisted the meaning of her comment.

"It's so different from anywhere I've ever been. Remember that I grew up in dark caves. And when I left, I moved from one city to another, trying to disappear in the crowds. So I exchanged one place of gray for another."

Her throat constricted at the thought of how empty her life had been before Alex, deadening her voice to a monotone. "Always surrounded by walls of stone."

The truth of those statements reduced her guilt for keeping him in the dark about how she might not be able to stay.

She peered up at him. "I didn't know if I would like it here. So isolated. So *green*. But I think I do."

He squeezed her. "Good. I like it too."

The surroundings *did* make it easy to ignore her problems for a moment—the ticking clock of Alex's business obligations, the mobsters who were searching for her, and her father and the new tools at his disposal.

Not to mention that without new treasure, she'd soon starve to death.

Chapter Thirty

AT A TABLE ON THE BEACH, ALEX USED THE SATELLITE antenna to check a package-tracking website on his laptop and swore. The order of jewelry he'd put in for Elaina *still* sat in customs. How many weeks did it take them to clear one carton? More likely, someone had confiscated the necklaces and bracelets for themselves.

Thank God he'd given her the ruby pendant just before they'd left. Hopefully, she'd be okay until he could have another package delivered. If that one disappeared as well, he'd have someone's head. Maybe several someones'.

Other than that hiccup to his plan, one day of their trip melded into the next with a comfortable routine. He wasn't sure why, but in addition to snorkeling, relaxing on the beach, and sailing on the *Revenge*, Elaina frequently wanted to visit the ruins of the main house on the exposed hill at the north end of the island. If she was disappointed in their cottage and wished for nicer accommodations, she never said so directly. Instead, she'd settle on the intact deck and look out over the water below the ridge. Perhaps she simply liked the view.

This afternoon, while he turned to catching up on emails, a hollow look crept over her face. "I'm going to search for pirate treasure."

"We're in the right place for it. This area was pirate central."

He paused mid-chuckle. Something about her expression

seemed more serious than just a whim.

"You've felt some out there." He closed his computer and leaned forward. "Where?"

She pivoted her laptop, showing him a satellite image of the island. "Here's the main house, almost centered on the bluff at the north end." She traced the northern shoreline. "This is all rocky, not like the beaches along the other sides. If someone had been searching for an easy place to bury something, they'd have dug into the soft sand. But this..." Her finger poked at the north coast. "This would have been harder. The question then becomes, why here?"

That explained why she'd wanted to hang out at the ruins of the main house so often. "A cave?"

Even in the bright sunlight, brilliant blue flared in her eyes. "Maybe. It'd have to be pretty hidden for no one to have noticed it though."

"How much do you think is there?"

"I don't know. Even though I've been concentrating on it for weeks, the impression I have is still weak. But if someone went through a lot of trouble to hide it, their intention would make the location as strong and protected as a safe. So even though whatever is there has long been abandoned, I can't summon it without being closer."

"Good." He flashed her a wink. "We wouldn't want this to be too easy."

Within the hour, Alex had the *Revenge* anchored in the water north of the island. The promise of adventure shone like the swords of light that cut across the water every night, five flashes every fifteen seconds, from the lighthouse in Hope Town. In contrast to his eagerness, Elaina perched at the boat's edge and seemed more agitated than excited, her brows etching her forehead.

"This is the place, but I don't see any openings. Do you?"

"No, but now that we're closer, can you summon whatever's there?" At her headshake, he tugged on the anchor rode's rope. The line's tension confirmed the anchor's flukes were well set. "I'll take a closer look."

He dove into the water and swam toward the rocky shore. The

solid mass of boulders at the foot of the cliff made it impossible to climb around without twisting an ankle. A half hour of swimming back and forth in front of the area Elaina had indicated revealed nothing even close to resembling an opening in the rock face.

Elaina's tight expression as she kept watch from the *Revenge* didn't improve when he spun toward her and shook his head. And with the tide moving out, they'd be driven farther from the cliff unless they decided to chance scrambling over the rocks at the base.

He returned to the first boulder he'd stopped near to gauge how fast the water level was dropping. Instead of seeing other rocks exposed near the surface, as he'd expected, waves lapped under the boulder. Under?

He sank below the surface to investigate. The mass of boulders at the shoreline had appeared solid because they *were* solid, a shelf of bumpy bedrock sticking out from the shore.

A minute later, water dripped from his limbs onto the *Revenge*'s deck. He balanced against the rolling waves and hopped into the cockpit area beside Elaina.

"Let's wait for the tide to go down more. Waves have eroded the bedrock under that ledge of boulders. It's possible an underwater cave opening is somewhere along there."

"An underwater cave?" She bounced on her toes. "That would explain why no one's discovered it yet. Especially if it's set back from the shoreline and hiding in the shadows."

"That's my thought."

She circled her arms around his neck and kissed him. Really kissed him. Tongue caressing, hands wandering, soft moaning type of kissing him.

Startled, he took a second to respond in kind. She hadn't kissed him like that recently, and he struggled to figure out when things had changed.

They'd had the confrontation in the closet and the difficult travel a couple of weeks back, but she'd seemed normal after they arrived. Hadn't she?

But now that he thought about it, she'd slowly become more withdrawn. So slowly that he hadn't noticed it until now.

She leaned back and gave him the radiant smile he'd missed.

"You're brilliant."

"I have to find *some* way to help you get treasure while we're here."

A shadow crossed her features so quickly he would have missed it if he'd blinked.

His grasp tightened on her hips. "Why didn't you tell me how bad it had gotten?"

"I did. Why do you think I mentioned taking those earrings weeks ago? Just to be difficult?"

His chest constricted, forcing a sour taste up the back of his throat. If the fatigue on her face and the slump of her shoulders didn't give it away, the dull, un-shimmery reflections off her skin made it clear. As if that wasn't enough evidence, her natural hair colors under the brunette shade she'd chosen for their stay here were pale and lethargic in their movement.

Whatever the signs were of a deathly ill dragon, she was displaying them. And he'd missed every warning.

All this work to keep her safe was killing her slowly. Despite his planning with the jewelry package, nothing had worked out, and he'd failed her again.

"That's why you've been sleeping with your lockbox at your back. And being in my arms at night hasn't helped you recover?"

"No." Her weight shifted from one foot to the other. "I think something about your proposal or my rejection of it broke whatever bond we had that was providing energy."

"Broke our bond?" His heart cracked, and the pieces plummeted into his churning gut. The weight behind his ribs squeezed his lungs so tightly he barely got enough air to put voice to his questions. "So you'd claimed me before, and now you've given up your claim?" Shivers crawled up his arms. "I'm not *yours* anymore?"

"I don't know." She pinned her arms against her stomach, adding distance between them. "I just know that a bunch of my energy drained away, and the travel in the cold stole the rest."

For a moment, her admission hurt even worse than her claim in the garage that she didn't love him. Hurt bad enough that he questioned whether trying to maintain a relationship with a dragon was worth it. Logically, between the effect on his companies and the effort to deal with her father, he *should* be questioning whether it made sense.

Just as quickly, his body answered with a compulsion his mind couldn't ignore. Maybe there would be a point where the trouble wasn't worth it, but he wasn't there yet. Good or bad, she was his obsession.

"Don't worry, I'll fix this. If I'd known it had gotten this bad, I'd have put in *ten* orders for jewelry, so at least one of them would make it through. We can head back, and I'll do that right now."

No, that would take too long. His skin itched under the evaporating seawater with the urge to take action immediately.

"Or I'll fight to keep you safe instead of hiding out here, find a way to prevent you from starving. Something."

"You can't be serious." She stepped back out of his hold. "See? This is why I didn't bring it up again. All you can think about is taking on more danger and risk when it would make the most sense for me to just leave until this blows over."

"Not an option." The fact that she'd kept him in the dark mattered more than her point. "You should have told me. We need to know we can trust each other."

"Right. Because you didn't lie to me for two months and have been completely honest with me about the effect all of this has had on your companies."

His body went so still the waves against the side of the boat sounded loud enough to be slaps. He couldn't deny a word she said. And the worst thing was that he'd lost her trust for nothing— he'd failed. Nothing he'd done had helped her live without fear.

"I do regret lying to you about the deal with the scumbag, more than you would believe. About as much as I regret failing to keep my promise."

"And what about the lying now?"

He tried to control his expression, but she saw through it, her brows arching high. He'd managed to keep up with voicemails, emails, and meetings, but in reality, his companies were at the mercy of the stock market. Any moment, the market might frown on his leadership—or lack of it—which would affect his companies' stock value. Even though he'd diversified his holdings over the years, he wouldn't be able to fix solvency problems from here for the stockholders or the employees.

"I didn't want you to worry."

"Uh-huh. Why does that excuse work for you and not for me?" Her shoulders rolled back, emphasizing her resolve. "I don't want you to worry about me hiding out on my own while you get back to work. You can't take an indefinite vacation, and I won't let you destroy your life for me."

"I said *no.*"

In his peripheral vision, he saw his hands had lifted instinctively, ready to...

He didn't know what. Restrain her? Or worse? His control when it came to her was nonexistent. If that was supposed to be a sign he should let her go, he refused to listen.

He clenched and unclenched his fists and picked up his snorkel gear. "I'm going to take a look. I'll let you know if I see anything."

Water slipped over his body, his dive carrying him below the waves. The flowing liquid contrasted with his solidifying determination.

He would win her back. He would earn her "claim" again. He *would* get this treasure for her.

Chapter Thirty-One

THEY'D DISCOVERED DRAGONS WEREN'T NATURALLY AT HOME in the water. She could swim, but wasn't comfortable with it. Now Alex could prove his ability to help her by fixing this problem.

Speckles of sunlight dotted the sea floor under the island's coastal ledge. The boulders overhead and the sandy bottom below left only a few feet of swimming space between them, but the outgoing tide created air pockets in the gaps among the rocks. Every minute, he expelled the water from the snorkel and took several deep breaths through one of the holes between the boulders.

He glanced back and gathered his bearings from Elaina's wavy form leaning over the *Revenge*'s side. Erosion had dug out a larger section under the rocky shelf than he'd thought, but his mask made it difficult to judge perspective. The shifting tide pushed and pulled him, and he verified his position with the boat every few minutes.

An odd splash caught his attention, and he made his way in that direction. Each wave swirled in an opening under the shelf and then made its way out with a *whoosh*.

Please let this be it. As he neared, the cavity in the wall revealed itself bigger than it appeared, the slanting rock face distorting its size. The gap was definitely big enough for a person. That had to be the place.

He pulled off his gear and swam back to the boat to fetch

Elaina. Despite her lack of swimming talent, she didn't need to breathe as much as humans—which explained why being encased in concrete by the mafia wouldn't kill her right away—and she could safely join him in checking out the cave.

She poked over the side of the boat, anxiety tightening her features. "See anything?"

"I think I found it. I didn't go inside, but I found an opening big enough to be a cave entrance. "

A splash punctuated the end of his sentence, her jump into the water landing her beside him. He replaced his snorkel, and together they plunged under the shelf.

She hadn't bothered with snorkeling equipment and crawled along the ocean bottom rather than attempting to swim. At the opening, she lifted herself over the bottom edge and climbed inside.

He cracked a glow stick and jabbed his snorkel through a break in the rocky ledge. After an extra deep breath, he followed her into the dark.

The feeble green light of his glow stick reflected off the sides of the passage, and the fog coating the inside of his mask didn't help him see their destination either. He felt his way along more than anything. At first, the rough walls sloped down, but then they curved upward, giving him hope of an air pocket ahead.

Not a minute too soon, the tunnel opened into a small cave overhead. He launched off the rocks and breached the water surface, gulping air.

In contrast, Elaina wasn't breathing heavy at all. "Oh, Alex, you were right."

Desperate for oxygen, he hadn't removed his fogged-over mask yet, but at her words, he slid off the mask.

A skeleton sprawled on a ledge in front of him.

His arms pinwheeled across the water. "Jesus!"

Her mouth curved into a mischievous grin. "How much you want to bet he was stabbed in the back?"

"Ha ha." At least his voice was steady, and the stick's pale glow hid the extent of his heebie-jeebies. The romanticized version of pirates was better than reality.

The cave was about ten feet across, but looked bigger because the side walls cut deeper above the waterline to create a rocky bench around the perimeter. Elaina clenched his forearm and focused behind him.

"I've never felt anything like this."

Trembles traveled into his arm from her fingers, and he tucked her into a protective embrace. "What is it?"

"I can see it, and I can sense it."

Her features screwed into a grimace, and he turned his back on the skeleton and checked out the other end of the cave. A large wooden chest sat on the shelf opposite the deceased pirate.

Alex lifted the glow stick for a better view. The green glow reflected off something through gaps in the dark, rotted wood.

She groaned. "But I can't get closer to it."

"What do you mean?"

"The protections around that chest are stronger than a bank vault." She noted the skeleton behind them. "Someone died to secure this place's secret. That created a barrier I can't get past."

"Like an invisible wall?"

"I could manipulate the metal walls of a safe, but this I can't touch. Literally. Whatever is inside there doesn't think it's been abandoned. The more I think about trying to claim it"—a quiver racked her body, making her point—"the more it pushes back, refusing to surrender to me."

"I'll make it happen." He passed her the glow stick. "Hold this for me."

He swam one-handed and towed her with his other arm. By the time they were directly in front of the chest, her trembles had intensified into full-body shudders.

"You okay?"

She shook her head, unable to speak.

"You want me to keep going?"

She met his gaze with soft, pleading eyes. He had a bad feeling about this, but he had to help her. No matter what.

He kept a tight grip on her forearm with one hand and heaved himself onto the ledge with the other. A seizure almost took her from his grasp. The glow stick fell from her fingers and rolled to a stop a few feet under the water along the curving cave walls. Before he lost her too, he hoisted her onto his lap.

Spasms threatened to send her back into the water, and he wrapped her in a firm embrace. "I have you."

He sat her facing forward on his lap and edged them closer. The light from the submerged stick was fainter now, but his vision had adjusted to the near darkness.

Up close, the chest's wood rot looked even worse. He bound one arm securely around Elaina and tapped the lid. The trunk collapsed like a house of cards. The rusty lock, hinges, and metal supports clattered to the rocky shelf.

As he'd suspected, the chest had held its form but none of its structure.

He brushed away the wood shreds and revealed a large pile of silver coins. Every legend of the Caribbean pirates came back to him at the sight of the Spanish dollars.

"Pieces of eight." He picked up one and angled it to catch the light from below.

The date was 17-something, but the glow was too dim to make out the rest. The opposite side displayed the name "Phillip V." If these were from the reign of King Phillip V, that would put the timeframe for this treasure hideout in the first part of the 1700s, which coincided with the golden age of piracy in the area.

He tossed the coin onto the pile and squeezed Elaina against his chest. "What now? Can you summon it from here?"

Her body shook a negative answer.

"Can you reach out to it?"

He couldn't see her face, but her shaking increased.

"Should I place your hand on it?"

Her head bumped his chin, which he assumed meant she was nodding.

He took her wrist and stretched her arm toward the coins. When he set her palm on the silver, her arm jerked away, like from a hot burner.

"Oh-kay. Do I need to hold it there for you?"

"Yeh—" Her teeth clacked together.

"Shh, it's okay. We'll figure this out."

He grasped her wrist again and placed her hand on the pile. Her muscles fought against him, and her body tried to escape his hold.

Was she in pain? The thought hollowed his chest, and he let her struggle wrench their arms back.

"You want me to do this, right? Even though it's hard or painful or whatever?"

Her head rocked against his chin again. Shit. He was going to have to force her, and the whole time, she was going to suffer.

But now was the time for him to prove they could trust each other. He had to trust that this was what she needed, and if watching her in distress put him through hell... Well, he loved her enough to go through hell.

He forced her hand back onto the mound. She was strong, damn strong. He leaned forward, shoving their torsos toward the silver and forcing her hand deeper into the coins. Air huffed between her teeth, her lungs spasming and hyperventilating.

An odd sound started deep in her throat, like a burbling motorboat. He couldn't see her expression to know what effect this was having on her, but it couldn't be good.

"If you want me to stop, smack me in the head or something."

Her muscles stiffened, as though determined to see this through. She'd claim these coins even if it meant using a mixture of brute force and determination. The sound grew louder, working its way up her throat.

A shriek ripped from her body. The cry echoed against the cave walls, shredding his eardrums. But he knew her agony was countless times worse. The scream continued, tearing from her throat, seemingly splitting her in half.

The sound destroyed him. The last thing he'd ever wanted to do was cause her pain, and now he was causing it, prolonging it, and forcing it.

"I'm sorry. I'm sorry. I'm sorry..."

Her yell changed volume only when she drew more air to keep it going, and her body shook violently in his arms.

He wanted to tell her that he couldn't do this anymore. He couldn't hurt her. He couldn't watch her be hurt.

But if he backed out, she'd starve.

On the other hand, was this killing her? All the times he'd worried about his accidental rough treatment, she'd told him he couldn't hurt her. She'd lied.

Now he *was* hurting her. On purpose.

How could he do this to her?

Light flashed, blinding his dark-adjusted eyes, and an electric shock laid him flat on his back along the rocky bench. His ears rang in the silent darkness. She lay limp in his arms.

"Elaina?" He jostled her and blinked, straining to make out her shape. "Elaina?"

No answer.

Oh God, no, no, no. A crushing weight held him in its grasp, like fingers of stone squeezing away his life. He sat up and drew her closer, unable to see if she was breathing.

"Come on, beautiful, stay with me." He lightly slapped her cheek. "Please, Elaina."

"Yeah?" Her slow, satisfied drawl told him what he needed to know.

The weight released him, and he sagged against the stone. Unconcerned that she'd notice his trembling, he hugged her tight and rocked back and forth.

"Thank God you're okay. Thank God you're okay."

"Oh yeah, I'm good. Really, really good." She twisted in his hold and nuzzled his neck. "How are you?"

"Freaked the hell out, but glad you're all right."

She pressed on his shoulders until he lay on the rough ledge, and then she straddled him. The light filling the cave was now blue instead of the glow stick's green. And it was coming from her. But when she rolled her hips and spread her fingers across his chest, he decided against interrupting her intentions to point out that her eyes weren't just glowing, but literally emitting light.

She leaned forward, and her breath hissed in his ear. "I'm better than all right." Her hips circled, pressing into his rapidly hardening cock. "And it's all thanks to you. My hero."

"It wasn't a big deal."

"Liar." She nibbled his ear lobe.

He sucked in a gulp of air. "Okay, it was the hardest thing I've ever had to do. I hated the thought of hurting you."

Her teeth nicked his neck. "Pain is often close to pleasure."

He closed his eyes, ignoring their surroundings and the reminder of what happened here. Not to mention the skeleton a few feet away.

"I like pleasure a lot more than pain."

Her nails trailed down his abs, and she circled his cock in his swim trunks. "Hmm, it feels as though you're up for pleasure right now."

In answer, he pulled off her bikini top and let her breasts fill his palms. Her throaty moan reverberated in the cave, setting his blood on fire. His hands slid to her ass and pried the stretchy fabric down her hips.

She knelt for a moment to remove her bikini bottom and returned the favor with his bathing suit. Cool air drifted over him, and water evaporated from his now-exposed skin. Before he could brace himself against the cold, her wet warmth surrounded him, taking him inside her.

Forget foreplay. Forget their arguments. Forget their lies.

The successful acquisition must have been enough of a turn-on for her to overcome practicalities. She pinned his wrists to the rock. Between her rush of energy, glowing eyes, and sexually charged mood, she clearly wanted to take control.

For once, he relaxed and let her lead. After nearly mistreating her on the boat, letting her lead was probably safer anyway. He didn't trust his shaky emotions.

"You're the most amazing and incredible man." She slid up and down on him, spreading her moisture. "I owe you everything."

"No, you d—"

Her teeth latched onto his lip in warning. "Shh. I'm talking now." Her hips lifted and pressed again.

He knew better than to argue, or even acknowledge her statement. Instead, he drank in the vision above him.

The sexiest woman on the planet was riding him, and although he'd lied to her, failed her, and caused her pain, she still wanted to be with him. Her rhythm increased, and she sat up, tossing her hair over her shoulder. She bit her lip in a sign of pleasure matching his.

He loved this woman. Far beyond just her looks, he loved her mind, her strength, and her determination.

The fierce expression on her face as she came drove him over the edge. He broke from her hold and dug his fingers into her hips, yanking her down for one last stroke, and then he let himself go.

A grunting yell escaped with his release. "God, I love you!"

Instead of reacting badly to his proclamation, she bent down to kiss him. "I know." She settled her head on his chest and gave a satisfied sigh. "And if I could love anyone, it would be you."

He hugged her and heard the words he knew she really meant. She loved him. More than she even thought herself capable of, she loved him.

And that secret knowledge was enough.

ELAINA CLIMBED THE ANCHOR'S ROPE, HER BODY TOO HEAVY TO swim to the surface. Alex had joined in her giddiness by decorating her body with coins, where they bonded to her skin for easy carrying. Despite the weight, she easily hauled herself up, strengthened by the addition to her hoard.

By far, that had been the most difficult claiming she'd ever attempted, and her success had repaid the effort a hundred times over. Now that the stress from worrying about her next meal had vanished, she could relax and figure out how to stay safe with Alex.

The boat rocked as he helped her over the edge. A teasing glint lit his face. "With all those coins plastering you from head to toe, you're like a walking silver statue. It's, uh, an interesting look for you."

"Be nice, or I won't let you help me take them off when we get back to the cottage."

He chuckled and brought up the anchor and set out to their beach. A sleek racing sailboat, the *Revenge* could be sailed single-handedly.

She settled onto the bench out of his way and watched him work from under her lowered lashes. Their days in the sun had bronzed his skin into a delicious shade, and he almost never wore a shirt anymore. Daily swimming and sailing had sculpted his muscles into mouthwatering perfection.

She licked her lips, but even the distraction of his gorgeousness couldn't stop her thoughts from replaying the events in the cave.

His acquiescence to her aggressiveness confirmed her suspicion of how hard that situation had been for him.

Normally, he'd have retaken control at some point, but he'd been rattled. Badly.

Love was more complicated and nuanced than she'd guessed. His understanding of her need—and his reaction to her pain—proved once more how much he loved her. Not that she really had any doubts, despite the lies.

Back at the cottage, the coins slowly overfilled her lockbox, and he worshiped each inch of her body revealed under the circles. Unlike his, her skin didn't tan, and the white sparkles of her microscopic scales matched the silver.

An unfamiliar feeling crept over her at his reverence. Beyond mere happiness, the idea that this bliss could survive anything and last forever bubbled into her thoughts. If that trial hadn't damaged their relationship, maybe her inability to love *didn't* matter.

Maybe this *was* real.

Chapter Thirty-Two

HOURS LATER, A TRILL STARTLED ELAINA FROM SLEEP. ALEX sprang from her side and searched for the source of the noise in the cottage. He lunged to the table and pulled his satellite phone from the laptop case.

"Hello?"

His tone matched her confusion. Only three members of his staff had their cell numbers, so they rarely received calls—and never this late. Middle-of-the-night calls were seldom good news.

"I don't have the satellite antenna up right now, but give me a minute." He hung up, threw on a T-shirt and shorts, and carried the equipment outside.

She shoved her arms into a robe and followed him onto the darkened beach, where he hooked up the antenna and started his laptop. "Something wrong?"

"That was George. He said he needed to show me something."

Visions of someone kidnapping George filled her limbs with icy dread. As soon as Alex's laptop was running, the video chat program dinged for an incoming call. He clicked the icon, and George's face appeared on the screen.

"Sorry to disturb you so late, but we have a problem."

His wrinkled brow seemed more worried than scared, so she tied her robe closed and stepped into range of the webcam. "Are you all right?"

His gaze moved with her. "Elaina, I'm glad you're there too.

Yes, I'm fine. This is about Dakon Fabricating."

He concentrated on her for another second, long enough for his words to sink in. This was about one of Alex's businesses, and yet George wanted her to be part of the conversation. Her chest tightened at his implied request for her help.

George's attention returned to Alex. "The chip fab plant in New York was firebombed a couple of hours ago."

Alex's sharp inhale echoed hers. The computer parts manufacturing company was one of his most successful.

George pushed a button and streamed live video onto Alex's screen. Tendrils of smoke rose from the ruins of a large, warehouse-sized building outlined by spotlights in the darkness. Emergency lights flashed red on the rubble. Portions of the structure were still standing, but fire had gutted most of the walls and the entire roof.

George's face appeared again. "No deaths, but eighteen wounded. Three critically."

Alex propped his forehead on his fingertips. "Do we know who's behind it?"

George's eyes shifted toward her for a split second, answering why he wanted her here. "An email arrived right after the bombing. The FBI already tracked it to New Jersey. They think it's the Albanian Mafia."

She cupped her mouth, and her muscles shook. Eighteen people injured. Because of her.

It had happened again. Despite everything she'd done to honor her vow not to hurt humans—or anyone—it had happened again.

Her knees weakened, and she clutched the back of Alex's chair. "Albania? You're sure?"

"I take it that means something to you?"

"Last I knew, that's where my father had his—" She caught herself. "Some property." The involvement of the Albanian Mafia explained how her father had been able to make contacts in the United States.

Alex's hand dropped from his temple. "What did the email say?"

"That you have twenty-four hours to turn her over, or they'll hit another facility."

"*What?* No, I can't—"

"George"—she straightened—"tell them I'm on my way."

While George acknowledged, Alex spun in his chair toward her. His expression curled into a grimace. "I *won't* let you do this."

Arguing was pointless. Instead, she focused on the screen over Alex's shoulder. "What does Alex need to do from a business standpoint?"

George's eyes locked with hers in silent agreement. "He needs to show his face in New York, support the injured, provide leadership. Or else the stock market will eat him alive."

"Bullshit." Alex pointed at the laptop. "You're exagger—"

"He'll be on a plane tomorrow." She'd make sure of that. Somehow.

Alex jostled the table and stood, crowding her. "Stop this. Both of you. I won't leave you here."

Behind Alex's back, George mouthed, "Good luck." The screen went blank.

A pulsing vein throbbed on Alex's forehead, warning her and serving as a reminder of his determination. But they weren't dealing with an enemy they could hide from anymore. All their efforts to cover their tracks during their journey here had only forced the mob to attack them a different way.

She'd seen plenty of evidence that he worried about being too much like his father, and his businesses—his successes in business—were wrapped together with his sense of being the better man. She wouldn't let him lose part of himself for her. She'd known this moment of choice was coming, and the fact that three people might die from injuries that were *her* fault only proved she should have done this long ago.

He had to go to New York, and she needed to get the Mafia off his case. Either they could attack this problem as a team, or she'd have to force it.

"Alex, we've talked about this. I won't let you destroy your companies for me. We tried it your way, and it didn't work."

He waved toward the laptop. "He's overstating the risk."

"He's not. People could have been *killed*. Innocent people. I can't give my father the excuse to escalate this. Who knows what will happen next time?"

"You heard George. He's already involved the FBI. There's not going to be a next time."

"You can't know that." When his mouth drew into a scornful twist, she held up a hand. "You can't. And I refuse to take that chance. Unless you're saying that I value human life more than you do, you *have* to let me do this."

"What are you proposing? That I let you sacrifice your *life* for my companies? For *money*? That's crazy."

"No, you're going to New York to take care of those issues, and I'm going to..."

She paused. If she told him the truth, would he use that knowledge to stop her? But she couldn't complain about him acting behind her back if she did the same.

"I'm going to leave enough of a trail so they know you're not hiding me anymore. Then I'm going to Europe."

He jerked back. "You're marching straight toward him? To do what? Surrender? Fight him?"

She didn't answer. She didn't know the answer herself yet.

"No, not until you show me right here"—his arm swept out, indicating the wide-open beach—"that you can shapeshift."

"I can't." Not even close.

But she didn't have a choice anymore. She wasn't the only one getting hurt.

Her best option for protecting Alex *and* having a chance to spend her life with him was to be proactive. Stop running. Take the fight to her father and convince him to leave her alone, just as Alex had convinced his father.

And to even the odds for a fair fight, as Alex was so fond of saying, she had to be able to shapeshift. Now.

A thought began to gel at the edge of her mind. The danger would be worth it if she could finally end this and be safe with Alex.

"If I steal the hoard of another dragon, an elderly one who can't keep up with me, I'll get stronger in a hurry. Then my father will think twice about coming after me."

"Christ." He pinned her in an embrace. "I can't let you do that alone. What if you needed my help, like you did this afternoon?"

His reaction didn't surprise her, but she'd hoped it wouldn't come to this. Would they ever be able to *not* lie to each other? How could they ever check the *respect* column on Peggy's list of healthy relationship traits if they couldn't trust each other's judgment?

But she didn't see another option. At least not one that didn't endanger him or other innocents.

She misdirected him, adding a touch of weakness to her tone. "Okay. What do you think we should do?"

Tension released from his muscles at her feigned submission. "Right now, we're going to go back to bed. It's way after midnight, too late to make arrangements for anything anyway, and we'll both think clearer in the morning."

"Okay, that sounds good." Just not for the reason he thought.

Chapter Thirty-Three

THREE HOURS LATER, SOFT MOONLIGHT FELL THROUGH THE curtains, highlighting Alex's body on the bed like a lover's caress. Elaina hated to do this to him, but it was the only way to prevent him from following her. The only way to protect him from her father. The only way to keep him alive so they'd have a chance at staying together forever.

She opened his laptop in front of his sleeping form, the tickets to New York she'd purchased for him displayed on the screen. That was the carrot to get him to do what he needed to do. The letter in her hand was the stick, an attack on the core of his abandonment fears in her heartbreaking attempt to convince him that he didn't have a choice.

The woodcarving he'd made for her a few days earlier leaned against the laptop. She longed to bring the small, vaguely dragon-shaped lump with her, but then he'd know how much she treasured the flawed chunk of wood. How much she treasured him.

Logically, she knew she should leave the engagement ring behind as well, but she couldn't do it. The reminder of what she hoped to return to, hoped to save, was her source of strength in carrying out this plan. With luck, he'd assume she'd taken his mother's ring simply because of its diamonds.

"Goodbye, Alex," she breathed, quieter than a whisper, and tucked the letter full of heartache beside him.

If their relationship was real, it would survive this lie.

She silently gathered her things and left the cottage behind. A stop at the island's greenhouse provided plastic sheeting for waterproofing, and she took the opportunity to reorganize her laptop bag. Traveling light and leaving no trace meant everything had to fit in this one case: laptop, phone, cash, the fake IDs and credit cards she'd never used in front of Alex, and whatever clothes she could stuff inside.

After covering herself with all the coins that didn't fit into her overflowing lockbox, she changed into her swimsuit. The clothes for later this morning went on top of the laptop bag, and she wrapped the plastic sheet around the pile, over and over, until watertight. Next, she needed to deal with her lockbox.

Down in the pitch-black underwater cave, the faint blue glow still shining from her eyes enhanced the night vision she naturally possessed from growing up in a cavern. She set the metal box on the shelf next to the remains of the pirate chest and opened the lid to her treasure.

Her talisman flickered in the low light. She picked up the palm-sized ruby and held it to her heart. "I'm not leaving you. I'm not abandoning you. I'm hiding you in a safe place."

She unburied the ruby necklace and fastened it around her neck while continuing to strengthen the bond to her talisman. "I'm bringing your friend with me so we can stay in contact. But it's too dangerous for all of you to go where I'm going. I need to know you're safe so I can do what I have to do."

She touched her talisman to the necklace, and the two gems cemented their connection to her and to each other. "I *will* come back for you."

Once she was certain her talisman understood her intentions, she placed the precious stone back into the lockbox. Hopefully, her discovery of the rubies' affinity for each other would hold even over thousands of miles. If not, this was going to be a short trip.

Other dragons had to have a way to leave their collections and yet tap into the full power of their hoard. Maybe this technique was part of the Dragon 101 training she'd missed by leaving early.

She grabbed a few of the lesser energy pieces, which might come in handy for bribes or extra cash, and the first gift from Alex, the diamond tennis bracelet. The extra room gave the coins stuck to her body a place to go. She added the silver discs to the safe and closed the lid. The combination locks wouldn't protect her treasure from someone desperate to get inside, but only Alex knew of this cave.

She double-checked the plastic wrap around her laptop case and strung it across her body, messenger-bag style. Her lungs filled with air, she lowered herself into the water again.

Outside the cave, moonlight filtered through the waves above her. Walking to the main island along the sea floor was easier than attempting to swim. Even so, moving through the dense water took longer than she hoped.

Time wasn't on her side for this part of her escape. She needed to get to Marsh Harbour before Alex awoke and thought he had a chance to catch her.

She monitored the surface for any boats, both for hitchhiking purposes and for Alex. But none passed overhead.

The physical exertion made her lungs ache for oxygen by the time she climbed onto Abaco Island, and she sucked in huge gulps of air. Luckily, the plastic wrap had done the trick, even after the long walk, and the clothes piled against the outside of her bag were dry. The dark night hid her change out of her swimsuit.

Once dressed, she stretched her senses to hunt for any metal on the water. One boat hull caught her attention a half mile down the coast. It didn't feel like the *Buttercup* or the *Revenge*. Maybe she could save herself the twelve-mile trek to the Marsh Harbour marina.

Her jog down the beach revealed she was on a barrier island, not Abaco Island proper. Damn. Would she have to rewrap her bag and change clothes again?

Her worry about how to get to the main island for the next step of her plan sharpened when she neared the metal hull she'd sensed. The vessel wasn't tied up to shore. Instead, the boat drifted in the sea several hundred feet away. Could she still get to the boat somehow and save herself the trouble of transferring off this barrier island and hiking to Marsh Harbour?

"Help! Is someone out there? I need help."

"Hal-lo?" A man's voice drowsily answered in an unfamiliar accent. A tourist, probably.

"Over here." She decided to go for blonde hair, and she carried her shoes and splashed a few feet into the waves. "I need help."

A sputtering motor churned, and the moonlight revealed a deep-sea fishing boat coming into view. The man at the helm sized her up with a leer. "What are you doing out here in the dark all by your lonesome, sugar?"

She hugged herself tight and bounced on her toes, faking worry. "Please, can you take me to Marsh Harbour?"

He stretched, peering behind her. "You running away from something?"

Latching onto this man was a risk, but she didn't have a choice if she didn't want to take the time—time she didn't have—to wade to Abaco Island and hike to Marsh Harbour. At least his obvious interest made her job easier, now that her time with Alex had honed her flirting skills.

"My father." She tilted her head and fluttered her eyelashes. "Will you please help me? You'd be my hero."

His lips curled into an unattractive smile. "Of course, sugar. Come on up."

She stepped farther into the water and let him help her aboard. Beer cans and chip bags littered the deck. The guy was probably living on the boat during his fishing vacation.

He eased out the throttle and popped open a beer for a pre-dawn breakfast. "Marsh Harbour, huh? What's in Marsh Harbour?"

"An airport. I need to escape before he hurts me."

"Oh now, why would anyone want to hurt such a sweet young thang? You sit right here next to ol' Phil, and I'll protect you."

She ignored his invitation and cast a faux-worried glance over the back of the boat. "Can this boat go faster?"

"Sure can, sugar." He revved the engine. "Let me show you how much power I've got for you."

His innuendos were tolerable as long as she was getting what she wanted. But right as they neared the lights of Marsh Harbour, he finished off his beer and cut the motor.

She stifled a groan. Of course he was going to try something.

He swaggered toward her, a hungry look in his eye, and started sliding down his shorts. "I'll take my payment for being your hero now."

The engine restarted just as he lifted one leg out of his shorts.

"What the—" He spun around and stumbled to the ignition key.

The motor spluttered more than it had before—she couldn't mentally control all its metal pieces and parts well—but the boat slowly carried them closer to land. Her would-be assailant didn't notice their approach, his concentration solely on the misbehaving engine. She braced for impact before the boat knocked against a half-submerged boulder.

Clunk.

Off balance and hobbled by the swimsuit around his ankles, the guy fell to the deck. While he was disoriented, she heaved him overboard.

"Bitch!" He splashed, his arms flailing in every direction, but got his feet under him. Lucky for him, the water was too shallow to let him drown. "What the hell you think you're doing?"

Despite his wild strokes, he closed in on the boat.

She grasped the wheel and steered away from the boulder. As she passed him on the other side of her circle, she threw an empty beer can at him and let her glowing eyes shine through her façade.

"You shouldn't drink and drive. Leads to hallucinations."

The guy recoiled enough that she had time to turn the ignition key before he reached the side. The motor now puttered more happily, and she had a chance to figure out how to work the boat.

Although she'd told the man she was running for the airport, the truth was that short of stealing an aircraft, no flights left from Marsh Harbour soon enough for her purposes. And her chances of being able to fly a stolen plane were somewhere between nil and none.

Boats were easier to operate. The only question was whether she'd take advantage of that slimeball and use this boat, or whether she should steal a different boat from the marina. A check of the fuel gauge told her the next stop needed to be the marina no matter what.

By the time she pulled up to the fuel pump on the marina's dock, she'd gotten a feel for the boat's controls. Meant to be a rental for fishing vacations, this craft was perfect for someone who didn't know what they were doing. Someone like her.

It wasn't the fastest thing she could get her hands on, but the ability to make it do what she wanted was important too. The fact that stealing a different boat—one whose owner hadn't done anything wrong—would twist her insides had nothing to do with her decision.

Nothing at all.

She snorted. Even *she* didn't believe her lies anymore. That fact had everything to do with her decision. Her time with Alex had irrevocably changed her, and she didn't want to change back.

More to the point, she wasn't *really* leaving him. She was just making him think she was. So her promise to follow human rules still applied.

On that note, she slid some cash under the door of the fuel and snack shop after filling the boat's tank. The old-fashioned pump's levers and switches had made it easy for her to turn on the flow of fuel without an employee in sight.

Next stop, Freeport. Most flights to the mainland went through Nassau, which meant if Alex chased her, Freeport would be safer. Freeport had one non-stop flight each morning to Fort Lauderdale, Florida. Like her decision to go through Freeport, Fort Lauderdale wasn't where they'd stopped before. Every choice was about trying to do what Alex wouldn't expect.

The waves were choppier than when they'd come through weeks before, and the dim light of sunrise made it impossible to see well, but she plowed through the breaking swells as fast as she could. Even though she pushed the engine, she reached the canals of the Queen's Cove neighborhood of Freeport with precious little time to spare. The subdivision was the closest place to dock a boat near the airport.

She killed the engine, left the keys in the ignition, and adjusted her bag across her chest before jumping onto shore. Her landing wobbled, and she took a second to get her land-legs back. A car approached on the main highway up ahead, and she scrambled to get there in time. The driver passed by her—and her thumb. She was about to make its engine quit when another car pulled up next to her.

An older woman with skin even darker than Uncle Lenny rolled down the window. "Where you going, chall?"

"The airport. My rental broke down, and I don't want to miss my flight." She bit her lip. Normally, she wouldn't let her desperation show. "I have money."

The woman swept her hand dismissively. "That's not but three minutes down the road. In with you, chall."

Elaina didn't argue. Sure enough, they arrived at the airport before the woman could interrogate her. After a sincere "Thank you," Elaina sprinted to the ticket counter.

Confirming her earlier research, seats were still available even though the plane was a small turboprop. Most tourists probably opted for the afternoon flight to extend their vacation for as long as possible.

An hour later, she sat heavily in a chair at her gate in the Fort Lauderdale airport. In her grasp was a one-way ticket for a non-stop flight to New York, where she'd find a way to get her father's attention right before she boarded for Europe.

More importantly, she'd be over North Carolina before the first flights from Marsh Harbour arrived. And that was if Alex guessed she'd come here rather than Miami.

Only one thing could stop her now. If Alex had seen—and remembered—her other fake identities, he might be able to pull strings to keep her in the States. But to do that, he'd probably need George's help.

She checked the time on her phone. Five minutes until they started boarding. That was time enough to see if George was on her side.

He picked up on the first ring. "Elaina?"

"Yes."

She waited. Would he quiz her on where she was?

At his sigh, she asked the only question that mattered. "Is he on his way to the plant, or is he chasing me?"

"He's not functional enough to chase you. What the hell did you tell him?"

Her eyes burned, and sharp pain shot through her, as if her ribcage had split open. She sank deeper into her chair, and cold crawled up her limbs. That answer was what she hoped for.

And what she'd dreaded.

Chapter Thirty-Four

ALEX GAZED BLANKLY AT HIS COMPUTER SCREEN IN HIS corporate office. Months of insomnia had taken its toll. His instincts for business strategy had strengthened his companies back into top form, but the rest of his life was consumed by a new obsession. The hope of finding Elaina was the only thing that kept him going at all.

Her absence had ripped away any sense of meaning from his life. Everything that had felt special in his life—special about him—had vanished. Without her, he was nothing.

Even the success of his Safe Home, Safe Child Foundation in breaking ground for domestic violence shelters across the state couldn't distract him. Each official function he attended served only as a reminder that he wished he could share the accomplishment with the one who'd gotten away.

The text streaming across his monitor confirmed his inability to leave the situation alone. His computer ran continuous internet searches on countless words: Elaina, Drake, Volus, Albania, dragon, jewelry, gold, silver, gem, theft, stolen, the description of every piece of her treasure he knew of, the fake name she'd used for their travels last fall, and anything else he could think of in every European language.

Whenever three or more keywords came up in an article, his search program flagged it for him to check. But months had passed with no trace.

The uncertainty of whether she was alive or dead killed him more each day.

The last record of her was a security photo taken at JFK airport the afternoon she'd left him. Despite her paranoia that had prevented him from having any pictures of her, much less of them together, she'd stood in front of a security camera at an Air France gate with a large sign that read *Këtu kam ardhur.* "Here I come" in Albanian.

The stunt had landed her in several newspapers and online news sites. Homeland Security had searched for her to see if she was a threat. They hadn't found her either. No doubt, however, her message to her father had been received.

A printed copy of that picture—one of the few pieces of evidence left behind of her existence—lay on his desk. Under that was her letter to him, the final proof of their life together. Together with the *A & E* ring he still wore, they seemed to hint at a hidden meaning beyond his grasp.

Or he liked to think so. Hoped so.

His eyes stung from staring at the screen, where he scanned search results long after everyone else had gone home for the day. He rubbed his eyelids and forced his shoulders back to prevent them from tensing up after his workout.

The strenuous gym routine was the other half of his obsession. He wanted to believe she'd gone to Europe to enact the harebrained idea she'd mentioned their last night together—steal the hoard of an elderly dragon. The workouts and internet searches were his way of helping her. He'd be prepared when she was ready to go up against her father.

But if that plan was her intention, why had she written the letter?

The letter. The essence of all his fears laid bare. The bitter truth that echoed the loudest voice in the back of his mind, which suspected she really *had* broken up with him.

At first, he'd hoped she'd written the note simply to make sure he did what she wanted—come back and take care of his companies. And he'd done that. Months ago.

If that was the explanation, why hadn't he heard from her?

His fingertips pressed on his temples. It didn't help. Getting angry at her cold "Dear John" method of leaving him wouldn't fix the situation.

Every accusation she'd written was one hundred percent accurate. He was the one who'd let things spin out of control.

Unable to help himself, he slid the photo across his desk, uncovering the letter. The words swam in front of his eyes, but they'd burned themselves into his memory.

Dear Alex,

By the time you read this letter, I'll be long gone. I can't stay with you any longer.

When we first met, you were strong. I liked that. I thought your strength would make us a good match. You're not strong anymore. Instead of spending your time building an empire, you're whittling scraps of wood.

When we first met, I was weak and needed to get strong. I thought you understood my needs. Instead, you've held me back from getting stronger, as though you thought rewarding me like a dog for good behavior would be acceptable. It's not.

I denied the truth for a long time, but I can't ignore it anymore. We don't belong together.

Don't bother to look for me. You're not good for me, and this is goodbye.

Elaina

Manipulation or not, her words scalded his heart every minute of every day. His attention landed on the woodcarving he'd made for her during their time on the island. The dragon sculpture seemed to mock him, but he hung on to it as a reminder of how special she was.

And how much he'd screwed up.

She'd told him that she suffered by not stealing, but he'd asked it of her anyway. The trinkets he'd given her *were* like a reward for obedience.

And then on the island, she'd nearly died in her attempt to

follow those rules. His rules.

Once again disrespecting her differences, he'd never accepted that she might *need* to steal sometimes. No, worse than that. He'd tried to control her.

A dragon. That had to be the stupidest thing ever attempted.

He'd ended up no better than his father.

Chapter Thirty-Five

ELAINA ZIPPED THE SKI JACKET UP TO HER CHIN. BITTER WIND swept down her neck anyway. Snowflakes stung her cheeks as she searched store windows in the fading light for a Wi-Fi sign.

Somewhere in this one-main-street village, there *had* to be one. Finally, a little pub claimed to have an internet signal.

The deep red walls and low ceiling made the small room look cozier than the reality of the cool indoor temperature, but being inside was better than being out in the blizzard. Fate was a twisted mistress, forcing a weak, immature dragon to explore mountainous territory in the dead of winter.

She missed Alex's heat—his everything. At this point, she had a better chance of freezing to death than dying by her father's hand.

She fumbled through ordering a coffee with her limited command of Hungarian. Most places didn't mind giving her the Wi-Fi password as long as she ordered something. Coffee was usually cheap, and more importantly, hot. She couldn't drink the stuff, but the mug warmed her hands.

Her laptop screen glowed to life with a map of the Carpathian Mountain range, and she marked off the regions she'd checked during the day.

Normally, that activity would give her a sense of accomplishment. Not today.

Today, the unchecked sections seemed larger than the checked areas. No, not *seemed.* They *were* larger.

And she had no resources left to continue. The situation was hopeless.

For the thousandth time, she debated her options. She could sell the car and hope to get a fraction of her money back—and save on gas too—but buses didn't go into the mountainous depths where undiscovered caves hid.

What was she supposed to do? Walk everywhere? That'd add months to her efforts.

Then for each extra day, she'd have to pay for a bed at a hostel or rooming house. Sleeping in a cold car would kill her, and sleeping in the open would do the same twice as fast.

Jobs required documents, which she'd have to buy to fake her legal right to work, and any time on a job would seriously cut into her time left to search. And with her traveling to different locations every few days to clear areas, she'd spend more time searching for short-term jobs than searching for caves.

The only option left was stealing, and that path led to a dead end if she was ever going to have a chance at earning Alex's forgiveness.

Before despair could drive her insane, she pulled out the European mobile phone she'd purchased and dialed the one person with whom she was still on speaking terms.

He answered on the first ring. "You're alive. Glad to hear that."

"So am I, George. So am I." If only he knew how uncertain that was.

"That bad, huh?"

"Remind me again what I'm doing here."

"I don't know. You refuse to tell me."

Even their standard opening banter didn't lighten her depression. She sagged into the bench and traced the red-and-white-checked pattern on the seat.

"Elaina, what *are* you doing there?" His words rushed from the phone. "I know you can't tell me what's going on, and that's okay, but if you don't have a plan for how to resolve things..." The speaker crackled with his sigh. "Well, maybe you should come home."

Home. How could one little word have so much power? Her

fingertip turned the square pattern into endless circles. Swirling, swirling, never getting anywhere. Stuck with no way out.

"Has the FBI captured everyone behind the explosion?" She knew the answer already, as George would have told her if they had. "As much as I'd love nothing more than to come back, I can't. We'd be in the same situation as when I left."

"Isn't there anything I can do to help? I promise I won't press you for details beyond what you're able to tell me."

"I—" She cut off her automatic response.

The last of her money sat too lightly in her pocket, but the memory of her last pawnshop visit burned her cheeks.

"I don't deserve your help."

"What? You're doing God-knows-what in God-knows-where all to protect Alex. How could you *not* deserve my help?"

"Because I sold my diamond tennis bracelet, the first gift Alex bought for me." Her throat thickened, straining her voice. "I'd brought it with me to remind myself of everything he'd done for me, not to sell it like a meaningless trinket."

"And you sold it because..." He trailed off, prompting.

Her pent-up frustration exploded in an aggravated burst.

"I didn't have a choice. I've maxed out my credit cards and sold off everything else I brought with me. Unless I started stealing things, I had to sell the bracelet or give up. This whole trip has turned out to be a bigger wild goose chase than I thought. I mean, who would have thought it'd be so damn hard to find an occupied cave in Europe? But *no*, they have to be all secretive and not put up 'Treasure for the Taking Here' signs. Stupid, paranoid dra—"

She coughed, covering up her words before she said too much. Idiot.

A guy watching hockey on the TV over the bar shushed her.

George didn't comment on her coughing fit. "Okay, I have no idea about half of what you just said—and I don't think I want to know—but I gathered that you're short of money. I can help with that."

"Didn't you hear me? I don't deserve it. I took something Alex gave me out of love or whatever, and I used it to pay for gas money and five-dollar-a-night beds so I wouldn't freeze."

"Uh-huh. You sold a bracelet that he can easily replace so you could survive another day. Sorry, not going to let you blame your-self for that."

She groaned. "Sometimes you're as stubborn as he is."

"Thank you." The smile in his voice carried over the mobile signal.

She didn't bother granting him a reply.

"So how can I get more money to you? Should I wire some to you? Should I pay off these credit cards for you? Tell me."

A quiet whisper fell from her lips. "Why do you want to help me?"

"Because, Elaina"—his tone turned her name into a sigh—"I want you to succeed with whatever you're doing so you can come home."

"Why?"

"Because..." He paused, seriousness coloring his answer. "Alex will never recover until you do."

She'd avoided asking how Alex was doing during these occasional phone calls. The last thing she needed was more guilt. But now, she couldn't help her question.

"Is it that bad?"

"It's worse. He's just going through the motions of living. Zombies are more alive than he is."

So she hadn't imagined his abandonment issues. Her insight into how to hurt him the most had served its purpose.

He had too many resources at his disposal to believe that she could ever cover her tracks well enough, so the only way to protect him was to ensure he didn't *want* to follow her. Even though that emotional pain was what she'd been counting on for keeping him safe at home, she still hated herself.

The diamond on her left ring finger chose that moment to catch her eye, and her chest seized as though she'd been stabbed. Several of the pawnshops she'd visited over the last couple of months had tried to get her to sell the ring from Alex's mother. She'd die first.

"I didn't want to break him, but I had to convince him to give up on us so he wouldn't follow me into a dangerous situation. I did it to protect him. I swear I never wanted to hurt him."

"I know you didn't mean it, but that's the reality. And that's why I want to do what I can to help bring you home faster."

"Do you think—?" She stopped, unsure if she wanted to know whether Alex would ever forgive her.

Instead, she asked the question that had haunted many of her internet searches. "Is Dakon Industries doing okay?"

"Around the office, we had a long-running joke that Alex could run ten companies in his sleep. We're learning how true that is. From a business perspective, he's better than fine."

Lightness in her chest released the air from her lungs. "That's good. Really good to hear."

At least her leaving to prevent one corporate crisis hadn't caused another.

"Listen, I haven't called or bothered you, and I haven't asked for anything from you because I know how much you've already sacrificed, but I'm going to insist on this. You have to let me help you."

"Would you really be able to keep it from Alex?"

He *tsk*'ed. "Such little faith you have."

The whirr of a drawer opening and the click of a pen carried through the phone.

His throat cleared, making his tone sound even more stubborn. "All right, give me those credit card numbers."

After she dug through her bag and rattled off the numbers from her various fake-name cards, he tapped on his keyboard. "Just in case they give me trouble paying those off for you, tell me where you're going to be tomorrow so I can send money directly."

She almost scoffed at his deceit. More likely, he'd try to do *both* the credit cards and a money transfer.

When she didn't answer, he made a sad *oh* noise. "You don't trust me enough to tell me where you are, do you?"

"That's not it. I—"

"So you'll tell me where you'll be tomorrow?"

She groaned at his double-layered trickery. "I don't even know where I am, to be honest. Some little town in Hungary with, like, twenty letters in the name."

"Hungary?"

"Yeah, I'm in the Bükk Mountains."

His keyboard clicked for a moment. "It looks as though the post offices there accept money transfers. Find out where you are, and

I'll have some cash waiting for you when they open tomorrow morning."

"There's a fine line between stubbornness and being annoying."

"You should know. You can thank me by bringing back a hot European guy for me."

She snorted in laughter.

"According to Google Translate, you should ask '*Mi ez a város?*'"

"And I'm supposed to believe you? You're probably having me tell them to put me in jail until you get here."

"Good idea. Let me look that up." He chuckled. "No, my dear girl, that's 'what is this town?'"

She groaned. "Fine. Hang on while I ask someone."

The bartender's answer didn't help, as it sounded like a long, consonant-heavy word, but he rewarded her attempt to speak their language by writing down the name for her.

After she spelled it three times for George, he took control of the conversation. "Feel better now?"

"Yes, I do. Thank you." It would be nice not to worry about money for a while.

"Do you have a plan for what you're going to do next?"

Her other worries returned. The banter with George had been a fun diversion, but the truth was that she didn't have a clue how to make her searching more efficient.

"Not really. All I can do is keep exploring. Eventually, I'll find what I'm searching for."

"Yeah, a cave or something, whatever. Can't someone there help you find it?"

Not likely. If humans had seen any dragons in their serpent form, her internet searches would have discovered it. No, the only ones who knew where to find the dragons were the dragons themsel—

Of course.

She *did* know where one dragon other than her father lived. She'd never steal treasure from her old teacher, Nastav, but maybe she could convince him to point her toward another dragon.

In fact, that might have been her subconscious's plan all along, explaining why she'd chosen to start in his home turf of the Carpathian Mountain range, rather than the Alps or somewhere else.

"Elaina? You there?"

"Yeah, and you gave me an idea. Thanks." Maybe she could figure this out after all.

"Excellent. Now remember that I like my men tall."

Her giddy laugh came easily now. "Tall. Got it."

"Okay, I'll let you go work on your cave project, but remember to pick up your money tomorr—oh." *Click.*

Odd. She stared at her phone, but the line was dead.

She debated calling him back. That was silly to do just so she could say goodbye, though. Instead, she brought up her map of the Carpathian Mountains.

Now she had a plan. Step one: Remember where she'd had her lessons with Nastav. Step two: Ask Nastav for help in finding another elderly dragon. Step three: Steal the treasure of said elderly dragon. Step four...

A charred taste rose up her throat. She hoped her father would leave her alone once she was stronger, the same way Alex's father had left him alone once it was a fair fight between them. But she couldn't count on the same psychology working. After all, her mother had been a full-dragon, and that hadn't prevented her death.

What would she do if her father wouldn't stop threatening her simply because she became a full-dragon? Or if she couldn't convince him to stop hurting Alex through proxy thugs?

She had to be prepared for the worst. If he didn't relent, the only way to protect Alex, the only way she could ever feel safe in returning to him, would be to give up her vow of non-violence long enough to get rid of the threat for good. Or die trying.

Her chest sank under the cold weight of facts, and she wrapped her arms around her ribs. But there was no escape from the truth of what she had to do.

Step four. Be prepared to kill her father.

Chapter Thirty-Six

THE VOICEMAIL ON ALEX'S PHONE CONFIRMED WHAT HE already knew.

"I'm sorry I couldn't make our lunch meeting today, Mr. Wyatt. Can we reschedule?"

Wasn't going to happen. No-shows were high on his list of those he didn't have the patience to deal with under normal circumstances, and the wasted trip in the middle of his day had worsened his mood.

He stopped at his secretary's empty desk and left a note to avoid rescheduling Mr. Townsend unless he had an excellent excuse. Alien abduction might qualify.

George's voice carried across the reception area from his office. For a second, Alex thought he heard him say "Elaina," but his mind constantly played tricks on him. That was one of the hazards of not sleeping enough—and having an obsession.

Alex stood outside George's office to tease him about working through his lunch hour.

George's attention was on his computer monitor. "Okay, I'll let you go work on your cave project, but remember to pick up your money tomorr—" He spotted Alex. "Oh."

He hung up the phone and closed a spiral notebook. "You're back from your lunch meeting already."

"A no-show."

Alex strode into George's office. The man moved his mouse and changed his screen. Was that behavior as suspicious as it seemed, or was this more mind tricks due to lack of sleep?

He pressed on his temple, but nothing could help his tenuous grasp on *normal.* "Something important going on to keep you from lunch?"

"No, a friend of mine is building a man-cave over his garage, and he wanted my advice. Like a *Queer Eye for the Straight Guy* thing." He shut down his computer. "I'm going to get food. Do you want anything?"

Did George usually turn off his computer when he left for lunch?

"No, I'm good. I ate while I was waiting at the restaurant."

"Smart." George grabbed his coat—and the notebook. "Okay, I'll see you in a few."

That was definitely unusual. George hated holding anything in his hands. He'd never carry around a notepad unless he had his laptop bag to slip it into later.

"Take your time."

George gave him a double take. "Is everything all right? I can order in if you need something."

Alex returned to the reception area and motioned to George from the doorway of his own office. "Go enjoy your lunch. Just remember we have the Powell meeting at two."

George's features relaxed, which only emphasized how tense he was before. "Sure thing, boss."

Alex turned his back to the man and sat at his desk. On his computer, he logged into the security camera feed and tracked George's progress to the elevator. He'd made security give him access a few years ago when paparazzi started trying to sneak onto his office floor.

Right as Alex switched over to the elevator feed, George glanced up at the camera, as though wondering if he was being watched. The man clutched the notepad tighter and strode out to the lobby on the first floor.

Lobby feed, lobby feed. Where the hell were the lobby cameras in the pull-down menu?

By the time he found them in the computer application, he was sure he'd missed George, yet there he was, buttoning up his coat and strolling outside. What had he done in the meantime? He was walking from a different direction than the elevators, and the notebook was nowhere to be seen.

Alex waited a minute to make sure George didn't double back, and then he called the lobby reception desk.

"How may I help you, Mr. Wyatt?"

"Did George talk to you while he was downstairs?"

"No, sir. Was he supposed to?"

"No, I'll take care of it. Thank you."

Either his obsession and sleep deprivation were turning into paranoia, or George *had* been acting suspiciously. The question would add to his fixation if he didn't discover the answer.

Alex went down to the lobby and stood in the same spot he'd last seen George, facing in the same direction. He spun around and tried to guess where the man had come from and what he might have been doing.

"Something I can help you with, Mr. Wyatt?"

He waved toward the lobby desk without taking his eyes off his target. "No, thank you."

The restroom? They were down that hallway, and if George suspected he was being watched, that'd be the only option without cameras.

Alex entered the bathroom. Empty. Most of the building was probably at lunch.

He removed the lid to the garbage can nearest the door. A notebook, which looked exactly like George's, sat on top of the pile of crumbled paper towels. Alex picked up the notepad.

Shreds of paper dangled from the spiral coil. He didn't remember seeing them in the notebook earlier.

Perhaps George had torn out a sheet of notes he wanted to keep before tossing the rest of the pad. If so, that was definitely suspicious.

Who would throw away a notebook when it had almost all of its pages? Only someone who couldn't stand to carry the whole notepad around, but needed to keep something on one of the sheets.

Alex tilted the top page to the light. No indentations left behind that he could see.

A few of the paper shreds fell from the spiral. Several chunks remained. Chunks. As in, more than one sheet had been ripped out.

Another garbage can on the other side of the sinks caught his eye. Would George have been that paranoid?

Alex replaced the lid for the first can and uncovered the second. Sure enough, several blank pages lay scattered over the top.

"George, you're a smart man, but not smart enough to out-think me this time."

He retrieved the pages and put them back into the notepad for safekeeping. At least one of the sheets had indentations, but he didn't want to risk messing up the evidence by running a pencil over it himself. After reassembling the second can and washing up, he called Governor Boyce's personal cell.

It was probably bad form to call the governor from a restroom—even while standing at the sinks—but he didn't care. Other than returning to his office, this was the best place for privacy.

"Alex, it's good to hear from you. To what do I owe this pleasure?"

"I need a favor, Roger."

"I believe I still owe you one for your security team's success with my wife's necklace last fall. What kind of favor are we talking about?"

"I need a couple of pages analyzed to see what was written on the sheet above them."

The man harrumphed. "That's an odd request. You mean like a forensic thing?"

"Yes. And I need them analyzed as soon as possible." It was overkill to go to the governor for this, but he didn't have the patience to deal with bureaucracy right now.

"Shouldn't be a problem. Let me make a few calls, and I'll get back to you."

After Roger hung up, Alex stared into the mirror over the sink. The face that looked back at him was nearly unrecognizable. The combination of poor sleep, his obsession, and the energy he now felt to solve this mystery left him resembling a reanimated corpse. If anyone knew how much worse his mental state was than his body's condition, he'd be committed.

His control over his emotions was more tenuous than ever, and he scrubbed his cheeks, pushing his chaotic thoughts below the surface. The motion brought something George had said to mind, something that would help him figure this out, but the specifics floated tantalizingly out of reach.

"Tell me." He struck the mirror. "Tell me what I need to know."

He pounded on his image, as though he could grab the memory from his double. The glass shattered under his fists. Fragments tinkled into the sink and pinged across the tile floor.

He jumped back from the shards, his hands empty of glass or answers. Jagged wedges of silver clung to the wall beyond the point of his attack. The remaining frame of sharp slices pierced the outline of his reflection, imitating the constant assault on his sanity.

He'd done that? Pinpricks of blood decorated the side of his hands.

Cold radiated from his core through his limbs. The evidence of his outburst surrounded him. He *had* done that. His grasp on his control was even worse than he'd feared.

He probably should be more concerned about his failure to restrain himself, but it was easier to chalk up his short temper to poor sleep. These slips didn't indicate a bigger problem. Did they?

Dismissing the question, he refocused on the immediate issue. Either he was completely losing his mind, or his assistant was trying very hard to hide something from him.

Neither option was good. And it was entirely possible that both were true.

Chapter Thirty-Seven

FIFTEEN MINUTES LATER, ALEX SENT JAMES TO THE FORENSIC Science Center at Chicago with the pages, a call from Governor Boyce clearing the way for a rush job. By the time George returned from lunch, Alex was at his desk and ready to pretend he was his normal put-together self *and* clueless about the man's duplicity.

In the middle of their two o'clock meeting, Alex's personal cell phone vibrated with a text. The lawyers for the purchase agreement of his latest business acquisition droned on, and George was busy marking up the negotiation's paperwork.

Alex held his phone under the edge of the table and read the message from James.

Have data. Doing research.

As soon as the meeting ended, Alex shut himself in his office and called his driver.

"What did you find out?"

"The scientists were able to pull several impressions off the paper—one foreign word and five strings of numbers. So far, we've discovered that the word is the name of a small town in Hungary, and—"

"Hungary?"

"Yeah, some place in the northeastern mountains. And we're

starting to analyze the numbers right now."

Hungary. Mountains. The clue that had teased him earlier came into view. *Cave.* He'd heard George say the word *cave.*

Only one person he could think of would have reason to go to the mountain caves of Europe. Elaina.

Had he *not* imagined George saying her name? New suspicions rose in his thoughts. Perhaps George had been in contact with her this whole time.

If so, she was still alive.

Alex sank into his chair, and his thoughts settled into a less shaky impression of sanity. Thank God. He'd hoped with every conscious and subconscious thought that she was safe, but the silence had dragged on for long enough that hope seemed dangerous.

Weight lifted off his shoulders, only to settle in his gut. George was *his* personal assistant. He was supposed to be unquestionably loyal to Alex, not flat-out deceiving him—hiding something *this* important—for months.

What the hell was going on?

"Tell me one of the numbers." The way James broke the long string into chunks for Alex to jot down the numbers triggered a thought. "Is it a credit card account number?"

"This one *is* sixteen digits." Rustling sounds erupted from the speaker as James adjusted the phone on his end. "See if those are credit card numbers."

A moment later, a woman's voice carried from the background. "It looks like it. We'll have to get in touch with the issuers to find the account owners."

James returned to the line. "I'll call you back as soon as we have the information."

"Thanks, James." At least there was one person he could still trust.

The betrayal burned in his chest. He'd been doing those internet searches for months so he could find her and help her, and here George and Elaina were colluding behind his back.

Even if she *was* trying to get away from him as her letter said, she shouldn't have stolen George's allegiance.

He uncovered her letter and spread his fingers over the paper.

The diamonds in the ring she'd made for him sparkled, focusing his thoughts even further.

For the first time, he might be close to tracking her down. He'd assumed he would go after her when that happened, but she seemed to be doing everything possible to avoid him. Should he stay away or force his help?

Unlike before, he now respected her strengths and needs as a dragon. She was no damsel in distress waiting for rescue.

But her problems with the pirate treasure remained sharp in his mind. She'd *needed* him to take control—while still following her lead.

He could be that way for her again, embracing his dominant temperament enough to be there *for* her. Her rock, her support, her protector. Not swooping in and trying to take control *from* her.

He'd rather she was alive and hating him for being there than if she was dead and alone.

His phone rang like the starting bell accompanying his decision.

"You have something, James?"

"We're still working on the rest, but we have information for one of the cards. Does the name Linda Jones mean anything to you?"

Linda Jones. He leaned forward, digging the information from the recesses of his memory.

Of course. Elaina had used the name for her job with that catering company last year. He'd forgotten about that fake identity of hers.

"Yes, it does. Anything else?"

"The card issuer had already flagged the account as one to watch because of suspicious activity. Gas purchases and lodging charges all over Europe, and then this afternoon, the account was paid off by a third party."

George. The pieces fell into place.

Was her father chasing her across Europe again? Why would she have left Alex's protection just to run straight to danger?

His heart wanted to believe her cat-and-mouse tactic was a sign that she still loved him. That like his mother, Elaina was expressing her love in a way he'd never expected.

But if she was attempting to distract her father simply to keep Alex safe, he couldn't stand by and watch. That plan was insane. It couldn't end well.

His mother had already sacrificed herself to save him, and he wouldn't let Elaina do the same. His decision to go to her hardened into a determined plan.

"Have the credit card companies keep me in the loop with new purchases on these."

"Should I ask them to put a hold on the accounts?"

"No, I want her using them."

"Got it. I'll let you know if we find anything else."

"Thanks, James."

He hung up and started searching for the fastest flights to Hungary. Whether she wanted it or not, he would be there for her.

Chapter Thirty-Eight

ELAINA TURNED OFF THE CAR AND PEERED UP AT THE LOW mountain range through the windshield. This edge of the Carpathian Mountains rose up more like gigantic hills than the other massive rocky formations she'd explored. From here, they didn't look promising, but her research had confirmed the existence of a cave-welcoming limestone base out there.

More importantly, the map's red dot claimed this was the place, even though this angle made her destination impossible to recognize. Every time she'd gone to Nastav's cave for her lessons, she'd ridden on her mother's back. Last night's studies of the satellite overlays for this area lined up with her memory of the various peaks and streams they'd flown over, so this was her best shot at finding his cave.

The blizzard had stopped during the night, leaving a pristine layer of snow on the ground. She laced her hiking boots and zipped up her jacket under her chin. A three-mile hike into the backcountry awaited her.

Before pulling on her gloves, she kissed the diamond on her ring finger and touched her ruby pendant. She owed a lot to the necklace from Alex. Its bond to her hoard had held up for months.

Good thing. If that part of her plan hadn't worked, she'd have been dead already.

"Wish me luck."

Her boots crunched prints into the snow as she climbed along

Jami Gold

the ravine from the faint trail she'd turned into a road. Sunshine warmed her face, and she shielded her eyes against the midday snow glare every couple of minutes to double-check her position. The outcropping she was aiming for still waited up ahead.

By the time she reached the rocky protrusion, she was certain this was the right place. At least, it *had* been where he'd kept his cave. Whether he was still here was another matter.

Her senses prickled as she rounded the outcropping and climbed into a side gorge toward the cave opening. Treasure. That was a good sign.

She pressed a palm against her sternum and let her head fall back on a deep breath. Honestly, that sensation was the best feedback she'd gotten yet that she *could* find another dragon. Maybe she could do this after all.

Tinkles sounded from dripping water, acting like a homing beacon for the cave entrance above her. Melting snow meant the cave was occupied. By a belly-full-of-fire, full-grown dragon. In dragon form.

Her steps slowed. She was walking into a dragon's cave without so much as a butter knife for a weapon.

Yet after coming this far, she forced her feet to move. Hopefully, her lack of armaments would help convince Nastav that she meant him no harm.

The small entrance was barely big enough for a person to wiggle through and led to a narrow tunnel, just how dragons preferred their homes. Tiny openings meant enemies couldn't surprise the cave's occupant in their dragon form. Only humans or those in human form could enter.

The tunnel wound down into the mountain's base for a quarter mile and then split into multiple passageways. This section looked familiar. Even without the heat flowing from the opening on the left, she'd know which one was her destination. If she remembered correctly, the other two paths formed a loop, leading nowhere.

She took the left fork and climbed a steep incline to the top of a subterranean cliff. The underground trail continued on a matching cliff on the other side of a wide abyss so deep and dark even her keen dragon eyesight couldn't make out the bottom.

This was where the rare human visitor would turn back. Only

serious cavers with ropes and rappelling equipment could hope to make it to the other side.

Of course, she had none of that gear. All she had was stubborn determination and a vague hope that she'd grown and strengthened in the years since her mother had helped her across the broad expanse.

Before nerves could take hold, she backed up several yards, ran, and pushed off the solid edge. *Thump.*

She landed hard on the far side, and pebbles skittered, echoing down the sheer drop. The chasm lay just behind her heel, and she teetered, almost slipping off the rim. She quickly shoved her balance forward.

Her wild leaning brought her to her knees, and her palms scraped over the cold, damp soil. Gravel ripped through her gloves. The torn fabric was better than the alternative.

That had been too close.

From this point, the path led down into the depths of the mountain's heart. Each step brought her closer to the treasure room and the pushback she felt from a dragon's ownership of the priceless artifacts. Her intention to *not* claim the hoard allowed her to press through the invisible, territorial barrier.

If it wasn't Nastav inside, this would be a very short visit.

Ahead of her, the tunnel opened into a cavernous room. She removed her gloves in the warm air and crept inside. Nothing happened.

In her native *Drakish* language, she called out. "Nastav? It is I, Elaina."

If it was Nastav, announcing herself should make her seem less threatening. And if it wasn't him, she was dead anyway.

His answer, breathy and rumbling, rolled around the cave's curving walls. "Come here, little one. Let me see you."

She rocked back and forth on her toes. So far, so good. His dragon-form voice was less strong than it had been years ago, but she recognized it regardless.

A dim orange glow emanating from the back of the cavern illuminated the loose hills of crowns, religious relics, and bejeweled swords she passed. Landslides of priceless artifacts accompanied her steps wherever she took shortcuts too close to the piled mountains.

At the far end of the cave, the light from Nastav's heart rippled from his belly like orange coals in a breeze. The smoldering radiance revealed him lying on a mound of coins separated from the rest of the treasure. This one collection of gold and silver was ten times larger than her old apartment.

She knelt prostrate at the edge of the low pile, the traditional Drakish greeting of a youngling to an elder coming easily to her lips. "Forgive me for disturbing you, Great One."

Heat blasted over her, fire erupting from Nastav's mouth.

Her chest tensed so quickly a cry squeaked out. She'd guessed wrong about Nastav. This was the end.

I'm sorry for everything, Alex.

But she didn't die. Instead, the cave exploded with light, the torches around the cave ignited by Nastav's flames.

"Rise, little one."

She stood on wobbly legs and faced the dragon. He was as big as she remembered, the size of a two-story house. The black parts of his body—the horns protruding from the top of his head, the frill along his spine, and his folded wings—contrasted with the dark blue of his scales and the armor plates running down his neck and belly.

It had been so long since she'd seen one of her own kind in dragon form she couldn't help staring. Evidence of his extreme age became more apparent the longer she studied him.

His wings drooped, their edges ragged. Instead of a bright royal blue, his scales were the dull, steel blue color of the Chicago River in winter. In places, patches of missing scales exposed soft tissue below.

She dropped her gaze. Interest in his poor health might be taken as a threat.

"Turn around. Let me look at you."

She did as she was told, despite the fact that she had to turn her back to the creature.

Once she faced him again, his blue eyes flashed.

"It is good to see you. When I heard about your parents, I feared the worst." He stretched out a foreleg and tapped a claw on the coins. "Sit. Tell me of your life."

She sat cross-legged on the rocky floor where she wouldn't accidentally touch his bed of treasure and seem aggressive.

"You feared the worst? What would have been worse than my father killing my mother?"

Smoke curled to the cave roof with his laugh. "If you had been killed, little one. The favorite of my students."

She dipped her chin, no longer too scared to take her eyes off him. "You are a good portion of my favorite memories as well."

After so many years around humans, Americans especially, the formal structure and limited vocabulary of the Drakish language sounded odd in her ears.

"Indulge an old one who does not get out anymore. Tell me of your journeys."

For the next couple of hours, she told him of her escape from her father, his continued hunt for her, and her eventual trip to the Americas. Her stories of the human world fascinated him, but most human inventions had no word in Drakish, so the telling took longer with her detailed descriptions to his questions.

"And now you have come back. Why?"

She slid her jacket's zipper up and down. Scorn awaited her for telling him the truth, but he'd always possessed an uncanny knack for detecting lies.

"I met someone in the United States. A human man. Alex knows what I am and loves me regardless. He was trying to help me get stronger, buying me jewelry to claim. But my father tracked me down and threatened Alex."

Instead of expressing disgust at her confession for latching onto a human, his eyes simply bore into hers.

A tense moment passed, and then he asked, "Do you love this human as well?"

She bounced to her feet. They refused to stay still, moving with itchy energy. "I–I cannot."

"Is that the truth? Or is that what you tell yourself?"

Her feet stuck to the rock. "Dragons cannot love. My mother was delusional."

"I have always loved you, little one. Will you dismiss me as a feeble old one the way you dismiss your mother?"

The cave blurred, and she blinked quickly. "I have always cared about you too. You are the best of the Great Ones."

"What do you think love is?"

She plopped down onto the cold stone, and her answer came out in a whisper. "I do not know what to think anymore."

Warmth wrapped around her with his slow laugh. "That is a start."

He stretched and curled his tail around his hind legs like a cat. "Volus might be watching the area, and yet you came. I am glad for your visit, but you did not come back for one last lesson from old Nastav. Why are you here?"

"I want to make things work with Alex, but to do that, I must convince my father to leave us alone."

"I fear that will not be so easy."

Her voice dropped, thickness choking her throat. "I worry I will have to kill my father."

A roar thundered through his words. "You are not strong enough for that."

"I know. Either way, I need to get more treasure first." She carved lines on the rocky floor with a fingernail. "And I do not have much time. I hurt Alex by leaving, and I do not know if he will forgive me, especially if I take too long to return to him."

"So you have come to kill me for my treasure?"

She scrambled backwards, hot itchiness filling her with nausea. "No! I would never kill you. I need to find an old one and take their hoard, yes. But not you. I just need your help finding one of the others."

Cli-cli-cli-clink, cli-cli-cli-clink. His claws tapped a repetitive rhythm on the coins, and the glow of his eyes dimmed.

"You think I would tell you where another Great One is so you could kill them?"

Oh... When he put it like that, her request sounded rather obscene.

Sure, she wasn't planning to *kill* a dragon to steal their treasure, but as Nastav's frailty proved, elderly dragons would *die* if their treasure were taken from them. The result would be the same, no matter how much she tried to distance herself from the act. She wouldn't need to wonder whether she had the emotional strength to kill her father because she would have already shattered her vow of non-violence with her theft.

"I am sorry. I should not have asked."

"No, you should not have."

His statement threw a bright light onto her selfishness. She'd expected another creature to give up their life so that she might enjoy hers.

She crumpled against her knees. "I am sorry. I did not know what else to do."

"Why did you come here?"

"I told you, I suspect I will need to kill my father so I can be with Alex."

"And why could you not be with him regardless?"

She stifled a groan at the circular conversation. "As I said, my father was threatening Alex."

"If your father had not done that, would you have stayed with Alex?" His Drakish accent turned the name into a hiss.

"Yes." Hadn't she just explained all this?

"So you came here *not* to kill your father. No, you left to protect Alex."

She rubbed her cheeks and peered into Nastav's unblinking gaze, waiting for his statement to make sense. The result would be the same either way. Killing someone was killing someone, right? There was no *good* way to look at that situation.

"Yes, little one, there is a difference." He seemed to understand her confusion better than she did. His powers of perception hadn't dimmed with age. "One is done out of vengeance, and the other is done out of love."

Her brain was still struggling to process his words when he stretched his long neck, putting her face-to-face with his sharp fangs.

"Do you hate your father?"

Weight pressed her shoulders down. Did she? The answer used to be easy, automatic.

"For the longest time, I did hate him."

"And now?"

"Once I met Alex, I was finally living my own life." Her fingertip stroked the ring on her hand. "My days were not simply about surviving, but about enjoying the present and imagining a future.

As to my father..."

She shrugged. "I think I pity him more than anything now."

"Pity?"

"Yes, because he had it all and lost it. Because even after my mother's murder, we did not have to come to this. Because someone loved him, and he did not treasure that as much as his gold."

Nastav touched his nose to hers, and then he curled his neck back and peered down at her. "Come embrace your great father one last time."

"Great father?"

"There are not many Drakish words for family. I am creating a new one. Volus, your father, is my son."

She whispered the word in English. "Grandfather."

He tried wrapping his large dragon tongue around the strange word. "Grandfather."

She climbed onto the mound of coins and draped her arms around his neck, speaking to him in Drakish once more. "I am proud to call you Great Father."

He rested his chin along her back. The sense of love and security coming off his body enveloped her like a blanket. There was no doubt that dragons *could* love.

"My great daughter, I have missed you. Seeing you one last time has made this old one very happy."

A few of his scales disintegrated at her touch. She pulled away and rubbed the powdery remains of his once-beautiful armor between her fingertips.

"You are not well, are you?"

He lowered his head and brought his eyes down to her level.

"Do not mourn for me. I have lived a full life. I have lived long enough to see the generations of our kind forget the Mythos homeland we lost to the faeries long ago. And I have lived long enough to see you as the one I hoped you would become."

"How can I help? I have a moving wagon. Should we get you more treasure?"

"To leave here, I would have to change into humanoid form. In that body, I would have died centuries ago. Only living in my dragon form, through which I can draw more strength from my collection, has kept my heart beating this long."

"Oh."

Spending time in their humanoid form shortened a dragon's lifespan? Her lack of knowledge about her own kind was appalling. No wonder she hadn't been successful in her searches.

Her muscles tensed at the thought of all the things she didn't know. Things she *needed* to know.

She wanted to know it all, but Nastav was dying right in front of her.

"There must be something I can do."

"Yes, my great daughter." He rolled onto his side, exposing his belly. "You can kill me."

Chapter Thirty-Nine

ELAINA RECOILED AND SLIPPED DOWN THE MOUND OF COINS. "No!"

Nastav ignored her. "You need treasure. I have no use for it any longer."

"It is not yet time for you to die. There is so much I need to learn."

"You have learned everything of importance. Giving my life in service to love is more than I had hoped."

"I will *not* do it."

"Even now, Volus is nearing this location, and I will not help you find another dragon in my place."

"Maybe I would rather die than kill you."

He gave an impatient snort. "Yes, I believe you would." A cloud of smoke puffed from his mouth in his version of a sigh. "Tell me, what is the significance of the ring on your hand? Why have you not claimed it?"

Against her will, her focus landed on her engagement ring. "It is from Alex."

She struggled to explain its meaning within the limited Drakish vocabulary. "It is a symbol of the promise he has made to me. That we would be committed to each other for the rest of our lives. It is meant to be seen by other humans."

"Would you break your promise to him?"

The argument that she hadn't promised him anything sat ready on her tongue, but she stopped herself. That fact was simply a technicality. In her heart, she *had* committed to him.

"Do it for him. Do it for me. Give my life meaning."

"I–I cannot."

Her vow of non-violence meant something, and she wasn't sure she could toss it away even for her murderous father. So she certainly couldn't violate her beliefs by killing someone she cared for.

His head reared up, and he snorted. "No. That is not possible." He concentrated on the cave entrance. "Great Daughter, get a sword. Your life is in danger."

The Drakish language had no way to express sarcasm, but her eye roll conveyed the message.

Smoke huffed from his nostrils. "I do not lie to you."

"Is it my father?"

His silence stretched on so long she was sure he was trying to make up an excuse. His eventual answer didn't change her mind. "Volus *is* in the region, but this... This is something else."

Her senses told her nothing. But maybe something was out there. Her abilities *were* minuscule compared to his.

His voice rumbled against her ribs. "Now."

The power behind his tone convinced her more than anything else. She sprinted to the treasure pile behind her and searched for a weapon. A bright silver sword caught her eye. She grasped the blade's hilt and returned to his side.

He captured her gaze. "Now kill me."

Her limbs went numb, and she staggered back. Kill him? What about the threat approaching the cave?

She was about to accuse him of tricking her when a glint shone on one of his scales. A teardrop rolled down his temple, leaving a trail of glittering amethyst blood.

The acrid taste of burnt tar singed up her throat. The last—and only—time she'd seen dragon blood was when her mother had been killed. Dragons didn't bleed without severe injury. They just didn't.

Tears were rare enough, much less a bloody one.

How damaged was he inside?

"Great Daughter, you need to gain strength for whatever is coming. You need it now. But if you will not do it for yourself, do it for me. For love."

The sparkling line of blood seized her thoughts. How much pain was he in? How long had he waited alone in this cave for someone to come and release him from his suffering?

Whether or not something dangerous neared their location, this great and noble creature shouldn't suffer because she was too weak to do what he asked. Her fingers tightened on the hilt. She couldn't fail him.

She'd do it for mercy. For him.

For love.

She tried not to think about what she was doing. Murdering her grandfather. A creature wiser than any she had known.

"For love," she repeated.

She plunged the sword between the overlapping armor plates on his belly, below the dragon-equivalent of his sternum, where his glowing heart lay under the slight gap between the plates. His head dropped onto the coins, jingling them as they scattered.

He enunciated the Drakish words clearly and strongly, "*Szörë waj dosarý načini zhè vadëkus.*" This is a good way to die.

As his heart beat its last, his body shrank, changing to his natural humanoid form. The ruffled collar and sleeveless coat he wore with that form were centuries out-of-date, proving how long he'd been restricted to this cave, slowly dying.

For the first time, she saw her grandfather's true features and recognized the resemblance to her own. A smile grew upon his face, filling her with peace and warmth.

And then, all too soon, the blue glow of his eyes faded. He was gone.

The cave felt colder—and countless times emptier.

No... What had she done?

"I'm so sorry." She fell to her knees at his side, her chest a solid lump of lead. The mass weighed on her lungs, and she couldn't breathe. Couldn't express her sorrow.

The orange glow grew in his torso. Flames escaped his pierced heart and consumed his body from the inside out. Within seconds, only a charred shape remained.

She sagged on her hands and knees. How could she live with herself?

Murderer.

So much wasted life, and for what? Her fingertips dug into the coins. It was metal. Only metal. Dragons could survive on a pile a fraction this size. But no, they were the ultimate greedy addicts.

She wanted to crush the coins. Punish them for being responsible for all the heartbreak in her life. Punish them for turning her into someone she didn't want to be.

Murderer.

She opened her senses, wanting to reshape the circles into a grotesque form to match her emotions. Power surged through her palms into the treasure.

Rather than deforming the metal, the energy made her one with the gold and silver. Before she could stop it, she became part of the pile, and the pile became part of her. Against her intentions, she claimed the mound of coins Nastav had used for a bed.

The rush of power roared in her ears, her eyes, her head. Heat burned in her torso, searing her organs. The tiny pilot light in her heart exploded into a full, blazing fire.

Dizziness forced her to collapse, and prickles stung her skin so hard her limbs became numb. Her mourning dulled the normal inebriated sensation. Instead, she felt adrift, uncertain where she ended and her new treasure stockpile began.

She'd succeeded in getting stronger, but the victory was hollow. She'd lost yet another family member who loved her.

Blackness prodded her temples, tempting her to sleep off the vertigo. She didn't resist.

Death would be a welcome fate.

Chapter Forty

SOMETIME LATER—SHE HAD NO IDEA HOW LONG—AWARENESS of a presence yanked her awake. She sat up just as her father's bright red hair crested the nearest mountain of treasure. His spiked locks framed the pale face that next came into view. That much had remained the same.

He stopped at the top of the hill and took in the scene. She gulped down a whimper at the sight of his full body. His clothes had changed since the last time she'd seen him in humanoid form. The stylish, modern outfit reinforced how much he'd integrated into human society.

Unless he'd killed a man for his shirt and pants. She wouldn't put that past him either.

But the bright glow shining through his shirt below his ribcage made the biggest impression on her. If the intensity of his heart's fire was any indication, he'd gotten stronger. Damn.

He scrutinized her, fixating on her torso. "Nastav is dead?"

His slender build and average height wouldn't intimidate humans. She knew better.

She stood slowly and deliberately to hide her fear. At least she'd awoken before he changed into his dragon form. "Yes."

"You killed him?"

Would he care that she'd killed his father? Just in case, she let her tone reveal her sadness. "Yes."

"But you have not yet claimed all his treasure."

He hadn't worded it as a question, so she only lifted her chin in answer.

His arms spread wide. "Is this why you came here? To kill and take?"

"To protect and defend."

He laughed, the cruel sound echoing throughout the cavern. "That human boy of yours?"

Her gut clenched at his mention—his knowledge—of Alex.

She covered up her reaction by removing her jacket and tossing it aside. No longer bothered by the cold, she didn't want the bulky coat getting in her way.

"How did you find me?"

His scan of the cave brushed the ashen form of Nastav, the evidence of her sin. "I knew you would visit him, and I sensed when you came into your own."

"And why did *you* come here? To kill me?"

His expression hardened. "I cannot let you live."

"Is that what your father would have wanted you to do?"

"Did my *father* also tell you how this is all his fault?" His eyes narrowed, searching for an understanding she didn't have. "He neglected to tell you that part, did he not?"

"We are responsible for our own choices. You cannot blame him for what you have done. But you can make new choices now. Just let me go. Let me live my life the way I want with the man I want."

He ignored her, his features twisting into a hideous mask. His face reddened, nearly matching the color of his hair.

"*He* is the one who put those ideas in my mind. *He* is the one who worshipped my mother's weakness and thought they had something meaningful. *He* is the one who told me I could *love*."

His hair rippled into the leading edge of the frill along the back of his neck and then faded back into his locks. Despite her intention to show no fear, she inched away.

Stable dragons would never flicker between forms like that. Stable, he was not.

He stormed down the treasure pile faster than she could decide on a plan of action. Waves of fury rolled off him as he approached.

"He was *wrong*."

His strides brought him within inches of her. His body shook, and his focus landed on the remains of Nastav.

He repeated his words, their Drakish consonants turning into a quiet, terrifying hiss.

"*Sè. Ishë. Greşis.*" He. Was. Wrong.

Ten years of running from her father had brought her to this—standing toe-to-toe with him and no way to escape. Ten years of trying to build up her strength, all to recognize too late that physical strength didn't give her the power to convince or the potential to murder without remorse.

For too long, her refusal to kill for treasure had defined her, separated her from other dragons. And now, especially so soon after Nastav's death, she couldn't change that decision she'd made to respect life.

She couldn't take the first step toward ridding herself of him. She couldn't be the aggressor and strike first. She couldn't end it like this.

"I am sorry, Father."

His head jerked back, his reaction matching how she felt. But she'd told Nastav the truth. She did pity her father.

He reached out and stroked her cheek. She willed herself not to flinch.

"You are so like her. My beautiful Saština."

A memory floated back to her of the countless times her father had said that about her mother. His beautiful Saština.

After the murder, it had been easy to forget how devoted he'd been to her mother. How much they had acted like a family. How much it seemed as though he *had* loved her.

Her father inspected her appearance, and his fingers trailed through her locks. "You have her hair. Do you know how rare it is, the changeling hair of the fae?"

His hand fisted in her waves and yanked. An *eep* leaked from her mouth despite her closed lips.

He's unstable. Very unstable.

This doesn't mean he's being aggressive. This doesn't mean he's going to kill me now.

Her pep talk didn't help, but she still couldn't take the step to escalate this encounter. For all she knew, her mother had been killed because she'd accidentally set him off. Maybe this didn't have to end in death.

His eyes sought hers again, this time with sadness reflected in their blue depths. "I wish you did not look so much like her."

"I know, Father. I am sorry."

"You understand." He leaned closer, his voice nearly a whisper. "That is why you returned, yes?"

"Yes," she lied, hoping she understood where his twisted mind was going.

"Good." He released her hair and sauntered back, nodding to himself. "Your understanding of why I have to do it will make killing you easier."

Damn! She hadn't meant to be understanding about *that*. Damn, damn, damn. She needed to distract him from his current thoughts.

"Do you remember the time you took me to Loch Ness? When you teased that we would visit my long-lost cousin, Nessie?"

A smile—a real smile—formed on his face, and for a second, he was the striking male dragon from her youngling memories. Flaming red hair, bright blue eyes, and a brighter grin. She understood why her mother loved him.

"I remember. I had you fooled, did I not? You thought you would get to meet the Loch Ness monster." His smile faded. "Saština was not happy about that trip. She never liked the water."

"But you like the water, Father. So do I." Finding common ground couldn't hurt. "I even went swimming a few months ago."

He stared at her without blinking. She couldn't tell if he was patronizing her with his interest or not.

"I swam where the water is warm, blue, and clear. We should go there together, and I will show you where we can sit underwater and watch the fish swim by."

"I would like that." His brows slammed together, as though he was surprised by the thought.

"So would I." She forced her lips to curve up, but a few trembles might have given her away.

"I wish I could love you. If I could love anyone, it would be you."

A fluttery feeling in her belly knocked her off balance. Similar words had passed her lips months ago, the day before she'd left Alex. Did that mean her father *did* feel something for her, just as she cared for Alex?

He pressed his fist against his torso and swayed. "My mind will not let me though. I wish you had not taken the ruby she gave me." He held his hands, palms up, in front of him. "I have to finish what I started."

"Why? Why can we not be happy together?"

His fingertips curled and clenched. "Because she condemns me from your eyes."

She flinched. Was that it? Maybe he hadn't been chasing her this whole time simply because she'd witnessed his crime and taken something from him. Maybe he'd come after her because she looked like the one he'd loved, and she reminded him too much of what he'd destroyed. Or because her talisman ruby was special to him too, a gift from the woman he loved. Or maybe it was a combination of all of it.

No matter his reasons, she understood him so much better now. On some level, she could sympathize with every one of those motives.

She folded his hands in hers. "You do not want to kill me, do you?"

He growled and tugged out of her grasp. "It does not matter."

"Yes, it does." She stepped closer. "It does not have to be like this. I forgive you."

His gaze snapped to hers.

She repeated herself, slowly and clearly. "I *forgive* you. There is no condemnation here."

Humans wouldn't understand her decision to forgive her father, but dragons would. The effect of treasure on dragons wasn't something humans could comprehend. For dragons, treasure was food, energy—*life*—and so much more.

The temptation to kill for acquisition was something she'd fought for ten years, and the lure of precious metals and gems was something she'd learned to resist while with Alex. Following his rules, starting a company to *sell* jewelry instead of claiming it, not taking everything she could—all that made her able to control her instinct more than any other dragon in history.

Treasured Claim

The simultaneous temptation and repulsion of living near another's hoard would drive any other dragon crazy. Her mother had known the risk. Had accepted the risk. Had chosen the risk.

Her mother had chosen love over her life.

And her father had paid the price several times over with his sanity. So yes, she forgave him.

"I believe you." He stared at her with clear vision for a moment. Then he broke eye contact. "But I cannot forgive myself."

"Killing me will not solve that."

"I know." His voice quieted. "It will condemn me even more."

He grabbed her arm and lifted it, palm up. The tragic tone of his acknowledgement held her frozen. He pushed her sleeve up past her elbow. She didn't resist.

His calm descended into a deeper pitch. "Condemnation is what I deserve."

His talon gouged into the micro-scales of her skin at her forearm. She sucked in a hiss and stiffened. Blood leaked from the line he cut, all the way from her elbow to her wrist.

She stood transfixed by the sparkling purple liquid escaping through the gash. In the back of her mind, she knew she should pull away, fight back—something.

The pain, more excruciating than she'd thought possible, stunted her thoughts and actions. And the blood. All the blood.

She'd never seen her own blood before.

"I am sorry, my daughter. I am sorry."

Even now, after he'd taken the first strike, she couldn't find the will to stop him, much less attack him. How could she punish him for doing something he didn't want to do? For making the same mistake she'd made? For letting his belief that dragons couldn't love determine his actions and hold him back from life's potential?

She'd die like her mother, with words of forgiveness and love on her lips.

Chapter Forty-One

HER FATHER STARTLED AND DROPPED HER BLEEDING ARM. Elaina collapsed onto the coins, released from the mesmerizing moment.

Had he rethought his actions? Maybe she'd survive after all.

Or maybe she'd stop being a damn coward and find the strength to do what needed to be done.

She buried her injured limb in the cool metal coins and twisted to check on him.

His focus was on the cave entrance. "We have a visitor." His head tilted. "*No*. Not merely a visitor. A *legend*."

He spotted the position of her forearm under the coins.

"Good. Call on your treasure to heal. We want to be at our best for this."

He faced the entrance again before she could register his words. He was giving her tips on how to heal the injury he'd made? The unpredictable nature of his insanity was enough to drive *her* crazy.

She concentrated on the gold and silver around her, drawing energy from the pile. A moment later, the pain receded, and she slid her arm back. No trace of the slash remained on her skin.

Her father had fallen into a wary crouch at the edge of the coin mound. She stood and shook out her wrist. Even though the healing was complete, odd tingles still exploded over her body.

She stepped alongside him, but not too close. "What is it?"

"Stay behind me. You are too young to fight this ancient enemy on your own."

Now he was being protective of her?

"Yes, but what *is* it, Father?" She shook out her arm again, the prickles continuing to excite her skin.

He straightened and called out in deep, growling Drakish, "We are ready for you, beast."

A running humanoid figure rounded the nearest mountain of treasure and skidded to a stop.

No, not a figure.

Not a beast.

Alex.

Her thoughts slammed into each other. What was Alex doing here? How had he found her? How had he made it over the chasm? How could she protect him now?

Her father spouted another warning, the Drakish words hard and guttural. "As you can see, you are outnumbered, beast. We will fight you, and you will lose."

Alex drew himself up and lifted his chin. "I did not come here to fight, dragon."

There was something terribly wrong with this conversation, but her mind was still stuck on the fact that Alex was *here*.

"You are not here to fight?" Her father scoffed. "Why else would a knight enter a dragon's cave?"

Knight? Not this again. Her father's assumption snapped her brain out of neutral.

"He is not a knight, Father."

Both men startled and gaped at her.

"*This* is your father?"

"Of course he is a knight."

She tackled her father's surprise first. His instability was dangerous enough. If he felt threatened by a knight, he'd be even more unpredictable.

"I know it feels as if he is a knight, but he is not one. I tested him. He cannot see a dragon's heart. Trust me, Father."

His brows pulled together, judging her as the stupidest dragon alive.

"Then tell me, my daughter," he paused, emphasizing his disappointment at her ignorance, "*how* is he able to understand and speak *Drakish*?"

Uh. Her brain crunched to a stop. She blinked, contemplated Alex, and blinked again. His incredulous stare matched hers.

Was this a hallucination? Maybe the size of her last claiming had driven her into a drunken dream. But her father's slicing of her forearm had hurt more like a nightmare.

Making sure she was speaking Drakish, she asked Alex, "How did you get here?"

"I—" He stopped, and his jaw circled, as though he was trying to figure out how his tongue was forming the sounds. "This is Drakish? How do I know it?"

She didn't want to think about that. "Answer my question. How did you get here?"

"I followed George and found your"—his lips pressed together, and then he apparently gave up trying to find a suitable word in Drakish and switched to English—"credit card numbers. You made a gas purchase in the town down the mountain this morning. From there, I followed my instincts." He grinned and conceded with a shrug. "And your footprints in the snow."

Her father's gaze bounced between them, his eyes narrow slits. She didn't know how much he understood English, but she needed to have this conversation with Alex.

"How did you make it over the abyss?"

A glint shone in his eye. "I'm stronger than I seem."

Before she could decide if that was a good or bad thing, his smile tightened.

He tipped his chin toward her father. "Does Volus's talk of teamwork mean things are patched up between you two, or did I interrupt something?"

Under her watchful eye, her father hadn't made any threatening moves or reacted to any of their English so far, so she risked prolonging the conversation to give Alex the background. "Only if you count him slitting my arm open as something."

He stiffened, and his focus jumped to her rolled up sleeve.

"It's better now. He taught me how to heal it."

"I don't understand."

"Neither do I, to be honest." She gave him an apologetic smile and shrugged. "He's very unstable. I'm afraid I'd be dead now if you hadn't showed up and interrupted him, but I don't think he *wants* to kill me."

The warning sign she'd been watching for flamed across her father's cheeks in a splash of red. In Drakish, he roared, "*This* is your male? A knight?"

Uh-oh. Her smile had probably given away their relationship.

"He is not a—"

"You tested him *before* your heart ignited. There was nothing to see."

No... She staggered back, stumbling under the weight of her body. Her movement drew Alex's attention. Was it her imagination, or did he glance at the bottom of her ribs?

She examined herself. Her torso now glowed, just as her father's did. Alex hadn't seen her heart before, but then again, neither had she. The claiming of Nastav's pile of coins had ignited her heart and potentially changed everything.

Her father didn't give her the chance to retest Alex. "I can feel that he is a knight. I can feel his power over my skin. And he feels it too. Do you not, beast? You feel our power. You cannot deny it. You cannot fight it. You are compelled to *contain* us. *Oppress* us. *Kill* us."

Each threat sent shivers skittering over her skin, and each shudder grew in strength, building like a tidal wave. Especially because Alex knew exactly how to carry out all of them. She'd unintentionally taught him about every dragon weakness, including the vulnerability of a dragon's heart. Her mouth grew as dry as coal dust.

No, it couldn't be true. She swallowed past the lies in her parched throat.

He'd given her a logical explanation for how he'd found her—credit cards and footprints. It wasn't as if he'd used a knight's instincts to hunt her down. And sure, he was aggressive, but that didn't mean he was a monster out to kill her. They'd even shared a smile a moment ago, as though he'd forgiven her for her lie in the letter and everything. He *couldn't* be a knight.

She waited for Alex to deny her father. He didn't have those urges. He wasn't a threat. He wasn't a monster. He loved her.

He drew himself up straight and answered in Drakish, "Yes,

but—"

"See, my daughter? Even Nastav would tell you, this man cannot ignore his instincts. He is a beast. He is our enemy. He—"

Her father stopped his tirade at the look on her face. Whatever expression it held brought pity to his eyes.

Alex had said *yes*. He hadn't denied a *need* to kill her.

For months, her body had known better than she did. The dangerous vibe. The warmth from his power. The energy between them, as no mere human could fill her with strength, claim or no claim. No, the energy came from her claim of a man with unnatural abilities of his own.

Understanding flowed through her, burning away her naïveté. He *needed* to fulfill his instincts, just as much as she *needed* treasure. He wouldn't be able to ignore his urge to kill her now that she was full-dragon, no matter what they'd shared in the past.

Her ribcage was hollow and empty inside, everything scorched into unrecognizable, meaningless husks. She would die here—either Alex would kill her, or her father would.

But she didn't—couldn't—care. She was beyond caring about maintaining a brave façade in front of her father. She was beyond caring if she left this cave alive. She was beyond caring about anything.

There was no happy life waiting for her at "home."

No, more than that. Her breaths stopped, and her new-and-improved heart ached with a heavy thud. Charred nausea singed her throat.

From this point forward, she *had* no life. No home. No one. Nothing.

"I am sorry, my daughter. No matter who you thought he was before, back when you were an immature dragon, now his instinct will be stronger, just as you are stronger."

Alex strode toward her. "Do not listen to him, Elaina."

Her father hissed and edged closer too. "Do you deny that your instincts are stronger now?"

"No, but—"

"Stop it, both of you." She picked up the sword she'd used on Nastav and held it in front of her. The blade tip swung back and forth, pointing at each of them. She wanted both of them to leave her alone so she could mourn Nastav and her lost dreams in peace.

Alex halted his advance, and his gaze flicked to her torso and back several times, clearly noticing the change in her heart's fire. Her father's expression hardened, and he strode to Nastav's charred body beyond the reach of her sword.

"You!" He knelt in front of what was left of the corpse. "You did this to her. You ruined my daughter just as you ruined me. All because of my *precious* mother."

He picked up the charcoal-like form of scorched remains and threw them at the cavern wall. They smashed into a black cloud of dust. A soft patter of ash rained down and then faded. Nastav was truly gone.

Her sword drooped, and her father sauntered toward her. She tightened her grip and pointed it at his sternum. "Stop." She spoke past the lump in her throat. "Nastav loved me."

That fact seemed like the only thing she had left that wasn't a lie.

"Nastav did not care about you. You were simply his latest attempt to justify his worship of my mother."

The whisper fell from her lips. "That is not true."

"What do *you* know of my mother?"

Considering that she hadn't even known Nastav was her grandfather, she had to admit her knowledge of her grandmother was a big, fat zero.

At her silence, her father scoffed. "My *mother* was a weak human."

Human? Was that even possible? Pregnancy between a dragon and a human?

No wonder Nastav hadn't freaked out when she'd told him about Alex.

Her father swept his hand down his front. "She died birthing me. Nastav convinced himself that he loved her out of guilt. My whole youngling phase, he talked about the loving sacrifice she'd made to give me life. Told me to find a female I could love the way he loved her."

"And you did." Her tone didn't disguise her sorrow. The puzzle of her father's life assembled into a tragic picture.

"I tried." His fingers curled into fists. "But Nastav forgot that loving a human woman was different from loving a competitor. And the *idea* of love is easier than actual love. He never had to *live* for years with the one he loved. Always trying to make it work." He unfurled and contemplated his hands. "I could not do it. I failed."

"I do not blame you."

She really didn't. Memories told her that he'd tried to make it work. He'd tried to create the first dragon family.

Her father focused on Alex. "Now you know why you must let me kill him."

What? In her peripheral vision, Alex backed up a few steps.

"You know it is true, my daughter. He will kill us both if he gets a chance."

"No." Alex's protest went ignored by both her and her father.

"I know he would." She thrust the sword closer to her father in warning. "But that does not mean you should kill him."

"Why do you protect him? For as difficult as Saština and my struggles were, any attempt you make to force it to work with *him* would be countless times worse. He is your *enemy.*" He stared into nothingness. "You would go to sleep as lovers and wake with his weapon impaling your heart."

"Wrong." Alex's empty denial echoed through the cavern. "I would never hurt her."

Her father's voice deepened into cold hatred. "That is what I said too."

Alex strode toward them, and she raised her palm for him to stop. His deceptions weren't convincing—or helping.

He halted and squared his shoulders. "I am not a beast or a monster. I would not hurt her."

"I will prove you a liar."

Before she could tell her father that he didn't need to prove anything because she already believed him, he smacked her backward. Her sword flew from her grasp and clattered along the rocky floor. She crashed onto her pile of coins, scattering them in her wake.

"Elaina!" Alex started toward her, but a growl from her father stopped him in his tracks.

She mouthed *no* to Alex to keep him from upsetting the situation more. Her father calmly strode away from them, heading to the open area between treasure mounds at the far wall.

Once he was in the open space, his form rippled, changed, grew. Her father crouched in his magnificent dragon form. Bright red scales covered his head, back, and limbs. Bone-white horns framed the top of the crimson frill standing up along his spine. Scarlet armor plates coated the front of his neck and belly. Air circulated in the cave from the beats of his devil-red, bat-like wings.

Alex's mouth hung open, an understandable reaction to seeing his first dragon in dragon form.

Her father's spiked red tail swished back and forth. "You feel it even more now, beast. Do you not?"

Alex's body shook, but he tried to deny it. "No."

"You want to pick up that sword behind you."

"I will not do it." Alex used his left hand to yank his right wrist behind his back, as though afraid his right arm had a mind of its own. His habitual gesture took on new meaning in the face of this temptation. It was the instincts of someone who knew a weapon in his hands would be deadly.

"You want to attack. You want to kill."

No doubt her father's taunting was having an effect. Alex's limbs squirmed in a one-man arm-wrestling match. Still, he fought his impulses. "You are wrong. I am not the monster you think I am."

"I will not let you trick and lie to my daughter."

Her father reared his head back and inhaled. A jolt electrified her chest in recognition, and her heart thrashed, clawing at her ribs, desperate to stop the inevitable.

"No!"

Her instincts drove her to rush between the males. It didn't matter that she and Alex couldn't be together. He didn't deserve to die in a ridiculous trial by her father.

Her instincts compelled her to prepare to block the flames. It didn't matter how much damage she'd have to endure. She would protect him.

Her instincts urged her to change into her dragon form. Her heart's fire spread to every cell of her body, forging a new form. A new existence.

Jami Gold

Her instincts accepted the mission to defend the man she loved. Love was worth more than her life.

ALEX'S CONCENTRATION ON HOLDING BACK HIS URGES WAVERED AT the sight of Elaina leaping into the open area between him and Volus. At the top of her graceful jump, the space around her body undulated. By the time she landed and challenged Volus, she was a dragon.

Elaina. A dragon.

A beautiful dragon—worthy of walking among gods.

Tension drained from his body, and a "whoa" sighed from his throat.

Every aspect that was fierce and terrifying about Volus was exquisite and stunning on her. White scales shimmered with blinding rainbows over her body. The ridge along her spine flowed with shades of yellow, amber, and brown. She opened her wings, displaying the same color pattern in hypnotizing swirls.

She was perfection. And he couldn't look away from her magnificence.

Then the flames hit.

Chapter Forty-Two

A ROAR FILLED THE CAVERN WITH THE POWER OF VOLUS'S fiery attack. Above Alex, the dragon he loved spread her wings over him, protecting him from the deadly inferno.

Tongues of fire licked at the edges of her wings, tearing them ragged. Puffs of white rained to the dirt, her scales disintegrating under the assault. An unholy shriek ripped from her body, and still, she held her ground.

"Damn it, Elaina, no!"

Alex tried to wrestle his way past her, but her tail flicked out and caught him across his chest. She slammed him to the ground, and the air burst from his lungs. The weight of her tail pinned him down and kept him from getting a deep breath to yell at her over the howl of the flames. Instead, he shoved against the appendage, freeing himself one centimeter at a time. It was taking too damn long.

Minute after agonizing minute, he was helpless as the woman he loved took the brunt of the flames meant for him. She was too brave for her own good. Each time Volus stopped to inhale, Alex hoped that would be the end of it, only to have another wall of fire blocked by her body.

Sweat dripped off his forehead from the desert-hot air in the cave. The fact that he was still wearing his ski jacket didn't help.

He searched for anything he could use to lever her tail off his chest. A few stray coins that had rolled near her feet during her

Jami Gold

leap were melting, giving evidence of the intense heat Elaina directed away from him. The heat she endured for him.

Crash. One of the large plates on her belly shattered as it fell and hit the ground.

He'd come here to protect her, and instead, she was protecting him. Dying for him.

The sword she'd dropped glinted in the firelight a few feet behind him. He stretched, pushing off the ground with the heels of his boots. His damp fingertips slipped over the pommel at the end. Almost.

He twisted his body and stretched again. His fingertips dragged the pommel closer, and he wrapped his fingers around the grip. Got it.

He slid the blade alongside his torso and strained to lift the hilt. The extra space allowed him to draw a deep breath. Hot, oven-like air burned his lungs. The acrid smell of burning flesh made his stomach heave.

Crash, crash, crash. He didn't take the time to check, but he guessed several more of her armored plates were smashing onto the rocky floor of the cave. The scent of singed hair curled around from the back of his neck in the increasingly deadly heat.

They were running out of time. With superhuman strength, he stiffened his wrists and forced the hilt up. One inch. Two inches. Three inches.

He sat up as far as he could and slipped the tip of the blade farther along his legs. At the same time, he scooted backward and pulled one leg and then the other toward him. Finally, her tail rested only on his lower legs, and he was able to bend his knees to get out the rest of the way.

He stood, tore off his sticky jacket, and spun toward the attack. *No...*

Ninety percent of her scales were missing. Glittering purple liquid oozed from open wounds covering her body. Her wings were completely gone, and only stubs remained of the limbs that had held them up.

The scream ripped from him without conscious thought. "No!"

His hand clenched the grip of the sword. Every urge he'd restrained before rushed to the surface. He held the blade aloft and charged forward into the wall of heat. He would fix this or die trying.

Right as he reached Elaina's side, the fire burst ended.

Volus's head curled back. "The beast has picked up a weapon. As I knew he would."

After the roar of the flames, the silence of the cave now sounded oppressive. A soft moan broke the quiet.

Elaina shrank into her humanoid form and collapsed to the ground beside him. If possible, she appeared more injured in this form. Instead of skin, open sores of charred purple burns covered every inch of her body, including where her hair should have been. Was there a level beyond third degree burns? Her ruby necklace and clothes were intact, but deep amethyst liquid immediately soaked through, staining the fabric.

No, no, no. "Oh God, Elaina. How can I help? Tell me what to do."

Even as he asked, he knew she couldn't answer him. Her lips and nose were damaged beyond function. Hell, for that matter, so were her eyelids.

He couldn't tell if her heart still glowed, if she was still alive. But he had to believe she was. He had to believe.

Heated air ruffled his hair. Too late, he remembered he'd turned his back to Volus.

The impulse to attack and kill the monster who'd done this to her seared through him, but he channeled that energy by focusing on her. He straightened, hefted the sword, and pivoted toward Volus.

"Tell me how to help her."

"Use that sword and kill her." Volus's voice sounded rough, as though the prolonged fire-breathing had damaged his throat.

Alex strode forward and jabbed the sword toward the dragon. "I am not the one trying to kill her. *You* are. Now tell me how to help your daughter."

"I did. It is too late for her. Put her out of her misery."

"She is stronger than you think. She *will* make it." She had to.

"If you will not kill her, I will."

Alex stepped in front of Elaina. "You will have to go through me first."

"You are not doing her a favor." Smoke huffed from Volus and ended in a cough. "I am trying to save her from the pain her mother endured."

"She is not her mother, and I am not you. Do not pretend you know how this will end."

"You think you love her, beast? What about when she needs more treasure? Will you help her kill to get it?"

"She is not like you. She has never killed for treasure."

"Fool. Who do you think killed Nastav?"

Alex paused. Yes, Nastav was obviously dead, but she'd seemed sad about that fact.

He glared up at the dragon towering over him. "If she wanted to kill, do you not think she would have returned your attack? You cut her arm and burned her alive, and yet she never moved to stop you. Why do you think that is?"

Volus grunted and pulled back. Alex stayed on the offensive and marched closer to the monster. "She is not a killer. She claims her treasure in other ways, and yes, I will help her."

"Your instincts will urge you to kill her first."

His muscles hardened at the thought. "Never. You do not know what we have already been through. You do not know the first thing about me."

"You like power. Your position in business proves that. What happens when you decide you want more, when the power you'd gain from killing her becomes too tempting?"

Alex glanced behind him. Elaina's glittering blood pooled next to the puddle of melted coins. Her broken form twisted his chest into a million pieces, each wishing he could fix her, heal her, save her. He ached at his helplessness.

"I would give up everything I have for her."

"You are *not* better than me." Volus snarled. "I trusted my *love*, and her mother paid the price. Instincts are stronger than love. Trust is an illusion."

"I am sorry for what happened to you, but you are wrong. Elaina and I can find happiness despite our instincts."

A growl shredded the quiet of the cave, reverberating in the curving chambers. "A beast like you does not deserve happiness."

Volus's claws scratched the rocky ground, and he scrambled

forward. Alex sprinted to the nearest treasure pile and grabbed a shield with his left hand.

"Come and get me."

Alex skirted the hills, leading Volus away from Elaina. Rubble fell from above as Volus followed, his wings bashing into the outcroppings on the cavern's ceiling. At the farthest clear area between the mountains of treasure, Alex stopped and confronted the dragon.

This wasn't how he'd pictured the day playing out while he'd dozed on the redeye flight to Europe. This wasn't what he'd expected to discover when he'd raced from Budapest to Northeastern Hungary during the afternoon. And this wasn't how he'd intended to help Elaina when he'd made his decision to come. How the hell had he ended up fighting a full-grown dragon alone while she all-too-quickly bled to death?

He tried not to think about her injuries. She would live. She was a survivor. And he would make sure she had the best chance possible.

Volus galloped around the edge of the treasure, his tail sweeping goblets and vases across the floor. He wasn't going to slow down for another chat.

"Shit." This was it.

Alex climbed the tallest pile to compensate for the dragon's height advantage. Volus snapped at him, his fangs barely missing Alex's boots.

At the top of the mound, Alex whirled to challenge the monster. Hopefully, Volus's throat damage was too bad to launch more fire. His horns and red scales and leathery wings added up to the demonic version of a dragon, nothing like Elaina's angelic form.

Volus's neck stretched in preparation for another biting attack. Alex swung out his left arm and bashed the monster's head to the side with the shield. His shoulder burned with the impact. He ignored the pain and thrust with the sword into the open side of Volus's mouth. The blade punctured the monster's tongue.

Alex drew the sword back. Thick purple liquid smeared the metal.

He could hardly believe it, whispering his surprise, "I scored the first hit."

Jami Gold

Energy crackled through his limbs, zigzagging to every cell like a lightning bolt. The additional power he'd sensed when Volus first changed now transformed into hardened strength. Like cold-tempered steel, he could endure this challenge. He welcomed it.

The blade in his right hand glowed for a second. Then the shield in his left did the same. They were no longer simple weapons or mere objects. They were an extension of his arms, an extension of him. The sword and shield felt as natural in his grip as a pen or cell phone.

"I am not going to be such an easy kill anymore, am I?"

Volus had pulled back in surprise, whether from the injury or because he sensed the power surge, Alex wasn't sure.

"All the more reason to kill you." The words slurred with Volus's damaged tongue. "I will not let you threaten my daughter."

Christ. An insane devil-dragon who was also stubborn as all get out. "I am not a threat. I am not the one hurting her. *You* are."

Instead of listening, Volus struck again with an open mouth. This time, Alex tilted his shield and clipped him. The sharp edge sheared off the nearest fang. How plain metal could cut through thick bone, he didn't know, but he didn't question it.

The long tooth clattered onto the treasure at Alex's feet. A grin broke across his features as Volus roared. Two hits. Maybe he could do this. Maybe he could save Elaina.

Volus swiped at him. Alex leaned back, his shield held up for protection. The dragon's claw snagged the shield, and an intense wrenching pain burned Alex's shoulder.

Shit! Alex kept his grip on the shield, but his arm hung useless, his shoulder out of joint. He breathed in quick, shuddering grunts and swayed from the pain.

Focus. Focus.

A menacing laugh rumbled from Volus. "My first hit."

Playtime was over.

The shield hung limp from Alex's arm. All the abuse he suffered as a child had given him plenty of experience with the "gentle manipulation" method of fixing his shoulder. But he didn't have time for that, and no doctors or physical therapists were around anyway.

Instead, he needed to knock his dislocated shoulder back into the socket. The only thing solid enough nearby was Volus's body.

Alex skated down the pile and slammed his shoulder against Volus's leg. He held in his grunt this time.

His shoulder still hung worthless. Not quite back into place yet.

The spiked tail whipped around, and Alex ducked underneath only to stumble on a rocky projection. The uneven ground made it difficult to keep his footing while dodging, but it was better than the sliding pile of treasure.

Alex sprinted around the tail and aimed for the inner side of Volus's far leg. Under the monster's belly, he'd be safe from the swishing appendage.

Again, he held in his cry from the collision. His shoulder popped into place.

"You can't hide there." Volus struck out with his forelegs.

Alex spun away from the dragon's claws. The monster swatted at him in a flurry of limbs. Alex dodged, ducked, and twisted away from the lethal talons.

Volus stood on his hind legs, ready to crush him under his forelegs. That's when Alex saw it. The glow of the dragon's heart from between two of the armor plates low on his belly.

This was no longer a dance to distract Volus while trying to keep Elaina and himself alive. If Volus didn't back off, this last attempt at negotiation would end with a fight to the death.

And Alex knew how to win.

"You can stop this. Let Elaina and me go." He left out the *please* to avoid seeming too weak, but his tone carried his wish to escape this without anyone's death.

Volus smashed down onto his forelegs, missing Alex by an inch. "Never."

Alex skittered out of the way, leaving Volus's heavy feet to stomp around him. "How can I prove to you that I will not hurt her?"

"You cannot. I cannot even trust myself not to hurt her. I could *never* trust you."

The words rumbled through the cave, crushing every hope of avoiding further bloodshed. The monster wouldn't trust Alex, and he'd kill his daughter to "protect" her from imagined suffering—what option was left? Self-preservation? Maybe he'd change his mind after a cut near his vulnerable heart.

Alex whirled into action, leaping over the swinging tail and weaving between the four limbs. But there were too many dangers to watch at once. One of Volus's wings caught him and slammed him against the cave wall.

The blow crushed the air out of Alex's lungs, and he swayed, struggling to regain his stance. Volus scrabbled over the ground to reach him.

Alex rushed toward the running dragon and dropped to his knees on a large golden platter. Skating under the monster's belly, he thrust up with the sword.

A miss on the heart, but he nicked the underside of the armor plate. Volus's screech rent the air. "No!"

The dragon turned around, and his tail swept Alex off his feet and sent him flying into a treasure pile. Priceless bowls and plates clunked to the ground with his fall.

Alex ran up the mound. He needed a second to plan, to think. Now Volus would be ready for him. Treasure slid under his feet with his climb. This wasn't the most stable place to stage an offensive.

He reached the top and panted for breath. "Now do you yield? Will you let us go?"

Volus approached his position warily. He kept his hind legs and lower belly down on the rock, away from Alex's blade. The dragon stretched his upper body and neck low over the gold and gems, the angle of the pile granting protection.

"If I cannot kill you, I will kill her." Purple liquid splattered the air with the hiss of Drakish consonants on his tongue.

The twisted mind of this demon was beyond Alex's understanding. He'd rather kill his daughter than let her take a chance with Alex? Elaina hadn't exaggerated her father's insanity. How could he care about his daughter and yet think killing her was *protecting* her? How could he love his daughter enough to *want* to protect her and yet believe that death was safer than love?

Alex's own need to protect Elaina joined with the urge to destroy this creature. Every violent impulse he'd had over the past several months now felt natural. His body had been maturing in power, readying for this confrontation. Instead of fighting the bloodthirsty compulsion, he embraced it.

He was dominant for a reason—and it had nothing to do with his father. His knightly instincts were more a part of him than his history. He was born to protect humans from the threat of dangerous dragons. And this unstable, unpredictable creature was as dangerous as they came.

Alex's temperament made perfect sense now, and he'd use it to the best of his ability. He trusted himself. He trusted his instincts. He'd never again restrain his impulses.

He'd kill this devil-dragon *and* save Elaina.

The monster struck out, mouth gaping. Alex leaped away from Volus's fangs—and landed right in the path of his claws. He couldn't dodge in time. Long, sharp talons ripped through Alex's jeans, slicing into his hip. *Shit!*

Alex stumbled to his feet before Volus could repeat the attack. White-hot pain shot down from his hip. His right leg didn't want to move on command. He forced it to obey anyway.

The next swipe of Volus's claw missed, but stooping made Alex's legs buckle under him. Too quickly, Volus moved in. His fangs opened right above Alex's head. His outstretched shield stopped the jaws from closing.

Volus opened his mouth wider and tipped the shield horizontal with his tongue. Fangs crushed Alex's bicep.

With nothing more than a grunt, Alex twisted his wrist and tilted the shield inside Volus's mouth, cutting into the tender flesh. Then a yank brought his arm and his shield out. Sharp teeth shredded his muscles on the way.

Alex dropped the shield, unable to do anything with that limb anyway. Random tendons and bone connected the limb to his shoulder, but barely. Black dots formed over his vision, and fiery agony sliced through him, burning the nerves of the left half of his body.

Blood freely flowed down his forearm, coating the treasure. The precarious stability of the treasure pile grew worse with the slippery liquid.

Another hit would be the end of him.

He staggered to his feet, but couldn't keep his balance. Any second now, he was going to slide down the hill on his ass.

Down on his ass. That was what he'd do.

Volus gnashed his teeth, as though perturbed by the injury Alex had inflicted to the inside of his mouth. Sparkling deep purple blood dripped from both sides of his jaw, adding to the slick surface below.

Alex limped along the top of the pile and lined himself up with Volus's length. The dragon's neck curved away in preparation for the deathblow.

Alex pressed his heels into the treasure and let gravity take over, sending him sliding down the hill on his back. Volus's armor plates were only two feet above him. Forelegs passed by. And then the limbs holding the wings taut whizzed above him.

Just before he reached Volus's back legs, Alex jammed his good leg up against the dragon's belly. The abrupt stop jolted his muscles and drove his knee against his chest. A glow shimmered behind the armor directly over him.

He angled the tip of his blade and aimed for the small gap between the armor plates. Volus started to roll away from his defenseless position. The extra space only made it easier to line up the weapon.

Alex thrust the sword into the gap. The blade sank easily into the vulnerable flesh. Light flashed, the blow puncturing Volus's heart.

Alex rolled onto his stomach in the opposite direction from the monster. Hard edges of treasure poked into his shredded right leg. He pulled his knees under him in a failed attempt to stand and defend himself.

There was no point.

Volus lay beside him, humanoid again. He gripped Alex's wrist. "Please."

What now? Alex searched for his sword, or any weapon, and came up empty. Volus repeated his plea. The multiple hits to his mouth mangled his pronunciation, but Alex got the gist.

"Please, what?"

"Promise me. Do not hurt my daughter."

A solid lump landed in Alex's gut. He'd just fought and fatally injured Elaina's father. No matter how insane Volus's method of *protecting* her was, Alex understood the emotions behind the actions. The urge to destroy this creature turned sour in his throat.

"Yes, of course. I promise."

"Tell her." Volus sucked in a breath. "Tell her I love her."

Before Alex could reply to the confession, the blue glow in Volus's eyes faded, and his hand fell from Alex's wrist. Then an orange radiance grew in his torso. Flames burst from Volus's rib-cage and engulfed his body. Just as quickly, the fire snuffed itself out, and only a blackened form remained.

Alex tumbled back on his ass, his limbs shocked by the do-it-yourself funeral pyre. Echoing the dragon's fiery death, energy surged through Alex again, and power thrust into every cell, singe-ing away everything he was and leaving a new form in the embers.

Electrified, his body went rigid, and his skull slammed down on the rock. Dizziness swooped and twirled in his chaotic brain like a swarm of drunk fireflies. His consciousness scattered, no longer under his control. If this was supposed to be the universe's way of congratulating him for a job well done, it didn't feel like much of a grand prize.

Just as he wondered if that would be his last coherent thought, the energy focused, infusing him with indescribable strength. His ragged wounds ceased bleeding, and new skin formed, healing un-til only a dull ache remained. Violent impulses coursed through him, and he sprang to his feet.

He found his sword on the other side of Volus's corpse. The blade was part of his body, and his hand itched to hold it.

The steel once again in his grasp, the drunk fireflies transferred their mood to him. He was a knight. He was powerful. He was invincible.

Holy fuck, killing dragons was one hell of a rush.

Chapter Forty-Three

URIED IN HER TREASURE, ELAINA WOKE, TIRED AND ACHING with pain. Why was she so exhausted?

Oh... The events of however-long-ago came back to her in a vivid nightmare.

She couldn't deny any longer that she loved Alex. Months before, she'd marveled at his strength for enduring years of abuse to protect his mother.

She'd thought she'd never be capable of such a thing. She'd proven herself wrong.

Bittersweet tears made tracks down her temples. Like her mother, she'd chosen love over her life. But at what cost?

She was in love with her enemy. A man who was driven to kill her.

She pushed up to her elbows to scope out the situation. Coins jingled off her as she moved. Something shifted alongside her and pressed against her back, helping her up.

Her eyelids didn't want to open. A gasp beside her told her why. She wasn't done healing, and her eyes hadn't yet recovered.

Being ninety-nine percent dead tended to require a lot of energy to heal. And she'd used up this pile.

Well, whoever was beside her was either going to kill her while she was helpless and blind or not. There wasn't a damn thing she could do about it except ask for help and see if it came.

She rasped out the barely intelligible words. "Need new

treasure."

"This other pile over here?"

She shouldn't have been surprised to learn it was Alex next to her, but she stiffened anyway. Then the whole *I'm dead either way* attitude came back to her.

"Yes."

He lifted her to her feet and led her forward. Stuck in darkness, she could only follow. The toes of her boots hit another treasure mound, and he assisted her in lying down.

The reason for Nastav making his bed on the coins was immediately apparent. This pile was decidedly less comfortable, with sharp corners and gems poking her from all sides, especially as Alex buried her under a layer.

Maybe he was making sure she was at full-strength before killing her. If so, that whole "wanting a fair fight" thing was buying her more time, but for what? A long and drawn-out death instead a peaceful one in her sleep?

Metallic scrapes and clangs nearby indicated he cleared a spot and sat next to her. She wanted to protest that she didn't want him there, but that wasn't true. If he *did* kill her now, at least sharing this time with him would be her last conscious memory.

After settling in, she molded the metal objects around her body for comfort and in the process, claimed the hill of treasure. As one mound rolled into the next, her claiming encompassed half the riches in the cave.

The new energy under her control immediately went to work knitting her body back together. In her delirious state, she'd have sworn she felt Alex's hand connect with hers, but sleep came too quickly for her to confirm.

When she next woke, her body felt whole once more. Her fingers twitched, but dream or not, Alex's hand wasn't within her grasp.

She sat up. Golden cups and bowls clattered to the ground, waking him where he lay several feet away on the rocky floor.

A sword—the same sword she'd used on Nastav—rested on the ground beside him. The torches throughout the cavern had long-since burned out, and now only a single torch lying near Alex filled the cave with flickering light that couldn't compete with the glow from her recharged, full-dragon heart.

An eager glint in his expression outshone the feeble flames. "You're better." He scrubbed the back of his neck. "You are, aren't you? You're healed now?"

"Yes, I think so. Close enough anyway."

It probably wasn't smart to let an enemy know she wasn't up to full strength yet. Then again, he'd had plenty of chances to kill her already.

He stood and leaned, checking out her head from the side. "Even your hair grew back."

Her hand went to her scalp. "My hair was gone?"

"How much do you remember about your injuries? And how did you make it into your treasure pile anyway? When I left to fight your father, you were..." He wiped his face. "I found you by following a smeared trail of blood and chunks of flesh."

At the description, she recoiled, her lips pulled tight. "Well, I remember that everything hurt a lot at first, but then the pain went away." She rubbed her forehead at the memory. "I thought I was dead. That I'd died." She scanned the battlefield, trying to re-member. "I think a puddle of melted coins dribbled down to my fingers. That gave me the strength to crawl to my treasure."

He grunted an acknowledgment but didn't say anything.

"How bad was I?"

"I don't know if I should tell you." Before she could protest, he relented. "The reason the pain went away is because your skin and nerves were gone. You were one big open wound."

"Eww." She shuddered, her stiff, blood-soaked-and-dried clothes giving evidence of his words. "I'm glad I didn't realize that."

His chin angled toward the cavern's ceiling. "It was rather..." He took another deep breath. "Horrifying."

"I'm sorry." She wasn't sure what she was apologizing for, but he seemed traumatized by the experience.

His gaze latched on to hers. "Are you?"

"Am I what?"

"Sorry that you saved me? Sorry that you endured all that for me?"

"No, I'm not sorry about that. I'm—" One corner of her lips

curved up. "I'm sorry you had to see me like that. So much for thinking I'm beautiful anymore, huh?"

"How can you joke about that?" He strode toward her, but stopped when she shrank back. "I *saw* you as a dragon. I've never seen anything more amazing in my life, and then to witness you destroying yourself for me?"

He swore under his breath and looked away. "I don't deserve such a gift."

She knew the answer, knew he would say he didn't deserve her sacrifice when he was going to kill her anyway, but she asked regardless. "Why?"

"Your father was right. I *am* a knight."

Even though she'd known that truth, his simple statement landed hard enough in her gut to drive stinging moisture to her eyes.

He nudged the blade on the ground with his foot. "This sword bonded to me, probably similarly to how you connect to your treasure." His arms hung limp. "I was able to see your father's heart, and I killed him."

His voice quieted. "His last words were asking me to tell you that he loved you."

She pressed her fingers against her lips. A confused mess of love, despair, and guilt bubbled beneath the surface. Her father had finally admitted the truth to himself, but it had been too late to save his sanity, to convince him to trust his feelings.

The bloodied shreds of Alex's sleeve and pants made it obvious the two had fought. Brutally.

All those years of struggling to get stronger, and when it was necessary, she couldn't hurt her father. Alex had no such trouble.

Honestly, she was grateful he'd done what needed to be done. What her father had probably wanted her to do—release him from his guilt-driven insanity. Alex had saved her father from his mental anguish and her from her cowardice.

She climbed out of the pile and met her enemy. "Well, you've been even more patient than Inigo Montoya waiting to kill the Man in Black. I'm ready now."

"What?"

"You know, *The Princess Bride*? You were waiting for me to heal enough so you could kill me honorably. The whole 'fair fight' thing."

Of course being a coward, she would have preferred him to kill her in her sleep, but she didn't confess that fact.

He grunted and ran his fingers through his hair. "Is that what you think of me?"

"Yes." What was he getting at? "You're a great and noble warrior. I meant it as a compliment."

"So we're supposed to fight to the death now?"

"No. I won't fight back. I—" Her arms crossed in front of her against her will, and she forced them to relax at her sides. "I've discovered I'm a coward. I'm not brave enough to hurt someone."

"*You* are the furthest thing from a coward possible."

She ignored his placating words. Her right hand sought the ring on her left finger for strength.

"I can't hurt someone—especially when I love them."

He took a half step back, his eyes widened, and his mouth hung open for a second. "You..." His voice lowered to a hesitant whisper. "You love me? You're actually saying the words? You *love* me."

"Yes. I love you." She gave him a teasing smile. "You don't think I'd go through all that for just anyone, do you?"

"I'm confused. You love me, and yet you're prepared for me to kill you."

"I don't blame you for what you have to do. Instinct is instinct. So yes, I love you even though you're going to kill me."

He ambled toward her, and despite her brave words, she moved back. Accepting that she would die was different from being ready for it this second.

He sighed and scrubbed his face. "I'm not going to kill you, Elaina."

"It's okay. I understand. Please... Just don't lie to me." Her heart couldn't take any more lies.

"But I'm *not* going to kill you. Not today. Not tomorrow. Not ever."

She couldn't breathe. Hope and denial battled in her lungs, leaving no room for air. She shook her head. "No more lies. Please, no more lies."

His tone grew dead serious. "I swear on my mother's grave that

I'm not lying to you."

"No." She stomped her foot and swept her hand in front of her, indicating everything she'd witnessed. "I *heard* you. You admitted you needed to contain, oppress, and kill us. And I *saw* you. You were shaking with the effort to hold yourself back from attacking my father. You'll go insane like him if you try to deny those urges."

His brow lifted, making him too sexy by half. "How I felt about your father is entirely different from how I feel about you. He insisted I could never prove I won't hurt you. I'll prove him wrong."

She scoffed, mostly to convince herself to hold on to her anger and ignore his attractiveness. His words weren't evidence of anything. Not when it came to the murderous impulses of a knight.

"So you're claiming you don't have any urges to kill me? Pick up that sword. Show me."

He hefted the sword and tossed it from hand to hand a couple of times. Then the blade became a blur as he spun and danced, fighting and parrying an imaginary enemy. The air sang, the metal whistling through the space around him.

The sight was beautiful and terrifying. She should have used the opportunity to put a few more yards between them, but she stood awestruck by his skill and the nimble motions of his body.

This was why she'd always felt the tingle of danger from him. Before, only the potential of this power had resided within him. Now he'd unleashed it. And fool that she was, she still wanted to be with him.

If anything, seeing him like this had increased her desire. His dangerous aspects had been a turn-on before, but now they were irresistible.

As quickly as he'd started, he straightened. The flat of the blade slapped his palm, and he swaggered toward her.

"Nope. I still don't want to kill you."

She shrank back from his power. The cavern wall right behind her interrupted her retreat, and she nearly bumped into it. She scooted around the edge of the treasure so he couldn't trap her against the rock.

He followed with his slow stride. The more arrogance he showed, the more she wanted to go to him, surrender to him, put herself at his mercy.

She resisted.

Until his hand stroked her jaw and slid into her hair.

Then her legs weakened, and she dropped to her knees in front of him. She stared up at him, and her breath caught at the sexy image of his dominance.

"You submit to me, beautiful?" His voice was low, rumbling, and even more dangerous.

She couldn't answer, but if her expression reflected any of the take-me-now craving burning through her body, he probably guessed the truth.

"And that's yet another reason why I'll never have the urge to kill you."

She lowered her gaze and broke the spell. No, a knight's instincts couldn't work like that. Could they?

She had to make him stop these lies before hope let her heart believe. Words still weren't enough to prove anything. Maybe there was a way to get him to take her seriously and back off at the same time.

She scrambled backward and stood. "What if I change to my dragon form?"

That had amplified Alex's reaction to her father. Surely, it would do the same for her.

His eyes flashed in the dim light. "Yes, I want to see that again."

She blinked. His response wasn't quite what she'd expected, and she wasn't positive she knew how to transform. Last time, her intuition had taken over.

She closed her eyes and imagined herself as a dragon, bigger, stronger, winged. Energy gathered around her, coalescing, and her body complied, growing into her dragon form.

Air swirled with an experimental flap of her wings, and she checked out the parts of her body she could see. Her tail swished happily at the view of white scales and changeling wings. Nothing like her father's appearance. For a second, she forgot to worry about Alex.

He approached, his swagger gone, his sword lowered. "May I touch you?"

His tentative tone caught her off guard. She held herself still and answered in Drakish, her dragon tongue unable to handle English. "Yes."

His hand skimmed over her scales, her wings, and her tail, exploring her body. The touch of his skin against her, massaging and stroking, once again filled her with warm tingling—the good kind. Hope tickled the back of her mind.

Then he placed his palm against her snout. "You're beautiful. Renaissance artists had it all wrong. Angels should look like you."

Her head pressed into his hand, just as she did in humanoid form. In Drakish, she asked, "You do not want to kill me?"

He blinked slowly, entranced. "I want to worship you."

She wanted to believe him. Oh, did she want to believe him. But one last test of his instincts remained.

She pulled back and moved to the edge of the remaining unclaimed treasure. "What if I become more powerful? Will that not make me more of a threat?"

He followed and captured her jaw between his palms. "Do it. Claim it all."

She reached across the cave with her senses and sought all of the unclaimed riches. One after another, the priceless objects fell under her control.

Her wings spread, unable to contain the energy. Power surged through her, and she shuddered with the effort to keep from flying in the constrictive cavern.

He yanked back and shook out his arms as though they'd been shocked. "That's right, beautiful. Be stronger."

Once her collection encompassed the entire hoard, she curled her neck back and peered down at Alex. His adoring gaze never left hers.

She had to concentrate over her dizziness to form her question. "You still do not want to kill me?"

He sank to one knee, bowed his head, and raised both hands, lifting his sword in offering.

"I hereby do homage and swear fealty to the life of Elaina Drake, Angel of the Dragons, to serve her in all things, to enrich her with my talents and abilities, and to never cause her harm. Here by my honor, my sword, and my heart swear I, Alexander Wyatt."

His words rang with authority, filling the cavern with resonant power. If there was any truth to the mysticism of knights, he'd pledged his life to hers with an unbreakable oath of loyalty, no matter what urges his knightly nature might provoke.

She returned to her humanoid form and accepted the offered sword. An instinct beyond her understanding brought the words to her lips.

"I accept your homage and fealty and pledge to you that from this day forward, I will honor and trust you, just as I will protect the trust with which you have graced me."

At the final word, tingles burst over her skin, as though their mutual energies celebrated their bond, their claim on each other. He stood and wrapped one arm around her waist. His other hand took the sword from her grasp and laid it on the ground.

He slipped his fingers into her hair, concentrating the tingles to her scalp. "Everything you wrote in the letter was a lie."

"Yes." A lump formed in her throat, and her voice cracked over the obstruction. "I'm sorry about that. I was trying to protect you, keep you from following me into who-knew-what dangerous situation."

"I forgive you." He raised his hand, showing the ring he'd never taken off, even after all the hurt she'd inflicted. His eyes glinted with the power of steel, but warmth rippled under the silvery-gray. "I believe in us."

He caressed her cheek, and her head pressed into his palm. The advice James's girlfriend, Peggy, had given her months ago for how to know when a relationship was real floated in from a memory.

Commitment? Between his oath and wearing of the ring, he'd proven his commitment to her both as a knight to a dragon and as a man to a woman.

Respect? This arrogant man had bowed to her and made himself defenseless by granting her his sword, all in his determination to respect her concerns.

Best friends? He understood her like no one else on the planet.

And on top of all that, he loved her, and she truly loved him.

Teasing danced in his eyes. "Does this mean you've *claimed* me again?"

"Yep." She stroked his biceps, grateful he'd healed. Tingles along where they touched were all present and accounted for. "This time for keeps."

His expression turned serious. "And now will you marry me?"

The warmth spreading through her chest competed with the fire in her heart. Her answer came easily. "Yes, of course. *Yes.*"

He kissed her as though there was no yesterday and no tomorrow, no worries and no lies. Truth, only truth, between them now. His lips and tongue meshed against hers with equal parts gentleness and passion, and all hurts were forgiven and forgotten.

Her giddy energy rush made her want to climb on top of him, but he leaned back and scanned her. "I've been waiting for this. No knights, no dragons, no fathers, no fear. Just us."

Her heart felt lighter, but she still worried. "I don't understand. How is it possible? Why aren't your instincts forcing you to defeat me?"

One side of his mouth curved up in a devilish smile, and he edged her backward, closer to the pile of her hoard. "Oh, I *do* want to defeat you. But not on the battlefield. When it comes to you, all my urges to dominate come out in a different way."

"A different way?" Were his words alluding to what she hoped?

He lowered her onto the treasure, which she reformed to get rid of the pointy bits. His breath floated in her hair, and he nestled near her ear.

"Yes." He trapped her wrists with one of his large hands. "With you…"

His other hand gathered a fistful of her shirt and yanked, ripping the stiff fabric away.

She gasped, and her heart raced in anticipation, thumping wildly in her belly. She *did* love this about him.

His palm molded her breast, and his thumb stroked her nipple. "I want to control your pleasure."

She arched into him and moaned. Oh yes, she'd missed this. Very much.

"I want to own your body." He unzipped her pants and maneuvered them down her legs.

"You have it. Take me."

"I want to own you."

"I'm yours."

He removed the tatters of his jeans and set himself at her opening. His expression hardened and became fierce.

If he were anyone else, she'd be terrified. Instead, she squirmed with need. She needed him, in all his arrogant, domineering, controlling glory.

He separated her wrists and restrained them on either side of her head. His hips pressed threateningly.

His eyes glinted like steel. "I want to fuck you so hard I break you."

She wiggled her brows in challenge. "I want to see you try."

And with that, he thrust into her.

The force of his impact, repeated again and again, set off a landslide of treasure, nearly burying them in priceless riches. She laughed, unable to contain her happiness.

This was everything she'd ever wanted. And more.

This time, when they both came, she was the one to shout. "God, I love you!"

His yearning sounded in her ear as he crushed her to him. "More than anything else, I want to keep you forever."

The words resonated deep within her, revealing the truth: Their future was whatever they wanted it to be.

She'd proven she'd give up everything for him, and he'd done the same. But now, they didn't *need* to give up anything.

She could claim the fortune waiting in her father's cave, and Alex could use the spent treasure for his philanthropy projects. Now that her body was mature, they might even be able to have the children he wanted. All in all, they had as much chance to make it as any other couple.

The world might want them to be enemies, but they didn't have to submit to anyone or anything but each other. In fact, now that she thought about it, a dragon and knight could be an unstoppable team.

She squeezed him in return, matching his intensity.

"Forever."

Be part of all
the love stories found in the...

Thank you for reading *Treasured Claim*! I hope you enjoyed meeting Elaina and Alex. The next book in the Mythos Legacy series is also available. Read on to learn more!

~ Jami

- If you enjoyed being part of the Mythos world, sign up for Jami's email list at *jamigold.com/mail*. Learn when her new books become available and **take advantage of her pre-order-only sale prices**!
- At *jamigold.com*, find information for all of Jami's books, including extra content for this book, and connect with her on social media.
- Reviews help other readers discover new books! If you have a moment, please leave a review on Goodreads, Amazon, and/or your favorite online retailer.

Pure Sacrifice, the second novel-length story
in the Mythos Legacy series,
features a **unicorn-shifter hero**.
Go to *jamigold.com/ps* to order!

PURE SACRIFICE

**To save his race,
a shapeshifting unicorn
must keep the chosen Virgin pure.
But she has other plans...**

A shapeshifting unicorn desperate to save his race...

The last hope for his kind, Markos Ambrostead must keep the chosen Virgin untainted. But when an attacker breaches his protective magic, he must reveal himself to prevent her death.

A tenacious woman who refuses to be ignored...

As far as the world is concerned, Celia Hawkins is a nobody. Nearly invisible. After a narrow escape from an attempted rape, she wants answers from the stranger who saved her—starting with why he noticed her at all.

Rules were made to be broken...

Markos can't risk being tempted by the Virgin, yet emboldened by his rescue, Celia's determined to make them friends. Maybe more. Maybe much more. Now only his crumbling willpower can maintain her purity—and prevent his tribe's extinction.

For more about *Pure Sacrifice*,
go to *jamigold.com/ps* to read an excerpt
and **order your copy!**

About the Author

After escaping a dragon with all her fingers and toes intact, Jami Gold moved to Arizona and decided to become a writer, where she could put her talent for making up stuff to good use. Fortunately, her muse, an arrogant male who delights in causing her to sound as insane as possible, rewards her with unique and rich story ideas.

Fueled by chocolate, she writes paranormal romance and urban fantasy tales that range from dark to humorous, but one thing remains the same: Normal need not apply. Just ask her family—and zombie cat.

Sign up for news on upcoming releases, find preview excerpts, and connect with Jami on social media by visiting *jamigold.com*.

Acknowledgements

Movies would have us believe that becoming a published author is a solitary achievement, where we slave away in our office. Alone. The truth is that book publishing is much closer to being a group project (and believe it or not, I'm not referring to the group of voices in my head).

I couldn't have completed this book without the unfailing support of my family. You tolerate my insanity and encourage my dreams. You're the best anyone could wish for and I'm endlessly grateful in every way.

I send hugs and thanks to my beta readers: Jay, Angela, Wendy, Suzanne, Susan, Janice, Murphy, Rachel, Melinda, Buffy, and P.W. You all helped me make this story better. *listens to mental whispers* And Alex and Elaina thank you too.

My wonderful editors improved this story in countless ways, so many thanks go out to Marcy, Erynn, and Julie. Thanks again to Laird for the wonderful cover too. All of you helped me make this book match the vision in my head.

Thanks also to the amazing writing community, those who gave me the confidence to pursue publication: the contest judges (especially those who awarded this story all its wins and finals) and the many readers of my blog. Thanks to my Twitter and Facebook friends who support my social media addiction and to those who helped spread the word (and for debating whether the rule to capitalize the word *Internet* could be broken without seeming like a grammar heathen). You all make my corner of the world a little brighter and happier.

And most of all, to my readers, the joy of writing wouldn't be the same without you!